Kingdom of Broken Iron

KINGDOM OF BROKEN IRON

ISBN: 978-1-7775132-3-8

Map by Lizard Ink Maps
Edited by Emerald Barnes, Raven Eckman and Brenna Bailey-Davies
Cover by Cora Graphics
Art by Lauren Richelieu
Interior formatting by Dark Wish Designs

PRAISE FOR KINGDOM OF BROKEN IRON

"McCartney strings together another brilliant story full of beautiful writing, action, and swoon. An addicting ride that I didn't want to end." – **Candace Robinson, author of Quinsey Wolfe's Glass Vault**

"Kingdom of Broken Iron is devastating heartbreak in pretty packaging. Scattered and broken, the last of the Black Dawn rebellion use their magic and wits to claw their way to power under the crushing weight of destiny. The only thing standing in their way is themselves. Can they overcome their secrets and loss in time to save Kiero?

Join the cause! Fight the dark forces in the name of family, freedom and a better future for all!

If power struggles, political maneuvering, magic, monsters and utter betrayal are for you, then look no further than the Black Dawn series. Dark forces and dangerous secrets abound. And yes, there's even a little steam for you lovers out there." – **Amy Poirier, Bookseller**

"A world to lose yourself in... Its ancient magic and fierce warriors will capture your heart in this dark and dangerous tale." – **Christine Rees, author of The Hidden Legacy**

"This is a wonderful story with exciting worlds that readers will enjoy exploring. The conflict is multifaceted and it follows multiple plot lines. The plot is cleverly written, featuring characters who are multidimensional, secrets being uncovered, and intrigue building on multiple fronts while the sense of urgency grows with the stakes." - **Grace Masso, Readers' Favorite**

For Matt and all the roads we've taken.
Thank you for reminding me on that night, in the words of one of our favorite musicals,

"Courage is when we face our fear." — Jack Feldman

You stood by me as I faced mine.

Trigger Warnings:
Extreme graphic violence
Suicide

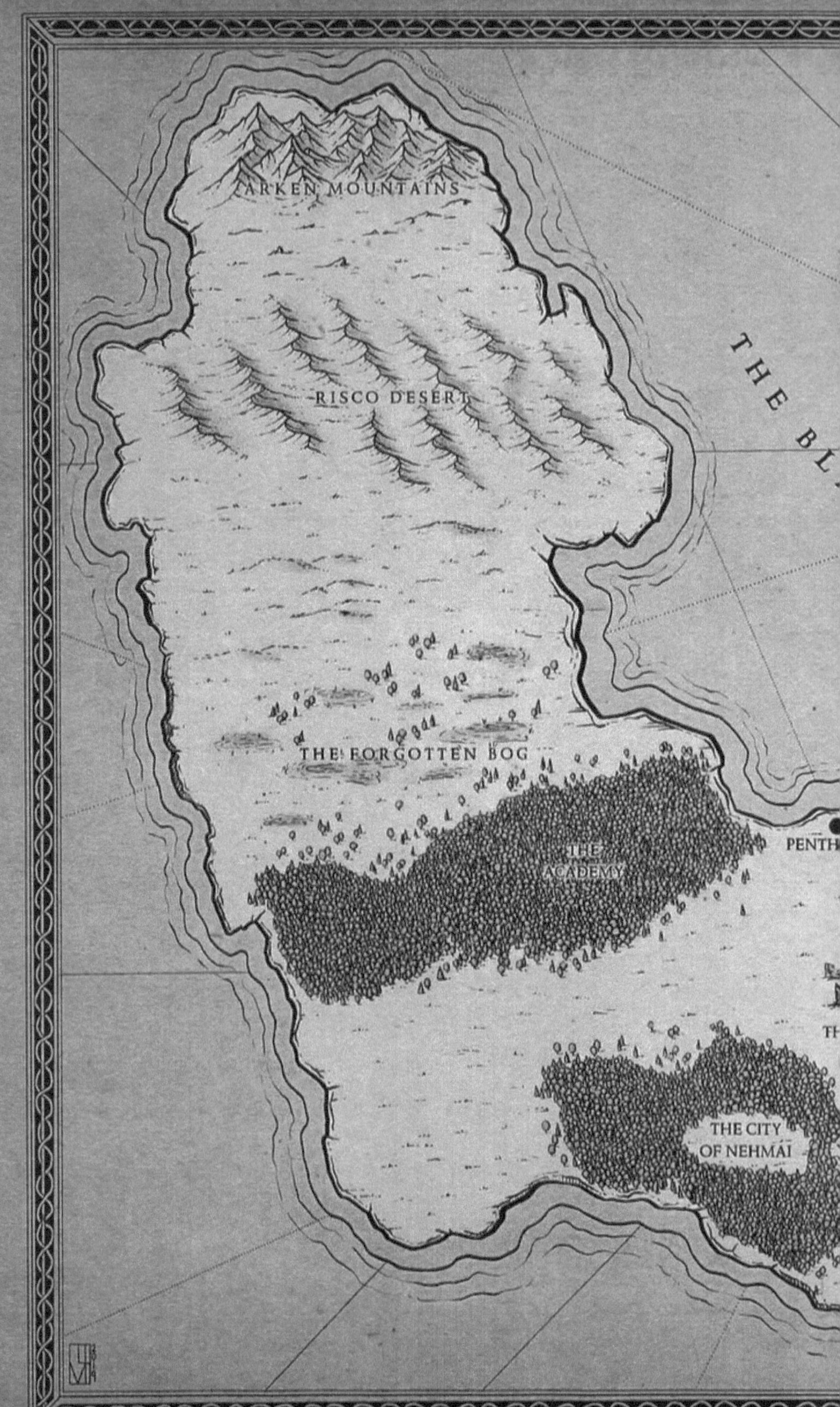
ARKEN MOUNTAINS
RISCO DESERT
THE FORGOTTEN BOG
THE ACADEMY
THE CITY OF NEHMAI

KIERO

THE SHATTERED ISLES

1. HARBOUR OF NEWSOLL
2. TERDES HARBOUR DISTRICT
3. HRISTE
4. OAKLAND WHARF DISTRICT
5. DURDOVER PORT

Kingdom of Broken Iron

BLACK DAWN SERIES BOOK THREE

MALLORY MCCARTNEY

PART ONE:

HARVEST EQUINOX

PROLOGUE

LANA

The saol eile was stuff of legend.

In Lana's world, Langther, the afterlife wasn't feared. In fact, it was a great honor to find one's peace with generations of your family waiting to greet you in the everlasting light. Death didn't scare her; she had been preparing for it since being trapped in Kiero. Now, the dark, unrelenting claws of death had her in their hold, and Lana wished she had more time with Azarius.

Her heart wrenching, she took a deep breath as the sounds of her *home* reached her, teased her . . .

Lana was on her knees, the waves of the Keiv Ocean crashing in the distance, the heat caressing her cheeks when she tipped her face toward the warm sunlight. Langther was tropical against the bleak war in Kiero that she had left behind.

That she had died for.

Greenery stretched as far as she could see: ancient vines crawling up the bases of trees. In her peripheral vision, she saw a flicker of movement—a small filieacan drifting toward her. Its vibrant yellow wings reflected the spattering of sunlight, its long antennae moving back and forth. Lana assumed it was taking in her scent. Fluttering, soft silver dust floated from the filieacan, touching the grass underneath as it grew before Lana's eyes, becoming lusher and healthier. The small creatures were always said to be a sign of vitality. Brows furrowing, she looked down at her fighting leathers—now stripped clean. No remnants of her blood, no trace of the clashing of ash and fire. Even the fissures of pain that had broken her were now only a memory.

Blinking at the landscape, she thought it would be busier. Yet no generations of windwalkers greeted her. No perytons clawed through the skies. No crystal champagne. No feast. No one disrupted the harrowing silence.

She stepped forward, and fear slithered down her spine. Lana tentatively called out, "Hello? Anybody?"

You're alone.

Alone.

The jungle absorbed her cautious footfalls as she walked in search of someone or *anything.*

"Lana?"

She closed her eyes at the sound of that voice, and her heart started to pound.

There, appearing among the thick green foliage, was her mother. She hadn't aged, looking exactly as she did in Lana's memories. Her skin was honey-gold, and she wore a simple green top and high-waisted black pants that flowed loosely toward her ankles, which were bound in leather sandals. Their gazes met, and Lana thought she would combust from the joy filling her.

Her mother made no move toward her. Instead, seemingly frozen, her mother paled. "No. No. *No.* What are you doing here? It's not your time yet." Her mother's face pinched in concern, her deep chestnut hair shining in the sun.

The familiarity of her and the fact she was *here* ripped a hole in Lana's chest at the time lost. "Hello to you too, Mom." Lana chortled. "That's a grand assumption to make."

Closing the space, her mother grabbed her wrists—hard. "*Lana, you have to listen to me.* I have seen it in the eternal winds. The whispers of your essence found me. You're *stuck*, my love, between life and death."

Cold sweat collected in Lana's palms. Echoes of memories churned in her heart—of the Oilean's dark ritual, how they had used her life, her magic, to rip open the channel between Kiero and Daer, how the menacing army had flooded the Noctis Woods before the end embraced her.

Her mother's understanding eyes held hers, and Lana choked out, "I went to distract Adair, thinking I could grant the Rebellion more time. The Oilean caught my scent, and I was caught off guard. They followed me back to Pentharrow, and to Azarius. It was the least I could do, Mom, to buy them the time to escape. I couldn't let them die."

She leaned into her mother's hands when her mother cupped Lana's face. "I know, my love, I *know*."

"Mom . . ."

Her mother kissed her forehead, soft and assuring. "Go back, Lana. Go back to him. Azarius Walsh needs you. Kiero needs you."

Tears slipped fast and silent down Lana's cheeks. She watched her mother step away from her. The wind picked up, dirt and pieces of green leaves ripping off the branches, spinning around her. The warm and familiar scents of cinnamon and sea salt filled her senses. Pure wonder radiated through Lana at how much a single scent could grant strength.

A moment was all it took to remember what exactly she was fighting for. What her mother had died for. Protecting generations of secrets and her dream to be able to live a life free from war.

One with *Azarius*.

Taking in a sharp breath, Lana couldn't react as her mother's hands connected with her chest, shoving her back.

And Lana fell, gravity leaving her in one swooping moment.

She *fell*.

And fell.

She gasped, and her eyes snapped open. Her soul reconnected to her physical self in a jarring rush, causing her to shudder.

Cold, heavy chains weighed down her wrists. She was still stretched and pinned to the trees in a *T* formation. The residue of the Oilean's magic covered her like a poison. Dried blood caked her skin, and Lana blinked against the soft purple light of the Noctis Woods. *It must be the middle of the night*, she thought. Downy snowflakes drifted lazily around her as she focused on what was in front of her.

The ring was charred, smoke still drifting up from it. Where the rocks had once been, tiny craters were grooved into the frozen earth. Frost clawed its way over the bark of the surrounding trees like rays of the moonlight, and the ice stretched as far as she could see.

Except for in the ring.

Her thoughts collided into her. The Oilean had opened the channel; the power they had funneled into the emerald stones had come from *her*. In horror, she had tried to fight against the weight of how the Oilean used her in the ways of forbidden magic . . . She hadn't stopped it, stopped them. They had left her body to rot in the ancient woods, her remaining power left to deteriorate with it.

Closing her eyes, Lana heard the earth churning, recoiling. And it was there, on the sigh of the wind, that the lingering magic spoke to her.

Run.

Run.

Run.

When her eyes opened, her resolve set. She had time. If war wasn't ripping Kiero apart at this moment, then there was still hope in the Rebellion. In Azarius.

Sucking in a deep breath, Lana dipped into her thread of depleted power. Thanks to her mother, the Oilean didn't foresee her coming back from death, so they had left a small ribbon of her ability.

In a plume of smoke, the chains disintegrated. She landed on her knees, and pain ripped through her. Panting, she forced herself to move, her legs shaking like a newborn peryton's. Lana stood, then tumbled. Flakes of snow caught on her eyelashes, melting against her skin.

She took one step; her mind spun.

If the Oilean wanted a body to display and relish in their victories, they would get one. With a flick of her hand, she carved an imprint with the last threads of her ability. Born from the wind, pieced together from the earth, held together by her spilled blood, the body appeared, strung up in the tree—a replica of her corpse.

Ripping herself from the grim scene, Lana fled into the night. Each painful step jarred her back to the present moment, pushing her to find Azarius. The whisper of the world curled around her.

Run.

Run.

Run.

CHAPTER ONE

DECLAN

Dipping his index finger in the spattering of ruby blood on the throne's arm, Declan licked it off the tip of his finger. Eyes closing, the Dark King could hear the previous man's screams, and that fear was still laced in his blood. Each prisoner that was brought to him amused him with their will to live and to fight back.

As if they ever had a chance.

The throne of bones he sat in was cool beneath him. Declan uncrossed and crossed his legs, glaring at the guards that were his puppets. Consuming souls was intoxicating and usually made his life extremely easy in what he hoped to accomplish.

No one could stop him.

Adair Stratton had been conditioned as his vessel for years by the Oilean and with the Book of Old's magic in the boy.

After years of meddling and consuming dark energy and magic in Daer, like his father, Declan was not a man anymore. He was raw power and rage; he was destruction. But only in a vessel who could contain him. The only other power that could sustain him would be a naithe warrior from Nehmai. But that city had died long ago, along with its elitist mentality. Without it, his essence was a whisper, a shadow.

He chewed his lower lip, and annoyance flickered at the years of planning to prove to himself and to his father's memory that Declan had been *more* than what his father had said:

A disappointment of a son and a waste of ability.

"Another," he said in a lazy drawl.

What weak man could eat the souls of people? Could steal their magic? Pushing the thoughts down, Declan steeled himself against the whispers of his dead father in his mind. He, Declan, would destroy Kiero until it was nothing more than a dying star, blinking out of existence. Oh, how he would enjoy watching it burn so brightly.

The guards swiftly complied, entities of his dark magic bowing to his every will, every command. Their silver eyes were empty of emotion; they had no recognition of the world around them. These *vessels* were for his practical uses and nothing more.

Drumming his fingers, he heard the screams coming down the hallway. The guards brought in the man, bloodied, sweating, frantic.

Declan stood, the Oilean materializing beside him, bowing in one motion.

"Our King." Their voices were quiet purrs.

Flicking his gaze to them, he demanded, "If you have nothing new to report, you have one second to get out of my sight."

"Emory Fae and Brokk Foster have seemingly . . . disappeared from Kiero."

"Then I suggest you look harder." Declan walked across the smooth black marble toward the next prisoner. The man paled, whispering intangible sentences while shaking his head. It only made the experience that much more pleasurable.

The rank tang of fear clogged Declan's senses. Stroking the man's face, Declan cooed, "Now, what's *your* ability?"

No words came out of the man's mouth, only choking hiccups.

Declan tutted. "Why must everything be a surprise?"

Declan's hand connected with the man's wrist, and the surge of raw ability filled every crevice of his new body. It expanded into him, easing his weakness, sating his hunger. He sighed in pleasure and dropped the man—now nothing more than a corpse—blood trickling from his mouth.

Rolling his shoulders, Declan addressed the guards nonchalantly. "Dispose of the body with the rest." Fire sprang to his fingertips, the silver flames mesmerizing. "By far, one of my favorites," he mused, more to himself.

Bringing his attention back to the assassins, Declan situated himself on his throne once again, inspecting his fingernails. "Now, I suggest that if you can't find them, you get creative. Draw them out. Set the whole world on fire if you must. Just get Emory Fae and Brokk Foster *back*. I will be ready, but I need what the girl stole from me."

The key.

His heart.

Part of the dark power that Adair had running through his veins.

The sisters bowed their heads, saying nothing.

"It is all worthless unless we get her back. I'm fragmented, broken. The power of the Book of Old has always been the key to my plan. But the power must be *whole*. This strength is only temporary. In a few hours' time, I will be nothing more than smoke and ash again."

"Understood, our King."

He sized them up, silver fire dancing along his forearms. "I suggest you fix your mistakes."

Bowing lowly once more, they disappeared in a plume of smoke.

Cracking his neck, Declan sized up the cavernous room and its unnecessary luxury. He would make fine work of Kiero. His army would sweep over the land, upturning every hidden rock and secret that lay underneath. He began to pace, fire crackling from his hands as it licked up his skin. Staring at the embers drifting to the ground, he fantasized about how exactly he would welcome the queen and prince back to *his* kingdom.

His head tilted back, and he stared up at the open ceiling. The serenade of screams floated up to him from far below; the humans he hadn't drained yet awaited their fate. Fear was such an effective weapon, and it was spreading as his presence became more known.

Declan held on to the fact that until he was at full strength, he would savor watching each prisoner be brought up to him. He would experience ecstasy while feeding off their abilities.

He would soon drain this world like he did Daer.

CHAPTER TWO

MARQUIS

Marquis stood on the cliff's edge. The night was flawless against the raging ocean as the torches flew toward the water, sizzling when they met their end.

Patches of clear sky poked out from the clouds, bathing the Isles in an incandescent wash of moonlight. Marquis chewed his lip, taking in his people who always had his back. They were awaiting instructions.

The waves continuously crashed against the cliff face, and Marquis couldn't wrench his gaze away from where Emory Fae had flung herself, disappearing into the Black Sea. In a moment, she had jumped, and doubt about this plan flooded into him. Why did he always have to push people to their limits?

Emory had assumed Marquis needed liberation, and that had pissed him off. What had given her the right to strut back into Kiero, the unflawed hero, to save them all from Adair? His pride and arrogance fueled his actions, and now he had to decide how to deal with the consequences. He clenched and unclenched his hands as if the movement would jar him out of this nightmare. The longer the silence grew, the more agitated he became.

Running a shaking hand over his mouth, he devoured the waves with his gaze, looking for movement, his heart lodged in his throat.

"Mar?" His best friend slid up next to him; Diedre Lucion's luminous eyes were wide.

He ripped his jacket off, pushing it toward her. "Hold this. I just bought it last week and there is no way I'm ruining it. Don't get it dirty, Dee."

Glancing back where Hriste lay, Marquis wondered if the two immortal warriors had burned it down yet. He would have to wait a little longer for that answer. First, he had to get Emory and Brokk out alive from the violent hold of the Black Sea. The wind howled around him, the hairs on his arms rising.

He took a step toward the cliff's edge then stopped and looked to the horizon where Kiero was nestled hundreds of miles away. How many times had he looked to that horizon, thinking about the Mad King who ruled there? And now . . . that fantasy was lost as well.

Grief pulled deep in his gut at the thought of Adair. Most had only seen him as a monster, someone who was beyond any kind of redemption. But did being human and making mistakes form you into something evil? Marquis thought the opposite. Everyone who claimed to love Adair had let *him* down by allowing him to feel worthless to the point where he felt that his dark intentions were his only option. Marquis remembered the intelligent, loyal-to-a-fault young man Adair had been. Someone who had to prove to the world that he was *more* than what the Academy had deemed him as—a dangerous outcast.

The darkness, one that Marquis to this day still didn't understand, had preyed on that, had feasted on it, and made Adair into the person he swore he would never become. And here, standing on the edge of the towering cliff face, foreboding washed over Marquis so strongly, he took a steadying breath. For years, he had left it behind: Kiero, the Academy, Adair Stratton. All the unsaid things lingering on his tongue that he had wanted to tell that mysterious boy. But that was a lifetime ago, before the world was torn apart by Adair's wrath.

Leaning over the edge, giving in to his adrenaline, Marquis knew he would never know the full truth of what happened in the last six years. He would only find pieces of it, scouring the broken path of lies. From Emory Fae, from the cage his father had built and trapped him in, from this entire world cloaked in madness, all starting with Adair.

Marquis was just another pawn, another player after years of building his own wall.

The wind smelled like salt and seaweed. Marquis pushed off the edge of the cliff and fell. In that space and time, the cold wind made tears swell in his eyes. Despite the jump, his thoughts refused to let him go. He would give anything in the world just for a moment to find out the truth from *Adair.* To have the chance to see him one last time, to tell him the truth . . .

I loved him.

Gravity seemed to transcend time and space as he braced for the impact of the roaring waves rushing up to meet him. He dove into the ice water, cutting through the waves with well-practiced grace. The strength of the ocean pulled him farther down, shock ringing through his body. His breath was knocked out of his chest, and for a second, he was weightless, at the mercy of the tide. His ability expanded from him, shuddering through the waves. Immediately, he could feel the shift as Marquis now commanded the wildness of the Black Sea.

Even now, his ability intoxicated him—the raw power he could harness on a whim. His arms cut through the water, propelling him forward, the moonlight casting the underwater dimension into one of dark beauty. He knew every nook, every cranny. Every reef and shipwreck. And he knew what lay in the shadows, watching who dared to pass through.

He swam faster, and the tide roared up behind him, but instead of sucking him into its treacherous grasp, it pushed him. Speeding up, Marquis sliced through the water seamlessly. Down, he soared into the dark with his heart in his throat. Everything became a blur, the energy within him building.

A split second and his world had crumbled.

The ice settled in his chest; his lungs burned, begging for relief. *What would I say,* could *I say to find even ground with Emory after this?* Screaming, Marquis dropped as bubbles escaped his mouth. All around him, the ocean churned, a massive underwater cyclone that he created. He was sucked into the eye of the massive underwater twister, frothing bubbles spinning around him faster than he could register. Concentrating, he willed the water to push him down, straight to the ocean floor.

Landing heavily, Marquis pushed his ability out in ripples. He pictured the dome in his mind, then watched in awe as the ocean arched above him, creating a protective barrier as blissful oxygen greeted him. He shook his head, salty water raining from his hair. Half drowned, he stood and marveled at the scene around him. The water bowed to his command, creating a protective shield. All around him was night, flashes of silver as schools of fish skittered by, their scales creating glimpses of silver light before being swallowed whole by the darkness.

Sucking in blissful oxygen, Marquis took the first step, his makeshift dome following. He craned his neck, looking up to the Isles.

"I hope your lover boy is worth it, Emory," he muttered.

At the water's silence, he shook his head and walked toward the small cave, the entrance only visible if one was looking and smart enough to stay away. The human skulls weren't hidden. Slabs of coral supported them, the peerless white beckoning to him. He swore under his breath, and a pit grew in his stomach. Marquis didn't falter, knowing what awaited him behind those walls, but for the first time in a long time, fear shot through every fiber of his core.

CHAPTER THREE

EMORY

'BROKK!" Emory's screams tore from her, panic overwhelming her.

All she could see was the deepening shadows as she swam, trying to find Brokk lost among the Black Sea. Her heart plummeted; she would not lose him now. Pumping her arms faster, she cut down against the tide, fresh oxygen flowing thanks to her makeshift face mask. One thought flared through her mind: He could not swim.

But then she saw the flash of silver, and she spotted Brokk, held by knifepoint, the assailant hidden in the shadows.

She was going to lose him.

Swimming faster, she cut down before her world turned into nothing but pain. Looking down, she saw the amethyst slam against her chest, her shirt having pulled loose. The gem fused into her flesh, starting to melt, her burned skin bubbling . . .

Gasping, Emory awoke with a start; panic and confusion washed over into her reality. Blinking rapidly, she stared at the rock face above her. A cold sweat coated her body, and her face scrunched. *Where am I?* With a groan, she closed her eyes, trying to remember what happened after she had seen Brokk.

Her mother's necklace had fused to her flesh . . . She remembered fire roping from her chest down to her arms—which was impossible. Her pulse thrummed, her muscles screaming; her nerve endings flared to life. Something dug into her back, her skin turning numb from the pressure. There had been a split second of freedom, of defiance. Her breath came out in a slow wheeze, fluid in her lungs choking her, drowning her. Then there had been pain splintering down through her bones until she saw nothing but red.

Eyes fluttering open once more, Emory squinted up at the ceiling. Stalactites clung to the dark-gray stone, glowing ominously. Water slid quietly down the walls around her, keeping the cave damp. Had Marquis imprisoned them again? Anger flared in her chest, and she wriggled against the restraints, then she heard them.

"She's awake!"

"Should we prod her?"

"Why are her eyes like that?"

"Do you truly think it's *her*?"

The voices overlapped, becoming too much, too fast. She sat up, and the world tilted. Emory rasped, "Where am I? Where is he? Where's Brokk?"

Dead silence followed as the entire room spun from the pain radiating through her body. Emory's wrists were tied behind her back, and she fought harder against the restraints. "Where is he?"

From the shadows of the cave, four figures slowly came into focus, wearing shimmering green V-neck shirts. The material looked like fish scales in the half light. Leather pants and boots finished their identical outfits. Their long, lustrous gray hair was unbound, tumbling past their shoulders. From their lithe and curved bodies, Emory guessed they were women, but their features were obscured by beautifully carved masks . . .

Her heart dropped into her stomach when she realized these strangers were wearing snarling wolf masks that looked to be carved from *bone. What the hell?* The exaggerated bone fangs jutted out above their lips, and the pointed ears rose above their foreheads. But the matching violet eyes glowing from behind each mask made ice rush through Emory's veins.

Breathing hard, Emory sat up, her core burning from the strain. Trying to logically assess her situation, Emory bit her lip. Blood welled, the sea salt stinging the wound.

The group pressed closer, and she realized they were watching the ruby droplet splash onto the cavern floor.

"If you have hurt him—"

"Calm down, Princess. Or should I say, *Queen*?" Three of them laughed, their bodies shaking. Heat blossomed in her cheeks as the speaker squatted in front of her, her gaze probing. "So, the rumors were true."

Emory's breath grew ragged; she searched the bare cavern walls for any sign of where she was being held or if Brokk was alive.

"You know, here we were, just minding our own business, like any other day. My sisters and I, devastatingly hungry, having been exiled and trapped in this boring cage, when you and your friend showed up. We were lucky." The woman slowly unsheathed a knife from the belt she wore on her hip.

Panic rose in Emory as the stranger ran her finger along the blade's edge. Without warning, the woman flipped the grip on the knife's hilt, cutting into her own palm. Her violet gaze filled with anger, never leaving Emory's, not even as her own blood started to splatter on the cave's floor in a steady drip. Emory watched in horror as the woman raised her wound to her lips and drank her own blood in heady gulps.

After a minute, she stopped, and Emory watched as the wound healed itself over.

"We were once like you. Desperate to prove ourselves to the Isles. Young, beautiful, powerful women." Shifting closer, she ran the blade along Emory's cheek, the rancid smell of decay rolling from her mouth. "But the world was unkind and cruel. Now, all of that is but a distant memory. We no longer care about the ploys of kings and queens. The only thing left for us is *hunger*."

Sweat trickled down the back of Emory's neck. "Then why do you care about me?"

"My dear thing, I don't. I care about what runs through your veins. What encases your heart, your blood, and your muscles. We both know that dark magic is not yours to keep. We all know that you stole it from the Mad King."

Any words died on Emory's tongue when she pressed her lips into a thin line. *There had been pain.* Emory blinked hard. *Pain as the gem had deteriorated, burning her skin, and that darkness had ravaged her. Had* become *her, no longer trapped within the amethyst.*

Emory tried to hide her horror at the realization. She tilted her head, hoping to sound braver than she felt. "Oh, I think you are wrong about that."

The woman closed the space between them, pressing the blade's edge—still wet with her own blood—against Emory's throat. Emory tried not to move; the pressure felt like it was already cutting into her skin.

"Those demons who hunt you will cross the sea for you." The woman's breath smelled like blood; she spoke into Emory's face. "They will never stop looking until they have the dark magic back and you are dead. Truly, I am doing you a favor. I will kill you before we eat you. It will be a mercy compared to what the Oilean would do."

The others behind her started to sway, a deep humming reverberating in the cave. Craning away, all Emory could feel was the heat clawing through her, a newfound force demanding her attention. *Who are these cannibals? How can they know so much about me and the Oilean?* Emory shoved the thought down, and her ability rose, the power building beneath her skin.

Keeping her face slack, the woman pressed on. "Now, don't make a scene. We wouldn't want to ruin the surprise for your companion."

Throwing her weight forward, Emory cracked her forehead against her captor's. The knife between them cut into Emory's flesh, down to her collarbone. She swayed against the wound and flaring pain, and blood trickled down her forehead as she staggered up. Heat flared around her wrists and the binds disintegrated. *Did I do that?*

Feeling lightheaded, Emory touched her throat, expecting to be bleeding out, but instead, she felt her skin knitting back together with inhuman speed. *My ability has changed because of the gem holding Adair's power.* Pushing down the shocking thought, Emory watched her opponent drop, clutching her mask. The other masked strangers brandished their daggers, closing in around her. Emory felt her skin flush, that humming building within her, begging to be released, and she wanted to obey its demand.

But only one thing mattered: Brokk.

Her captors froze when she rolled her neck, bones cracking. Closing her eyes, Emory relished in the movement. "You know, I was hoping it wouldn't come to this. But you give me no other choice."

Emory heard the hiss of the blade cutting through the air. She bowed her body backward, and the knife slashed where her throat had just been. Straightening up, she lunged, allowing the power, her anger, and grief to rise to the surface, raging through her core. And it was there that she found herself limitless.

The cave was a blur as her knuckles slammed into the jawbone of one of her captors, blood spattering as bone cracked. As the woman stumbled back, the mask clattered to the ground. The hollowed woman stood before her, pale skin stark, eyes boring into Emory's. Emory's skin ignited as if fire was incinerating her blood, her heart.

"Where is he?"

The rest of the company charged at her as a response. Emory met them, picturing Anithe clearly in her mind as the sword was born from the embers and ashes, materializing from thin air.

Adair's voice whispered through her mind, *"With my ability, I could raise an army from the dead."*

Shaking, Emory took in the inky metal, deep hues of red and orange flickering against the dim cave light. If her ability had no limits, then breathing Anithe into life didn't seem out of the question. Gripping Anithe's hilt, Emory bent her knees, planting her left foot behind her right, brandishing the flaming steel in front of her.

The women were circling her, grinning, daggers brandished as if toying with her. Again, Adair's voice slithered into her mind, whispering as if he were standing beside her, murmuring into her ear, "*You've taken on more formidable enemies than these. Me, for instance. Remember, don't stand still. Try to use this cave to your advantage.*"

Raking her gaze quickly around her environment, she noticed that the bare walls offered nothing she could immediately use. Emory dodged the first attack. One woman threw her dagger, aiming for Emory's heart, as the other lunged toward Emory, driving her back.

Flames roared from Anithe, making the woman who was charging toward Emory falter for a split second. Emory ducked fast, and the dagger flew past her cheek by a hairsbreadth. She fell into an unwavering, steady focus. She rolled, her calves burning, and her right leg connected with one woman's groin as she stood, the feint kick hard as Emory drove Anithe into the woman's chest cavity. Blood sprayed the cavern's closest wall.

Heaving Anithe back, Emory spun, panting; she parried the ramming attack that met her. The stranger yelled, trying to drive her dagger into Emory's throat. Shoving the woman hard, Emory rammed her right elbow into the woman's gut as the dagger clattered onto the floor between them. Moving fast, Emory brought Anithe down, cleaving through the woman, the wound splitting from her shoulder to hip. Blood sprayed into Emory's face, but she was numb.

Running forward, the remaining two threw their daggers simultaneously. Emory swung Anithe fast and low, deflecting the two blades. Sparks flew as she stumbled slightly over her footing, ten steps ahead of her mind.

Adair sighed in her mind. "*Concentrate, Em. Allow yourself to breathe. Move with the weapon.*"

Exhaling hard, she quickly assessed the cavern: the smooth walls, the table where she was bound, high ceilings . . . But there, to the left, a small shimmering of movement. Yelling, she slammed the blade down, catching the woman's shoulder. Emory's eyes widened as her attacker dropped, the woman's right arm almost fully severed from the socket, blood pooling at an alarming rate.

Wrenching Anithe from the bone, Emory circled the remaining woman. Parrying, Emory ducked as another knife flew, cutting through the negative space. Sweat trickled down her back, and pain seared up her triceps. The woman had run behind her, and Emory felt the hot blood pouring down her skin, felt the steel bite into her flesh from behind. Swinging, Emory blocked the next attack. Everything was a blur, their yells becoming white noise. Emory was relentless, Anithe an extension of her arm.

Adair's whisper curled around her mind, saying, "*Now. Do it* now."

Tucking her elbows in, Emory crouched low, gritting her teeth as the sword met hers, sparks flying.

The woman she fought said, "You are ours, Emory Fae. Give up."

Kicking, Emory slammed her foot into the woman's shin, hearing bone crack from the impact. Propelling forward, she slammed Anithe into the stone, and it cut into the floor like butter. *Impossible.*

The ground shuddered, and a hairline fracture shivered up the blade's edge. Not stopping, Emory ran, and Anithe exploded behind her, exactly as she had willed it. Debris bounced off the wall, screams climbing behind her.

To her left, another cave wall exploded, throwing her sideways. Black spots erupted in her vision, and her stomach lurched. Choking on dust, she staggered, trying to get up. *Where is Brokk?* Running, she stopped as a voice rang out behind her.

"Emory!" Through the dust and debris, Marquis Maher closed the space between them, chest heaving. Emory stilled, her pulse thundering in her ears. She watched his face turn ashen as he stopped dead in his tracks at the sight of her. Emory screamed as a woman appeared behind Marquis and threw a knife. The blade nicked the edge of his ear, and he broke out of his trance.

Marquis was a blur as he ripped his blades from their sheaths. He ducked as the last standing woman charged him, her bloodlust plain.

Adair's voice snapped, "*Now, escape.*"

Emory fought against ever fiber in her body as she turned around. Heat flared through her veins, a wild unharnessed thing. The energy closed in around her heart, her footfalls echoing as she calmly walked back toward the first cavern.

Then, a crack of electricity exploded from her.

The force knocked Marquis to the ground. The power was like a spider web, and Emory created it, commanded it, and was learning its depth like the back of her hand. The threads lined up to each one of her captors, their beating hearts echoing to her. *How could they possibly still be alive?*

Emory pinned them, her newfound ability roaring in pleasure as she sank her claws deeper into their minds, taking over their bodies. Memories flashed before her, of pain, of blood. Of every victim they had lured and captured in their nightmarish cave and had preyed on, without mercy, to gain the abilities and strengths that flesh yielded. Eventually, this turned them into monsters; they called themselves *diams.* Emory relished how they struggled beneath her invisible grasp. Their fear was tangible, and she pressed harder, the thrumming in her blood drowning out everything else.

In that moment, she wanted them to know what it was like to be hunted, to be afraid.

"Em?" Brokk's voice sounded behind her.

It was one feeble word. How Brokk said her name, held it, and protected it. Emory loosened a breath, and her ability shattered around her, bringing her smashing back into reality. She spun to face him, and his golden eyes found hers. The fire running through her veins was quenched.

Brokk staggered forward, blood running down his temple. He reached for her. "Em. Help me." Unsteady, he collapsed to the ground, his eyes rolling into his head, and all she could see and smell was blood.

"Brokk!"

Her feet couldn't carry her fast enough, the cannibals screaming behind her. Her heart was lodged in her throat; fear gripped her tightly.

Dropping to her knees, she clutched Brokk's face, frantic. "No, no, no!"

His skin was feverish and clammy, his blood wet as it dripped through her fingers. His breath quick and shallow. Her fingers scrambled as she tried to pinpoint the wound in his chest. Someone clawed at her back, ripping her jacket, ripping her away from him.

"Emory, move!" Marquis rammed his shoulder into her.

Stumbling back, she looked to see Marquis throwing his knife. It sliced through the air, finding its mark. The woman's yowl cut through the cave. Her body dropped, the knife lodged in her heart. Black blood seeped everywhere.

The rest of the diams looked to them. Defying all logic, soaked in their own blood, they made their way toward Emory one staggering step at a time.

Grabbing Brokk, Marquis threw him over his shoulder, bellowing at Emory to move, to follow, but his yells were drowned out by her shock. She licked her cracked lips.

The women charged, their fingernails sprouting into long, pale claws.

One. Emory braced herself, clenching her fists, feeling the tide of energy trying to pull her under.

Two. Blackened veins pulsed under her skin, and for a split second, she marveled at this terrible, beautiful, endless power. Instead of scaring her or disgusting her, the thrill of possibilities electrified her.

Three. She ran, her body fueled by her adrenaline, her ability acting first. Shooting down that web, her claws sank into the hearts of the remaining three, and Emory didn't falter.

"*Make your decision, Princess,*" Adair purred.

Yelling, she slammed down with her ability, breaking all threads, and the bodies dropped before her.

"By the . . . Black Sea." Marquis's voice bounced around the small space; his footsteps were heavy and coming from behind her.

Chest heaving, she couldn't look away from the broken masks and scattered bodies. The blood.

"Emory?" Marquis's hand was there, on hers, and she wrenched her gaze away from the bodies. Slowly and gently, he placed Brokk back on the ground. "Princess?"

Moving away from him, she seethed, "Get away from me! Get away from him!" The air stirred, Anithe materializing once again in her grasp.

The king of the Shattered Isles, his features dark, looked at the sword. "I am not your enemy."

Emory arched her brow. "Oh no? You locked us up only to shove Brokk over a cliff, where conveniently ancient *cannibals* waited for us."

Marquis huffed. "I didn't think you would jump. It was meant to be a test, all of it. What do you think ruling is? Allowing whoever sails across the sea onto our shores, welcome them with open arms and no questions? Again, you haven't the first clue what you have gotten into. Yes, I did shove Brokk off the cliff, and yes, you did jump. I also locked you up for a time so I could think about what exactly I was going to do. It allowed me to talk to my people, to address what you have brought to our shores. Am I a criminal for giving the Isles freedom to speak, to digest? To choose?"

He continued, "You have come back from the dead! You are bringing war upon us and asking my people to die for you. Asking me to trust you. You and I don't know the first thing about each other."

"So what? Am I your prisoner? While we argue, dark forces are working against us. We don't have time for this childish behavior!"

He shook his head. "Don't begin to tell me about the danger we are in. I can see it."

"And what is that supposed to mean?"

"Either you and your party leave now, or you start listening to me. I just saved your life. The diams were cursed exiles, their power bleeding into madness as they fed on their prisoners. No one, in thousands of years, has walked away from them and been able to tell the tale."

Marquis looked down at Brokk's unconscious body and back up to her, his green eyebrows arching to match his condescending tone. "You are brave, Emory Fae. You are powerful. But you can't win this war alone. You will find allies here if you allow yourself the time to learn about what it means to rule."

"So, you're saying yes? You will help us?" Emory countered.

"I'm saying you need friends. A court. A shield to front the onslaught that is coming for us all. I'm saying that you need to grow into your potential. Your parents started a revolution in the Academy only to have it go up in flames because of the secrets they kept. I'm not saying my dad did much better ruling the Isles; he only got his throne by killing your grandfather. I'm proposing that you and I both do better than the examples left for us." He paused and took a breath. "So, I suppose in a way, I am agreeing."

Exhaling hard, she deflated, looking down to Brokk. *You're wasting time. Brokk needs help now.* Marquis's words resonated through her. When she was a teenager, the promise of court had been in her mind with Adair beside her. Her throat became thick at the reminder. She sheathed Anithe across her back, the scabbard materializing as she did so, her ability anticipating her thoughts.

"And you would want to teach me, after everything I have done? After I killed Adair? You would trust me?"

Marquis closed the space between them, grabbing her chin with his fingers. "It's all about trust, Princess. I trust that you gave him every chance. That you weren't as hasty as the others, that you knew there was more to his story than becoming the Mad King. There has always been more. I'm willing to put my feelings of animosity toward you aside for this alliance. For survival. Are you willing to do the same?"

At her silence, he gently shoved her back and picked up Brokk, raising that emerald eyebrow at her.

Heat rushed up to her cheeks, flushing her face as she digested his words. Guilt tugged at her stomach. Had she truly given Adair every chance he deserved?

No.

Trying to forget about Adair, she said, "I want to do the same, but we will all talk. Riona, Kiana, and Brokk. It's not just my decision."

"I wouldn't expect anything else." Marquis smirked.

Emory held up a finger. "And no more cells."

With a shrug, he walked away from her, and with one last look at the massacre she was leaving behind, she followed Marquis out of the cave.

He slipped through a small archway, and she could feel the shift in his ability. It was like a shield all around them, keeping the oxygen in and defying the rules of the ocean. There was a small stone walkway down, and she followed, in awe as she glimpsed the world around her. The tinges of the night were bleeding away, golden light starting to filter in ribbons through the water. Landing on the ocean floor, she walked, the schools of fish swimming far above them, the reefs clambering up like castles. Exhaustion nipped at her body, but she pushed on, following Marquis, lost in thought.

He was their only way back to Kiero. Back to the Black Dawn Rebellion. To face the Oilean and the Dark King.

The thought of facing Declan made her stomach churn, anxiety clawing through her. But every single step brought her closer to helping Brokk. To seeing the warriors again. To have a fighting chance in this war, she needed Marquis as much as he needed her.

Sighing, she cooed, "Oh, noble king?"

"What?" Marquis sighed.

"How do you propose we get out of the ocean?" He faced her and his dangerous expression made her falter. She paused. "Marquis?"

Suddenly his ability was like an electric current running through the ocean, bringing it to life. He said, "Hold on."

The ocean churned, and she was swallowed whole.

The shield of air vanished as she was ripped upward, the water responding to its king's demands. Emory twisted; her body flipped upside down. Her palms smacked her face, her arms spinning wildly. Her legs flailed, trying to find solid ground, but any connectedness had vanished under Marquis's command.

Emory screamed. She was wrenched around, faster and faster. She broke through the surface, her screams a gurgled mass trapped in her throat. The roaring waves pushed her up, rising with the sun. Everything moved too fast as she saw the swell crashing toward the cliff face. Gravity disappeared, and then she dropped, soaking wet. Closing her eyes, she expected to be met with open air, falling endlessly.

She landed hard, and blood and dirt filled her mouth. *Shit.* Groaning, Emory rolled over, blinking against the new morning light. Murmurs erupted around her, the noise sounding like the sighs of the wind. There was a crack like thunder, and she watched another colossal wave rise. Marquis, still holding Brokk, descended in front of her with much more grace. Landing beside her, he smirked before the wave crashed back to the ocean, froth spraying them all.

"Mar!" The woman was a blur as she collided with the king, hugging him fiercely. Breaking free, Marquis gently lowered Brokk to the ground, talking in hushed tones to the group forming around them. The woman handed him an elegant black collared jacket. Marquis lit up at the sight of it, donning it over his sodden clothes.

Emory coughed, and the woman snapped her attention to her lying on the ground. "And what about this one?"

Marquis looked to her, voice lowering. "Diedre, we talked about this."

Diedre looked at Emory, skepticism bright in her eyes. "I can't trust that she won't murder us in our sleep." Her gazed raked over Emory as she tilted her head. "Well, time will tell. Though a note for you, Emory, is that I would destroy you in a fight. No funny business."

Standing and wheezing slightly, Emory met the woman's intensity head-on. "Noted. But Brokk is our priority right now. Nothing else."

"Diedre, please take Brokk to see Elle immediately with the others. Now, Emory, with me," Marquis ordered.

A bitter taste filled Emory's mouth. She watched as Brokk was ushered away. Heart lodged in her throat, she drank in Brokk's pallor, his limp body covered in blood. Faltering, Emory tried not to think about the possibility of losing him. Her teeth chattered; the crisp morning promised that winter was looming over them.

Looking to the rolling hills, she whispered, "And where, exactly, is the city?"

Marquis nodded to the empty, rugged horizon. "Not far. Come on, Princess. There is a lot to discuss."

The wind howled and the sun crested, touching the Shattered Isles. The lush green valleys dipped and rolled, the vastness of this land leaving Emory breathless. Hunching her shoulders against the wind, Emory followed.

For several moments, the only sounds were the crashing of the Black Sea, the gulls in the distance, and the crunching of their footfalls against the loose rubble flowing into the field before them. They walked into the bowing grassland, leaving the mammoth cliff faces behind. In the wind, sea salt crusted her lips. Emory took in the scenery for a moment as she stared at the rolling plains, nothing in sight for miles.

The contrast between here and Kiero was stark. Here, there were no ancient forests or dancing shadows within them. On the Isles, nothing could hide for miles, and the unfamiliarity filled her with nervousness. She was brought back to when she had run away from the Academy in the first week of being brought back to Kiero. Her fear and adrenaline had spiked at the wildness of the world around her, at the impossibility that she was there, a part of it. That same feeling started to creep into her heart now. Walking beside Marquis, Emory realized that over the months she had been in Kiero, without realizing it, it had become her home once again in all its flaws and unforgiving history.

Home.

"What happened to the necklace you had? The one that had Adair's dark magic trapped within it?"

The waves crashing against the shoreline filled the silence between them, and Emory said nothing.

"Our relationship is not off to a good start if you can't answer a simple question honestly," Marquis pressed.

Emory replied, "It's not simple to explain."

"Then enlighten me."

"No. Who's Elle?" Emory asked, changing the subject.

"Elle is the healer in Hriste, the capital of the Shattered Isles." He paused. "I have my theory, you know. About how the necklace is conveniently missing."

It was all too much: the game, the imminent war. Alliances and friendships were being bled dry as they spoke. Soon Kiero would consist of nothing more than monsters ripping and tearing everything apart. Then nothing would remain but the corpses left behind.

"Remember what we talked about," Marquis gently pressed.

The ground dipped as Emory walked, her heartbeat becoming louder as if she were being stripped away from her body. The world was this constant beat, pulling her forward.

Running a hand through her soaking hair, she shook her head. "I don't understand half of what is happening to me. Of what happened when I killed Adair . . ."

Marquis whispered her name.

The words escaped her. "Winning this world means fighting against impossible odds. How do I know that you won't hand me over to the Oilean? How do I know that you won't betray everything I am fighting for?"

"And what exactly are you fighting for?"

Exasperated, she shot back, "Freedom. A better world than the one my parents left behind. Peace. So that none of us are prisoners of war."

"I want that future, too, Emory. But remember you are on my kingdom's terms now. You don't get to return from the dead and expect my people to abandon the Isles to follow a new queen. You must earn that trust and respect. I know we are off to a rough start, but I want to work together to win this. When you first told me about Adair . . . I was unprepared. Hurt."

Whipping around, she pressed her finger into his chest. "And you didn't stop to think for a *minute* that I am hurting as well?"

"Oh, I am banking that you *are*," he rebutted.

Her voice was coarse as she slammed her hands into his chest. "I *loved* Adair once. Even if you are too small-minded to understand the depths of it, I did. He was a part of my family. He was one of my best friends. And the Oilean—they turned him into a weapon.

Into something beyond recognition. Into my *enemy.*" She sucked in a breath. "And now I'm the monster, a ruthless killer, and there is no turning back from what I have done. The darkness that was in Adair is a *part* of me. Where is that dark magic now, you ask? It's running through my veins, Marquis."

"Even so, you're the reason he is dead. *You* drove the dagger into his heart. Your *darkness* and the consequence of that choice is yours to bear."

Marquis was so close. Emory took in his spattering of freckles, his unyielding emerald eyes. Turning his back to her, he made his way through the swaying fields.

The grass shone, churning like molten gold. As the light danced across their path, Emory was transported to a simpler time. A time when, as a young girl, she would watch the leaves fall from the trees outside of the Academy, floating down to where they would rest on the forest floor. Back then, she had wondered if all time would pass like this—something so fragile that, if you weren't paying attention, it would fade away into a delicate memory. She swallowed past the lump in her throat, trying not to think about how much had slipped through her fingers.

"Princess?" Marquis's voice brought her slamming down back into reality. Sighing, she put one foot in front of the other, forcing her breath into an even rhythm.

"I was lost in thought. You're right. I am trying to live with the consequence of killing Adair, but I came here for help, and what I'm going through doesn't change that. You must promise that you will follow through on your end. But first, I need another promise from you."

"I'm listening."

Emory looked around, breathing in the salty air as they cut through the rolling expanse of grassland. Her voice was soft, but she knew he heard every word. "Not a word to Brokk or the warriors about the necklace. That is my business, and I'm not beyond killing kings. Never forget that."

A beat passed.

And another.

Grumbling, Marquis narrowed his eyes. "I'm choosing not to take what you just said as a threat. But you should heed my warning . . ." His lip curled up. "One look at you, Emory, and they will figure out that you are changed."

"And what is that supposed to mean?"

Marquis stopped and faced her. His hands cupped together, and water pooled between them instantly, swirling, creating a flat oval surface.

She stepped closer, and her hands shook as she reached out. Ice immediately flared beneath her touch, and the world shrank into the background. Emory looked at her reflection in the icy mirror. Her hair was sopping, blazing red ends clinging to her shoulders. She took in her pale skin, the huge dark circles bruising underneath her eyes. The mirror started to frost along the edges, and Emory couldn't look away.

She had her father's eyes once. But now black swirled around her irises, sucking any trace of the emerald out, leaving an echo, an imprint, of something more sinister. A constant reminder of the dark magic pumping through her veins. *No, no, no, no.* Her limbs trembled as the new fire pooled in her belly. Intoxicating, it commanded her, slithering through her muscles, her sinew, her bones. Emory closed her eyes. Her nerve endings burning.

The echo of energy surged through her, never leaving her grasp. It was like she was coaching the power forward—it became her heart, her will. With Adair's power, she was able to bring her normal appearance back, hiding her secret. Opening her eyes, Emory smirked and shrugged past Marquis, her now-green eyes flashing in the ice. "As I said, not a word."

The ice cracked behind her, followed by Marquis's footfalls, and Emory's frustration grew.

"Emory . . ."

Spinning around, she said firmly, "Not a word, Marquis. I will meet you halfway, but trust me, this is my compromise. It's not your truth to tell. Especially not to Brokk."

Running a hand through his green hair, he shrugged. "*Okay*. Okay. But if you bring the war to my shores because you won't tell lover boy what happened to you down there, then I will be the first to kill you."

"I wouldn't expect anything less."

***

The sun hung high in the sky, the amber light washing over every crevice. The last time she experienced an afternoon like this, she was on Earth, sipping iced coffee, tucked beneath an umbrella at her favorite café. She was in no rush, soaking up the last nice days of summer, the promise of fall in the air.

The simplicity of that life was gone.

Now, every time she closed her eyes, Emory saw the knife in her grip as she sliced into Adair's chest. She saw Brokk falling into the ocean. She saw the Rebellion burning. Her reality now made up her nightmares. She would lie awake for hours at night, thinking of decisions she could have made differently. Would Adair be alive now? Could she have figured out a less bloody route to save Kiero as well as the Mad King? Or at the end of the day, was she as bad as her parents, thinking she was acting out of love? Thinking that she could make a difference against dark forces such as the Oilean?

It was a dangerous path to go down, but despite her doubts about herself, Emory knew within her heart that Brokk was part of her hope. If he was alive, there would be hope for Kiero's future, no matter what happened. If winning this war meant Emory had to walk behind another arrogant king and omit telling her company what happened when she killed Adair, then so be it.

Sweat slithered down her spine, and Emory glared at Marquis's back, trying to figure out how he was so unnervingly calm.

They hadn't moved past the rolling hills and, judging from her now-dry clothes and hair, they had been trudging for hours. The terrain had grown rockier, the sounds of the distant crashing waves the tempo to her thoughts. Emory tried to hold on to her resolve as her consciousness debated her decision.

She could leave Marquis, but who would she turn to in this war? What would that prove except that she couldn't be a potential ally? Marquis was arrogant and annoyingly stubborn. But who else could rally behind her? She had no other option.

She gritted her teeth, and her breath hitched. *I am a queen, not a prisoner.* Squinting, Emory tried to see any sign of a city, let alone another person. *Brokk is depending on me. Kiana and Riona are depending on me to be there for Brokk.* Clenching her fists, her nails digging into her palms, Emory held her head high, trying to steady her nerves.

"Princess?" Marquis's voice was silken, and she stopped, taking in his darkened expression. He stepped toward her and his eyes churned, emotions flickering through them so fast, Emory couldn't pinpoint what exactly he was feeling. The movement was quick, his hand wrapping around her wrist, gripping hard. She waited for the normal rush of his ability flooding through her body, but nothing came.

He pulled her in closer, a smirk on his face. "Remember, I am the only one who can neutralize your ability." He paused. "Now listen closely. Do exactly what I say and follow my lead. You are on my lands, asking for my help. Are you willing to do whatever it takes?"

"Of course. We need to join forces, to help unite the rebels. We need to rebuild the Black Dawn Rebellion and join armadas."

Marquis nodded and letting go, he said, "A tip for you before we continue. Hold on to whatever you are feeling now, and don't forget that you need my resources, not only to help rebuild your scattered Rebellion, but also in this war. How can you feed an army? Clothe them, provide them with weapons? I can make that a reality, but alliances come at a different price here on the Isles."

Her heart lodged in her throat as Marquis turned.

Unbuckling the knife from his belt, Marquis sliced it hard across his palm; blood bubbled from the wound. Kneeling, he pressed it to the ground, murmuring softly.

Wide-eyed, Emory felt the tremor in the ground shudder up her body. The wind picked up, and déjà vu washed through Emory. Adair had entered his kingdom the same way—with a payment of blood. The ground cracked, the fissure racing down the land, then Marquis turned to her, hand outreached.

"Trust me."

Staring at his palm, she licked her cracked lips, the power of her ability thrumming through her veins, wrapping around her heart. Her shaking fingers intertwined with his as the grass and dirt disappeared from underneath them . . .

. . . and they fell.

She clamped her mouth shut to hold in her scream. Marquis squeezed her hand so hard she was sure it would break, but the rest of her limbs flailed. Flashes of green and gold burned through her vision.

Her fear broke through, panic welling at what she was trying to accomplish. Emory was just a woman fighting for a broken crown within a broken kingdom. She was navigating a sea of strangers in the Isles; how could *she* win them over? Her memories were still like burned fragments, some whole, some still just echoes of feelings guided by blurred images. She knew Marquis had once been enough for her to like as a friend. Was that enough to trust him as an ally?

As they dropped through time and space, dread shredded her piece by piece. Who was she to Marquis but a result of a broken government? Of a broken dream where Kiero and the Shattered Isles had been united?

Emory opened her eyes to see the rushing expanse of blue before it swallowed them whole. The water crushed her lungs, and they begged for air. The freezing water electrified her, and Marquis let go of her hand. She felt her clothes dragging her down, but she fought, kicking and clawing her way up. Numbness radiated through her arms and legs; water filled her lungs. Energy exploded from her; the water churned as Emory, with the help of her ability, swam toward the surface.

She crashed through the water, and the waves bucked beneath her, shoving her harshly onto the shore. Gravity took hold, and she landed heavily on grass. She coughed as water spilled through her lips, her lungs burning and tears pricking her eyes. With a gag, she emptied her stomach then gasped for air. Her fingers dug into the grass and dirt. Ears ringing, Emory blinked, the sunlight making it hard to focus. Bile still stung her throat.

Trying to get her bearings, she focused on the scenery around her. It was like she was in a massive stadium, the cliff ledges dropping into a deep bowl where the capital of the Shattered Isles was hidden. Looking behind her, she saw a small lake with a waterfall crashing into it from the cliff face above. She would have to ask Marquis later if he specifically made it for visitors entering Hriste.

Then she noticed them. Ten men and women dressed in vivid clothing stood around her in a half circle. She had gotten used to the black-and-gray clothing of the Rebellion. Here, she took in the deep purple, blue, and pink-to-canary-yellow tops. Some of the women were adorned with gold bracelets that wrapped from their wrists to their upper shoulders. Emory spotted full tattoo sleeves on both the men and women, capturing beasts she'd never seen before and capturing life, magic, and wonder at first glance. She breathed in the culture she had only just begun to glimpse. Behind them, she spotted a bustling city—hundreds of houses sprawling for miles—and in the distance, people rushed down the cobblestone streets, going about their day. They were on the outskirts of Hriste.

She breathed hard, and the thud in front of her made her look up, stunned. Diedre glared down at her, the sword she had tossed to Emory lying before her. The blade was gorgeous, deep-blue and gleaming. The hilt was carved like a wolf howling toward the sky, mocking her.

Emory stared past the sword, to the black boots that moved toward her. “Marquis . . .”

He was sopping wet as he kneeled in front of her. Loud enough for the crowd to hear, Marquis said, “Emory Fae, did you and your guests come to the Isles for aid and shelter? Asking not only for this but for our help in the looming war?”

Her throat became like cotton. Feeling thick and clumsy, she squinted at Marquis, his face darkening. Standing slowly, he rose with her, picking up the blade and handing it out to her—an invitation. Focusing more, Emory took in the deep cuts of rock face that rose toward the sky, closing them in and shielding Hriste. Marquis’s eyebrows rose, his eyes challenging her.

Flipping her hair back, Emory anchored her body, her left foot sliding back, finding balance. Accepting Marquis’s silent request, Emory took the sword, palming the hilt and adjusting to its feel and weight.

Her voice was steady as she finally responded. “I do. Kiero is burning. The Black Dawn Rebellion has scattered. I need your help, *all* of your help. I can’t win this war alone.”

“Nor can you gain our trust instantly. It’s time to prove yourself, and only *we* can give you a proper Isles’ greeting.”

“What—?”

The crowed chortled, the energy around them spiking as Marquis smirked. “Come on, Princess. Give me your best shot.”

Emory’s fear and pounding heartbeat engaged her ability. She tried to focus on Marquis’s sudden demeanor change in front of the crowd. His voice, his tone, was so much like Adair’s. She was transported to a million other times when Adair had said those exact words in the Noctis Woods. Moments where Adair fought against the dark forces controlling him—when he wasn’t a monster, when he was just a man. An empty shell of someone she had loved and known.

She took a deep breath in, steadying her grip. Adair’s voice whispered through her mind, *“Remember not to show them what true power flows through your blood. Most aren't like Marquis. Most won't understand that you aren't a threat."*

Holding on to that reminder, Emory tried to quench the building power running down her arms as Marquis matched her stance. Her ability wanted to break free, to overcome Marquis and every person watching.

Careful.

A trickle of sweat rolled down the back of her neck. The sunlight was right in her line of vision, making it difficult to see. She needed to get Marquis where she was standing. Her biceps burned as she threw the sword Marquis had given her, sending it careening toward him. Marquis staggered back, caught off guard as the blade imbedded itself in the grass before his boots.

Emory commanded her ability to match her intention, and her sword materialized behind her back. She swung Anithe in front of her, and it gleamed in the afternoon light. Marquis lunged to grab the wolf-hilted blade, brandishing it to block hers. Emory exhaled as she took in the familiar black steel and blood-red edges of Anithe. Gripping the hilt, Emory met Marquis's gaze as everything within her world fell silent. Her knuckles turned white, and she trusted her instincts, her training.

The world broke away as she charged, fire pooling in her core. Marquis ducked, swiping at her abdomen, but she arched back. The wind churned, singing around them. The familiar burn of her muscles made Emory grin as she aimed her blow down toward Marquis's shoulders. He sidestepped to his left, and at an inhuman speed, Emory swung Anithe at his thighs, forcing Marquis to jump, retreating.

Sweat gathered at his temples. "You were taught well."

Emory picked up her relentless pace, forcing Marquis to block her attacks continuously. Swearing, he unsheathed a knife from his belt with a *snick* and threw it, forcing her to jump back just as an orb of roaring water swallowed her whole. Anithe dissolved as the water hit her and knocked the breath from her chest. She closed her eyes, and her heartbeat thrummed faster and faster. Her command filled her entirely, and she felt the shift.

When her eyes opened, her breath came in a misty puff, the ice globe encasing her, distorting Marquis. Emory stroked the flawless ice, marveling at how clear it was—like glass. Using a little of her new ability wouldn't hurt if Marquis was going to play dirty. The crack shivered beneath her touch, lines expanding all around her until the ice exploded. Heat hit her like a wave as Anithe materialized once again within her grip.

Running toward Marquis, she pushed faster. At the last minute, Emory drove Anithe deep into the ground. Abandoning her weapon, she dove low, her arms wrapped around Marquis's waist. Hard muscle met her touch, and they went flying. The element of surprise worked to her advantage as Marquis lost his grip on his sword. He scrambled, but Emory pinned him, her hands pressing down on his wrists, the darkness rising in her and slamming into him before she could control it. She was met with an iron wall.

He gasped when her fist rammed into his jaw.

"This is your idea of acceptance?" Emory asked.

Wriggling, he shifted his weight, rolling, flipping her over. The back of her head slammed into the ground. Emory bit her tongue hard, and blood pooled in her mouth. A sharp ringing filled her mind from the radiating pain. Heat rushed up her body, flushing her cheeks.

Leaning in close, he breathed, "Are you done yet, Princess?"

At his words, Emory pressed her lips into a thin line, swallowing her reply as a flood of frustration welled up inside her. This was all just a show, some sick rite of passage for his people to enjoy.

Her mother had deep roots in the Isles, and as heat licked through her body, Emory allowed herself to feel every inch of anger at what happened to her family. Anger at Marquis's father for killing her grandfather, anger at never getting the chance to grow up in Kiero because of her fear that Adair would kill her—to not be an outsider anymore. Emory pushed both physically and mentally, and the king of the Shattered Isles flew back.

Thunder rumbled in the distance, and the ground beneath her shuddered. She felt that hold, that grasp of new power thrumming through her, and it expanded, uncontrollable.

Marquis shot up, the crowd around them protesting, their complaints lost on her ears. He placed his hands low in front of him when she drew nearer, and Emory could swear she saw excitement flashing in his eyes at the challenge. Another point to prove that she was worth helping, worth risking their lives for in this war.

He wouldn't want her as his enemy.

Adrenaline rushed through her, and she ran toward Marquis. When he clapped his hands, wind that carried thousands of snowflakes bellowed around her, trying to disorient her. The blizzard thickened, turning her world into an alabaster washboard. As a last resort, Emory crouched, touching the ground with her fingertips. The ground shook more violently under her command, and the snow stopped as soon as Emory stood.

Marquis dropped into the pit she'd created.

Climbing out of the pit, Marquis landed in front of her, the knife in his hold slashing toward her shoulder. Emory grabbed his wrist mid-stroke, and her knee connected with his gut. He doubled over, dropping the blade.

Kicking it away, she purred, "Come now. What's the point of this, Marquis?"

Lunging at her, he wheezed, "A test of strength. Of resilience." His fist flew toward her jaw, but the darkness within her reacted first and she materialized behind him. Raising an eyebrow in disbelief, he spun, spouting more of his moral justification. "Of character. Of endurance."

His body became a blur. Blocking his onslaught, her forearms protected her face, and each blow sent vibrations through her bones. When she arched to the right, his fist connected with her side, sending Emory reeling. She gasped for air, and her vision spun as his other fist slammed into her jaw; she felt the crack resonate though her.

Her body collided with the ground.

"And to show you that there is always more to learn."

Emory blacked out.

***

In her dreams, he was waiting for her.

Declan.

The Dark King cracked his neck, reaching for her in the darkness. "Hello there, Emory."

She staggered back and realized that she was standing in a thick fog, no shape recognizable except for him since he was right in front of her.

Nostrils flaring, he breathed deeply. "I can smell your fear. And you should be afraid. I won't stop hunting you. Neither will the Oilean."

Tears slipped down her face, and she clamped her mouth shut.

Prowling around her, he sighed. "You are making this harder than it has to be. Do you want more bloodshed? You want your friends to die? You will never win. You will never best me."

Her heart broke as she looked at the familiar body. *He isn't Adair.* Her friend was dead by her own hand. He was gone, and he was never coming back. She bit her lip so hard it split.

The Dark King ran a smooth hand over his chin. "Come back to me, and all will be forgiven. Come back to me, Emory."

Emory ran, cutting through the never-ending fog, trying to escape him.

His whispers followed her. *"Come back to me. Come back to me."*

***

Emory woke, shooting up so fast she nearly slammed her head into Marquis's forehead. She blinked, disoriented. Where was she? The small room came into focus—a window, soft light filtering through the panes, warm downy bedsheets, and tea steaming next to her, lemon and ginger.

"Is this how you treat everyone who visits the Isles?" Emory asked.

"Only the ones I want to make sure no one is soon to forget."

Emory closed her eyes as she laid back. "Yeah, that makes sense."

Marquis sat down in the chair beside the bed, and mischief danced in his features. "It would be boring if everywhere you went had the same customs and traditions, no? The Isles may be rough around the edges compared to the finery Kiero offered you."

"I wouldn't say any place in Kiero is offering finery with war looming over the country for six years. Why don't you make yourself useful and tell me something about the Isles? Do you know anything about my mother? Her family?"

Leaning back, Marquis murmured, "You spoke of monsters earlier. My father, Tadeas, became more of one after the war at the Academy. He wanted to cut all ties with Kiero, and after we left, he did. Your mothers' sisters were slaughtered weeks later. Anyone who had any association with your mother went into hiding, fleeing the Isles."

Her heart dropped into her stomach, tears pricking against her swollen face, her wounds bruising her skin. She knew her ability could easily heal her superficial wounds, but if Marquis told the others about her initiation, it would seem suspicious if she came out unscathed. It would lead to questions she didn't want to answer from Kiana, Riona, and especially Brokk.

Her gut twisted at the thought of keeping the truth from him, but she could not take killing Adair back. This was the price, one maybe branded in her destiny since her birth. Emory didn't know what her future held, but she had to make the alliance work with the Shattered Isles, just in case something happened to her.

"I'm sorry." Marquis rubbed his jaw.

She let out a deep breath, unsure of what to say.

"You know, though, Nei was not only a healer. She was one of our best teachers. Teaching women and young girls how to fight, when traditionally in the past it was only the men who were allowed. And how to sail, too. People tend to forget that she was a warrior first. That she inspired others, and that she taught people the most important lessons in life: how to fight and never give up. How to be strong, both physically and mentally."

"Tell me more, please."

Settling into the sound of his voice, Emory listened as Marquis told her about a woman who was known to be kind but also fearless. Who would do anything for her people and her kingdom.

"I see her in you, in the best ways possible. It gives me hope, Princess."

CHAPTER FOUR

BROKK

Not for the first time in his life, Brokk woke up to find himself bound in chains. He groaned, and his chin slumped against his chest. His surroundings came into clarity in snippets: brick walls, the red stone weathered. A small, barred window to the right, filtering in soft light that he blinked against. His tongue felt thick, as if he had bit down on it, the skin having split. Breathing slowly, he leaned back, closing his eyes.

"So, what did you do to get yourself in here?" a voice asked from the shadows.

Opening his eyes once more, he peered into the shadows, croaking, "Kiana?"

Kiana emerged from the far left of the room, alive and untouched. She smiled at him, her silver gaze glowing when she asked, "Are you okay?"

"Not even close, but I'm alive. Where is Riona? And what, by fire and flame, is happening?"

His memories were a distorted mess. The first one that flooded to the surface was his lips meeting Emory's while Marquis held them in a cell. Heat pooled in his stomach at the thought, his pulse elevating. In that second, Brokk could see a future where they could help each other mend the wounds and broken parts of their souls together, and he willed to any gods listening that she felt a fraction of what he felt for her.

But then one thought after the other came, and his mind tried to make sense of it all.

He remembered Marquis taking them out to the cliffs—how every stranger's face Brokk looked at held malice in its features. The torches, the pounding of their feet, the crashing of the Black Sea. Then all he saw was Emory, her face darkening in pain, in *fear*, before he had fallen. Next came the screams of a far distant cry before the ocean had swallowed him whole. He remembered salt water burning his throat as he had tried to claw against the might of the tide, the panic in knowing he couldn't swim. He faintly remembered seeing a flash of silver—and then, nothing.

Nothing but blackness until he had come into consciousness in that cave, and at first, he had thought Emory a dream. His angel of death was more like it, especially how she had fought off their captors.

Sighing, Brokk tried to relax.

Emory had killed Adair, had died, had been shackled, broken. Tortured. Orchestrated to be a weapon. And coming back, things had been hard but okay until they had gotten here.

"Prince, stop thinking so hard. You will hurt yourself." Riona's snarky voice came up beside him when she sat down. Brokk looked at her with raised brows, assuming the warriors had used their magic to set both her and Kiana free. The blacksmith grinned, punching his shoulder. "Well, I'm glad you're not dead."

"Same to you both. But do you mind setting *me* free?" He addressed Kiana, practically feeling Riona's wicked glint burning into his side.

Kiana's ancient eyes softened. She closed the space between them. Her hands acted fast, and her voice was soft. "We were taken here, the chains spelled with Kieroian steel. It doesn't affect our power but—"

"What Kiana is trying to say is that we are being polite to this Marquis by not breaking free from this cell and kicking his ass." Riona smirked.

Kiana shook her head, but a small smile tugged the corner of her lips.

Deciding not to comment on Riona's statement, Brokk watched in awe as Kiana's hands hovered above the chains enclosing his wrists and then ankles. A soft white light started to pulse as the iron turned into a drifting silver mist, dissolving into nothing. There was pressure and then a flood of relief.

He massaged his wrists, and his blood pounded beneath his skin. "So, what do we do now? Where is Emory?" At their silence, he stood and began pacing, the sisters watching him. Brokk bristled when Riona stepped in front of him.

"We are treading on dangerous ground. You are our priority, not Emory. When the guards brought you in, they said you were lucky to be alive—despite your abilities."

Baring his teeth, he could feel the claws wanting to erupt from his knuckles. "Emory is *my* priority."

Riona rolled her eyes, sauntering to the farthest corner, arms crossed. "Not that I expected you to say anything else . . . Though, before we argue more, there is the matter of getting food sometime in this century."

"And here I thought you immortals were above such things," he stated.

Licking her lips suggestively, Riona purred, "It's all about the enjoyment, *Prince*."

Heat rose to his cheeks. Brokk went back to pacing, glancing up at the ceiling. It loomed above them, creating almost a dome at the top as if they were in a tower. He felt Kiana's presence behind him like a steadying caress.

"What happened, Brokk?"

"Exactly what I was afraid of. Marquis hasn't changed a bit. He always has a flair for the dramatics." He jumped into the tale, and the sisters listened. They were as still as statues, their faces revealing nothing. His voice was clipped as he recalled what he could remember about Marquis. The king's impulsive, arrogant nature, and the fact that Marquis had shoved him off the cliff.

Naturally, Riona was the first to react. "Well, that confirms it. We need to get off these blasted Isles and get back to Nehmai. Navigate this war from the safety of our own city. Rebuild it."

"The city my parents were slaughtered in? A city long thought to lie in its grave? We need to protect Nehmai by not sitting in it for the Dark King to find us. We *need* allies," Brokk countered.

"Like people who think it's acceptable to push people off cliffs?" Riona prowled around the room, assessing and weighing.

Taking a deep breath, he retorted, "Yes. We are in Marquis's land. Let him assess and make his own decision instead of us forcing his hand. There has been too much of that in the past years."

"Do you trust him?" Riona asked.

Brokk snorted. "No. But let's see what the Shattered Isles have been hiding all these years and make our own choice whether Marquis can be trusted."

We just need time. Time that we don't have. Brokk could feel the tension in his jaw, in his shoulders, in his very core. How long had he wanted to act? How many years had he spent wondering what more could he do to move Memphis's hand? He shivered and hunger clawed at his belly, which did nothing to lift his mood. How many more weeks—or months—would they have to endure here to move forward? Sighing, he ran his hand through his hair, slowly lowering himself back down to the ground.

"You've got to be *kidding me*." Riona was in front of him in a second, jumping down his throat. "Your plan is to wait for the Dark King, the Oilean, defenseless, *here*?"

"And what is your plan, sister?" Kiana shot back. "Escape, and be a threat to the Isles? Burn whatever chance we have at this alliance? We've been out of court too long, Riona. We have each been living in our own nightmare of isolation. Politics is a well-maneuvered fight; one wins with the power of words and antics not by brute force and rushed decisions."

Riona shook her head, grumbling under her breath. She sat down beside him with a drawn-out sigh.

Kiana's energy swirled around the room in soothing flickers of stardust as the silence grew between them. Her magic hung above them, weaving illuminated orbs that pulsed down bursts of heat against the cold in the cell.

Relaxing, Brokk took in the sisters. Riona and Kiana made up his court if he accepted his true title. His naithe warriors, his friends, and those loyal to *him*. But when the time came, would they understand that he would always choose Emory first?

Brokk chewed on his inner cheek, whispering, "It's probably best if we put the shackles back on."

Without a word, he felt the magic shift through the small space, wrapping around the three of them. The weight returned to his wrists and ankles. Brokk watched the iron materialize over Riona's wrists and ankles, first nothing more than speckles of light. Then, the magic wove in brilliant ribbons, taking no more than a minute. Riona's eyes were narrow slits, and she glared at Brokk. He picked out at least three swear words in the same sentence while she muttered to herself and looked away.

Riona's darkening mood spread in the small space like a storm cloud, and soon her protests grew loud enough that he bet Marquis could hear them past the brick walls and out to the Black Sea.

At his right, Kiana raised her eyebrows.

Sighing, Brokk settled in for a long night.

***

The creak of the door was slow. Stirring out of an uneasy sleep, Brokk blinked up at the illuminated figure standing in the doorway. The woman wore a long red coat, and swirling wave tattoos decorated her hands. The woman had a half-shaved head, and Brokk took in the lanky tree tattooed on her skull. Her silver hair was like moonlight, and her eyes gleamed as she stared at him. She wore comfortable-looking slacks, knee-high boots, and the edges of a silken shirt peeked out from underneath her jacket. One impression stood out to him— this stranger had the luxury of owning expensive clothing. A small reflection of a life untouched by the Mad King.

Her features gave nothing away while she warily eyed his companions. "The king will see you now." She snapped her fingers, and the shackles vanished. "This trust goes both ways. It will be in your best interest not to break it."

He stumbled to stand, his heart in his throat. When she began walking, he casted a wary glance at the warriors. They flanked him, and all three began to walk.

They descended the winding staircase. It was windowless, and the darkness closed in with no indication of what time it was. Their footfalls echoed, becoming their personal tempo.

Clenching his fists, Brokk asked, "So, who the hell are you?"

Her back stiffened, and for a moment, she didn't reply. "My name is Diedre Lucion. I'm Marquis's second-in-command. I'm also the woman who brought you to our healer, Elle."

He glanced over his shoulder, and Riona raised her eyebrows at him.

Chewing over his thoughts before he spoke, he settled on, "A pleasure."

Continuing in silence, he wanted to drown in the unsaid words rattling in his mind. Why had they been imprisoned? Was there any word on what was happening in Kiero? Was Emory okay? Had anyone heard if the Rebellion was still alive? Or did the Dark King they had left enraged in Kiero turn everything to ruin?

Pushing the thoughts down, Brokk settled on mulling over seeing Emory again. She was familiar to him, and he loved staring into her emerald eyes that reminded him so much of the heart of a forest, her easy smile, and kind heart. They had always been there for each other, through all the good and the bad. Brokk had found his way back to her and Emory to him.

A second wave of elation broke over him at the new possibility growing between them. He once thought he understood what it meant to love Emory, but over the last couple of months, he had realized what he felt for her was wild and consuming . . . And it scared him to think he would ever lose it.

If she was hurt, he would end Marquis.

He tried to stay calm, a lick of nervousness erupting in his anger. *What if she had regrets about me kissing her?* Swallowing hard, Brokk dug deep to find his courage, a small amount blooming within his heart. He refused to allow his doubts to fill the crevices of his insecurities.

The spiral staircase seemed endless as they descended from the cells. Finally, they reached a weathered plank doorway. Diedre swung it wide open, and Brokk stopped in his tracks.

The blanket of night covered the deep cliff faces. The steady rhythm of waterfalls sounded in the distance as his animal instincts perked up. The air tasted of salt, the crashing of the Black Sea echoing far off. Houses lined almost every inch of the valley; their bright colors were bathed in cool moonlight. Not a person stirred; the city was in a deep sleep.

Riona was the first to voice what they were all thinking. "So, are you going to kill us all at once, or one by one?"

Diedre spun, amusement dancing in her eyes. "And what makes you think I am going to kill you? We wouldn't waste resources on locking you up. If that's what Marquis wanted, you would already be dead."

Brokk bristled as Diedre chortled, shutting the door behind them. The tower stretched toward the sky, and all he wished was that wherever Emory was, she was not bound in chains in the dark.

As they twisted down the empty streets, he took in every detail he could. The weathered shingles, the flowers clinging to the fronts and sides of houses. Even though the cool caress of autumn was upon them, he felt the kiss of winter approaching in the air. He shivered as the group turned left. The alley was short, but the house in front of them was slender; it stretched toward the sky.

Diedre stopped in front of the soft light pulsing from inside, dancing in the window. Brokk sensed ripples of unease from Riona and Kiana as the king's second pulled the sleek door open, revealing who was inside …

Brokk shattered.

He saw the bruises on her skin first. Deep purples and yellows covered her jaw, and her lip was split. Emory's skin looked translucent, shadows underneath her eyes. The wounds had been cleaned, and her hair was tied back in a loose braid, the red ends glowing in the firelight, which crackled merrily behind them. She wore a simple green shirt, black pants, and tie-up boots. Time seemed to slow, but eventually, he ripped his gaze from Emory and met deep-green eyes.

Marquis stood, a tiny smile dancing in the corner of his mouth. He half turned and motioned for them to sit. "Please, do come in. You must be famished."

The door shut behind them, the lock clicking into place. Seated in the dining room, Emory said nothing, staring at the ground, her hands trembling.

No one moved, the electricity in the room sparking. *Just look at me, Em. C'mon.* Brokk's fingers curled into fists, his nails biting into his palms.

Lifting his eyebrows, Marquis turned, putting an iron kettle over the fire and murmuring, "Diedre, I think I need to have a private visit with my guests."

With a wicked glint in her eyes, she sketched a bow, leaving them.

The king straightened his emerald jacket, his voice turning hard. "Now, I must insist. *Sit.*"

Again, no one moved.

Emory's eyes finally found Brokk's, urgency burning in them. Swallowing hard, Brokk moved; his boots padded lightly on the tiled floor. He couldn't hide the tremor in his hand when he pulled his chair back, sitting. Riona and Kiana followed his lead, sitting on either side of him as they looked to Emory across from them.

He couldn't stop staring, trying to pick apart her wounds and what would cause them. Or *who.* His rage crept up, making his blood rush to his face. His imagination ran wild.

"Excellent. Tea anyone?" Marquis placed the china down, savory smells wafting from the small kitchen.

Brokk furrowed his brow, and his voice was low. Guttural. "What did you do to her?"

"Whatever do you mean?" Marquis asked.

The table creaked beneath Brokk's grasp, the wood threatening to break. "She has obviously been hurt!"

Marquis stood and moved toward the whistling pot. "Nothing more than a tradition of initiation in the Shattered Isles."

Brokk scowled. "Secondly, you shoved me off a cliff."

"A misunderstanding."

"*I can't swim.*" He took a deep breath. "Then you locked us up like common criminals. And Emory . . ." Brokk tried to find his words, but they were lost.

Turning, Marquis moved around the table, pouring the boiling water into waiting cups. "Obviously, I didn't know you couldn't swim. And I locked you up because I was unsure what exactly to do with you after you were healed. Emory and I had other *personal* matters to deal with."

Bastard. Brokk reined in his thundering anger, a slow blush creeping up the back of his neck.

Marquis shot him a sly smirk before he sat. He reached toward a small porcelain dish where tea bags layered one another. Grabbing a bag, he stirred it into his cup, not breaking Brokk's gaze. "Now, you have risked traveling the Black Sea to ask for my aid. You are asking my people to die for your cause when we have lived in peace for years—separate from Kiero. Why would I consider breaking that now?"

Riona and Kiana were statues beside Brokk. Too still. Too calm.

Brokk countered, "Because if you don't, we will all die."

The king sat, stirring his tea mindfully. "Perhaps."

Brokk pushed his chair back. He couldn't hold it in anymore. "There was a time, *King,* that you and your father begged us to find refuge on the Isles. For us to become a part of your society."

"Things change."

Both Kiana and Riona had risen beside him, swords half drawn from their sheaths.

Chuckling darkly, Brokk spat, "And by that, you mean, Adair is dead."

He regretted the words as soon as they left his mouth. He looked at Emory, bathed in the warm glow of the fire, shadows dancing across her face, a deep sadness flooding her eyes. He hated the power that one name had over her, a reminder of what she had done.

Marquis took a sip of his tea, lips smacking together. "Brokk Foster, you are a guest in the capital of Hriste and will be treated as such only if you can command yourself in a manner suited to reaching a compromise. I am not your enemy."

Brokk was torn between wanting to rip Marquis's throat out and sitting back down. Exhaling hard, he sat, his warriors following suit.

Appraising them, Marquis said, "The most influential people of Kiero sit at my table, and you wonder why you were locked up? Pushed off a cliff? Challenged? Because I refuse to make the same mistakes my father did and bow to others' demands before my own. We have come too far to be killed in another nameless war. And over what?"

"It is no longer the greed of men that dictates the tide of this war." Kiana's voice was cool.

"True. Instead, it is the greed of a much more dangerous enemy. How do you propose to win, even if we did ally together?" Marquis asked. Not giving them a chance to reply, Marquis snapped his fingers and waited.

A young woman came out, setting plates down before them as the most delicious smells danced from the room behind her. She flitted around, fast, cutlery following the plates. She ducked back into the kitchen and returned with steaming dishes, placing them on the table: freshly baked buns and steamed vegetables, luscious and green.

Plates of grilled meat and fish were placed in front of Brokk, and he had to swallow back his hunger. When was the last time he had properly eaten? As he licked his lips, his gaze rose, and Marquis was looking at him intently.

"Please don't wait on my accord, Prince."

It hit Brokk like a blow. A fake title. A condemned title. Trying to ignore Marquis's antics, Brokk dug in. The fish was glazed, sweet and savory, and the tender meat seemed flaky on his tongue. Swallowing, Brokk tried to stop himself from scarfing the rest of the piece down. It was delicious—not that he would be jumping to shower Marquis with praise.

"Or should I say *king* now?" Marquis mused, talking with his fork, food hanging off the end.

The room grew too small.

Riona glared at Marquis. "Enough," she said through gritted teeth.

"Oh, but isn't it true? And what about our proposed queen? Is the true nature of your birthplace none of her business?"

Sweat trickled down his neck when he looked at Emory, who was back to avoiding his gaze. Picking up a piece of meat, Brokk slapped it onto his plate. "Emory already knows. Get to your point, Marquis."

"Really, you do need to work on your manners." Marquis cut into his dinner with meticulous, precise strokes. He chewed and swallowed. "The future is at our fingertips. This *war* is at our fingertips."

"Marquis, stop dancing around your answer." Emory's voice was gravelly, broken. She pushed some vegetables around on her plate, eyeing Marquis skeptically.

"My *point* is that now is the time to negotiate. You came to me first, remember." He cleared his throat. "I sit with the prospective Queen of Kiero, and my guess would be the King of Nehmai?"

The sisters glared, and Marquis's grin grew.

Dread pooled in Brokk's belly. "How do you know about Nehmai?"

"Call it a lucky guess for someone who has access to a well-stocked library. You're not the only one familiar with the myths and legends . . . Now, there is something you want, and something I can give you, *if* you help me first."

Emory slammed her utensils down. "At what cost?"

Sipping his tea, Marquis mused, "You make this sound one-sided, Princess. I am merely voicing options. How do you expect us to work together if we don't all trust one another? If there is no give-and-take for us as a collective? To fight alongside one another and potentially die for one another. It all starts now." His eyes narrowed. "Do you want the Isles' assistance or not?"

Brokk looked at Emory, his heart pounding. Meeting his gaze, her green eyes churned, and she whispered, "I do. Brokk?"

The division she just drew cleaved through him, and he wanted to reach out, to just hold her. To allow her honey scent to wash over him, to transport him from this reality. "Yes," he croaked in agreement.

Emory nodded. "We also need the Rebellion."

Marquis lifted his eyebrows. "If they are still alive."

"They are," Brokk said, blood pounding in his ears. Marquis looked at him as if he were a child.

Riona cut in. "Just to be clear, what are you providing to win this war?"

"Numbers. Ships. An army. An alliance that survives after everything is said and done."

Drinking deeply, Brokk took them all in. He could feel it—that shimmering energy as tangible as autumn turning into winter—that everything had already begun to irrevocably change.

Leaning back, Marquis sighed. "Now, it's your turn to listen to my terms."

***

Brokk's mind was reeling from what Marquis had said, what he had *asked* of them. His stomach was churning, and a cold sweat broke out over his upper lip. He would not murder innocents on the accord of Marquis's ego. These other royals who were opposing Marquis did not warrant a death sentence.

He left the warmth of the cottage, and the cold night air seeped through to his core. His hands shook as he stuffed them into his jacket pockets, looking to the sprawling night sky. The moon was nestled in the clouds, Hriste flaring to life underneath it. If Sarthaven had once been the city under the stars, this city was born from one. It was something created from a dream. This beautiful, rugged world stole his breath away. For years, it was protected, untouched by the ugliness of the world. Of Adair. Of the darkness that had been Brokk's life for so long.

As he walked down the deserted street, Emory's voice rang out behind him. "Brokk."

He stopped, his breath coming in misty puffs, his heart in his throat. Riona and Kiana dipped their heads at him as they continued, leaving him to have some privacy.

Brokk felt the pressure of Emory's fingers on his arm. At her touch, fire pooled in his belly, jolting his nerves. He turned to face her. Finally, it was just them. No distractions of alliances and wars. And in the late hours of the night, Brokk allowed himself to hope. This moment was untouchable and completely their own.

The moonlight hit her face when she looked up at him. He tried to ignore the bruises that lined her skin. They stared at one another; words lost in the moment. His mouth ran dry, and a small smile tugged at her lips.

"I'm glad you're okay," she said.

"Thanks. My ability healed most of my wounds once I was out of that place. And you? Em, what *happened* to you?" he asked.

Her eyes flitted over him, fast and unreadable. "You know I swore to myself that if he hurt you, I would end Marquis. End it all. But it's so much more than you and me7 now, isn't it?"

Brokk's fingers found hers. Emory's were shaking and cold. He pressed, "Did he hurt you?"

Her eyes fell, and she pulled away. "I'm not some clueless girl you have to rescue, you know? We are in a *war*. It was a test, Brokk, and I somehow doubt it will be the last."

"Em, I just wanted to make sure you're . . . okay." The words fell flat and awkward between them.

"If I'm *okay*?" Her voice rose.

For a second, Brokk thought he saw Emory's eyes turn pitch black, a hardness filling in her features. Tremors ran up her arms, and she stepped back.

"Brokk, we were almost killed by bloodthirsty cannibals. I didn't even know if you were alive, if Marquis had kept his word and had Elle help you. All I knew was I had to keep going, because when I saw you last, you were drenched in your own blood." Her voice broke. "There is so much at stake; I had to remind myself that no matter what, I must keep going. This is just another game, another trial that we all have to survive."

"Em, talk to me. Please. I didn't mean to upset you."

His heart nearly stopped as she continued to back away from him. "You should consider Marquis's offer. Because as much as you say we are in this together, we all must decide how much we are willing to sacrifice. Are you willing to give your heart and soul to fight for Kiero? Even if it destroys you?"

Blood roared in his ears, but before he could answer, Emory slipped into the night, her words floating on the wind. "Goodnight, Brokk. I'll see you in the morning. We all have a lot of thinking to do."

CHAPTER FIVE

EMORY

What the hell was *wrong* with her? Exhaustion washed over every sense as she mulled over what she had said to Brokk. It wasn't his fault the Dark King haunted every dream she had, and she was weary. It wasn't Brokk's fault that she was falling in love with him but wished they didn't have to navigate the throes of alliances and war. It wasn't his fault she was terrified to tell him the truth of what she had become, of what ran through her blood. *Dark power. Stolen magic.*

Emory wandered through the unknown capital, down the cobbled street washed in silver moonlight, trying to remember Marquis's directions and pushing down everything else.

Turn right at Oak Street. Left on Port Street. Continue until you hit the cluster of cottages with shuttered windows and the wraparound porches. Those are my guest suites.

Hot, bubbling anger burned in her gut as she prowled through the night, watching for the street names. She exhaled hard, and her body screamed at the simple movement of walking. The arches of her feet felt bruised, shooting pain lacing up her calf. Bruises ran along her rib cage, making it feel like she was short of breath. But the pain was a reminder of the cost of her so-called *freedom.*

The words Adair had said to her weeks prior echoed through her mind. "*Status will not keep you alive. It will feed your ego and your arrogance, but it will do nothing against an opponent who wants you in the ground.*"

Considering recent events, Emory thought truer words had never been spoken. What was Adair's stolen crown and bloodied kingdom to him when she had driven her sword through him? How could she protect Kiero with no army, no allies, and yet another bargain to appease before she could begin to take the right steps to win back her country? Not to mention that the Dark King could be pinpointing exactly where she was hiding. They were all already on borrowed time.

Looking at midnight-blue sky stretching endlessly above, Emory allowed—just for a fleeting moment—for the events of the last month to sink into her.

She had killed Adair and had died.

Brokk had found her in between life and death.

She had chosen to come back, and thanks to Brokk, she could.

They had fled the Draken Mountains—barely—with their lives, so they could ally with Marquis Maher.

She had chosen to fight for the life she was robbed of here.

To fight for Kiero.

Tears slipped quietly down her face as that abyss of numbness tried to swallow her up. *Murderer.* Frustrated, she wiped away her tears, determined to find these elusive cottages. She craved nothing more than a hot bath and to be alone, but Marquis's proposition weighed heavily on her. He had a fleet, an army, and the resources to provide food and weapons—to give them a fighting chance. Alone against the Dark King, even with her stolen ability, she knew in her heart she wouldn't stand a chance. Marquis was her key to securing an army and to finding the Rebellion.

Was she ready to pay what that would cost?

To distract herself, Emory soaked in the world around her. It felt like a lifetime ago since she had kissed Brokk, since they had finally found safety in each other, their feelings clear and true. Fear laced through her heart. Now, falling in love with Brokk seemed reckless. She couldn't lose another person in her life—especially him. Loving Brokk would make an easy target for the Dark King to use against her. Marquis could even use him against her . . .

Emory passed a closed tea shop, butcher's, hairdresser's, tattoo shop, and a clothing shop unlike anything she had seen before back on Earth. In the window, brilliant jackets were on display and in every style you could imagine. They had high collars, buttons, cloaks, and capes, and there were what looked like jackets with armor built into them. They seemed to come in every color from black, gray, gold, and silver to bright pink and electric blue. *Marquis and his jacket fetish.*

A small smile tugged at her lips.

***

The cottage was small but quaint. The ocean-blue wraparound porch, white shutters, and white doors seemed stark in the night. A warm glow emitted from the cottage beside it, and Emory regretted looking up at the window. Riona stood there with pursed lips, palming a knife. With her gut twisting, Emory's mind wandered to Brokk, wondering if he had made it back yet. She masked her features, giving Riona a stoic look before making her way up to the first cottage door and going inside.

Shutting the door behind her, Emory relaxed against the door, burying her face in her palms. A cold sweat drenched her skin, and she quickly shrugged her jacket off, placing it on the back of a chair. The air felt stuffy as her eyes adjusted to the darkness.

In the living room, a small brown couch was along the left wall, a brick fireplace the main focal point. Along the adjacent wall, three bookcases devoured the wall space. Making a mental note to explore that tomorrow, Emory practically ran up the wide staircase to the second floor. It was like a loft apartment: a small kitchen to her right, and to her left, a bedroom beckoned. Trying to do too many things at once, she untied one boot, kicking it off, and then the other. Not caring if she was leaving a clothing trail, she ripped her sweaty shirt off and opened the door.

The bed was *massive*. A king size with a plush midnight-blue comforter and marshmallow-looking pillows. She brushed her fingers along the satin fabric, giddy from the luxury.

A bay window allowed the moonlight to ignite the room with its cool wash. Emory made her way to the washroom, stepping onto the tiled floor. A lamp was secured on the wall, a huge unlit white wax pillar candle within it. Dipping into her ability, Emory touched her fingertip to the wick, and black flame jumped from her skin. A clawfoot tub was before her, and at least four or five different bars of soap lined a floating shelf above it. But it was her reflection in an oval mirror that made her turn slowly, drinking in her own image.

Her dark hair was braided, the blood-red ends shimmering in the candlelight. Dark bruises peppered her skin beneath her eyes and along her jaw. And her eyes . . . Now that she was alone, in the bathroom, the endless black gaze stared back at her. Gone were her emerald irises. Flicking her focus down, she almost threw up.

Black streaked veins webbed from where the amethyst necklace once had been. Raised scarred skin was left in its wake, and her veins webbed down her abdomen, past her lace bra, climbing up her throat and down her arms like a poison.

"Oh my *god*." Her shaking fingertips traced the lines, the echo of the dark power running through her.

Dashing to the toilet just in time, she emptied the traces of the rich food from her stomach, gasping from the acidity. Tears pricked her eyes. She pulled the lever, and her vomit flushed down, the rancid smell hanging in the air. A cold sweat peppered her brow and Emory leaned away from the toilet.

Sitting in the middle of the bathroom, she spread her knees, hanging her head in between them. Breathing deeply, she willed the room to stop spinning, trying to wrap her mind around her thoughts. Did it make her a monster that she knew she would accept Marquis's terms? That even though Adair had manipulated her to murder the thieves and so-called criminals of his kingdom, that she would do anything to save Kiero? Even if the price would cost her everything?

Sweat dripped down her collarbone, her spine. The walls seemed to close in. In having accepted this life, this *world,* and her position in it, what kind of queen would it make her if she did accept Marquis's terms? *A smart one, if you survive.* The thought ate its way into her heart; she felt the finality of her decision. She had come to Kiero a naïve girl. She had gone to Adair as a reckless, selfless sacrifice. And now, she was no longer anyone's savior, nor was she so naïve. If she were to be played a pawn, she would ensure each move she made would be her own—that Marquis couldn't control her in the end.

As she brought her head up, realization settled into her. She had taken Adair's ability from him. She hadn't come back from death to be weak. To be played a fool. *You decide what kind of queen you will be.*

Slowly standing, with the poison of dark magic running through her veins, Emory drew a bath. Steam curled in the room as she removed the rest of her undergarments before submerging her bruised and aching body into the blissful water. The heat dragged the tension away.

Emory grabbed an ivory bar of soap that smelled like lemon and verbena, and the luscious suds unfurled as she scrubbed her skin raw, repeating the affirmation that no matter what, she would *be* a strong queen. With each scrub, tension lifted and faded away along with the already complicated politics Marquis presented. Breathing deeply, Emory sank into the steamy waters, her eyes fluttering shut.

Within the quiet, her mind drifted to Brokk.

Her heart clambered to find a rational way they could explore the possibilities of a relationship. The echo of their kiss made her toes curl, heat pooling in her belly. It was branded into her mind how his eyes lit with excitement in that moment of realization between them. When they both wanted what the other desired and it crashed down upon them. In the fear of the unknown, they had grasped it, not wanting to let it go.

But now? She would do everything within her power to protect him. Even if it meant protecting him from herself.

***

Early morning bled on the horizon, the buttery sunlight tingeing the clouds, the cliffs visible through her window. The calls of sea birds floated on the wind as Emory tripped around the room, trying to finish getting dressed. The bruising had deepened overnight, her jaw swollen. She could heal herself with her new ability, but that would only lead to unanswerable questions.

She found clean black pants and a green long-sleeved shirt, the sleeves coming to points on the tops her hands. Swearing, she buckled a knife on her hip, casting one last look in the mirror. Jutting her chin out, she scowled at her black irises. With the use of her ability, her eyes returned to their once-normal emerald, the wound from her chest hidden along with her blackened veins.

"There. That's better," she murmured.

Emory grabbed a pair of knee-high boots, lacing them up. A black high-collared jacket hung in her closet, which she also grabbed. Dressed, she threw her hair up in a top bun. Turning toward the door, she found Anithe in the corner of the room. Her skin prickled when she tried to remember if the sword had always been there or if her ability had manifested it there . . .

Striding across the hardwood floor, she grabbed Anithe in its scabbard and buckled it across her back.

Not giving the room a second look, she left, walking down the stairs and out the front door. It clicked behind her, and the crisp autumn air slapped her senses alive, driving any nervousness away.

Adair's voice cut through her mind again. "*You have to find that place within yourself. Where everything goes quiet, except you and your intention.*"

"Well, let's see if this ability can track a person down," she muttered aloud.

Emory stepped off the porch, slowly walking up the deserted street, all the while diving into that abyss of power. Her ability had always been as natural as breathing. But *Adair's* ability added into that was like diving into an ocean of ice, the sheer immensity of the power encompassing her. It pushed every human thought she had down, clearing her body of emotion. Gone were the fear, the second thoughts, the yearning and wondering if Brokk was thinking about her as much as she had been about him. Gone were the insecurities about her future. There was a certain clarity in the intoxication of power. Her pulse was thundering, and background noises bled into nothing as ability and intention became one.

"Marquis, are you sure?"

She felt the question in her mind. It felt like an echo, as if she were standing in a cave, the power stretching across Hriste like thousands of winking stars. She searched until Marquis's voice rattled through her consciousness so loud that Emory startled.

"*Diedre, I'm telling you, I know they will come together and help us. We are all desperate.*"

Emory held on to the connection, walking faster in the early dawn.

"If you believe that, then why are you so nervous?" Diedre's voice was dry.

Turning, Emory headed into an alleyway. A droning had filled her senses, and she pushed their conversation to the side for a moment, responding to the intense pull in her gut. Jogging now, Emory tried to spot a door or hidden passage among the dull brick.

By this point, it wouldn't surprise her if in Marquis's world he had an intricate underground travel system.

The unyielding droning grew within her mind. Pressure built along her temples, a deep throbbing resonating through her. Emory tried to sever her hold on the power, on the conversation she followed, but her power dipped further into that void. She stumbled in pain, and it felt like the ground was tipping up, making everything spin.

Gravity shifted, and Emory fell to her knees, feeling the cold, cobbled stone underneath her. Groaning, she shut her eyes, pulling at the connection with her ability, desperately trying to break it. It was *too much*. The pain ran through her jaw, in her mind . . .

"Emory?" Marquis asked at the exact moment she broke free from the abyss. Focusing, she took in his silver jacket, deep-blue pants, and gleaming leather boots. His hair was disheveled, and he had bags underneath his eyes like sleep had eluded him after their meeting.

"Why are you on your knees in this alleyway?" He scoffed, uncertainty bleeding into his voice.

"Looking for you. I need to talk to you, *alone*."

Diedre poked her head out when Emory stood.

"Diedre, kindly give Emory and me a moment alone."

"Mar—"

"I'm not asking."

Dipping her head, Diedre made sure to shoot a scathing gaze in Emory's direction before disappearing back inside.

Appraising Emory warily, Marquis sighed. "Alright, come in then."

Standing, Emory moved, walking to the opening of the door. As she went to pass him, Marquis's fingers dug into her forearm, stilling her. He leaned in, and his breath was hot against her cheek in the cool morning air. "Putting your new ability to good use, I see. Though some practice may be in order since you look like death."

Shrugging out of his hold, Emory smirked. "Always such a gentleman. As I said, I need to talk to you."

"After you, Princess."

Stepping through the threshold, she heard Marquis shut the door behind them. "Where are we?"

Marquis ran a hand through his hair, and a light blush crept across his cheeks. "It's a hidden study of mine. To be honest, it's mostly where Diedre and I come to hash out political matters within the Isles, which lately has been a daily meeting. But it's also a safe place for me, away from prying eyes so that I can think and not have to worry about keeping up appearances. A place where I can truly be myself."

There were oak tables in the room filled with maps and books, and huge couches lined an entire wall. The ceiling above them mocked the night sky, deep purples and blues and thousands of orbs hanging above them, acting like hundreds of constellations. It was gorgeous.

"I like it. It's surprisingly homey," she replied.

"What? Were you expecting a dungeon where I hatch my newest evil plans?"

Chuckling, Emory strode over to a couch, throwing her aching body down on the cushions. "Not in the slightest. If I'm being honest, I didn't know what to expect. You're a hard person to figure out, Marquis, and we haven't been reacquainted that long."

"Before we get into what I expect will be an interesting conversation, would you like something to drink? No offense, but you look terrible."

"Yes. Thanks," she said drily. She watched him walk over to a kitchen island and open a container of brown beans, preparing what looked like a carafe. The smell—like chocolate and roasted hazelnuts—washed over the small space, and her mouth watered.

"We call this dochase, a drink that I can't live without, to be honest. It will help you wake up," Marquis said.

"Like coffee."

"Like what?"

"There is something similar on Earth. I loved it," Emory said softly.

"Ah."

"How can you have such . . . normalcy here?" The question erupted out of her—it wasn't how she wanted to start her negotiation.

The dochase starting percolating as he poured water into the pot. "Well, a lot of it goes back to protecting ourselves, separating ourselves from the war. It allowed traders to flourish within the Isles and different businesses to grow. And of course, magic. The core of the Isles isn't that different from Kiero, and my father mimicked your father's technologies. We draw it from the ground—magic for engineering truly has been life changing."

"And from Adair's kingdom," Emory added.

"That was after my father was dead, though. Never forget that our peace here came at a great price."

Emory tried not to fidget with her jacket as she sat back. "Cream would be fine for me if you have it, thanks."

Smirking, Marquis shook his head. "You certainly are a direct woman. I can see why Adair had such a fascination with you."

It felt like a blow to her gut, and any words she was about to speak died on her tongue.

Marquis brought her steaming cup over, handing it to her. Accepting it, she inhaled the deep scent, instantly more at ease.

"Forgive me," he said.

"When it comes to Adair, you have nothing that needs forgiving. If I'm speaking freely . . . everything feels immensely complicated," Emory murmured before taking the first delicious sip of her drink.

"And here I sit, completely taken aback by that comment. I would have thought that you and your Rebellion would hate the Isles for what we have done. Separating from the rest of the world and ensuring our connection with Adair wasn't one he could destroy. As you may have already guessed, my heart got in the way of going to war with him." He stared defiantly into her eyes, steam curling from his cup.

"You did what you had to do to survive, Marquis. Isn't that what everyone has been doing for the last six years? We can't hold each other as enemies for following our instincts, or for falling in love. I'm not going to lecture you about the looming war and complications of human emotion." She shrugged. "You could sit with me here, saying it was treason that I left Kiero, but to move forward, I agree with what you said yesterday. We need to trust each other. You and I have more in common than you may think." Taking another much-needed gulp of her dochase, Emory swallowed. "Which brings me to our early morning meeting. I just wanted to say again that I'm sorry about Adair. I know what he meant to you." *What he meant to both of us.*

Staring at his drink, Marquis whispered, "You and a select few possess the ability to see the truth when it came to Adair and me."

Nodding, she pushed on. "It's hard to grieve over a villain when the rest of the world rejoices. It breaks my heart that who he was before is nothing more than a memory. People won't remember Adair as a kid who once had dreams. The Oilean dehumanized him. He will be remembered as the Mad King. And especially now since this Dark King has taken over his body. He was a weapon, nothing more than a tool for this foreign king from Daer. His life was ended for that." Anger encompassed her heart. "I don't plan for anyone else I love to become a pawn or a weapon. But this is war, and we are all pawns on the board right now. Which is why I want to make a bargain with *you*."

"I'm listening." Marquis's eyes sparkled with intrigue.

"I agree to the terms you proposed last night. I will help you assassinate this royal from Durdover Port. But no matter what Brokk and his warriors say, please agree to help me get them off this Isle. They are safer away from me."

"Trouble in paradise?" he purred.

"The Oilean will be coming, Marquis. It's only a matter of time, and I refuse to lose him because of my actions. You and I both know the Oilean won't rest." Desperation bled into her voice. "With Brokk, if he is alive, there is hope. Hope for the Rebellion and hope for Kiero. Please, promise me you will help me." Setting her mug down, Emory implored, "If given the chance, would you have done anything to save Adair's life?"

His gaze darkened. "I warned you if you brought the Oilean here, I would kill you."

"I know I'm asking a lot, but so are you. I don't know that they are hunting us for sure or if they will even find us here, but I do know that Declan needs Adair's magic. The same magic I now have running through my veins. I'm making a calculated guess that also means the Oilean are out there looking for it. For me."

"By the Back Sea, Emory," Marquis snapped.

"I will help you, Marquis, but this is the price. The risk of having me here for us to work together."

Letting out a frustrated groan, he shook his head. "I had a feeling we would be in this situation. Well, it seems we have a busy couple of weeks ahead of us, Princess."

Nodding, she loosened her knife. "You won't mind making this promise binding?"

"Trust issues?"

She smiled. "I will take no more unnecessary risks, Marquis."

"Very well then. Can I see your knife, please?"

Handing it over, she watched him slice the blade—unflinchingly—across his palm, nodding at her to do the same. Taking the hilt, she mimicked the movement, biting her lip as the steel sliced into her flesh, her inky blood pooling.

Marquis raised his brow at the color but said nothing more as he clasped her hand, his voice rough when he said, "Emory Fae, I promise to uphold our agreement by getting Brokk Foster and his company off the Isles and away from you, for their own safety."

"And Marquis Maher, I promise to help you kill this royal that will visit on the Harvest Equinox. I promise to be at your disposal, and in return, you will aid me in this war against the Dark King."

Heat flared beneath their intertwined fingers, and Emory watched with wide eyes as their blood mixed and turned incandescent, like liquid moonlight.

Emory shivered against the magic when the blood soaked back into their wounds, their promise binding them together.

Marquis held her gaze, his emerald irises darkening. "And so, it will be done."

He broke away first. Trying to hide her surprise, Emory asked, "Now can you give me more background information about these royals I am going to help you kill? Strengths or weaknesses I should know about?"

Giving her a mischievous grin, he said, "That is an answer you will find out later. Now go, Emory, or we will raise more questions than we want, especially since you don't want Brokk catching on to your newly acquired *talents*."

Scowling, she drained her mug in one glorious gulp. Putting it back on the table, she stood to leave but not before steadying her gaze at him one more time. "Just so you know, Marquis, if you betray me, I *will* kill you."

"I wouldn't expect anything less," he replied with a whisper of a smile on his lips.

She walked out of the secret study, and the door clicked shut behind her.

CHAPTER SIX

BROKK

For the first time in his life, Brokk dreamed of Nehmai.

Singing streams webbed through the forest outside the city, and bubbles foamed along the shore in gold and silver washes. Forest creatures unlike anything he had seen before stared back at him, their doe-like eyes blinking as they ruffled their downy wings, hooves pawing the ground. As he walked toward the white city farther away from the dense forest, flowers bloomed before the soaring, shimmering gates. The petals were huge, a golden yellow. The gate's iron was incandescent in the sunlight as if it were made from pearl.

In his dream, the gate opened as he made his way down the streets, the residents there inhuman—their pointed ears and unearthly beauty foreign to him. Faces of pleasure, of *pride*, met his gaze as the fey bowed, murmuring, "My king."

It was only when he stopped at the heart of the city, at the roaring fountain, that he saw the blood flowing down the peerless cobblestone, the whispers churning around him. He watched the entire city turn to ash, disappearing in an instant.

He shot upright, sweat dripping down his bare chest to his lower abdomen.

"Bad dream?" Riona sat at the end of his bed, her gaze unreadable.

"Do you have any understanding of privacy?" Brokk shot, trying to gather the sheets around him.

"Oh, get over yourself. You're not my type anyway. I'm here to let you know you have a visitor." At that, she padded over to the already open door, and his heart shuddered to a halt as he focused on who stood there.

Emory looked regal despite her bruises. The look suited her: her hair in a high bun, those piercing emerald eyes, and her mostly black outfit and leather boots. A small smile curved his lips.

"Emory."

"Brokk. Can I come in?" she asked.

Behind Emory's shoulder, Riona waggled her eyebrows, and he scowled. "As long as you shut the door behind you."

When the door clicked shut, he was suddenly hyper aware of his lack of clothing and of Riona laughing down the hallway with Kiana. Blushing, he cleared his throat, watching as Emory walked over to him. He was at a complete loss for words when she sat on the edge of his bed. He could hardly breathe from the electricity churning between them.

"Sorry if I woke you, and for my unannounced visit," she started.

"No, it's okay. I was hoping we would have a chance to talk." *After last night. After we left so many things unsaid.*

Nodding, she stared at the wall, her features a cool mask. Trying not to panic at his inexperience in talking to girls, Brokk abruptly asked, "So, do you think he is trustworthy? Do you think he is worth killing someone for?" His mind was still reeling from the possibilities, the madness of it all, and Marquis's proposal.

Emory smiled at him. "You know, this time last year, I was working at a secondhand bookshop, my future completely at my fingertips. Would I go to college? What program would I take? How would I navigate that path alone? I was struggling, but everyone was. I had a best friend; her name was Moore. I had a life."

Brokk's brows furrowed; the situation she was describing was foreign to him. But he didn't interrupt.

"Now, I'm here, this world at my feet. I've tried to be the savior for the Rebellion and failed. I bested Adair only to reveal a darker enemy. But I do think trusting Marquis is essential to Kiero's survival. I think we all must learn to trust again. We *need* his army. I need the Isles behind Kiero. So, yeah, I think it's worth helping him."

Brokk nodded, understanding the soldier's train of thought. But his gut pooled with dread of the thought of letting the king of the Shattered Isles close to them. Wiping the sleep from his eyes, he asked, "What's college?"

Bursting out laughing, Emory asked, "That's what you're worried about?"

"I'm trying to understand your world."

"This is my world. Earth was just the void where I was placed and forced to forget about Kiero," Emory snapped, their relaxed conversation turning. Her words hit him like a blow to the chest.

"Right," Brokk said flatly. Looking up at the ceiling, he tried to push past his guilt. But it was never enough. It chipped away at him bit by bit, and nothing he could say would ever make up for it as it threatened to drown him, to suffocate him.

"Brokk—" she started, her eyes softening, but he shook his head.

"You have every right to be angry. Every right to feel betrayed." His voice shook. Emory shimmied closer as he kept going. "I should have questioned what we were doing. I should have done something more to make you stay. Because now—"

"Stop. I don't blame you for anything. It was Memphis. He stripped away my choices. My memories. My right to know about our world. About you all."

Brokk had forgiven Memphis for a lot of things over the years. He still loved him like a brother. But Brokk wouldn't forgive him for taking away Emory's memories, manipulating her. Heat pooled in the bottom of his belly, igniting something completely new. Running his weathered hand over his lips, Brokk murmured, "Humor me for a minute."

Curiosity bloomed in her gaze, burning like green embers. The prospect of war swept into his reality, his fears at the loss of time driving one primal thing—a priority. To not lose any more time with Emory. All he had ever wanted was right in front of him, bruised and exhausted, but despite all the odds, they were here. Together.

How many times did he envision this moment? Had dreamed of it? He took in Emory, how she held herself. On the surface, she seemed . . . determined. She was suppressing the wounds he knew ran deep. He saw it in small flickers—how much Adair had broken her. How deep his claws truly went.

Heat flared in him, his mouth running dry. The Oilean whispered to him in his own nightmares, and he could practically feel the phantom blades carving into his flesh. The lies blended with reality, and he struggled against the cage in his own mind.

Roque Fae was not your father. You are the heir to the lost city of Nehmai. The legends are real. Kiero's light is not gone.

It is not gone.

It is not.

"Brokk?" Emory's voice was soft. Not prying, but offering.

"You know, for years I didn't even know if you had survived. The weight of what we had done, what *I* had done, crippled me. Every single day. And I allowed myself to turn into a man I swore I would never be."

"How can you blame yourself for something I pleaded with you to do?" she countered.

"I should have tried harder. Without you, the world forgot about the strides it had made. It fell back into ruin, into fear, and years turned into hiding. Into war. Our life turned into nothing more than a movement to beat Adair. You turned into that movement. I will never forgive myself for that. For taking your life in Kiero away from you."

It was there, bathed in the early sunlight in his bedroom, that Emory pinned her gaze on him, a tight frown pulling at her lips. "Did you tell me to come in so we could argue?"

He faltered, and heat rose within him again. He allowed the sheets to drop from his grasp, his heart hammering so hard against his rib cage. Brokk realized that he was afraid. He was a lethal soldier, harrower of death. He had become a monster, a beast, a shadow of a man. But as his fingers shakily tipped her chin up toward him, he was stripped raw. "No. I wanted to explain, so you can begin to understand."

Emory stilled, eyes flitting over him. Each part of his body touched by her gaze felt like it roared into flames.

Smirking, he ran his thumb lightly along her jaw, and she shivered underneath his touch. "It was always for you, Em. Everything I did. I thought I was protecting you. I thought to myself that if you were safe and alive, it would be good enough. But Kiero needs you. It has always needed you. And so have I."

His voice was rough, the last sentence a near whisper. Fear sliced through him at a possible rejection. Their last kiss, after their brush with death in the Draken Mountains, was maybe nothing more than that. Just a kiss. He would have to learn to live with whichever outcome.

Her breath was shaky. "You mean so much to me, Brokk. More than I can put into words."

A full smile broke across his face. Brokk pulled her into a bone-crushing hug, resting his chin on her head. "Just remember you're not alone in this. Every step, we will navigate this together."

This alliance, this war, this world. *Together.*

This time, Emory's fingers found his, weaving through them, heat blazing through his core as her cool skin brushed against his. He was shaking. He hadn't noticed how much she had truly changed in the last months. Her body was lean with muscle.

She closed the distance between them completely, her eyes glowing. "I think we should pick up where we left off in the cells."

Fire erupted all along his body just at that look. Her conviction, his longing . . . it broke him. In a moment, the space between them was gone. His hands brushed along her jaw, feather light. "Is this okay?"

Leaning in, Emory whispered against his ear, "Better than okay."

Everything bled away.

Slowly, his fingers brushed down her neck, her collarbone, down her sides, her hips and thighs. Emory's breath hitched as his hands roamed back up to her hips his hand gripping her and lifting her up. Excitement shot through him as Emory straddled him, a wicked glint forming in her gaze. It was pure reaction, their bodies knowing what to do, their heartbeats thundering as one. With swift fingers, he unbuckled Anithe and the knife belt around her hip, both weapons clattering to the floor. Biting his lip, holding in the groan that wanted to break free from him, Brokk breathed in her lemony scent.

Emory's legs wrapped around his waist, her arms looping around the back of his neck. He breathed heavily. Their foreheads rested on one another, blood thundering, and all he could smell was the sea and the soft scents that made her up. Like after a storm in the woods or in the morning dew clutching to the grass. She was light, familiar. She was everything to him.

Swallowing hard, Emory lowered her lips, exploring every inch and crevice of Brokk's neck, roaming over his raised scars as shivers of pleasure ran up and down his spine. *Gods above.* Lifting her, he rolled, pinning her, and she chuckled breathlessly. Brokk lowered his lips to hers, and he was lost. His tongue tasted hers, and they fell into the unspoken language.

Memories flickered; they were back in that cage, in that dungeon, fighting for one another. Emory's hands were bold, showing him what she wanted. His body demanded more of her—*wanted* all of her—but Brokk was under her command.

The shadow of the world dimmed as she leaned in, his muscles quivering, her breath hot on his lips, igniting him. "Thank you for believing in me. For bringing me back. For fighting," she whispered.

A deep rumble reverberated through his chest as her lips collided with his own, shattering him utterly. It was fire and ice that raced through his veins, consuming him. Emory's hands grappled for more, *more*. They never broke apart, his tongue roguishly tasted her, and he could feel her shaking underneath him. Panting, he smoothed back her hair, kissing her neck, her cheek, every inch of her he wanted. Burning together, slowly, like embers pulsing in the night.

Nipping lightly at her ear, he whispered, "I will never have enough of you, of *this*. War or no war, I stand beside you, Emory Fae."

Unsaid words hung in between them, but he conveyed them in slow kisses as she closed her eyes, sighing, melting against him. Traveling down lazily, he took his time, enjoying every quiver, every light moan.

Her hands stopped him, rasping, "Brokk. *Brokk*."

Coming back up, he kissed her deeply, his voice a low growl. "Yes?"

But before she could say anything more, Kiana burst into the room, clearing her throat. "Sorry to interrupt—ah!"

Heat flushed his cheeks. He sat up, glaring at his friend. "What, Kiana?"

"It's just time for breakfast," she said, not meeting their gazes.

Smirking, Emory nodded to him, and Brokk sighed. "Alright."

He felt as if he could never eat again, and he would be fine. He wanted to exist in this moment forever. But reality and bodily needs pressed.

Kiana left, her pointed ears flaming red.

Brokk glanced at Emory, and her cheeks tinged pink before she burst out laughing. Partly mortified and feeling like a teenager, Brokk couldn't stifle his laughter either.

"Ready to go to a slightly awkward breakfast?" Standing, Brokk offered his hand, which Emory eagerly took.

"I wouldn't dream of missing it. You know it's only awkward if you make it awkward, right?"

Pulling her in close, Brokk kissed her forehead. His actions were a vow, a promise. "Yeah, sure. Kiana only feels like my immortal mother." But even as he said it, Brokk couldn't stop his wide grin.

Everything was so still, etched in time: the crumpled blanket beneath them, the luscious plum tones ignited in the crisp sunlight coming in through the massive bay windows, the deserted city outside coming to life with sound.

"I just need a minute."

"I can meet you downstairs." Emory beamed.

Lowering his mouth to hers, Brokk stole another kiss, murmuring against her mouth, "I'll be fast."

When they broke apart, Emory's cheeks were flushed, her hair rumpled from the bed. "Good."

She grabbed her knife and Anithe, and Brokk watched her buckle them back onto her body. He listened as she made her way down the stairs.

Moving quickly, he slipped into the small bathroom adjacent to the room before balking at the luxury. The shower stall was lean, glass doors leading to green tile. The sink was deep, the silver handles holding his reflection like a mirror. Closing the door, he turned on the shower, the hiss of water and steam beckoning to him.

As if in a trance, he ripped off his boxers and stepped under the steady stream.

Muddy water began rinsing down the drain. Resting his forehead against the cool wall, he shut his eyes as the water pressure battered his tight muscles, the heat soaking into his skin. How long had it been since he *could* shower?

Breathing deep, he took his time, soaking in every precious second. Grabbing the small bar of yellow soap, he lathered himself, the scents of lemon and sea salt filling his senses. Rinse. Repeat. Feeling clearer headed, he stepped out, toweling himself off. Sweeping his golden hair out of his eyes, he wiped steam off the lone mirror in the room.

He took in his face: his golden eyes, his hair slicked back, the raised scars traced along his jaw, his neck, his arms. Shaking, he couldn't look away from the scars, a hollowness pushing through him, drowning him. Immobilizing him. The mirror fogged again from the shower steam, and bringing up a shaky hand, Brokk wiped the glass clean.

The gaping holes of the Oilean's features gazed back at him, their long, stringy black hair hanging limply. Ice rooted Brokk in place, panic building in him. The Oilean slowly tilted their heads in unison to the right, their pinned smiles unnatural, their pointed teeth gleaming beneath their thin lips.

Stumbling back, Brokk slipped out of the hallucination. The Oilean disappeared with his movement. His heart walloped against his rib cage, a cold sweat breaking over his skin, the walls spinning. He couldn't catch his breath. The panic attack had him in its hold. He had never seen the Oilean like that. It was as if they were haunting his waking moments, the nightmare of their existence never truly leaving him.

Your name is Brokk Foster, and you will not break.

He said this repeatedly, cupping his head in between his legs until his pulse slowed. His vision stopped spinning, and all that remained was his body, slicked in sweat. Slowly standing, he couldn't bring himself to look in the mirror as he left the bathroom.

A slow drip of fear trickled down his spine. He tried to let go of the attack, but it hung over him, gripping him as he wondered if he would ever be free from those demons and the scars they had left, visible and invisible. With each second, the fear slipped. Brokk walked farther into his room, filling his mind with what happened before the shower—how Emory had felt in his arms. Holding on to that and feeling like a man fully emerging from his shadowy depths, Brokk started to get ready for the day.

He looked at the small dresser; there was a stack of towels on top. Grabbing one, he tied it around his waist. *Let's see what kind of clothes Marquis has stocked here.* Rummaging around, he found close to his usual attire: black pants, black shirt, and a padded jacket with gleaming silver buttons. Making a mental note to find weapons and some boots, he dressed then left the room, running down the staircase, looking for Emory but finding an empty house.

"Em? Riona? Kiana?" he called out. *Where are they?* Panic started to thrum in his blood until he spotted a pair of leather boots beside the door. Making fast work, he put them on; they were a bit big but would do. As he left the cottage, freezing air whirled around him, his body trembling.

Shutting the door, he blinked up at Hriste.

At the end of Port Street, men and women set up tables and vendor carts. Walking to them, Brokk took in ceramic pottery, beautiful bowls, glasses, and art pieces. Walking farther along what he guessed was the market, he saw delicious-looking fruits stacked high in bowls. The next vendor had a wide spread of different styles of clothing: jackets, tops, pants, embroidered scarves, and matching mittens and hats. For a moment, Brokk just stood there, drinking in the normalcy of the lives of the people of Hriste. Jealously bubbled up within him, leaving a bitter taste in his mouth. He noticed a man appraising him, and the stranger said, "They are in the courtyard at the end of the main road."

Brokk whispered his thanks and ducked his head. What they must think of them all, warriors from across the sea. A princess returned from the dead. *And me.* If he knew anything about Marquis, he wouldn't keep it a secret who Brokk was: time manipulator, shape shifter, Prince of Nehmai. *Brokk Falkov.*

Picking up his pace, he kept his head down, his heart beating a little too fast. How long had it been since he had been out in public? No missions. No imminent death. No maps and endless nights wanting to bash his head against the wall, trying to figure out how they could end Adair. Sweat collected in his palms, and his ears perked up at the sound of swords clashing. He jogged toward the noise, and two figures came into sight.

Riona ducked, laughing as she spun, her hammer striking precisely where her sister had just been. The cobblestones exploded into shards. Riona furrowed her brows just as her sister reappeared behind her. Blades drawn, slicing down, Riona defied gravity, bending backward, enough to flip—her hands pushing her into the air before she landed back on her feet. The crowd around them cheered.

He watched as some people shook their heads at the display of power while others were handed heavy bags of coins from winning their wagers. The different emotions charging through the crowd left his head spinning. But Kiana and Riona seemed to feed off it. Rolling his eyes and pushing forward, he made it to the railing where Emory raised her brows at him.

"Breakfast was forgotten when they decided to get their exercise in," Emory said.

"And, of course, they had to show off. Em, I tell you, these immortals are annoying sometimes." He huffed.

Riona sprinted, Kiana meeting her, sparks flying from the metal as everything became a blur. It was like watching lightning strike the earth; the warriors were untouchable and incomparable. Everything bled away as Brokk lost himself in the fight, his soldier's mind unable to do anything but weigh the odds. Riona was fast but predictable, her anger fueling her body. Kiana, on the other hand, thought logically, and it showed in her sparring. Playing on her sister's emotions, Kiana made sure Riona was riled up, draining her faster, making her use all the space of the court.

Riona rolled, slicing at Kiana's ankles, forcing her back, but Kiana's blade flew up to meet the metal. However, Riona had the upper hand, pressing her sister down to her knees. The crowd's energy picked up . . . It reminded him so much of the Ring and the bloodlust of the Academy.

His voice cut above all the rest, "Riona, let's have a fair fight, shall we?"

She stopped, head snapping toward him as she sized him up. A flare sparked in her eyes, that desperation Brokk was also familiar with. That hole that could never be filled, the reminder of everything they had lost. That hollowness. Riona lifted her free hand, waving him over. The challenge to a fight masked as an invitation to train.

Jumping over the railing, Kiana backed away, and Brokk felt a vibration in his bones, a shuddering through the earth. Landing, his growls tore through him as he lowered his weight, his head dipping. Riona nodded as if to say, *Come get me.* Brokk's muscles tensed, his claws digging into the dirt, preparing for a fight. His heart thundered in his chest.

Boots came into focus as he snapped his jaw, lifting his gaze. Marquis stood in between them, a golden jacket shimmering in the morning light. Marquis frowned.

Shifting back, Brokk snapped, "Out of our way. We are training."

"My, my, Foster, you really have flourished into a moodier version of yourself, haven't you? May I gently remind you that training is not meant to be a show? Violence is not meant to be glorified. Never forget that."

"Even when it's with my own court?" he asked. Kiana and Riona stood a little straighter.

Marquis walked around him, nodding and smiling to the now-dissipating crowd. Coming back to face him, Marquis breathed, "Especially when it's with your own *court.* Now, if you're done getting your aggression out, let's all take a walk, shall we?"

With no room to decline, Brokk shrugged, looking back to Emory. She nodded at him, and they soon fell in stride with Marquis, Riona and Kiana mumbling behind them. The crowd went about their business as if nothing had happened.

Walking to the top of the street, Brokk drawled, "Where are we off to?"

"It's time to hear your decisions about my proposal, Foster. Naturally, over a good meal."

Brokk kept his emotions in check. Marquis had a certain talent of getting under his skin. They were preparing for war—there was no time, no room, for anything other than the immediate threat. He was living proof that the demons came later to claim their dues. "Any word of what is happening in Kiero?"

"No," Marquis replied.

"Any idea of when *we* will be going back to the war?"

"Why? Is this life not appealing to you? Not enough slaughter to sate your bloodlust? Besides, you all came to *me,* remember?" The challenge rang clear in Marquis's voice, and Brokk shrugged, stopping in the street.

An arrangement of blue-and-white buildings lined the street. Shutters opened. Red-and-gray brick lined every home. Some people had even put out decorations for the upcoming Equinox. It made him feel sick that they would be celebrating only to stain the festival with murdering these royals for Marquis. It was a never-ending circle of violence and resolving other people's feuds. When would the killing end? How could they break out of the cycle when they were already in the middle of fighting for Kiero?

That empty hole in his chest spread wider as he whispered, "You know, Adair had what was coming to him. I'm only sad I wasn't the one who drove the knife through his heart."

It happened fast. Marquis was face-to-face with him and slammed his hands into Brokk's chest. Brokk's head cracked against the cobblestone when he fell, pain lacing through his skull. He bit his tongue. Blood bubbled up, and he swallowed past the coppery taste filling his mouth.

Marquis's shadow fell over him, and Brokk spat, "Come on then. Let's go."

"Marquis, Brokk! Stop." Emory was there, pulling them apart, eyes flashing. Riona and Kiana drew their knives, the steel pointing at Marquis's chest.

The King of the Isles was visibly shaken, clenching and unclenching his fists. Brokk waited. For the moment, he *willed* Marquis to react. He needed to blow off some steam in a way he knew how.

Exhaling hard, Marquis adjusted his golden collar. "Forgive me. I forget myself. Some wounds are fresher than others."

Brokk stood up, chest heaving. In a second, he could have the upper hand; Marquis's guard was down. Brokk's blood boiled as his heart dropped into his stomach, that small voice pulling at the back of his mind. *Not a monster. Not a monster.* Stilling, he was transported back to years ago when he was a teenager gripping his humanity like a lifeline. To prove that his life was more than being groomed to be a soldier. What would that boy say now, to see the man he had become? How many lives had he taken without blinking an eye?

Swallowing past the lump in his throat, past that hole in his chest, he tipped his head to Marquis. "Forgiven."

The king's face shadowed. He dusted off his clothes and set off again, taking them to gods knew where.

Kiana fell into step with Brokk, whispering, "Careful."

"I slipped. It won't happen again," he replied.

From his other side, Riona purred, "You would think after spending the morning with the queen, you would be in a better mood."

Heat washed over him, crawling up the back of his neck. "Watch it, Riona, or I won't be so kind when we train next."

Brokk felt heat spreading across his cheeks as he watched Emory walk up beside Marquis.

"I believe I hit a nerve." Riona flashed a toothy smile at him, and he rolled his eyes.

All the houses looked quaint and well-tended; flags of the Shattered Isles' sigil flapped in the gentle breeze. Various shops opened for the day. Book stores, bakeries, clothing shops, forges, jewelry shops, and fine goods stores streaked by him. He was numb. How could an entire country have all this and more at their fingertips? From what Brokk could see, the Isles' main concern was the drama that accompanied Marquis. But to not be lacking in the necessities of life or worrying about surviving another attack from a deranged king? Hriste did not know how lucky they were.

Brokk's mood continued to darken, and he concentrated on breathing. From his peripheral vision, he saw Kiana shuffle closer.

Her breath was light when she asked, "So, do you have a plan yet?"

Shooting her a sideways look, he muttered, "It's not just my call."

"I'm surprised with you. You're now bowing to a woman we literally almost died for; in fact, she *did die*, and you almost did too." Her deep silver eyes held his for a second before she looked away, pretending to observe the city bustling to life around her. "Listen to me. We have been here for less than a week and have observed one thing. We are *disposable* to this king. Emory is not. I would find out why and tread carefully. I'm not agreeing to kill anybody, alliance or no. We can establish our own army."

Digesting the words, Brokk walked on, whispering, "I will, and I wasn't planning on agreeing. Marquis's personal vendettas are his own business. But that doesn't mean we can't lie to him and grant ourselves the upper hand."

Looking ahead, he almost didn't catch what she said under her breath. "That's all I ask."

His eyes followed Marquis as he talked to Emory: his mannerisms, what he looked at, whom he stopped to talk to as he led them deeper and deeper into the throng of his world toward the secrets that lay at its heart.

CHAPTER SEVEN

EMORY

The street was a burst of color and life. She was in stride with Marquis, and the king muttered beside her, "Your boyfriend has a talent of annoying me."

Chortling, she shot back, "I think that feeling is mutual. And he's not my boyfriend."

Mischief lit in Marquis's gaze as he whispered, "Keep telling yourself that."

Shaking her head, Emory couldn't wipe the stupid smirk off her face. There was so much happening so fast, but her heart pounded with the memory of her body against Brokk's warm flesh . . . his disheveled hair, his molten eyes. She could lose herself in him completely. *It's not a crime to allow yourself to be happy, to fall in love. Only, when the time comes, you will have to let him go.* The thought tore through her senses, and the undertone of dread left a bitter taste in her mouth. In time, she would tell Brokk what had happened with Adair's ability. She *would* tell him the truth.

Shooting a sideways glance at Marquis, she mulled over her decision to bind herself to him. For Kiero and for this war, she would be his shadow, his assassin. Swallowing, she looked at the shop windows. The path she was headed down wouldn't have a happy ending.

She stuffed her hands in her pockets, and the world suddenly fell away. The street disappeared, and Marquis with it.

The room she stood in was massive. There was no ceiling; instead, the walls climbed higher and higher, bleeding into the swirling sky far above. She shivered, and goosebumps raced on her skin, her breaths coming out in misty puffs before her. The walls were black, like a smooth curtain, capturing the reflections of the clouds dancing above. *Don't panic.*

"Hello?" The echo of her voice bounced around the room, becoming more distant.

The walls churned the farther she traveled until a forest erupted around her. The dense, ancient trees with gnarled bark and weathered roots poked out from the earth as she slowly gained her bearings. *Where am I?* The forest exploded into clarity, the empty room bleeding away until all she could smell was the moist earth and heady scents of the woods. She weaved between the trees, her hands trailing along them lightly; the bark was rough, pricking her skin. She loosened a shaky breath and closed her eyes, feeling the wind sift through her hair.

Emory didn't know what was happening, but she felt a shiver of connection to the forest. The vision felt so real . . . She took a moment to stand there in the dappled green light, the towering trees and lush leaves creating a natural cathedral. What was the difference between fantasy and reality when in both she *felt* alive? Stepping forward, she anticipated the soft moist ground underneath her boots, but instead was met with hardness. As she looked down, the scene changed, the marble smooth beneath her feet.

"Ah."

Emory knew that voice. But she couldn't stop looking at her feet, her chest heaving. That voice claimed her darkest nights and tried to claim her every waking moment. The nightmare had become her reality.

"It would seem we meet again. Now, let's talk like adults, shall we?" Declan asked.

How? How? How?

Fear burned through her core; Emory couldn't move. She dragged her gaze up. At first glance, the obsidian crown seemed like it was sitting on a base of clear quartz. Looking closer, Emory felt sick as she realized that teeth were piled up, the edges smoothed to make up the base, and the obsidian gem was smoke. A green glow emitted from within each spear that made up the crown, which was made from flesh and more smoke. It looked luminous in the soft light, and Declan's black eyes devoured her. His slender hands drummed lightly against the throne's arms, the ghost of a smile on his features.

"You left me in quite the predicament. Would you mind telling me where you are?"

It was Adair's voice, but it was not him. It was his body, but there was no trace of Adair left. The fragile piece of her mind broke.

"Emory, are you hearing me?" Declan snapped.

The knife, heavy in her hands, chaos breaking out around them. But it was always leading up to this moment.

"Where are you?"

Blood, there was so much blood as Adair fell.

Backing up, she shook her head, breathing, "This isn't real."

The Dark King arched his eyebrow. "Define *real.* I find that surprising, especially coming from you. Tell me, was it real the last time someone found you in your dreams? All those special years spent with Memphis weren't real?"

Ice splintered through her body; the throne room was identical, the ceiling opening to the skies. Swaying, she shook her head. "No . . . It . . . This can't be happening again."

Standing, the Dark King mused, "Far from the truth. Now listen closely, *Queen.* Tell me where you are, and we can reach terms. I'm most interested in what is flowing through your body as we speak. An unexpected turn of events, though I'm guessing not entirely what you wanted."

Emory's retort died within her when she stared at his smooth inky shirt and black pants, the crooked crown plastering his midnight hair almost into his eyes. He nodded. "You do know that I will find you. The Rebellion is dead, Emory. You are alone. Why fight in a war you cannot possibly win?"

He was so close to her, but she couldn't form the words. *Stop. Stop. Stop.* They were face-to-face, his pitch-black eyes acting like a mirror, her pale reflection staring back at her.

"Where are you?"

Vision blurring, she breathed, "It will not end like this."

His hand cupped her cheek. "It already has."

***

Vaguely, she was aware that she had bit her tongue. The coppery taste of blood filled her mouth, and, blinking, she stared up into Brokk's face.

"Stop fussing over her, Foster. She obviously just passed out. Nothing a solid breakfast won't solve," Marquis said behind him, arms folded across his chest, but his dark gaze said the complete opposite.

"Em, I'm here. Are you okay?" Brokk asked.

Tell me where you are.

Pushing Declan's voice from her mind, she focused on Brokk. "I'm okay. Just as Marquis said, I need to eat." She breathed deeply, and the trace of the Dark King faded. Finding her feet, she tried to place her features in a neutral mask, not allowing the fear to control her. "Let's continue. The faster I get some food in me, the better."

Finding her footing back on the street, she noted Brokk trailing her like a shadow, obviously not convinced by her explanation.

She couldn't look at any of them. They passed vendor after vendor with customers lined up. A woman walked by her, head half shaved, tattoos sprawling on the exposed skin, trailing down past her neck and onto her arms. Men were in gorgeous clothing, wearing jackets of all colors from gold to black. Kids ran in the streets, yelling about their products, from the best fruit you would ever taste to hair serums that were sealed with magic. Standing there, all Emory could do for a moment was take it all in, no one paying her much attention.

"Miss?" The voice was squeaky. As she looked down, she saw a boy no older than thirteen. His ashen hair was shaggy, and he pushed it out of his eyes. He wore a simple green shirt, black pants, and boots. She took in the black lines on the tops of his hands—the start of two anchors beautifully drawn there—she couldn't help herself.

"What do those mean?"

His blue eyes looked down at the ink, and he proudly looked back up at her. "They are my clan's sigils. Before moving to Hriste, we hailed from the south, in Oakland Wharf district." He smiled at Marquis then sputtered, "The room is ready, milord."

Blunt and to the point.

Marquis motioned to him. "Lead the way for our guests, Adi."

Adi wasted no time diving into the crowd, and Emory lurched, picking up her speed to trail after him. The whispers started as they walked; trying to ignore them, Emory asked, "So, what is this all about? The upcoming celebration?"

The boy shook his head, offering a tentative smile. "No, this is just our everyday artisans' market. You know, everyone's different livelihoods."

The normalcy of it struck like a knife. Swallowing, she nodded. "I once lived in a city that did a similar thing. It's great for the community."

Adi's eyes went wide as he stared ahead, no reply. *Alright, my past is a forbidden topic.* They passed a cart with beautiful baked goods, from tarts to breads, and it was all she could do to make herself keep walking. Swallowing against her hunger, she asked, "So how many different clans are there within the Isles?"

Adi eyed her skeptically. "Well, Hriste is only the capital. There are hundreds of small towns within the Isles. But there are four main districts: Terdes Harbor, Oakland Wharf, Harbor of Newsoll, and Durdover Port. But Durdover Port is trying to separate from the Isles."

Hundreds. Nodding and digesting that information, she assumed the self-proclaimed royals of Durdover Port were going to be their target. How many clans followed Marquis loyally and would side with them? How many clans followed this other proclaimed king from Durdover Port? Marquis's plan seemed less obtuse with that key point of information. They had thousands of people, hundreds of towns to convince that their cause, their war, was worth it.

As they walked, her body slowly woke up, the bruises still tender, still swollen. As the cobbled streets slanted up, her thighs burned. The crowd started to thin. Soon, they cut to the left onto a side street, where there was barely anyone. Lost in her thoughts, she clenched and unclenched her fists, her nails biting into her skin.

Catching Brokk's worried gaze trailing her, she tried to smile reassuringly. How much of this morning was because she wanted Brokk and she was terrified she would never get the chance again? The man who had defied death *for her.* Defied the laws of time and space to save *her.* Dread filled her, but there was nothing left to do now except tell him the truth.

Oh, yes, Brokk, you know when we both almost died, and we were caught by ancient cannibals? Well, the dark magic that was in Adair is in me now—permanently. Trapped in a magical necklace left by my own mother; it exploded, melded into my blood and bone, and I don't know how much time I have left. I don't know what to do.

Oh, and I think the Dark King is hunting me in my dreams, and I am putting us all in danger just by existing. Also, I went behind your back and promised Marquis I would kill for him to attain an army for Kiero. Not only that, but he'll help me get you and your warriors to safety. Away from me.

Biting the inside of her cheek, she jumped as Adi asked, "Miss, did you hear me?"

"Sorry, no," she replied.

He motioned to the building in front of them, and her jaw dropped. The building was *massive*. It looked to be built out of flawless marble, and it stuck out like a sore thumb among the cozy houses of Hriste. Pillars framed the wide staircase, beautiful carvings in their bodies of ships riding on the waves of the Black Sea. Emory was entranced by the portrayal of the creatures carved into the marble, lurking deep beneath the ocean's surface.

"Beautiful, isn't it?" Marquis sidled up beside her.

"Yes, it is."

Riona and Kiana looked with skepticism at the building while Brokk met Emory's eyes, concern flooding his own. Emory broke the gaze first. Trying to get her bearings about where they were, Emory noticed they were closer to the enclosed field, the waterfall roaring in the distance. *We're on the outskirts of Hriste.*

"Just straight through the doors," Adi said. Glancing back, she was about to ask why he wasn't coming in, but the boy was already gone.

Marquis nodded at them all. "Welcome to the heart of Hriste."

Breathing fast, she climbed up the stairs, Brokk maneuvering beside her, with Kiana, Riona, and Marquis following. The cool wind whipped across her face, and her heart pounded with her lies. How would she tell them? How could she? Especially Brokk, who had always believed in her. But when he found out about the darkness in her? The deceit? What would happen then?

She stalled at the door—torn in two, yet again. Pressing her eyes closed, she fought against the hollowness. Most of her memories had come back: her parents, her younger years, her friends, the Academy, the first war, the essence of who she was, who she wanted to be. And yet, there was an empty hole in her chest that had only widened since being here. Her parents had been good people; she had loved them. But everyone had secrets, and their motives were blank pages to her.

She had *nothing.*

Opening her eyes, she whispered under her breath, "Show them who you are meant to be."

"What was that?" Brokk asked.

"Nothing." She opened the door. Faltering, Emory took in how lavish the room was. Her boots thumped lightly on the smooth marble flooring as she and the others filed in. The bay windows surrounding them made the room light and everything seemed sharper.

"Welcome to my council room." Marquis breezed past them all, heading toward the round table in the middle of the empty room. Those blazing green eyes singed into her, as if saying, *Now our future changes.* The freckles danced along his cheeks as his mouth curved upward. "Please, let's all be seated. We have matters to discuss."

He beamed, motioning for them to sit. The chair was hard as she pulled it back; it screeched against the floor. Brokk moved fast, sitting beside her, Riona and Kiana following suit.

Marquis clapped his hands, his voice bouncing around them. "Now, let's get down to business. Emory Fae, you and your company have asked us for your help in the upcoming war, have come to *my* shores bearing the news that you have killed Adair, more commonly known as the Mad King. You stated that there are forces possessing his lands and body that none of us have ever seen before and that they are coming for us all. You are without an army. Without a court. I have discussed this with my advisors, and, in short, my people who support my ruling will rally with you. You all know my terms."

Marquis paused, looking only at her. Trying to still her frantic pulse, Emory focused on her decision, her heart turning to ice.

"First, I have one more condition." Marquis sighed. "We hold on to as much normalcy as we can. Before the winter takes ahold of us, we celebrate the change of seasons. The Harvest Equinox pulls all the clans together, as we celebrate for days. Before my men and women go to war, we will hold on to this. That is where the royals from Durdover Port will bless us with their presence. And it is where, with your help, King Iain and Queen Skena will die, their rebellion against me dying with them."

Emory's palms were clammy. "And you promise that once these two are killed, the rest of the Isles will follow you into war with us?"

"To the very end. Durdover Port is the last clan who has remained faithful to my father's reign. They don't recognize me or my right to the Isles. We can't afford to fight two wars, and unfortunately, the Port holds most of the fleet." His voice was rough.

Brokk looked at her and then to the king. "What if you're lying? These two royals can't be persuaded for peace?"

This time, that dark expression overtook everything Marquis Maher was. "These two are the people who orchestrated and happily murdered the rest of Emory's living family under my father's command. I'm tired of oppression. Of having to always shield Hriste against the relentless attacks against me from Durdover. You aren't the only ones who have been navigating politics alone. Our parents did it backward, building their monarchy on lies. Kiero suffered for it. So, I'm proposing that in return for the Isles' resources, you will help me end these royals who thrive off gruesome violence. To leave behind the wounds of the past and work toward *healing*."

The room was too still, the air too thick.

Kiana and Riona practically snarled under their breaths.

Marquis looked pointedly at Emory. "It will be dangerous, but I'm determined that with us all being the most influential people in Kiero, we can manage." Nodding, Marquis glanced at them all. "Brokk. Thoughts?"

Brokk's voice was low, and Emory's heart plummeted. "I've thought about it, and I will not kill unless I absolutely have to. This war is happening with or without you, Marquis, and my hands are already covered in enough blood. It's your choice if you want to join, but I will not buy you over by doing your dirty work."

Riona chipped in, "And I follow Brokk and Brokk alone. I stand with Nehmai, having seen Kiero ripped apart by its own doing for centuries. I didn't think coming here was a good idea. We should be home, planning how to get rid of this *Dark King*. Not here, planning a harvest equinox and how to assassinate two people. I frankly don't care if they have been causing you grief or not." Heat rose in Emory's cheeks when Riona shot her a pointed glare.

Emory knew what she would say, whose alliances she was true to. Kiana met her gaze, unreadable emotions flitting in her silver eyes. "Marquis, I am sure you know my answer."

Marquis shrugged.

Loosening a shaky breath, Emory shifted her gaze to Brokk, her voice curt. "What happened to you saying we are stronger together? What about our promise to ourselves that we will overcome anything for Kiero? If we are divided now, then how will we defeat Declan and the Oilean?"

"Killing these two people isn't the answer." Brokk locked his gaze on her.

"Then what is the answer? Building an army in Nehmai? With *whom*?" Emory countered.

"The answer is the Rebellion. We have wasted enough time here with him," Brokk shot back.

"I disagree." Silence fell, and Emory glanced to Marquis, her words ringing through the air. "Look at the pattern of the last couple of months. I am brought back to ignite the Rebellion, who in turn disrespect me for being kept safe. That's on all of us. The Rebellion was ripped apart at the seams. People died because of the ripples I caused, Brokk. I went to Adair to try to grant us time. I killed people to keep Adair from catching on to my true intentions. I died. And through all of that, what have we heard of the Rebellion? We *are* the Rebellion, and we have a chance at gaining an army. Gaining another ally. If that means sacrificing more of ourselves so we can free our world, then so be it. I will help you, Marquis, if it means you are with us."

Marquis winked at her from across the table. Emory looked at the king. "Are we in agreement?"

"Yes, Princess. We have an agreement."

Emory lifted her gaze to Brokk's, his molten gaze afire.

***

Emory leaned back, her eyes fluttering shut for the briefest second, feeling like she could sleep for a decade. The savory and sweet tastes from their breakfast lingered on her tongue. The clink of silverware and the voices of Riona and Kiana collided with each other around her. She opened her eyes, reaching for another sip of tea and noticed Brokk eyeing the silverware warily across from her.

Marquis had led them back to his home, and the dining room they were in was small. The soft gray walls held hints of blue and green décor, making her feel like she was trapped in sea glass—pieces of beauty everywhere. The sizzle and crackle from the stovetop wove above them while more meat cooked.

Emory didn't want to know exactly what it was, but it was the closest meal she had had to bacon and eggs since arriving in Kiero, and honestly, it was bliss. Freshly baked buns rested in a woven basket, and Marquis nodded to Diedre, who had joined them. "The second round should be almost done."

Diedre stood, making her way around the table to gather their plates to be refilled.

Riona groaned, flashing her teeth in a feral grin. "I don't like you, but I will say, you know how to entertain."

With a shrug, Marquis replied, "It's my job and duty. But you are also all worthless to me starved." He pointedly looked at Emory, and she could feel the tension rippling from Brokk.

Diedre returned from the kitchen, placing another heaping plate in front of her, and Emory reached for the biscuits and jam. Cutting into the crusty bread, she asked, "So, what is the course of action then?"

"Well, the Harvest Equinox is planned for three weeks from now," Marquis responded. "That's when we will act. After that, we will set off to Kiero before the winter sets in."

Emory chewed her food carefully before saying, "That's not a lot of time."

"*Trust* me, Emory. It will be enough. I will remind you of one thing, though, and only once." He paused a moment. "If you back out of your promise, you will die. Then what? What was the point of you killing Adair? What was the point of you returning? Take the time to learn while you are on the Isles. If you can't do that, then you are walking in the exact footsteps of your parents and mine. And our world will be lost."

No one said a word.

***

The early afternoon sunlight soaked into Emory's skin, relaxing her further after the filling breakfast. As a group, they wandered down the cobbled streets in silence, everyone seemingly lost in their own thoughts. She didn't have the energy to start a conversation, but she felt Brokk's gaze burning into her back.

They had each made their own decision, and she would see hers through.

For Adair.

For Brokk.

For Kiero.

Despite her conviction, she couldn't help but feel dread wash over her with every step. It was when her life became quiet that memories of Adair snuck in. At night, if she wasn't plagued by the living nightmares with Declan, she was with Adair in her dreams. Memories from the Academy when they were teenagers—distorted but loving—replayed in her mind. He had been her first best friend and that bond had not been broken in her, but it was a bleeding wound that worsened every day, the weight of his death heavy and unyielding.

Looking up as strangers now passed her in the streets of Hriste, Emory thought she saw Adair's eyes. His crooked smile, his inky hair. Her heart rate galloped at the seconds of hope that somehow it was truly her best friend passing her in the street. But that defied rational thought.

Traces of him burned through her like a poison, the guilt of what she had done twisting her thoughts. He had been the Mad King; he had blood staining his hands for years, had plummeted Kiero into ruin.

And yet . . .

If she had tried harder to get the Oilean's dark magic out of him, *saving him*, would he have been the same Adair she knew and loved? As she remembered him?

It was the possibility she never granted him that ate away at her, spreading like a rot and breeding doubt.

Taking a deep breath of the turning autumn air and balling her hands into fists, Emory tried to clear her mind. Adair was dead; she should let him go. She should be focusing on the tasks ahead—of making sure Brokk and the naithe warriors got off the Isles unscathed. Away from her and the raw dark ability that was building in her.

But, behind her every blink, it was Adair's face she saw, her heart yearning for her friend.

Passing shop after shop, Emory saw that the houses were thinning, the bustle of Hriste diminishing, and then the field came into view. In the distance, by the waterfall, a group was gathered. Emory watched the men and women pair up, the crash of swords ringing out across the plain.

Eventually the street stopped, and the grassy field met them.

Brokk nodded, hope brimming in his eyes for the first time today. "Are we training?"

"My other condition. You will meet here every afternoon and *learn*. The rest of your time is yours while you are on the Isles. Everything is accessible to you."

Her companions' faces lit up, and they eagerly drank in the scene below.

Crossing her arms, Emory looked to Marquis. "And where will you be?" It came out sharper than intended.

Sauntering up to her, Marquis breathed, "Don't worry. I will still check in with you; besides, you and I have some coordinating to do. But first we must give the people what they want. Together, we will show a front of unity despite our different decisions." Dread pooled in her stomach when he nodded. "Go. The rest will come. You will see, Princess."

Turning, he left without a backward glance.

Sighing, Emory looked to Brokk, exhaustion filling her body as he motioned toward the fighters. "Shall we?"

Not having a choice, Emory walked to the group with the others close behind.

Riona jabbed, "It's time I pummeled you, Emory. This whole trip has caused some pent-up frustration toward you, *Princess.*"

Anger flickered through her chest, but she didn't react to the immortal. Suddenly, vertigo washed over her, making her stumble. Everything fell into the background. Emory saw Brokk's lips move in slow motion, but she couldn't hear a single word he was saying.

A high-pitched ringing cut through her hearing, and Emory winced. Her heart dropped into her stomach as pain erupted through her. Her soul seemed to crack, and anger licked up her arms, pooling in her core. It felt as if she were being torn in two. Emory felt the darkness rise in her, hungry.

Declan's voice filled her mind, echoing in the folds of her consciousness. "*Emory, this is yours to take.*" Stopping midstride, she blinked, expecting to see the Dark King in front of her. The imposter *wearing* Adair. "*Destroy them, and come back to me. Together, we could be unstoppable. It's not too late to turn yourself in. To make yourself known.*"

Warmth bloomed on her hands. She realized blood trickled down her wrist, her nails having sliced through her flesh. Gently, the pain brought her back, Declan's voice fading away. She focused on Brokk standing in front of her with furrowed brows.

"Em?"

She plastered a fake smile on her lips. "I'm okay. Let's go."

The group was maybe a couple yards away from them, but some of the people had stopped, taking in her display. Brokk fell into step with her, his steadiness and warmth momentarily chasing her demons away. He didn't prod, but his gaze was burning into her, branding his questions: *What's wrong? What can I do?*

Emory pressed her lips into a thin line; grief was waiting for her in company with her guilt. Brokk wouldn't understand what she was going through. How she mourned the man who had slaughtered her parents, had destroyed her life. Adair had destroyed Brokk's life, had slaughtered his friends. His rebellion. Adair had cultivated hatred in every action, but she wanted to scream.

What would they have done if they were in Adair's situation?

Sadness welled up in her for the fallen Mad King, consuming her. A thousand times, Emory replayed the moment she drove the blade into Adair's heart. Her eyes stung, but she blinked the tears back. The clanging of iron was her tempo as she pushed herself forward, the memories of her last training session lurking in the shadows of her mind.

They reached the group, and Emory watched a woman bring her fingers to her lips, whistling shrilly as the group of about forty ceased their fighting. The woman had gleaming indigo hair and two silver rings in her nose. She stalked toward them. She wore a dark-green top, black pants, and knee-high leather boots. A full sleeve of all nautical-themed tattoos covered both of her arms. Emory noticed two anchors on the tops of her hands, identical to Adi's.

Her stern hazel eyes drank Emory's group in as she sheathed her long broadsword at her hip, crossing her arms over her chest.

"Well, everyone, it seems we finally get to meet the group everyone has been so *distracted* by." Snickers followed her words; Emory felt sheepish, heat creeping up the back of her neck. "My name is Nasiea. I expect you all to drop your titles and everything you think you know about the art of fighting. While you are on the Isles, you will follow my lessons like every other student. Have an open mind and an open heart, and maybe you will learn something."

Well, this is going to go well.

Stepping up first, Brokk held his hand out, his voice even when he said, "My name is Brokk Foster, and these are my companions, Kiana and Riona."

The warriors dipped their heads in sync, but the woman brushed past them, focusing on Emory. "And you. The Fae girl who has risen from the dead."

It wasn't a question. Emory jutted her chin out. "Yes."

Nasiea looked like she had swallowed something sour. "Well, isn't that convenient."

Riona frowned as she took in Nasiea. Naturally, Kiana smiled softly.

Nasiea looked Emory up and down, making her blush deeper before she walked past the rest of their company. "Well, let's begin."

Emory's mouth felt dry, like she had sawdust in it. She stood there, heart pumping unnaturally fast. That flicker, like a cloud passing over the sun, encompassed her once more. All she felt was the ice, the wrath churning underneath her skin.

Kiana gripped Riona's wrist, pulling her off to the side. Brokk's fingers interlaced with Emory's own, dried blood flaking off as he gently pulled her to the side as well.

"Emory, we need to talk."

Her breath hitched as she took in the intense look in his eyes, his lips, the tiny freckles on his nose that she had never noticed before, every detail that was him.

He exhaled, and his voice was just a whisper. "There you are. Sometimes I feel like you're not here, in this moment."

She stepped back, unsure of what to say. Brokk smiled, looking optimistic, like the conversation they were going to have later could go well. Trying to reciprocate his warmth, Emory felt like her smile was a grimace instead. Brokk's smile faltered.

Emory looked to Nasiea, who walked toward them.

"Now, before you will ever touch a weapon, it's time to learn how to harness your energy."

"Seriously?" Riona rolled her eyes.

Brokk drawled, "Shut up, Riona, and listen."

The warrior stuck her tongue out at him, but Nasiea ignored their banter.

"Mastering the sword is only half the battle. What about your mind? If you're at war with yourself, you are already defeated."

Every word felt directed at Emory, like their instructor knew. As if she could sense what Emory was feeling. Emory feared the worst as Nasiea continued, "Until you master the art of meditation, you will not touch a weapon in my class."

You are already defeated.

She trembled as fear tore through her.

"Find somewhere comfortable and begin. Start by concentrating on your breath. In for three counts, inhaling deeply into your belly. Exhale through your nose."

Looking confused, Brokk watched as the rest of the class resumed their sparring. Riona muttered; Emory only imagined what colorful words she chose to use. Kiana sat on the grass, her sister soon following suit.

Sighing, Emory left them, making her way toward the waterfall, away from everyone else. She didn't want to explain—*couldn't* explain—what was rampaging through her mind. Grimacing, she lowered herself onto the ground, the soft grass cushioning her body. Closing her eyes, she felt stupid as she crossed her legs, resting her hands on her knees, concentrating on her breath, and tried to still her hammering pulse.

"How will you ever rise if you are hiding the truth from yourself?" Nasiea circled around her, making her jump. Her tone was soft, so no one could hear her except Emory.

The words landed like a blow, and she flinched against the shadow. Trying to keep her face soft, Emory replied, "I know the concepts behind stilling your mind."

"Ah, you may know, Queen, but that means nothing when confronting your fear. Do you have the courage to confront what you fear most?"

Stiffly, Emory said, "I don't know what you're talking about."

Nasiea didn't reply, which left the lie clinging thick and bitter on Emory's tongue. With a sigh, Emory pushed the thought of the bold instructor out of her mind. Nasiea knew *nothing* about the weight that sat on her shoulders.

While Emory concentrated on her inhales and exhales, her mind ran circles. What was happening to Memphis? To Alby? Azarius? Even Nyx? As Emory sat in the grass, how much time did Black Dawn Rebellion have left? If they were even alive. Did they even have an inclination of what lurked in the Draken Mountains? What was lurking in Adair's body?

Her breathing morphed into a rattling gasp, thick and unsettled. Maybe her whole life was an hourglass, split between her two realities, and this world, *this* one, may have tipped the scale. But ultimately, she had paved her course, had chosen to sacrifice and die for this cause. But with that came *this*. Her choice to lie to Brokk about what really coursed through her and who hunted the stolen power. Allying with Marquis to *kill* in order to gain an army, bickering over capitals and titles while Kiero burned. Her nails bit into her palms, the fresh wounds laced with pain. Again, she breathed deeply, trying to harness her fear.

"Emory." In and out, the Dark King's voice drawled in her mind. "*Come back. Come back to me. Come back. Come back. Come back . . .*"

She was sure if anyone gave her a second of attention, they'd see her face pinched in fear. In her consciousness, Emory couldn't escape the poison in her veins and whatever this connection was. It was an unwavering reminder. Every second of every day, the Dark King searched for her. Calling to her very soul to *obey* him.

The waterfall crashed behind her, and she stood up, shaking. Nasiea's steady gaze pierced through her. Behind her, Brokk was peaceful, on the brink of sleep as he sat, the warriors serene beside him. The rest of the class sparred, their swords continuously clashing.

Emory's breath was ragged, tears burning her eyes. No one except Nasiea, who Emory could have sworn was smirking, saw her leave the class behind.

Her emotions slipped. She concentrated on her footfalls, and her steps became a constant rhythm.

One.

"Destroy them and come back to me."

Two.

"Destroy them."

Three.

"I will find you, Emory."

Declan's voice chased her thoughts, anxiety making her stomach churn. Since she had come back to Kiero, she had trusted one thing—that she was meant to be here, deserved to be here. Not only to stand alongside the Rebellion but to be the missing piece to help liberate Kiero.

Now, she wasn't so sure anymore.

This dark magic from the Book of Old had controlled Adair, destroying the friend she had once known. How would she be any different? How long would it be before she lost herself to its alluring power?

Swallowing hard, Emory entered Hriste once more, swept up in the bustling streets. The houses she passed were in washes of blue, yellow, gray, and orange. Strangers passed her in wide berths, their mistrusting gazes doing nothing but deepening her worry.

With no specific route in mind, she delved deeper into the heart of the city. She stuffed her hands in her jacket pockets, and the sun's warmth bathed the back of her neck, but nothing could stave off the chill of autumn clinging to the breeze.

They were all running out of time.

"Hey!" a young voice rang out.

Looking up, she saw Adi launch himself off the brick wall he had been sitting on, racing over to her.

"Hey, yourself." Emory smiled, shifting to the side of the busy street.

"Are you lost? Why aren't you with your company?" Adi asked, tilting his bronzed head.

"I'm pretty sure I was dismissed from my lesson with Nasiea."

Scrunching up his face, Adi stuck out his tongue. "Nasiea is mean."

Chuckling, Emory took in her young guide. "I think she is just brutally honest."

Adi shrugged. "Where are you heading?"

"To be honest, I guess I was hoping to find somewhere quiet I could sit for a while."

Nodding, Adi tugged on her sleeve. "Follow me."

Some of the tension lifted from this morning as Emory jogged after him, trying not to lose him in the crowd.

"You know, my parents think your arrival here is punishment by the gods for Marquis not fighting against the Mad King."

Heat rushed to her cheeks as Adi slowed his pace, waiting for her answer. "You don't say? But you know that building an alliance with the Mad King has kept the Isles out of war all these years."

Adi frowned. "Many believe he is a coward."

"And what do *you* think?"

Adi looked at a passing fruit stand with hopeful eyes, tossing a coin to the vendor before swiping a deep-blue fruit. "I think you're probably not a demon witch like my mom thinks. And Marquis . . . he treats me well. He gives me work when most won't. I would rather judge him on what I know, and he is a good person."

"Then you are already wise beyond your years." Emory smiled.

Stopping in front of the shop, Adi beamed. "The best tea in Hriste. You won't be disappointed, I promise."

"I owe you one, Adi. Thank you."

With a dip of his head, he left, disappearing into the bustling city once more.

A tiny bell trilled as Emory opened the door and entered, waves of lemongrass and lavender welcoming her. Small round tables were scattered among the shelves of loose-leaf teas, instantly creating a space of peace and comfort. A man looked up at her from behind the counter, paling.

"Hello." Emory smiled softly, trying to ease the man's discomfort.

"Milady, the shop owners were told our guests may grace us by visiting. Whatever you desire is yours."

"Thank you . . . uh . . ."

"Kee," he said pleasantly, going about his work, sifting through different tins strewn behind the counter.

"Thank you, Kee," Emory said, picking a seat by the window and concentrating on what tea she would try first.

***

Emory sat, staring out the arched window, her third cup of lavender tea steaming in front of her. The shop was quaint with gray walls with bookshelves filling every possible space. The countertop sported an assortment of glass jars filled with baked goods and every tea leaf possible. And *then* some. Sighing, Emory cupped the mug in her hands, watching the pink hues bleeding into the sky. How could it be dusk already?

Turmoil had taken over her. Was it the right decision to stay, to help Marquis? Dark thoughts had crept in in the hours she had been alone, doubts at the impossibility of her task before her. She didn't even know how to truly harness the power buried within her. Would it destroy her, as it did with Adair in the end?

Anger licked through her veins as she fought her thoughts. She had not come so far just to fall into the oblivion—that devastatingly enticing void—to give up.

Emory eyed Kee for the hundredth time, wondering if he was getting unnerved yet. She sipped the velvety tea that warmed her core. Watching people pass the front window, she tried to calm herself. There was time to make sure they had secured an army before Declan found her.

There was time before her end would come . . .

Panic clutched at her heart. The thought of dying and leaving Kiero behind—truly leaving it—scared her more than anything. Pure desperation to find an answer to defeat the dark power within her—to stay alive—overwhelmed her. A tremor shuddered through her, and she clutched her cup with shaking hands.

And then . . .

Would Brokk still support her if he knew the truth about what had happened? Once he understood what this dark power that ran through her veins meant?

Feeling sick, Emory pulled her attention to the streets outside once again. The families shopping. Couples in conversation. Emory caught lingering looks, hidden smiles. Shop owners discussing products with their customers. Did they even realize the war that was waiting for them all?

A clang in front of her made her jump. Kee smiled softly, and the sandwich in front of her looked divine. But a voice drawled behind her, making her skin crawl. "You do know it's almost dinner time, don't you?"

Marquis had changed, his leather boots softly padding on the floor. A deep-green button-down shirt made his eyes ignite. His black jacket and black pants tied his outfit together. The king plunked down across from her.

"Thank you, Kee."

The clerk bowed lowly, leaving them in peace.

Scowling, Emory brought her attention back to the window, trying to keep her voice steady. "I'm really not in the mood."

"And do you think I care?" Marquis replied.

Her scowl deepened. "How did you find me anyways?"

Leaning over, Marquis grabbed half her sandwich, taking a hearty bite. Groaning, he chewed mindfully as she glared at him. "Are you actually thinking word doesn't spread that a dead girl, who is now proclaimed royalty, has been sitting in Kee's shop for hours?"

Sighing, Emory picked up the other half, the fresh lettuce and layered meats taunting her. She was starving. As she bit into the soft bread, bursts of flavor danced along her taste buds. Sweet and spicy, crunchy and savory.

Leaning back after she finished, Emory nodded. "Yeah, and here I thought I could get away with just being Emory Fae, wanting some alone time."

"When will you realize you can never just *be*? Here, you are my guest, but a lot of my kingdom hates Kiero and the years of slavery they pushed on the Isles. A proclaimed Queen of Kiero is going to take time. They don't see you as just a person. They see you as a threat who has asked them to put their lives on the line, and for what? For *who*?"

"Is this why we are going through with the Harvest Equinox first?" she asked.

"Part of the reason. The other motive is just to enjoy a celebration. I feel like you have forgotten your humanity ever since you have returned."

Emory scoffed. "My humanity? My humanity is the only reason I am here with you now. The Rebellion was lost. You think, in my sacrifices, I am not reminded every day of my guilt? Of my anger? My love? My fear? If that's not humanity, I don't know what is."

"Touché. But even still, now more than ever, you need to keep that part of your heart burning—the part that feels all those emotions so deeply. Allow yourself to feel them." His voice was gentle, and she hated Marquis for that. For the pity that clung to his voice.

Clenching and unclenching her fists, she replied quietly, "What I need is to get back to Kiero."

"Before what?" His question hung in between them as her chest heaved. She held every breath steady. *We need him, we need him, we need him.* Leaning closer, Marquis whispered, "Have you told Brokk your little secret yet, Princess?"

Emory shoved her chair back and stalked to the exit. Over her shoulder, she nodded to Kee. "Thank you for your hospitality."

As she pulled the door open, the crisp air swept her breath from her lungs. The world was quiet as she walked down the street, her anger and sadness festering. Who did Marquis think he was? He didn't have the *right* to keep throwing in her face the fact that she was lying to Brokk. Maybe it was Marquis's mission to make her as miserable as possible, since that's the way his great love with Adair ended up going.

Footfalls sounded behind her, and Emory gritted her teeth in annoyance. When she turned down the side streets, soft melodies of families at home drifted on the wind. The last of the soft pink streaks in the sky faded away as night swept in. Turning to her right, she leaned against the brick, heaving as pain laced through her stomach.

"Princess?"

Tears streamed down her cheeks as she rasped, "He is hunting me, Marquis. Declan won't stop until he has it back. And now . . . it is *in me*. This dark magic. I'm the weapon."

In the shadows, he leaned closer, breathing, "I know."

Hiccupping, she blearily asked, "How could Brokk ever accept that? Am I selfish for wanting whatever time I have left with him to be happy?"

"He deserves to know the truth, Emory. Before it is too late to tell him. Trust me. I know how that feels." Marquis leaned in closer, his breath hot against her cheek. For the first time since being on the Isles, in the shadows of the alley, Marquis opened his arms, folding her into his chest.

At first, her body stiffened, not sure how to accept Marquis's empathy. Instinctively, Emory nestled her face into the crook of his neck, her tears pouring down her cheeks and raking sobs shaking through her core. They stood there for what felt like hours until Emory's face was swollen and no more tears came.

And in the silence, they broke apart.

CHAPTER EIGHT

BROKK

The pub was a heartbeat, pulsing raw energy all around them. The sisters had *insisted* they go after spotting it in their afternoon exploration—just them since Emory had disappeared from the class. He didn't have the heart to turn them down. The music soared around Brokk while he sipped his drink, the ale making him feel warm and relaxed. For the first time in years, his pain ebbed into the background.

He grinned at Riona and Kiana dancing in the crowd. Beside him, strangers were having boisterous conversations, the bartender watching his customers with eager eyes. There was a tapestry of men and women behind him on the dance floor, their bodies swaying to the upbeat of the cluster of stringed instruments that were seemingly playing themselves.

No one talked about the war coming; no one talked of death and loss, of the rebels across the sea. And for the first time, Brokk could see why Marquis was reluctant to give this up to their cause. Sighing, he finished his drink, wondering where Emory was and why she had been avoiding him. He knew her wounds ran deep, but he had promised her she wouldn't be alone in this. She would never have to deal with her pain alone, despite their differences.

The bartender set down another drink in front of him, nodding. "On the house."

Half smiling, Brokk kept the amber liquid close as all around him time stopped and slipped away in the same breath. The music climbed and climbed, and his thoughts became more disjointed.

For his entire life, Brokk had been tortured by his moral compass for placing Emory on Earth, for the Black Dawn Rebellion losing to Adair, attack after attack for years. He was still having trouble digesting the last month, especially the lies he had eaten from the Oilean about Roque being his father when his past in Nehmai had been waiting for him all along. How he finally learned about his true name and family: *Brokk Falkov.* All he had done since then was navigate broken kingdom after broken kingdom, moving nowhere toward a resolution.

Brokk tipped his drink back, looking for answers in the bottom of his glass that he knew weren't there.

The bell above the door rang as the door opened. Crisp air flooded into the pub before the door closed. Blinking up, Brokk narrowed his eyes. Marquis Maher, looking as tired as Brokk felt, locked his gaze onto Brokk before crossing the room.

"Foster, glad you seem to be settling in."

Not looking at the king, Brokk sighed. "What do you want, Marquis?"

"Can't a king join his people for a drink?" Marquis sat down beside him, flagging down the bartender. "My usual, please, Jare."

It wasn't until the amber whiskey was placed in front of Marquis that he continued, "I heard Emory walked out of training today."

"Yes, she did."

"Do you know why?" Marquis asked through sips.

"You two seem close enough. Why don't you ask her yourself?"

"Jealousy doesn't suit you, you know."

Brokk had no reply to that.

Throwing his head back, Marquis finished his drink. Clinking the glass down, hard, on the counter, he asked, "Will you walk with me?"

Maybe Brokk's judgment was skewed from too many drinks, maybe he was tired of chasing after answers, or maybe he was ready to stop worrying about Emory. In any case, his curiosity was piqued. "Sure."

Slipping from the stool, Brokk caught Kiana's eye in the pulsing crowd. She nodded. He could read her wishes in her features, by the burning in her eyes. *Learn his secrets.*

Dodging the dancing bodies, they left the pub. The quietness of the street seemed unnerving as Brokk pulled his jacket tighter around him. He pushed down his bitterness toward Marquis, and they fell into stride.

"I like Nasiea," Brokk said.

"She has been helping teach sparring since she was in her teens, along with Emory's mom. Nasiea has graciously kept them going." That caught Brokk off guard as Marquis led him farther down the street, heading toward the grotto. "She is very skilled at what she does. But I didn't bring you out here to talk about her," Marquis continued.

Far above them, the crescent moon hung in the sky, stars stretching for as far as Brokk could see. The ever-distant lull of crashing waves reminded him even more of the miles between him and the Rebellion. *If they are still alive.* When Brokk looked up, the king's expression was unreadable, and Brokk suddenly felt uneasy. "If this is about the royals from Durdover and me not agreeing to kill them . . ."

"Funny enough, I had a feeling that your response would be as such. You are a lot of things, Foster, but you are loyal to *your* cause. You always have been. I would have been surprised if you decided to delve into the gray areas of morality this late in the game."

"Then you must know that the warriors and I seek to sail for Kiero immediately," Brokk whispered.

Marquis nodded. "That's why I have found you. I have received news from Kiero."

Blanching, Brokk stopped. "How?"

"I have hired spies that work for me. Information is power."

"Shouldn't Emory be here?"

"She needs to rest, as both you and I know. Now move, Foster. My contact doesn't like tardiness."

As they moved through the night lithely, Brokk's heart was in his throat. Houses blurred around him, his mind spinning. Rarely had he ever felt so raw in his life, his control slipping thanks to the bartender and his own bad judgment. Every second wasted here could mean life or death for the Rebellion.

Yet his heart strained against his promise to Emory, that no matter what, he would be loyal to her. *How could he stay true to his word?* Sweat collected at the base of his neck, his muscles straining to coordinate movement after the hours spent at the pub. His breath hitched in his chest, and the road dipped into the grassy plain. Marquis jogged toward the crashing waterfall. In the moonlight, the grass swayed in the light wind, mimicking a silver ocean. Rushing after Marquis, Brokk reached the pool's edge as the king dropped to his knees, and Brokk stood back.

Marquis bent, lowering his lips against the churning surface of the water, and spoke plainly, "Iria, I'm here."

Underneath the freezing spray of the waterfall, two luminous doe-like brown eyes blinked from below the surface. Straightening his upper body, Marquis waited. Ripples shuddered over the surface as Iria revealed herself. Her blue hair was electric, her brazen scaled skin breathtaking in the moonlight. Her scales shimmered every color of the rainbow in the light, her body exposed to the elements except her fins. *Merpeople.* Heat rushed up Brokk's neck as he tried to look anywhere except at her exposed body. Fixating on him, Iria bared her sharpened teeth.

"Marquis, you have finally brought me a handsome friend. A trade for the news, I hope?" Her voice was satin smooth and alluring.

Brokk's stomach churned, but Marquis brushed the idea off. "As much as I am enjoying him looking like a blushing maiden, no, he is not for you. Iria, may I introduce Brokk Foster, a rebel from the Black Dawn, the prince of Nehmai, and my guest."

Snarling in distaste, Iria focused back on Marquis. "Why tease me? That's hardly fair for the distance I have traveled."

"I pay you handsomely, Iria, as you already know."

Watching the back and forth, Brokk shifted his weight as Iria swam closer to the edge, bringing her scaled arms closer to Marquis. "Then let me claim my payment, dear *King*."

Brokk couldn't move, couldn't form words as Marquis lowered himself to the mermaid, baring his neck for her. Horror washed through Brokk's body when Iria closed her eyes and pressed her wet lips against Marquis's skin. His heightened senses picked up on the sudden tang on magic that clung around them. Iria began sucking on Marquis's skin, but not drinking his blood. Brokk staggered back, Marquis writhing underneath Iria's touch. His veins bulged, his skin turned dull, and his eyes rolled into the back of his head.

"Enough! Stop!" Brokk's voice was hoarse when Iria broke away, smacking her lips. Marquis sagged, and Brokk lunged to his knees, catching the king's weight.

"It's okay, Foster. This is nothing new for me," Marquis slurred, sweat droplets collecting on his forehead.

Iria smiled maliciously in the light up at them. "Unlike some, I'm not immortal. My price for my services of spying is taking years off the young king's life to extend my own. Tonight will be worth it, Marquis. Besides, Brokk, how did you think he knew how to find you and your company when you were sailing across the Black Sea? That it was luck that when the caine destroyed your ship, Marquis was there?"

Years off his life? Dumbstruck, Brokk looked to Marquis, who smiled up at him gravely. "I have to be resourceful sometimes. Now, Iria, please tell us what you have found out."

"Kiero is restless," she whispered, her voice dropping into hushed tones. "There have been whispers of death washing over the land like an infection, growing ripe with each passing day. Not only of Adair Stratton. Far in the east, news has reached us of a new leader of the raiders in the Dust Clans. Someone who isn't native to the Risco Desert."

Pausing, Iria locked her gaze on Brokk. "They say she goes by the name Nyx Astire, and that she has a fire burning in her soul and whispers of commanding the clans to join the war against the new Dark King. The raiders are worried that she will be caught up in the grief of her companion and not look to the future well-being of the clans."

The words dripped off her lips like honey, but they sliced into Brokk like knives. *Death of her companion. Death of her companion.* The world stilled, and it was like he was standing at the end of a tunnel, hearing himself ask, "And who was her companion that fell? Who was with her?"

In the moonlight, Iria replied, "A man named Memphis Carter."

Brokk felt his arms leave Marquis's body, and the young king staggered to the ground. Heat crawled up Brokk's arms, his legs, his throat. He tasted embers and ash, choking him. The world spun viciously, and Brokk numbly walked away. Behind him, Marquis's voice rippled out, "Foster, wait!"

But his paws were already digging into the damp earth. He loped back toward Hriste. He didn't remember shifting, but the seconds passed in clipped severity, all the while the words sinking deeper and deeper into his heart. *Memphis is dead.* How much would they all lose? How many more betrayals would they have to go through before the end? And even then, would they all make it back to what their purpose was as individuals? *Freedom. To not become a monster.*

But none of that seemed to matter anymore; it paled against the death of his best friend.

The autumn air had the cool kiss of winter on its wings. Brokk growled, the guttural sound tinged with a whine. He stood on the edge of raw emotion. As he pushed harder across the grassy plain and into Hriste, the questions haunted him. *Had Memphis thought dedicating his life to the Rebellion and ending Adair had been worth it? Or was he scared and alone as he died?* Houses blurred, people shouting as he barreled past. The night held no answers for him, only the stars embedded far above, twinkling down like a thousand gems. The silver light was his guide. The houses started to fade out until they eventually blurred in his peripheral vision.

Breathing hard, he pushed faster, *farther.*

"Foster."

Slamming to a stop, he shifted back to his human form. *That one voice.* Really, he had enough of it today, but he met Marquis's gaze.

"How, by fire and flame, did you get here so fast?" Brokk spat.

Marquis sagged, his skin looking gray, his hands shaking. "I can make the wind bow to me, as does the sea. I can use the elements to my advantage, you know. Just hear me out. I know you are hurting, and I'm *sorry.* Sincerely."

Blinking hard against the burning in his eyes, Brokk paced.

Marquis walked up beside him. "You know, I never really liked you. When we visited the Academy, I thought you unbearable. That if you were in a position of power, you would lead like the rest of Kiero already had—recklessly."

"Is that why you were drawn to Adair?" he replied.

Shadows danced across the king's face as he whispered, "Yes. But you have proved me wrong."

Surprise rippled through Brokk. "Why is that?"

"You love her. The true kind of love, Foster, the kind that defies everything you thought you knew on the subject. Yet, you will risk losing Emory to do what's *right*."

Brokk's heart dipped. Marquis held his hands out in front of him, low, like he was talking to a rabid animal. Chuckling darkly, Brokk shook his head. "But that doesn't even matter now. I may love her, but my best friend just died for a cause we have been fighting for our *entire lives*. Emory has chosen to help you; I will never be the man who cages her. But the Rebellion needs me. Nyx has secured the raiders; we have allies. The survivors of the Black Dawn Rebellion need to know they aren't alone."

"And I respect you all the more for that," Marquis replied.

"Let me tell her what has happened here tonight in my own way, Marquis."

Tipping his head back, Marquis drank in the stars. "Despite what you think, she can handle a lot more than we give her credit for. Allow her to have this time to reconnect with a part of who she is."

"I *know* she can handle a lot more."

Sighing, the king dipped his head, ignoring Brokk's response. "If you go back the way you came, past the waterfall, I have ensured there is staircase that will get you out of Hriste for tonight. Just in case you needed to know. I will open the gates at sunrise if you choose to return."

With that, Marquis left him, his footsteps fading.

Loosening a breath, Brokk shook his head, hating that Marquis was right. He propelled himself to shift, his muscles screaming and his bones cracking. That familiar pain was home to him. With the moon as his guide, he ran, his four paws colliding with the earth.

***

A flash of waterfall. A flash of stairway. Of climbing, up, up, *up*. Growling, Brokk flew, coming to an expanse of rolling hills, the waves crashing in the distance, and he allowed his wolf form to swallow him whole. Everything and nothing all at once met him as he pushed himself faster. The expanse ahead of him was endless. The stars and inky sky looked like they touched the grassy horizon, and it was achingly beautiful.

Heaving, he howled, his bay shattering the silence of the night. His howls climbed through the skies as the news hit him repeatedly, plowing deeper into his anguish. *Memphis is dead.* He pushed himself faster, but with every step, his friend's voice nipped at his heels. *Where are you running to, Brokk?*

His hackles rose as each footfall thundered, his resolve slipping into the darkness.

Eventually, he reached the cliff's edge that faced the Black Sea. When he shifted back, his body was slick with sweat, his limbs trembling. He paced back and forth, the silence of the night making his hair stand on end. And in the silence, in the isolation, he was surprised to be met by his anger.

"It wasn't supposed to end like this. Us worlds apart. The last time I saw you, I blamed you for Nyx's disappearance. For loving Emory. Even though it was *both* of us that had done wrong. It has always been both of us."

He shook, nails biting into his palms, his skin ripping open only to heal. "Now, I must take over, to make sure that the Dark King doesn't win. Of course, I *will* do this for you. For the Rebellion."

Tears slipped down his cheeks, silently, as he sat, the soft grass bending beneath him. Legs dangling over the edge, he watched the inky waves roll and crash. "But how can I move forward without you by my side? To leave her behind *again*? I'm at a crossroads, and I don't know what is right, Memph."

He sat there, listening to the raging ocean. Nothing to keep him company but his grief, sinking its claws into his core, not letting go . . . And Brokk gave in to it, watching the rhythmic motion of the waves until the darkness bled away and the sun started to climb on the horizon.

When the streaks of gold touched every corner of the Isles, Brokk stood up. Dusting his clothes off, he whispered on the wind, "I miss you, and I love you, brother. I hope you find peace, Memph."

Shifting, he ran back, his heart and his soul with Kiero, and the memory of his best friend erupting within him. He took in the Isles as he ran: the rugged, untamed landscape, the loose rocks in the dirt. The cliffs against the Black Sea. For miles, as far as the eye could see, were grasslands. No woods, nothing like the ancient trees that had circled the Academy. The expanse was unnerving and refreshing. He drank in the orchestra of foreign scents. His muscles screamed—the push and pull that he loved and that had carried him on endless nights.

In running, he found solace. And maybe he was running from his truth, savoring the time of just *existing,* but he could breathe. The nightmare that had been his life for years faded while running. It was just the open sky, the crisp air, and *him.*

The hours bled into one another until, finally, sides heaving, he spotted Marquis, arms crossed. Shifting back in a fluid motion, Brokk breathed, "You are quite punctual, aren't you?"

Those green eyes took in his soaked hair, heaving sides, and trembling limbs. "Long night?"

Shrugging, Brokk yawned. "Just working through some things."

Marquis ran a hand through his hair. "Come on, Foster. Back to our reality now."

Brokk looked down. "Where is the gate?"

He felt Marquis's hands shoving him forward, and he was screaming. The freefall was swift, the air howling around him, but not before he heard a whoop behind him. Gasping for air, he gulped before colliding with freezing water. It filled his nostrils as he dropped like a stone, his limbs flailing. *I can't swim. Can't swim.*

The water filled his lungs, choking him as he sank. The morning light filtered down to him in ribbons. Screaming, he tried to cut upward when Marquis crashed into the water. Air bubbles rippled in Brokk's vision; he sank lower. Everything in his mind pounded, his oxygen slowly cutting off. His arms lifted as he let go, gravity pulling him down farther.

Strong arms grabbed him around his waist, and he felt his weight lift. Kicking, his savior heaved them up, black spots swarming into view, but they broke through the surface, and Brokk spewed out a lungful of water.

"It's okay. I have you."

Blissful ground and air met them as he heaved himself out of the water, sodden. Marquis stood up, offering his hand. "Brokk, that's the gate."

"What the hell? Adi told me where you were headed, Marquis." Emory's voice rang out as she jogged across the plain toward them. Hands on her hips, Emory brought herself to full height, glaring at Marquis. "You have one second to explain." She looked sick with dark bruises underneath her eyes. She wore a black jacket and pants plus her usual knee-high boots, and Anithe was dutifully strapped to her back.

"Princess—"

"*One*."

"I was trying to help him. I knew he liked running through the woods at the Academy. I just thought he might want a fraction of familiarity."

Emory eyed Brokk. "Is this true?"

"Yes."

Looking back to Marquis, she narrowed her gaze. "But you knew he couldn't swim."

As Marquis shook his hair, water droplets flew from him, and he beamed. "Who says this life is meant to be lived dormant? I was seeing if he could learn."

After the initial shock, Brokk pressed his lips together. Emory moved toward him, and the weight lifted off his chest. Then, he couldn't hold it in anymore; the howl of laughter escaped him as he worked to catch his breath. Marquis chuckled, visibly relaxing, and they made their way back to the city, Emory muttering under her breath the entire way.

As the morning air shifted through Brokk's hair, his skin prickled against the cold—he felt alive.

***

Everything in Marquis's world had to be an affair. After Brokk had showered and changed his clothes, breakfast had been a parade of *finery*. An alabaster cloth was laid over the table without a crease in sight. Crystal flutes were filled with water, but Brokk wouldn't have been surprised if it had been wine. Porcelain teacups matched the plates, the delicate yellow flower designs looking hand painted. Polished knives, forks, and spoons were placed at either side of his plate, and the whole situation left him feeling uncomfortable.

Riona and Kiana, to his left and right, glowered at him, sensing something was wrong. Emory was across from him now, wearing a light-blue shirt, black pants, and a leather jacket. She chewed her assortment of fruits and steaming biscuits slowly. *If looks could kill.*

They were back in Marquis's quarters, Diedre on his left; the rest of his court they had only just met. A deep bellow vibrated across the room as Ennis threw his head back at something Marquis had said. Ennis, covered in tattoos and piercings, had caramel hair and striking features. To his right, Siobhan punched Ennis's arm, her red hair cascading around her freckled skin, and as Brokk caught her gaze, she winked for the fourth time at him this breakfast.

Emory's face darkened, and he bit back a smile. Brokk watched Emory glare at Siobhan, stabbing at her breakfast a little too aggressively.

"So, wolf boy, what's your story?"

Brokk practically choked on his biscuit and jam as he leaned past Kiana, meeting Siobhan's gaze.

"No story to tell, really." *Lies, lies, lies.* "Just part of a rebellion that needs your help." He said it all gruffly as he chased the food with crisp water.

"I have an uncanny feeling that you are lying. That's a cause I would die for." Siobhan layered the sarcasm on thick as the conversation died.

As she turned her head, Emory's eyes narrowed, and he could have sworn in that second her eyes turned *black*. When she blinked, the deep-emerald of her irises returned. "*Excuse me*?" It was a snarl, a challenge. Emory slowly tilted her head.

Siobhan flicked her hair over her shoulder. "I wasn't talking to you. The adults are talking."

Emory shoved her chair back, and Siobhan rose to meet her. Quickly getting up, Brokk stepped between the two, his voice low. "I wouldn't advise doing anything, Siobhan."

Glaring at the woman, he turned his back then grabbed Emory's hand and led her out of the room. Siobhan's words chased at his heels. "It's only a matter of time, lover boy, before you can't run anymore."

As Brokk slammed the door shut, Emory's whole body shook against him, tension rolling off her in waves.

"Em, come on. Let's walk it off."

The street unfolded before them; the bustle of the winding roads nestled in the rolling city. Far above, gulls called, cutting through the clouds, and salt trailed on the wind. Along Marquis's quaint house, golden bushes lined the sidewalk, shimmering leaves dropping to the ground as their breaths came out in misty puffs. She wouldn't look at him; she wouldn't stop pacing until finally his hands rested on the sides of her arms.

"Em, how can I help?" he whispered.

Raising those green eyes to his, she replied, the rising melodies of the city sounding around them, "You can't."

CHAPTER NINE

EMORY

In that moment, Emory hated herself for wrenching away. Gulping down air, she cut through the streets, everything blurring into the background. Everything *but* Declan's voice. It was getting intolerable and stronger with every waking second, pulling her back to that moment where she had killed Adair. Back into the darkness, where she didn't recognize herself.

Pulling her jacket closer, she shivered against the unseen king, feeling the claws of his essence sinking deeper.

"I will find you, Emory. I can practically taste your fear."

Ramming her lips together, she held in her scream as pain split through her mind. Tears pricked her eyes; the pain raced through her muscles under Declan's phantom grip. Concentrating on her steps, she pushed past the sinking in her stomach, past the hopelessness she felt as she fell deeper into her consciousness. And it was there, in the pit within herself, where she stood tall, baring arms. The pain ebbed, fading to a dull pulse behind her temples. She could use the time she had left to liberate the Isles and join the army with the Black Dawn Rebellion. She *would.*

"Hey, Princess. Fancy meeting you here." His voice snapped her back into reality, any trace of the Dark King vanishing. Marquis leaned against the wall; eyebrows raised.

Shaking her head, she snapped, "You really do have the gift of showing up at the worst moments."

Marquis rolled his eyes. "And here I thought you were taking my advice on how to defuse the situation."

"By defuse, you mean deter a king who is hunting me?"

"Why do you think I made training with Nasiea nonnegotiable? Your ability is strong and unique. You *are* strong, Emory, and a great fighter. But right now, the Oilean and the Dark King are stronger, and they have one target before they destroy the rest of Kiero. *You.*"

"You're annoying when you're right."

"It's my most charming attribute," he mused. Strolling down the alley, Marquis said, "You know, I think Siobhan admires you."

Snorting, Emory quipped, "And she shows it by causing her own war over breakfast?"

Nudging her, he murmured, "Don't take it personally. Siobhan likes a challenge."

"Yeah. Right."

"So, do I even want to know why you left lover boy in the dust back there?"

Her brows furrowed as she looked at him. "It's none of your damn business."

It was like a slap to the face, and his features darkened. "You do know that having a friend or two isn't a bad thing, right?"

She stopped, jabbing him in the chest, waiting for the familiar rise of her ability that never came. Breathing hard, she snapped, "Do you realize that you aren't privy to every thought I have?"

Standing there, they glared at each other. Finally, he broke away. "I'm sorry."

Nodding, she accepted it. "You know, if I'm being honest, I don't think Nasiea's training is going to help me."

"Oh?"

She had mulled over her next words all night. "I want to train with you."

"Pardon me?" he drawled.

As she walked down the alley, her words came fast and honest. "All I can think about is our plan, and time is against us. I know what is happening to me. I know you want to help me destroy this dark magic within me, but don't you see? There isn't a way to achieve that. But to use the dark power to my advantage, to hone it? *I* am the weapon now. There's no more going back, and you are the only one who knows, Marquis. Our priority is planning how we are going to kill this Iain and Skena from Durdover Port. And then, it's war."

The cool wind wrapped around them, and she watched his face fall.

"Marquis, think about it for a second. Our world's villain has fallen only to reveal a bigger threat. We will never win this if I don't use what is in me."

"Even if it destroys you?" he whispered.

"Even then. Allow me to explore this darkness. To strengthen it. You are the only person it won't hurt. That I *can't* hurt."

He ran his hands through his cropped emerald hair, exhaling hard. Lifting his gaze back to her, using her own words, he said, "You know you're annoying when you're right."

"So, you will help me?"

"Yes, even if I regret the decision later."

Her stomach flipped. "Okay then."

"And one more condition. You and your company will join me for the festivities leading up to the Harvest Equinox. Despite you thinking otherwise, I know what I am doing when it comes to my people and Hriste. They need to see a unified front."

"Fine." She stuck out her hand, and they shook hard, her ability flaring up to the touch. It was as if her body had known her decision all along, waiting for her heart to catch up. Dropping her arms back to her sides, she asked, "Well then. Shall we begin? We are down to the weeks, Marquis."

"I know the perfect place. It will take hours to get to, though."

At his words, Emory beamed. "No, it won't."

***

For the first time since being with Marquis, Emory thought he looked truly nervous. His skin drained of color; his freckles stood out. Crossing her arms, Emory said, "You do know this is payback for shoving me off a cliff, right?"

"You do know that I saved you? I wasn't about to let you die." He huffed.

"Oh, and that makes it justified? I was captured by cannibals. *Cannibals,* Marquis."

Pressing his lips into a thin line, he asked, "And you have done this before?"

Smirking, she crossed the space between them, shaking her head. "This is the first time."

Watching in pleasure as he paled even more, Emory clamped her hand around his wrist, and the world dissipated. *Fly*, she thought, imagining them cutting through the skies, infinite and free.

Now the vision of the seaside filled her mind, pushing her *down, down.* Her nerve endings erupted into fire, splitting through her body. Pain jarred through her teeth, making her wince. Emory was transported into memory.

She was transported to another cliff, to a day that felt like centuries ago. Fear had immobilized her, and Adair's eyes bore into her. That darkness that she had hated, resented, now resided in her, but despite that, she had still grasped his hand, and she had let go, trusting them. Trusting *him.* Until she drove that knife into his heart.

Vaguely, she realized Marquis was screaming. His hands were tight around her waist as they cut far above the Isles, her body barely more than deep purple smoke and ash, embers flying behind them.

The temperature dropped; Emory dipped further into the ability. This foreign power was limitless, the well within her begging her to use more, to become more. As she obliged, the guilt and anger dissipated.

In the thrill, they climbed up, up, *up*. The wind screamed around them, and Emory took in a breath.

They dropped.

As they sliced through the clouds, embers crackling around them, all she could think of was a fallen star, rushing toward the life below and what was at stake. Pushing faster, she could feel Marquis trembling, his hands scrambling until the crashing of waves became her world, and Emory collided with the sand. A dust cloud exploded around them, and Marquis rolled at least twenty feet from her.

Chest heaving, she was on all fours, in a crater the landing had created. The beach was private, the cliffs of the Shattered Isles looming far above her, gulls screeching along the coastline. The gray cliff face was wet, jagged edges slick with ocean spray. Emory breathed in the refreshing air, and the black water crashed and receded on the shore, creating this private enclosure. As Marquis had called it, the *perfect* training area.

"Are you insane?" Marquis spat, prowling back toward her. His lip was cut and bloodied. Emory stood, trying to ignore the ring of burned sand and embers. Marquis was in front of her, gripping her shoulders. "You have to be trying to kill me."

As she pushed him off, the air in front of her shimmered. Anithe materialized in front of her, and the handle in her grip felt familiar. Her image was reflected at her—the gaunt cheeks, the pitch-black eyes, deep bruising underneath them. Panic clawed through her as she blinked, her eyes changing back to emerald-green.

Finding her footing, she breathed, "What's your grand plan, Marquis? How will we pull off casually killing two political members?"

"The one thing you have to understand about Durdover Port is they won't hesitate to hurt my people, to hurt the Isles. Iain believes that he can control basic human rights by fearmongering. After your mother left for Kiero, they ambushed Hriste, murdering anyone who followed her beliefs in the streets. My father bowed to them after that. Understand, they will be coming to the Harvest Equinox to abuse that stolen power. They expect me to fight back, but our advantage is that they won't be expecting *you.*"

Marquis unsheathed two curved knives from his thighs and stepped back.

Emory replied, "True."

His face darkened. "When they least expect it, you will strike."

"Then let's make sure my sparring skills aren't rusty." Smoke spilled from her blade, drifting toward Marquis like a fog.

Emory ran and jumped, slamming her blade down to be met with empty air. Twisting low, Marquis was a flash of green as he ran. Her growl of frustration chased his heels.

"Why did your father do nothing about Durdover slaughtering my mom's sisters?" Emory asked.

Flashing her one of his charming smiles, Marquis replied from across the beach, "I thought I may get your attention with that. Iain and Skena hold on to old hate, especially when it comes to Kiero. Why be associated with the country that enslaved our people for centuries? Your mother was a constant reminder of her progressive thinking by joining herself to your father and, through him, Kiero."

Sand particles rose as she said, "They deserved better."

The sand shivered under her ability, black fog spreading around Marquis, masking him from her. The particles of sand rose, banding together, taking shape as spears. As the sand spears hovered above the beach, Emory harnessed her hold on them before loosening the storm brewing within her.

"By whatever means possible, I will do *better* for the people I love."

The fog twisted higher toward the sky like a funnel cloud. Relishing in the power building within her, Emory sent the spears flying, crashing toward the king. There was a gust of wind, and then silence fell.

Emory looked up, shock rippling through her. The wave was massive, and she crumpled, protecting her head as the icy water crashed into her . . .

She was sucked into the water.

Blinking hard, she kicked, realizing Marquis had trapped her yet again in a water sphere. Grinning, she reached out, her fingers caressing the water as it rippled. Light flared, and Emory watched the blackened water turn to ash all around her. Running, Emory tore into the fog, meeting Marquis, and swung her blade viciously. "You better get some new tricks; you're getting predictable."

Rolling, Marquis kicked her feet out from underneath her, making her land hard on the ground. Diving, his body collided with hers. Her ability attacked . . . She was met with nothing.

Marquis chuckled. "I could say the same to you."

All she felt was air around her as Emory soared backward. Her head cracked against a rock embedded in the sand, blood filling her mouth. Waves crashed, seafoam covering her side. Sputtering, she scrambled, but Marquis's boot connected with her gut. Winded, Emory crumpled.

Marquis was everywhere, his whispers as sharp as knives. "Show me what you got, *Princess*."

For months, how many people had demanded that from her? Put her on a pedestal, telling her who she was. Where she came from, a *legacy*. But who knew her? No one. Adair had devastated her by killing the person she used to be.

Spitting, she stood, realizing that life was slipping from her fingers. She wasn't a princess who needed to be saved. Who needed her hand held, guided and unsure. She was a *queen*. She had died believing that she couldn't make a difference. But she was given a second chance, one she would not waste.

Blood bubbled through her lips as she wheezed, "You mean like this?"

The ground shuddered.

Her attack was fast, escaping from her like smoke. Emory slithered into the depths of Marquis's mind, using Adair's ability, possessing Marquis's body. A wall had been there, but Marquis was taken by surprise, so she stripped it down. The world disappeared, and memories assaulted her as she sank deeper into Marquis, controlling his every move.

He always remembered that morning. The first time they had truly talked.

The morning air was crisp, though the fleeting summer had held on, the breeze warm and inviting. Marquis had always been one to rush to see the sunrise when the world was quiet, unfurling around him. That morning was no exception, even in a different country. The days had been spent negotiating, his father relentless, fighting for the years they had been restricted, forced to the Isles.

Chewing his lip, his heart sank at the violence, at how his dad had treated Adair. His blood pumped faster as the sun crested the horizon. Everything was washed in golden hues, then he heard the door slam in the distance. When he twisted, the dark hair and jacket were prominent, and everything in his world stopped.

His mind was already memorizing the twist of Adair's mouth, the furrow of his brow. How he popped the collar of his jacket up, his lanky body carrying him across the courtyard. Adair didn't realize Marquis was there, and Marquis felt heat bloom through his chest. He smiled, jumping down from the brick ledge.

He wanted to make himself known.

He needed to.

Marquis bucked underneath her hold, but she plunged deeper, another memory crashing into her.

The ship swayed, waves crashing, as the storm rolled in. All he could do was look back on the war they had left behind in Kiero. Who *he had left behind. Smoke curled up in the distance.*

He leaned against the rail, shaking.

"Marquis." His father's voice was quiet, almost predatory.

His breath quickened, but he couldn't tear himself away. He couldn't let go. The crew jumped to life aboard; thunder rolled through the humidity that was thick in the air.

"We did everything we could have, son. You must know that."

Tears streaked down his face, the taste of the life Kiero held vanishing. The darkness that held that country . . . its king.

All he could remember was the look in Adair's eyes. There had been no trace of Adair. Just an empty void. His dream gone with him.

"We must survive this, Marquis. That is our priority now."

He didn't look at his father. "You don't care about what has been lost, about who died today."

"No. My world is on this ship. The country we left behind already had the knife in its heart, an open wound bleeding out. What happened back there was just digging that knife deeper, this time finding its mark. Kiero is done."

The wind picked up as his dad left him, tiny water droplets spattering down around them. His hair was plastered to his forehead, rain mixing with his tears. It wasn't until the clouds blackened, lightning streaking against the sky, that Marquis wrenched himself away, heading below deck.

More memories. The years passed too quickly for Emory to keep track.

Marquis paced around his home, clutching the letter, not believing what he was reading. Catching his reflection in the mirror—his hard jaw; short, unruly green hair; a spattering of freckles—he frowned. Everyone claimed he was the epitome of his late father, Tadeas, and the thought made him want to throw up.

They had cowered in the corner for years of Adair's reign, leaving Marquis years to plan how he would approach the Mad King. He wasn't delusional; the horrors that rippled through Kiero made their way back here. But he had to hope. Hope that Emory wasn't dead, that Adair wasn't totally lost. That somewhere, somehow, hope would piece their world back together.

The handwriting was elegant and familiar. Adair had accepted his offer—an alliance. Marquis would provide Adair with produce, and in return, Adair wouldn't kill him.

Barking out a laugh, Marquis shook his head. Even after all these years, he would do anything to protect the memory of the broken boy who just wanted to live an adventure. To escape the life so neatly laid out in front of him.

Tears pricked his eyes. Marquis smoothed the letter, running his fingers over the ink, wondering if Adair ever thought about the fact that he had become a nightmare and what that meant to Marquis. If he even paused while writing his reply, knowing how much it meant to him.

Slammed out of the memory, Emory let go.

They both stood there, chests rising and falling, unable to say anything.

Waves crashed onto the shore as she trembled. Her heart pounded. *I had hoped, too. I didn't want to lose Adair. But we did long ago.* Opening and closing her mouth, Emory tried to figure out a way to tell Marquis she hadn't meant to cross that line. Panic filled her at the fact that, somehow, she *succeeded* in possessing him and ripping into such private memories like it meant nothing.

"Apparently, as your power grows, it defies all logic. You just broke through my ability like it was nothing. No one has ever done that, Emory. Has your point been made?" Marquis choked out the words. He tried to look anywhere but at her. One step forward, and he balked, shaking his head. "I can't learn your secrets, but you can steal mine?"

"No. Marquis, *no.* You have to understand it's not like that."

"No. *You* have to understand, to grasp, what I have been telling you since you arrived. You are spiraling into this madness. The lust of this darkness is consuming you. You need friends. Allies. But this road you are going down . . . no one can follow you. So, tread lightly."

The pit in her stomach grew. She was brought back for the rebels, the spark to end their war. Instead, she had begun one. Now the world was on fire, and she could do nothing but fan the flames. She had died for the Black Dawn Rebellion. Took on a tyrant for them. But would she learn to open up? To show her vulnerability?

"Let's head back."

She swallowed down all the questions she wanted to voice, and she and Marquis disappeared as she grabbed his arm again, becoming nothing more than smoke and ash.

***

Using Adair's ability was becoming muscle memory. Her thoughts swirled around her—was it worth exploring this power to lose everything else, to lose a future? *Her future.* At the edge of her vision, the field surrounding Hriste came back into view, and they streaked toward it.

Landing hard, she exhaled.

Marquis was pale but alive. Curtly nodding, he walked away, leaving her alone. She had crossed a line today. Emory sighed and started walking to the waterfall's edge.

It was late afternoon, the autumn air refreshing. Her skin soaked up the sun as the waterfall cascaded behind her when she sat at its edge. Ripples danced across the surface, and Emory wondered what she was doing. Coming to the Isles had been her hope for answers, for a clear alliance, but all she had found were more secrets and complications.

Pressing her eyes shut, she tilted her head back, concentrating on the lulling gurgle of the water behind her. The sunlight still washed over her, but nothing could distract her from the bitter taste in her mouth. What the hell was wrong with her? The first chance she had to fight without hiding her abilities, and she had slipped so badly.

Would Marquis forgive her?

I can't learn your secrets, but you can steal mine?

Groaning, she cupped her head in her hands.

"Em, we need to talk. I first want to say . . . do you know that I turned around?" Brokk's voice came to Emory unexpectedly, pulling her back into reality.

He lowered himself next to her and her heart dropped. How much had he seen? How long had he been waiting for her? Emory drank in how the light caught his hair. His strong jawline. That trace of a smile lingering in the corner of his lips. Heat rippled from him, and Emory sidled closer, her heart pounding.

"Hey. What do you mean?" she murmured.

Running a hand through his hair, he exhaled. "After I escaped the Oilean and went back to the Academy, all I found was its skeleton. My home—gone. But I followed your trail right to the Ruined City. I could have gone in there, but I turned around. I left."

She frowned, and coldness swept into her heart; she barked out a laugh. "You would have been mad to walk into that kingdom. Adair had his people under an iron rule. You would have been killed immediately. Adair probably would have relished in me being the one to kill you for a second time."

Brokk peeked at her. "I wanted to break down the walls, tear them apart, to find you. But it has always been bigger than just you and me. I wanted the truth, and to find it, it demanded that I go down a separate path than you."

Her mouth ran dry. "Did you find what you were looking for?"

He stilled, truly looking at her. "I found that I'm tired of people telling me what I should know. What I should believe. The Rebellion made a lot of mistakes, but trying to defeat Adair wasn't one of them. Bringing you back wasn't one of them. But coming here, to another king, with another pointless wager—we are wasting our time. We should be focusing on finding and putting the Rebellion back together instead of being scattered to the winds."

Exasperated, Emory asked, "But what do *we* do, Brokk? You have no idea who we are up against. To win a war, we need allies."

"Do you trust Marquis?"

The question caught her off guard. Looking past Brokk, she looked at the capital of the Shattered Isles. Hriste was protected by the cliffs surrounding the city like a shield. The afternoon light washed every building in its orange glow. It was beautiful, and Marquis had helped build this world. Why couldn't Kiero have the same?

Sighing, she met Brokk's gaze. "Yes, I do."

Sucking in a fast breath, Brokk nodded. "And I respect that. I just want you to know that no matter what happens, I meant what I said in the Draken Mountains. I will always be here for you, Em. I will always believe in *you.* I just don't know if I will be able to keep my promise. Which is why we really need to talk about something else."

Dread filled her. "Brokk, what is it?"

"Marquis received news from Kiero. I have been figuring out how to tell you, and then after this morning, I didn't understand what I did to make you so angry. So here goes."

Time stopped. Emory was transported, in a second, back to the Academy. Practically hearing Memphis. Alby. Even Nyx. "What news?"

"Memphis died." Brokk's voice broke.

Emory knew she had registered the words. Had heard them. But it didn't stop the world from falling under her. She was numb. Blankly, she felt her hands shake, her heart crashing into her stomach. She opened her mouth. Closed it. She was blinking too hard, too fast. *Dead.* Like Adair. Her parents. This *world.*

Somehow, she was standing, pacing like a caged beast. Her ability quivered, churning underneath her skin, the power begging to break loose. Her breath came hard, ice cutting into her. "How?"

Brokk was there, gently grabbing her wrists, the wind pulling across the grasses, coursing between them. The knives strapped across his chest reflected the afternoon light. Heat flared under his touch, and Emory wrenched her hands back. Still gentle, Brokk found her chin with his hand, forcing her to look at him.

"Memphis and Nyx went to the Dust Clan raiders. To persuade them to join the war."

"The Dust Clan?" It was an empty question, but the story pulled together in her mind, becoming vivid, slamming Emory back in time to the raider that had been in the woods outside of the Academy. The promise Emory had heard Memphis make, that if he ever went to the raiders again, he would be killed. Memphis had sought them out anyways.

Tears streamed down her face as she looked into Brokk's eyes. Exhaling hard, she nodded. "What are you thinking?"

"That I care about you, but I have to go back to Kiero. I can't stay here while my friends are dying. But I need you to choose me this time."

"You know I have already made my decision."

"Or is that what you have convinced yourself? Em, Memphis *died.* We know where Nyx is. Our main priority should be making sure the rebels know that we aren't lost."

"Brokk, I need you to trust me, but more than anything, I need you to understand I need to help Marquis to gain his armada. I need to give us a fighting chance. I've made my choice."

"But you won't talk to me. Every day, you pull away to a place where I can't reach you. But you want me to trust you?"

As Emory exhaled hard again, her tears ran faster. "Brokk, I want to—"

His eyes darkened, and Emory flinched.

"No, you don't," he retorted. "You don't want to tell me what you're thinking or what you're going through. Or even what's going on with you. On one hand, in the shadows, when it's just us, you show me that you have feelings for me. But now I'm asking you to come with me, and your answer is no? You cannot win this alone."

"Which is exactly why we need the Isles," Emory spat through clenched teeth.

"That is exactly why you need people you can trust! People who would have your best interests in mind. Are you sure that is Marquis?"

Exhaling, she looked around her. "Marquis would do anything to keep Hriste safe. His world. His people. But he also knows that war will find him, no matter how far he runs."

Clenching his fists, Brokk shook his head. "I don't think that's true. He has you in his grasp, and I think he intends to use you for more than this assassination. Why else would he prepare a ship for me, Kiana, and Riona, and fifty of his best men after the Harvest Equinox and not tell you about it?"

Relief coursed through her; Marquis *had* kept his promise to get Brokk off the Isles. *Good.* Time had run out for all of them, it would seem, and now she would rise, her darkened ability and her conviction a duet of bloody vengeance. Ready for the Oilean, for the Dark King.

As she held Brokk's gaze, a stony expression overcame his features. Deciding to swallow down all her doubts about her decisions, she said nothing, a coldness sweeping through her and settling into her core.

"I'm leaving the Isles, Em, and I hope in the end you will choose to fight for me. For us."

Standing there, Emory stared as he walked away. She was unable to move, unable to breathe. The world crashed around her, beating against her like a rock, her unease growing, and she succumbed to it.

In war, there was no room for love or vulnerability.

***

The days passed in numbing, repetitive routines. Eat breakfast. Train with Marquis. Try not to kill him as they pushed each other's boundaries. After lunch, she wandered the streets, her thoughts her only company. Emory's mood darkened in that time, the looming Harvest Equinox and *assassination.*

She hadn't seen Brokk more than in passing, her heart breaking every time she saw his clouded eyes and clenched fists.

Every time she wanted to stop him, the unsaid words repeated in her mind. *I'm putting you all in danger. He is hunting me. The Oilean's magic is in me. Is becoming me. You need to be far away from me.*

Today, the waves crashed with raw power. Sweat glistened on Marquis's brow, and Emory narrowed her eyes, her mind moving in calculated steps. Baring Anithe in front of her, she charged, Marquis smirking as he ran to meet her.

Her calf muscles burned, and the sand shifted beneath her boots while she sprinted. With a flick of her ability, she conjured up an echo of Adair, right in front of Marquis.

"Marquis?" the ghost of Adair asked.

"Oh, you've got to be kidding me!" he yelled.

But the second of distraction was all she needed. Running through the vision of Adair, she slammed Anithe into Marquis's broadsword, the impact jarring up her arm. Spinning, Emory parried, throwing sand up into Marquis's eyes with her left hand. Grunting, Marquis stumbled, and she slammed her foot into his gut.

When he fell, Anithe was at his throat in seconds.

"What's gotten into you today?"

"Someone once told me your enemies won't play fair. I'm using my resources." Emory shrugged, helping him up. Marquis sheathed his sword. Following suit, she then admitted, "It's all getting to me, Marquis. Everything."

Placing a hand on her shoulder, Marquis nodded. "I know. But you're doing everything you can."

"It doesn't feel like it's enough. I'm slipping, and I'm scared I'll fail again."

The blackened clouds churned above them as the wind picked up, the cold drying the sweat on her skin.

"That is understandable, considering what you've been through. But what options do we all have? We can give up, or we can try," Marquis countered.

Sighing, Emory stared out to the Black Sea, mulling over his words.

"Can I show you something?" he asked, holding out his hand.

Emory nodded, taking his hand.

"This way," he said.

They trekked across the sodden beach, the ocean salt spraying in her face. Emory gripped Marquis's fingers, thankful for his friendship when everything felt so lost over the last weeks. Among the cliffs, Marquis gestured to a ragged staircase, just hidden from view.

"I hope you're not afraid of a little climb?" he asked.

Looking up to a challenge, she ventured, "Never."

"Good."

***

The staircase was treacherous, and the climb even more so. Slicked with ocean spray, Emory's arms shook with effort as she pulled herself onto the next rockface step, her jacket flapping in the wind. She tried not to look down, and sweat dripped into her eyes as she pushed herself to keep going.

Marquis made the climb look annoyingly easy, scaling the cliff with practiced grace. They must have been climbing for twenty minutes and seemed no closer to the top. Emory breathed through her shaking and burning muscles.

Marquis yelled back at her, "Almost there!"

Where?

As far as she could see, there was only the cliff face, the rocks glistening with algae. Trusting Marquis, she lifted herself onto the next step, where he was waiting. For once, since she had known him, he looked sheepishly at her.

"This way."

Walking along a very narrow rockface path, Emory didn't look down.

"Trust me, Em. I should have shown you this when you first came."

Sucking in a steadying breath and pressing her back flush to the rock, she shuffled carefully after Marquis, focusing on his back.

At the end of the path, a small cave opening came into view, and Emory felt it: a shift in the energy, a shiver running along her spine. Marquis walked into the cave without trepidation, and she followed, entranced by the echoes of magic. Her heart recognized it, and her pulse raced as she entered. The howls of the wind suddenly cut off as if they were in a soundproof room.

Deep-blue gems flared to life, lining the walkway embedded in the stone of the cave. Marquis met her gaze. "You say that you feel lost. Today is the day you'll see that's wrong."

As they walked deeper into the cave, the walkway slanted, as if they were heading into the heart of the Isles.

"After my father killed your grandfather, he wanted this place to be destroyed. Any trace of your family's lineage gone. But, not even a mortal man can touch the magic that protects this cave. It is legend on the Shattered Isles that when a person dies, they are given to the Black Sea, their spirit feeding our magic and abilities, and that their power is returned to the earth. Much like the city of Nehmai being the origin of magic in Kiero, and the fall of the warriors creating people with abilities, magic comes at a price and rejuvenates in a cycle. The myth says that witches once lived along these coastlines, our great-great ancestors. Within these caves, they, with the help of their paisce, would collect the most esteemed warriors. It was the highest honor to be laid to rest here. To this day, the witches' magic still seeps within these walls, making our land thrive and our legends live on."

Completely spellbound by the tale, Emory asked, "What happened to your ancestors? And what is a paisce?"

"The witches who founded the Isles were mostly lost to bloodbaths as the generations grew and the Isles became more established. It was said that people feared the original coven's power and wanted to wipe it from our history. But it is rumored that a few still live on, hidden within the coast. Paisce are their steeds. First born from rays of moonlight washing over the rolling waves. They look like caines with their serpentine bodies and scales, except they have wings like crystals—each fiber of their wingspan pulled from the constellations themselves. They act as spirit guides.

"It's said that when the full moon hung high in the sky, you could see them emerging from the Black Sea for the witches to gather their bodies on the mortal land. Each witch would find peace in the next life, with the help of their paisce. After the paisce have helped the soul of the witch pass on, they fly among the highest stars, feasting upon the night until they are called upon once more."

"Wow."

"It is quite a tale, I know, but I promise it will tie together soon."

As they traveled deeper into the cave, the deep gems continued to flicker to life, washing them in their cool light.

"You see, Emory, I am obsessed with our ancestors. To be descended from witches . . . is that what makes people like you and me gifted? Is it the fates intertwining, bringing us together after all these years? Many from the Isles scoff at it, at the impossibility of it all. Yet, they believe Kiero's legends without blinking an eye and simply believe we get our abilities from the naithe warriors when they die."

"So you're a romantic. A believer of fantasy," Emory mused.

"I allow myself to dream, so I suppose so," Marquis replied.

"I think it's important to hold on to that."

"I wholeheartedly agree." A slow smile spread across his lips as he motioned for her to pass him.

The path had evened out when they stopped at the mouth of a small room. Hundreds of crystals and sea glass had been collected and strewn beautifully around the edge of the room. In the soft light behind them, all the colors of the gems ignited, deep purples, yellows, greens and blues climbing up the cave walls, transforming the room in ribbons of light.

It took her breath away.

Walking farther, Emory noticed that the cave stretched for miles, hundreds of tombstones side by side and an array of weapons lying gracefully on the stone coffins.

"Holy shit," Emory whispered.

Marquis stepped beside her. "Who is to say what is impossible? The possibilities are endless if there are people who dare to dream them, and it is that seed that breeds hope."

Marquis gestured to the closest tomb, and Emory walked toward it on shaking legs, her throat constricting. Upon the smooth stone, she read the words etched there:

May Nei Fae's spirit find her way back home, to where she was meant to find her final rest among the stars.

Dropping to her knees, Emory placed a hand on the tomb. Black roses materialized from her fingertips, growing where her mother was supposed to lie. Tears blurred her vision, emotion thick on her tongue.

"You see, Emory, your legacy is one of hope and inspiration. Please, show the world that, as your mother did," Marquis said, dropping down beside her.

She lay her head on his shoulder, weeping for the mother she never got to meet as an adult. Grief took her when Marquis wrapped an arm around her shoulders. They watched as the roses bloomed, their inky petals glistening in the cavern light.

***

Walking along the beach once more, Emory looked to the rolling pitch-black clouds above. The temperature had dropped significantly since they emerged from the caves. Marquis, seemingly comfortable in their silence, walked with her beside the raging ocean.

"Thank you for showing me that. It meant a lot, Marquis," she said.

"My pleasure, Princess. It looked like you needed a pick-me-up before tomorrow night."

How had the weeks gone by so fast? Tomorrow was the Harvest Equinox, where she would help Marquis end this false king from Durdover Port.

Smiling weakly, and in much need of a recharge, she asked, "So, changing the subject. About the couple from Durdover Port . . . Are you sure you need to go through with this? I think I may be the last person you want to hear this from, but that kind of blood hanging over your consciousness . . . It changes you. Their sentence seems . . ."

"Harsh?" he suggested.

Emory nodded.

"Remember Adi?" Marquis started.

"Of course."

"Well, I have helped out a lot of kids like him over the years, but in Durdover Port, Iain and Skena have a habit of installing slavery back into their city. Child slavery, specifically. They will go and intentionally make children orphans to profit off them, to sell them. That is just an example of their madness. I got Adi out, and he got adopted by one of the sweetest families I know. A lot of kids in Durdover Port don't meet the same fate."

She felt sick. "Marquis, I'm—"

"Don't say you're sorry. I just can't let the Isles fall into a world where slavery is accepted and money and greed only benefit those who make these practices. We fought against Kiero enslaving our people. I can't let it happen here anymore than it already has. Iain and Skena deserve what is coming to them, Princess."

Nodding, she looked to the storm looming. "We should get back."

He took her hand, wordlessly, and their world became smoke and ash as they soared above the Isles, making their way back to Hriste.

***

After arriving back in Hriste, Marquis agreed they both needed to gather themselves before the Harvest Equinox, and Emory found her way to the library. The library's peeling red paint and musty smell of weathered pages lulled her into relaxing. The storm raged outside now, thunder cracking, rain pattering against the glass. The temperature dropped significantly as she pulled her green jacket closer, the leather holding her body heat. No one had found her yet to pull her into the preparations for tonight or, even worse, *tomorrow*. The social obligations were tiresome and even more pointless.

Her fingers drummed against the table as she peeked down at the book in front of her. The history of the Isles was long, but the hours blended, her mind churning after what Marquis had told her this afternoon.

"After the mysterious death of Tadeas Maher, the smaller colonies along the coast separated themselves from the capital, not agreeing with the new king's decision to ally with Adair Stratton in a trade agreement. Others muse whether Tadeas's death was natural or something more sinister. To this day, those colonies remain defiant against Maher's rule, claiming their land and a new king—Iain Reesle of Durdover Port."

That was nothing new to her. She flipped the pages, and it continued into an even bloodier history than Kiero. Years filled with revolution and unrest. Narrowing her eyes, she stared at the paragraph in front of her, rereading it twice before snapping the book closed.

"The most infamous myth about the Isles is the curse that surrounds the Maher boy. A local seer projected he would lead the Isles to ruin, and a cloud of death clings to the Isles under his rule, even today. The clans that separated from Hriste think that the Maher boy worked with someone to ensure his father's end and the safety of the Isles."

The lights flickered as another clap of thunder rolled. Emory flicked her gaze over to the librarian; the older woman was nose-deep in another book, not paying her any attention. In a fluid motion, Emory stood, shifting the book into her pack. Then she left, stepping out into the storm.

The rain was freezing, cutting through her layers without mercy. She bowed her head, and her feet carried her onward. She was only a couple of blocks away from her temporary home. Truly, she relished in this time. Anywhere she went now, the Oilean would follow. Staying here for the last few weeks was a risk that had already gone on too long. They whispered to her in her sleep, dark forces spreading toward her. It was only a matter of time now, and she didn't have a lot of that.

The information she had collected was feeble, but it had to be enough. Marquis needed her—needed a strong alliance to smooth out the instability of his kingdom. He did a great job of hiding it, but in passing, the show started to fade. Maybe his people weren't bound to him out of loyalty but out of fear of what waited for them outside the borders. Maybe she wasn't the only one keeping secrets.

Walking with purpose, she turned down the street, straight to the king's home. The wind howled as Emory stomped up the steps, throwing the door open. Marquis sat at his table, lifting his gaze to her with wide eyes. She was sopping wet. "Do you have a moment?"

Dipping his head, he said, "For you, always."

She pulled the chair back and sat. "I've visited the library."

Marquis's eyes narrowed, and he nodded. "Go on."

"As much as I like reading for leisure, knowledge is the sharpest weapon if you know how to wield it. And I've decided you haven't been honest with me."

The smile was slow, spreading across his features with finesse. "Oh, *really*?"

Leaning across from him, she held his gaze, her ability pounding under her skin, feeling the shift. "Enough, Marquis. You say that Durdover Port is the sole source of the uprising on the Isles, but maybe they think they have reason to oppose you? Why did I find, in a history book, the whisper of uncertainty of whether your father died from natural causes? Perhaps you just made it seem like that? You preach about trusting each other. You were so upset when I broke into your mind, which I am sorry about. But what are you hiding? There are clearly documented rumors that you worked with someone . . . a witch?"

It was a flicker. A pause. But Emory jumped at it, pinning him. "You have ensured Brokk's survival. That he finds his way back to Kiero. But you? You need me more than you let on. All this talk of promise of the future, but I don't know how you acquired this kingdom. Through magic? By killing your father? Did you do it to feel closer to him? Did you think that a part of Adair needed you to survive? What lengths did you go to, Marquis?"

It came out in a harsh rush, and she trembled against her rage when she continued, "A part of me will always be changed. I can never forgive myself for what I did when I was in Adair's kingdom. The heaviness weighs on me. I hear their whispers at night, the death of innocent people becoming my demons. It's a constant reminder to be better. To *become* better. There is also no way that I can undo what happened to me. So how about you say we give Kiero a chance at survival, and you actually listen to what I have to say?"

Her heart was hammering, threatening to crack her bones.

His eyes were practically glowing, the smug smirk that had once lit him up—gone. Thunder rolled, lightning streaking as he nodded. "Now there is a peek of the queen everyone has been talking about. But you shouldn't believe everything you read in a dusty old book. If I genuinely believed I was cursed, I would have told you. My father was an evil man, Emory. I did what I thought necessary for Hriste, not because I was longing for Adair."

"I just wish you had told me."

"Yet, you are the only person on the Shattered Isles I have ever spoken the truth to about that question when confronted. Rehashing the past usually does nothing but reopen healing wounds."

Marquis was right. There were no more crossroads; there was only survival. And that left no room for error.

"I guess I get that. But I'm asking you to listen to what I'm about to say. I think we need to tweak a few things about our plan. To do what *I* think is necessary," Emory said.

CHAPTER TEN

BROKK

Staring up at the ceiling, Brokk listened to the natural symphony raging outside the window of his bedroom: clashes of thunder, trills of rain, the pounding of footsteps from the street below as people ran for cover from the storm, and their squeals of exhilaration. Honestly, it was too much. Hours and days had passed, each one a reminder that he should be trying harder to understand Emory's decision to gain Marquis as an ally.

Sighing, he closed his eyes, breathing in each knot of tension. Like Nasiea had said, *Master your mind. Master yourself.* Had it only been a little over a month since the Oilean? Since their knife had cut into his flesh, bleeding lies into his mind, his body, and his heart? Since he had left Memphis, angry for being so ignorant about Nyx?

Everything in his world had been about Emory. How to bring Emory back, how to tiptoe around her, how to make her *see* that he was never her enemy. But where did all those paths lead him? To igniting a war and rising to his own title, his best friend gone. Brokk tried to digest the knowledge that he never got to say goodbye to Memphis, that he would never get that chance.

Unexpectedly, the bedroom door creaked open, then he heard it shut quickly and softly, a shutter of mechanisms. His heart rate doubled as he sat up. One tentative footstep, and then a rush of steps. Emory came into view.

"Em?" he breathed, confused.

She was sopping wet, and her emerald-green jacket clung to her, her black T-shirt and pants suctioned to her skin. Her green eyes were ignited, simmering green twin flames. Chest heaving, she shrugged her jacket off, and it landed with a thud on the floor.

"Are you okay?"

Her face twisted, either in pain or in anger, he couldn't tell within the shadows.

"I came to tell you . . . no, I *needed* to tell you that you have to know . . ." Her voice was husky, low and urgent.

"Know what?"

Trembling, she closed the space in between them. "That I'm in love with you. Everything in our lives is complicated, but what I feel for you is pure. It's *good.* I can't leave things between us with how we last spoke. I'm sorry."

He stilled, heat flaring through every nerve ending, muscle, and bone. Every part of him bowed to those words, to her declaration, his frustration and hurt evaporating for the moment.

Mouth running dry, he cupped her face in between his hands, shivering in pleasure. "Em."

"Nothing feels right to me, Brokk, except you. I need you to understand that," Emory whispered.

It was easy when it was just them. No abilities, no titles, no war. No crossroads. He lifted her to him, and they fell back softly, her soaked clothes seeping onto him. He leaned in closer, and she smelled like sea salt and flowers, intoxicating his senses.

Her breath tickled his ear when she said, "I'm sorry. For everything. I'm *so* sorry."

Her kisses were slow, deliberate. Meaningful. Groaning low, he hated himself for pulling her attention from her current train of thought. "Me too. Will you promise to stand beside me, Em? Tell me you are coming back with us."

Say yes. Choose me. Choose us.

Dread pooled in his stomach as she rose, her voice ripping through him when she finally answered. "Yes."

Heat devoured Brokk's body at her words. He locked his gaze with hers, his breath coming quick as Emory's hands knitted behind his neck. Her fingers moved slowly, tracing each scar and sending ripples of pleasure shuddering through him. His hands found her waist, and he firmly grabbed her curves with hungry intent. Thunder rolled like a war drum as Brokk brought his lips to Emory's in the cover of night, his tongue tasting her, slow and wanting. Her heart slammed in time against his own. His fingers worked deftly as he lifted her shirt up over her head. It dropped to his bedroom floor with a wet thud. Slowly, his shaking fingertips traced her skin, starting from her hips, up her bare side, her neck, and gently brushing her jawline. Her skin pebbled under his touch.

Leaning into him, she held his hand pressed against her cheek, closing her eyes as she whispered, "I am so lucky to have you in my life, Brokk. No matter our differences, please always remember that."

A grin broke out across his face as lightning flashed outside. He enjoyed the power his touch had over her body. His fingers traced a map down her spine, ever so *slowly,* watching as her eyes became heavy lidded, a slight moan escaping from her. Emory lowered herself to him, her body responding, demanding more.

She smoothly unbuckled his pants, pulling them off. Unblinking, Brokk took her in, her bare skin lustrous against the inky cover of night, the swell of her breasts that were peaked, her flawless skin. She was the most beautiful woman he had seen, and everything else fell away in this moment. His pulse pounded within his flaming ears. Brokk was *there*, removing the rest of their boundaries. Nervousness and excitement tingled along his spine, his breaths coming fast.

"I love you," she whispered in his ear, nipping it lightly. Moaning, Brokk closed his eyes, ecstasy flowing through his entire body.

They became one, all other boundaries removed. Gods above. The feel of her was an explosion of starlight, consuming Brokk. He lost himself in her flame and salty kisses and pushed down every doubt screaming in his mind as he and Emory discovered themselves, and just for a night, he didn't question why he didn't believe that she was truly coming back to Kiero with him, nor did he question why this felt like goodbye.

***

The next morning greeted them with a thin layer of ice coating Hriste as Brokk looked out the cottage window. The sheen of ice casted a glazed look over the city, as if the city was captured in time. The change of seasons had always cultivated wonder in Brokk, but now . . . Now it was a reminder of how fast they were running out of time. After last night, he just wanted to hold on to this day, this *moment* of happiness a little longer.

Kiana buckled another blade to her leg, huffing. "Truly, dresses shouldn't even be an option. Jewels and makeup never won any wars, did they?"

"In the throes of politics, I'm sure politicians would beg to differ," Brokk replied with a smirk. His companion's cabin was the epitome of warm and welcoming. Orange walls and a quaint, roaring fireplace made the illusion that they were captured in amber.

He ran a hand over his face, saying for the millionth time, "Kiana, you are putting me on edge. Can you please tell me what you are so worried about? We are leaving tonight."

"The moment we are off this blasted island, I will relax. This has been a waste of time. We should be focusing on the Rebellion and building our base in Nehmai where *you* will be safe, and more importantly, where you *belong*."

Rolling his eyes, he caught Riona out of the corner of his vision, shaking her head. "You can't tell me that you don't think we should be trying to take back more men and women with us, despite what Marquis wants. He is already getting enough from Emory."

"The division within the Isles runs deep. Marquis does not realize that it will take years to heal his people, if it all. He has no court. He has no one."

Sighing, he sat down at the table, grabbing a lush yellow fruit from the bowl and biting into it. An explosion of flavors danced along his tongue, sweet and succulent.

Riona strode toward them, wearing thick armored pants and a chest plate, donning a midnight-blue jacket. The hammer strapped across her back tied it all together as she drawled, "And what of the Queen of Kiero? Will she sail with us? And has she given anything up about Marquis?"

Heat rushed up Brokk's neck as snippets from last night burned in his heart. Emory's lips, their skin against one another, their promises in the dark. The pleasure, the pure exhilaration of giving in to his most human instinct. *Love.*

"Yes. And some. Enough."

"That sounds like enough to get us all killed."

As he finished his breakfast, Brokk waggled his eyebrows. "Not everyone is going to the festival dressed for combat. I will see you both later." He couldn't make it to the shower fast enough, Riona and Kiana's gazes burning into his back.

***

It was late morning when Hriste started to stir. Every house and shop he passed had laid out flags from their windows and their balconies: the crest of the Shattered Isles—broken longswords, the iron shattered. Flag after flag followed him as he turned to the main street. It was *freezing,* his breath coming in quick misty puffs. He hadn't bothered waiting for Kiana and Riona. The sisters, despite their demeanor, were curious. They all were.

"Brokk."

Ice ran up his spine as he exhaled hard. "Siobhan." Her fiery red hair came into view, her emerald jacket and pants striking.

Her mouth twisted. "Fancy finding you here so early. Couldn't stay away, could you?"

"I'm just looking for Emory," he replied gruffly.

This only made her flash a wicked smirk before she grabbed at his hand. "Come on. You're about to miss it."

"Miss *what*?"

"If I told you, it wouldn't be a surprise, now, would it?"

They took off, his protests lost to the wind. In the distance, a crowd started to gather. The building behind them was golden, flaring in the new light, the clock tower at the very top intricately made. Structurally, the building was massive; winding staircases on each side led up to a central platform. The closer Brokk got, he realized this building, lying at the heart of the city, was golden brick.

Siobhan pushed through the crowd, making their way up to the front as a smooth voice boomed, "Welcome to the sixty-third celebration of the Harvest Equinox!"

Head snapping up, Brokk froze. Marquis, green hair combed back, wearing a silver jacket and boots, looked sharp—every ounce of the king he claimed to be.

Looking among the crowd, he locked eyes with Brokk. "May the festival begin."

Emory was nowhere to be seen.

The wind picked up, carrying the bite of winter on its wings. Pulling his jacket closer, Brokk tried to pinpoint what had changed within Marquis. He stood on his pedestal, the same smug smirk playing along his lips. But his eyes flitted across the crowd, and beneath his façade of indifference and arrogance, Brokk could see a smudge of fear bleeding through it all.

"Today is for celebrating, for us to remember that we are united. To forget our differences and focus on a common goal of peace and prosperity."

The crowd rippled. Brokk sniffed at the wintery air, a heavy scent lingering—one unrecognizable to him. More than one hundred people had gathered at this point; an array of rainbow-colored hair and icy-cool tones of clothing sent the plain square into vibrancy, every person burning with life. Women passed him, their skin painted with twirling silver-and-gold paint, mimicking downy flakes cascading across their skin. The men wore calmer attire, complementing their partners and reminding him of dawn and the night. Everywhere he looked, he saw symmetry and balance.

A low humming rose from the square as the bells behind Marquis chimed, slow at first but then picking up their tempo.

All around him, abilities exploded. Ice flew up beside the flames, water sizzling. The ground shuddered, and Brokk watched a man in his fifties in front of him stomping his feet, each impact exploding the stone street under his inhuman strength. A blaze of purple flames spouted in a roaring brilliance up toward the sky. Brokk spotted the girl in the crowd. She grinned widely, looking no more than fifteen, the flames dousing her in purple embers, looking more like gems falling around her.

Wind, rain, ice, and fire flickered—storms gathering on the horizon as thunder cracked. All under the command of the people around him.

Brokk clenched his teeth at the wild display until the humming became hollering, the showcase of abilities abruptly ending. The crowd erupted in cheers as friends, family, lovers, and strangers grabbed arms. Somewhere in the distance, music started. Marquis clapped his hands, rushing down the stairs, swallowed by the enthusiastic people.

"Brokk." Kiana materialized beside him, and Riona pushed her way past Siobhan, grumbling under her breath.

"Ladies. Ready to enjoy the Equinox?" Brokk tried to sound normal, but his voice came out flat, detached. The tempo of drums picked up as the crowd bowed to it. He watched the carefree dancing, the excitement, the celebration. A bitter taste filled his mouth, his eyes constantly watching for black hair with blood-red ends.

"Do not react to what I'm about to say," Kiana whispered, the pressure on his wrist increasing. "The next tradition of the Equinox is to welcome distant clans from the coast into the capital. It is a grand display of wealth, practically a pissing contest of power lasting several hours until the banquet and the party."

Looking ahead, Brokk whispered, "It's time, then."

"Listen to me, Brokk. I want you to truly grasp what I am saying here. We need to get off this Isle sooner rather than later. Now, in fact, would be an ideal time," Riona interrupted, looking drawn and pale against the celebrating crowd.

Kiana continued smoothly, "Just because I lived as a recluse doesn't mean I'm uncultured. Or know the ways of tradition. Anyways, my point is, Riona and I believe today would be the perfect distraction for spies to be here that have infiltrated from Kiero. I fear the Oilean will come for us, Brokk. For Emory."

"How do you know this?"

"Let's get this through your head. Kiana and I have felt a shift in the magic, and let's think where else we have felt this before." Riona paused. "Oh yes, in the Draken Mountain range with the *fucking* Oilean. We need to leave, and we need to leave *now*."

"Not without Emory."

Kiana pulled him, and together with Riona, they cut through the back of the crowd with ease. He knew what their body language meant—their lips pressing into a thin line. His heart pounded. Every face, every person he made eye contact with made him break out into a sweat.

Brokk prepared for the worst.

CHAPTER ELEVEN

EMORY

It's a stupid plan. Frowning at the mirror, Emory sighed. The package arrived early—and swiftly—just as Marquis said it would.

When she left Brokk's room at dawn, the golden rays were just starting to ignite the sky. Making her way up to her room, she had waited. And waited. Until a gentle knock on her front door brought a yawning and disgruntled looking Adi, bearing the package in his hand.

She had dressed mindfully, slowly, all the time thinking, *Is this what Nasiea meant about facing what I fear most?* Each action she took was devoid of thought. She couldn't wonder what would happen next or what could be. There was only now, and that would set her free.

The shirt was liquid silver, flowing over her skin like silk. The sleeves were short, the black jacket sliding over them with ease. Silver buttons lined the front, the sigil of Hriste over her heart, branding her. The sword with its iron shattered. Poetic. The pants were thick, armored. Two beautifully crafted knives were attached to her upper thighs, and Anithe was strapped across her back. She held her chin higher, and her black eyes blazed, not hiding any longer.

The promise she had made to herself felt like eons ago, but it resonated within her. *Show them the queen you are choosing to be.*

She tightened her half-braided hair; the rest fell loosely around her shoulders. Emory picked up the silver dusting of makeup; Marquis had been clear on his instructions.

Dipping the brush's end in a small jar filled with water on her dresser, she started from the bottom corner of her right eye. She followed her cheekbone and the silver paint shimmered, highlighting her bone structure. Before she met her hairline, she curled the brush in a semi wave. Doing this two more times, she connected the lines from the corners of her eyes. She then copied the same on her left side. From the middle of her forehead, she highlighted above her brow on both sides; the result was similar to an incandescent henna design. When the paint met her skin, it seemed to come alive, her strokes mimicking the Black Sea and its waves. If she dipped her chin, the paint shimmered, transforming to look like snowflakes. *Magic.* But with it framing her blackened gaze, she looked powerful.

Finishing, she laced up her knee-high boots, the leather gleaming while she waited for Diedre. The drums pounded outside, clear violins bringing in the start of the festival. Her pulse picked up to a sickening pace.

The door to her bedroom cracked open. Diedre stood there, dressed in a deep-green jacket and silver shirt, the sigil matching Emory's. "Are you ready?"

"This will work, Diedre." Emory held her gaze. "The Shattered Isles needs Kiero just as much as Kiero needs them. It's time to heal old wounds."

"It's just surprising that you are being so reasonable about this. Given the impression I had of you and Brokk," Diedre said smoothly.

Standing, Emory adjusted the jacket, her ability clawing underneath her skin, begging to break loose, making her palms itch.

"I have changed *nothing,* as I know Marquis made you aware of," Emory said. "This plan must work. Don't be nasty just because Marquis also trusts me. Brokk needs to go back to Kiero. They must live. How can they do that when the Oilean are knocking on your doorstep because of me? They need safe passage, but they would never leave if they knew the truth."

Diedre arched her eyebrow. "So, you are going to break his heart and then let him leave?"

Every word, every accusation shuddered through Emory. "This is war, Diedre. *War.* What I want doesn't matter anymore. Isn't that clear to you?"

Diedre's eyes softened, and she truly looked at Emory. "Well then, the festival awaits."

Nodding, Emory fell in stride with Diedre.

Emory processed what she was about to do in snippets: the last look of the room, the staircase as they walked down it. The living room, every crevice of this place riddled with memories of Brokk . . .

Diedre threw the door open, the street exploding before them. Crowds had collected on either side as an assortment of groups sauntered down the middle in all different shapes of carriages with magnificent creatures pulling them, like horses in looks except for their rainbow scales and stark-white manes.

The groups and titles flashed in her mind as Emory ticked them off. The silver carriage with blood-red streaks held representatives from Terdes Harbor. Apparently, they were brutal in their court manners, but some of the most talented swordsmiths in the world filled their district. Emory was excited to meet them. Behind them, a jet-black carriage came into view, which was Oakland Wharf: fishermen and trade district. Next, a peerless bone carriage, The Harbor of Newsoll: fruits distributors known for their vineyards. Her heart dropped as she craned her neck, looking behind herself at a shimmering golden carriage behind them all, guards following the steeds. Durdover Port.

Diedre, noticing her gaze, whispered, "Come. We must find Marquis. Time is of the essence now, Queen."

Queen, queen, queen.

Whispers chased at her heels, her heart begging her to find Brokk, to say a proper goodbye. He never realized that last night was the only time she could give him, the only memory to take with him, before everything shattered around them. This was never a fairy tale—she knew that. A princess who wasn't lost but chose to leave her friends behind. A family destroyed by secrets and built on lies. A boy king who was doomed from the beginning. Her own ending was never to get the prince and live happily ever after. Emory saw that, clearer than ever before.

Breath catching in her chest, she tried to place her features in a neutral position. To focus on the beat of her heart, the hum of her ability, the depth in it.

"That's it, my Queen. You want a war, you will get one." Declan's voice had never left her, but the Dark King had become her demon in the night who knew the darkest parts of her heart.

When she shivered, Diedre raised an eyebrow at her. Shaking her head, Emory took in the massive tower in front of them, the heart of Hriste and the pinpoint of the festival. Then Emory was fixated on the crowd, unable to look away at first. Some women had dyed their hair deep blue, pearl white, or silver to mimic the shades of the winter to come. And their attire—flowing dresses of black with dashes of purple and blue through it—was like the tailor had sewn pieces of the night sky. Others had dresses shaped like snowflakes.

Tuning the music out, she counted the guards, at least fifty, just flanking the hub of people and vendors starting to gather. *Good.*

"To your left." Diedre's voice was soft.

Marquis appeared from thin air, falling into step with her and pulling her from Diedre, leaving his second behind them. A warm lemon scent surrounded her, and Emory focused on that. His emerald hair was combed back, his clothes plain, but he emitted power in every step, in every sly smile.

"Breathe, Emory." His voice was soft.

The crowds parted for them, a question hanging in their eyes, flickering to their matching sigils and back up to her blackened gaze.

"We are almost there. Just follow my lead. This *will* work. Just like we planned, okay?"

It was easy to follow his voice.

Marquis was steady as they climbed on to the first level of the clock tower, the smooth marble shining in the midday light. They faced the crowd, the music still softly playing in the background, but everyone looked to them, waiting for their visitors to arrive. The carriages slowed to a stop in a line. The doors creaked open, and Marquis stood taller, putting on a façade, the one he wore like an armor.

He was right. I still have so much more to learn about ruling. And I will never get that time.

The representatives stepped out, eyeing one another cautiously. One burly man with a black goatee and a leather jacket bowed before Marquis, the woman behind him following suit. Her black hair shone in the sun, her weathered and scarred hands knitting together, muscles rippling up her forearms.

"Thank you, our King, for hosting us so graciously. May I introduce my wife, Ceridwen."

Marquis dipped his head. "Nolan. Ceridwen. Welcome." Marquis shook Nolan's hand, letting go to gingerly lower his lips to the top of Ceridwen's right hand. Emory tried to keep her composure as Marquis thrived in his charm.

"And who is this?" Nolan asked.

Emory realized *this* meant her. Choking, she could not seem to say it. There were so many people waiting for that exact answer.

Marquis didn't miss a beat as his hand found hers, warm, steadying. His voice boomed, the wind picking up and carrying his words. "May I introduce Emory Reia Fae, the Queen of Kiero and my fiancé."

If Nolan was shocked, he did a great job of hiding it. Ceridwen eyed her with interest as she and her husband bowed to her, murmuring, "A pleasure to meet you."

The crowd, on the other hand, churned, whispers filling the square.

Emory's body felt detached from her mind as she stiffly bowed then rose back up.

Behind them, Oakland Wharf graciously took the news, their excitement and questions about planning the wedding making her want to puke. Delaney and Reagan were twin flames, with coppery hair and inquisitive pale-green eyes. As they moved aside, Marquis squeezed her hand tighter.

The Harbor of Newsoll brought a stoic Calum and Isla, their gazes set above tight-lipped smiles, but Emory loved their electric-purple hair. They bowed without a word, moving aside for the last couple.

Durdover Port. My targets.

The couple had pale, luminous eyes, reminding Emory of moonlight. Their hair was shoulder length, honey-colored and braided back intricately. They wore simple gray shirts and black cloaks, boots, and pants. The woman took her hand, shaking it. "It's a pleasure to meet you, Emory."

Not Queen. Just Emory.

Marquis's mouth twitched as he drawled, "And I presume we are in the presence of the proclaimed royalty?"

The man stepped forward, and it seemed the entire kingdom held its breath as he clasped forearms with Marquis. "There is a time for politics later, I'm sure. For right now, we come as allies, to help celebrate as a country."

Marquis chuckled. "Of course."

"Well then, may I introduce my wife, Skena. My name is Iain."

Though Marquis nodded, talking to them both, Emory didn't miss the pressure tightening his hands or the shadow lurking in his gaze. The world was watching, and they just invited the snakes into the kingdom.

Loosening a breath, Emory gazed across the crowd, looking for one face.

Stepping up to her side, Marquis said loudly, "Let us show our guests Hriste's hospitality as we celebrate this special day of a new union between the Shattered Isles and Kiero!"

The crowd boomed, and Marquis leaned in closer, his breath tickling her ear. "Now remember, our show is just beginning."

Marquis stepped back, and Emory took a deep breath. Trying to smile, she waved out to the crowd, to the clapping and joyous yells meeting them. Her gaze roamed, though she promised herself she wouldn't look for Brokk.

***

The afternoon passed like they were walking on ice—constantly balancing while breathing life into their lie. Alone, Emory would never win this war. Without the fleets and army of the Shattered Isles, Kiero was on the executioner's block. If Emory was being honest with herself, her own time was slipping through an hourglass, waning by the second.

Dark whispers raced through her at random. "*Join me, Emory. Let go and give in to me.*"

Ignoring Declan's smooth voice, she allowed Marquis to guide her through the highlights of the festival; as they traveled to vendor after vendor, her taste buds exploded with flavor at the food and drink she tasted. From syrup frozen on chunks of ice, to charred fish, to meat skewers, to a variety of different ales, she was so full that tiredness pulled at her limbs and mind. But she had to hold on.

"How are you doing?" Marquis pulled her out of her thoughts.

"Fine." Another easy lie passing through her lips.

"No, you're not, but I'm glad that at least for this afternoon you are living in denial."

Rolling her eyes, she dipped her head at the constant sea of bodies passing by. *Smile. Just another kingdom you must convince. Another union. Another death. Another lie.*

Behind them trailed the visiting royals.

"How much longer until we act?"

Marquis chewed on his lip. "Given the intel we have, everything will boil down to tonight. If we stand as allies or if the other clans play another enemy in this war."

"The proclaimed king will be interested in talking to me?"

"Why wouldn't he? Everyone wanted to see this mysterious queen. Now that we added fiancé into the story, he will not be able to resist."

"More like dangerous," she quipped.

"Dangerous, mysterious. Emory, it's all the same. Whether you like it or not, you're a symbol. Kiero has fallen into shadows. Everyone wants to see who will make it whole again."

The words sank in as she nodded. "A day at a time."

"More like a war at a time. We have to be prepared."

"Marquis, I know. Trust me, I do. I won't mess this up." She adjusted her jacket; the late afternoon had turned cool, and in the distance, waves crashed.

Hriste had emptied out by now, people dancing in the streets, musicians of all kinds playing—they passed band after band. Marquis stalled, pausing in front of two drummers, one instrument player bowing his head as he plucked along with the fast song.

Emory squinted up at Marquis, already shaking her head. "Please don't—"

His hands grabbed hers, pulling her in against his chest. "A show. Remember, Princess? Give the Isles the vision of who they should look up to. Not a lost king and queen, but a king and queen who are unified. *Happy.* People they will trust and follow into war. A future they will want to fight for."

Nodding, she forced herself to relax, to lean into him. Marquis spun her out, pulling her back in, and she couldn't stop her lips from pulling up.

"You're not so bad at this." Emory commented.

"It comes with years of practicing with the broom, you know."

She chuckled, the music taking her into a different time, a different place.

A commander she had trusted. *Memphis.* The name hurt, chiseling a hole into her chest, her grief raw. He had sacrificed himself, knowing that Nyx could win over the raiders. Another ploy. Another pawn. Another *life. How many more will have to die?*

The music slowed, and they took their time breaking apart, clapping. The band bowed as Marquis took her arm again.

"That wasn't so hard now, was it, Princess?" Marquis beamed, and she couldn't help herself as she smiled warmly up at him.

The band picked up again as passersby dipped their heads, whispering well wishes and congratulations behind Emory and Marquis wherever they went. They walked, Emory noticing a slight shift in Marquis's demeanor when he whispered, "Assuming tonight goes off without a hitch, is there a way that you can sense if they Oilean have come? To the Isles?"

It was a simple question, yet her heart raced as she mentally checked the number of blades she had on her. The answer itself was the darkened whisper flowing through the air like electricity. Adair's ability had become more prominent with each passing day, her sense of self drowning within the desire to give in to the power. To overtake and destroy. Finally, that siren call was being answered—a private invitation just for her.

Her heart plummeted, and her gut twisted. Following in Marquis's stride, she whispered back, "Yes. It could be soon."

He lifted his brow. "I'm trusting you, Princess."

"I know."

Again, they wove through the crowd, the festival in full swing. There were booths upon booths of local businesses displaying goods from food to fine jewelry. Shimmering gems, polished bones. Canvases upon canvases of swirling colors. Deep greens capturing the rolling fields of the Isles. A stormy sea, the inky waters with purple lightning streaking far above. Paintings of children, running down the cobblestone streets, their futures inked on their arms and hands. Paintings of the harbor, row upon row of ships. Each painting held a memory of the Isles, of the culture, and all Emory could do was look. The innocence of it all, the normalcy of it all.

Tears welled in her eyes, and she swallowed hard. *This is war, Em. No room for tears. Or remorse.* Clinging to the thought like a lifeline, she murmured to Marquis, "What time does the dinner start?"

"At dusk. But first—"

"The council."

Marquis nodded, solemn.

Politics. It was all she could do not to tear her hair out. It was one small step at a time here on the Isles, while her friends were burning a world away.

Holding her head high, she turned, facing their guests. "May I suggest we all refresh ourselves?"

The group looked at her hungrily, a pack of wolves cornering their prey. It was Iain who spoke. "I couldn't agree more."

With Marquis pulling at her hand, Emory led them away from the festival. She knew the route to his place by now, her body falling into muscle memory. The wind cut around her; she closed her eyes, breathing deeply. One second, one moment of silence.

Opening her eyes, Emory stopped in her tracks, heart in her throat.

Across the crowd, Brokk's golden eyes met hers, wide with disbelief. Riona and Kiana flanked his sides, glaring at her and Marquis, at their interlaced fingers.

Marquis followed her gaze, features darkening. "Princess." His voice wasn't harsh—more like a steadying force reminding her what she was doing. What *they* were doing.

The sun sank lower, the party swinging more into life.

Emory shook her head, ever so slightly, hoping Brokk would see it all in her eyes. *I'm sorry. Go, Brokk. Leave. I'm not coming with you.* Exhaling hard, she turned her back, cutting through the crowd, memorizing his face as she left him behind, her head held high.

***

Emory could cut through the tension with a knife, it was so thick. All of them were seated around Marquis's table with no guards and no weapons; it put her on edge.

Marquis leaned back, a smirk tucked in the corner of his lip. No one spoke, the steaming pot of tea sitting in the middle, untouched. Outside, the intoxicating sounds of the party continued.

"Don't you think this day calls for something a little bit stronger?" Iain finally threw out.

"Not in the slightest. Besides, when have we all been in the same room as one another? Normally, not all of us come together to celebrate the Equinox. Clear minds demand clear intentions," Marquis stated.

Iain's face darkened. "Marquis, we are not talking alliances today."

"I beg to differ. You came to my capital to ogle at my future wife, and you honestly think I wouldn't arrange terms? That with Kiero and the Shattered Isles joining, there wouldn't be a cost to you all?"

"I knew it. You haven't changed a bit. Just as spineless as your father, trapping us in a corner and then biting. What are you demanding then? Me to step down and bow to only you?"

"On the contrary. Though I am going to ignore your insults. This one time." Marquis held the other man's gaze, his emerald eyes igniting. "I'm proposing that we decide not to fall into the traps and mistakes of our forebearers. I have made mistakes, and I will be the first to admit them. Let's ensure that Kiero doesn't lose this war. Fight with us. Let us unite the Shattered Isles. I can respect you being recognized as a leader. Let us unite our courts, our power. I'm asking you to treat us as equals."

Skena scoffed. "Never. You would never give up your crown."

"Our enemy is not within these walls," Emory bit out, anger flaring, as sparks danced from her fingertips. "If you don't follow us, you will die. If you do, I can protect this army. I can protect you. The choice is yours. Whoever wants to bicker over titles can do so later."

Iain looked positively dangerous as he leaned forward. "You are both alone in this. It is not our war. We came to show the people of the Shattered Isles that I am not hiding any longer. We came to show *you* that, Marquis. Your time ruling this country is slipping from underneath you. And I relish in that fact." Shoving his chair back, Iain spat, "I am sure I will have to clean up your mess later."

Skena followed, the honey curtain of her hair covering most of her face, cloaking her emotions. The door slammed behind them.

Marquis loosened a harsh exhale.

Looking to the rest of the group, Emory said what her fake fiancé could not. "If you want another future cleaved in blood, then walk out that door. But we implore you to help us rebuild. I killed Adair Stratton." His name tasted thick on her tongue, foreign and wrong. "This Dark King, this imposter, is just another pillar we must knock down. A resistance is forming, and we must rise. And we must do so together."

She could feel Marquis's gaze on her, the truth that rang in her words. Her friends, her family, had only known this darkness. This world of violence, of war. And it was time that they no longer had to live with that threat.

Sitting taller, she said, "Don't allow the Isles to become as divided as Kiero has been."

Marquis jumped in, pushing the rest of the group to enjoy the festivities, to take time to think over their proposition. Calum and Isla had kind faces, intrigued eyes. Nolan and Ceridwen nodded as they left, Delaney and Reagan close at their heels.

Shivering, Emory blinked as her stomach swooped, vertigo washing over her. The room slipped from underneath her, walls disappearing . . .

The Black Sea roared, inky waves frothing. The Oilean looked at the shoreline, rising from the ocean themselves. Nostrils flaring, they tasted the air and the ancient magic blanketing this land. Blood magic. But on the horizon, deep within the land, their own magic called to them, held on a leash by the woman who stole it.

They giggled as their bones cracked, spurting, transforming. Hiding in plain sight. The sister closest to the water's edge dipped her hand in the water, murmuring, "Come, rise up, diams, who have been banished to the darkness. Come help us devour this land."

The bubbles started, slowly at first. A wave crashed, pearly white bone flashing underneath the water, reflecting in the late afternoon sun. With their bodies changing—sinew strengthening, nails growing into claws, teeth into fangs—the Oilean growled in pleasure as the cannibals shook their bodies, emerging from the depths of the sea. Droplets of water flew, and violet eyes flashed.

They drew their blades, bowing in unison.

"You freed us, Ancient Ones. We crave the blood of the Fae girl who tried to kill us and failed."

The Oilean tilted their heads at the diams. "How do you know about Emory Fae?"

"She and the man traveling with her almost made us a delicious dinner, but she is stronger than we thought. She left us for dead, and as we recuperated, we hoped you would come and that we could make an alliance to end her."

"Your power calls to us as ours did to you. Help us tear the Isles apart. But Emory is ours," the Oilean said in unison.

Plumes of smoke poured from the Oilean's bodies, forging swords as the diams dipped their heads. "Let the hunt truly begin."

"No mercy!" the diams roared.

The Oilean bellowed, "No survivors."

The beach exploded around them, the shrubbery shriveling up in sparks, the fire devouring everything in their wake.

Emory was slammed back into her body and immediately vomited all over Marquis's table. The acid filled her sinuses, tears streaking down her cheeks, as she heaved again.

"Emory!" Marquis was there, rubbing her upper back.

"Don't touch me," she wheezed.

Stepping back slowly, Marquis replied, "What's happening? You and I are beginning a truly awful routine of this, you know."

"Marquis, *shut up*. It's happening. They're here. The Oilean are coming. Now."

There hadn't been enough time. The last time she had encountered the Oilean, they had infiltrated the Draken Mountains, setting up Declan's plan to take over his perfect vessel—Adair. She still had nightmares where she was running down the hallway, gripping Anithe, their whispers chasing at her heels.

"Emory."

The fear had choked her then as it did now; the Oilean were born from nightmares. Now they had come to claim their dues. Her ability.

Panic clawed at her throat as she wiped her mouth, standing. "You have the guards in place? The fleets?"

Marquis paled, nodding. "The people cannot know. Not until our plan is set in motion. How much time do we have?"

"Not long."

"It's time then, Em."

The empty room blurred around her, but Emory steadied herself and ran out of the house and into the heart of the festival, music blooming around her, weaving into her pulse, spiking her adrenaline more. *It's time to show them what kind of queen you are.* The weeks she had spent with Marquis, testing the depth of Adair's power, and the prior months training would all help one thing—her intention.

Anithe was strapped to her back, and two knives were sheathed on the outsides of her thighs. Yet, she felt bare going into battle until her ability subdued her fear into focus, demanding her power to be *more* than she ever thought possible. Dusk approached on the horizon, deep oranges rippling among the clouds as the promise of a bloody night unfurled. Slipping into that harrowing depth of power, Emory dissipated into smoke and ashes.

***

Iain and Skena were impossibly easy to find. They had almost made it back to the festival. Landing in front of them, Emory took a steadying breath and looked up at their blanched faces.

Marquis's voice erupted in her mind.

They couldn't ever imagine I would arrange a marriage in my favor. They will pretend to play nice, and we will only have to keep this lie up for a few hours. Enough time to distract them, enough time to hurt Brokk so he will leave you behind. Enough time to offer them to join us in this war, for Durdover to show their true colors. That's when we will unleash your ability.

Don't hold back, Em.

This is your promise.

Grabbing Anithe's hilt, she pulled, unsheathing the blade. As she brought the blade low in front of her, the steel erupted into a black flame in the dusk.

Iain stepped forward, shielding Skena. He started to open his mouth, in some threat or some incoherent statement, she assumed, but she didn't give him the chance to speak. She launched forward, throwing her body weight into the upper cut, and Anithe was liquid fire. Blood, bone, and sinew spattered against her silver outfit as the iron cleaved Iain cleanly from groin to head. The body dropped in front of Emory. Skena's screams reverberated through the night, but those were nothing against the pounding in Emory's heart, the ringing in her ears.

Emory stepped over the proclaimed king of Durdover Port, wiping Anithe clean on her upper thigh. "You really should have agreed to Marquis's terms."

As the sun finally dipped below the horizon, Emory dug deeper into that void of ability and was a blur as she reappeared behind Skena, plunging her sword through her upper back, driving it into her heart. In the street of the Harvest Equinox, Emory held Skena until she stopped breathing before lowering her body to the cobbled stones.

Distantly, she was aware of the screams of joy from the festival building and sounding closer to her with every second. Sheathing Anithe, Emory snapped her fingers, sparks erupting from them.

The fire caught, devouring the bodies and the evidence.

CHAPTER TWELVE

BROKK

The crowd was only becoming thicker, making the usually cool air seem suffocating. Sweat trickled down his spine, making Brokk shiver. Thousands of fairy lights ignited along the street sides as the sunset disappeared behind the cliffs that flanked Hriste. The clouds glowed from the last rays of the sun, igniting the festival in full swing as twilight blanketed the Shattered Isles—this beautiful, cruel country he hoped to never step foot in again.

At the edge of the crowd, the screams began. Music filled every possible empty space, fire and ice exploding toward the burnt orange sky. A show of abilities for beauty, for celebration. As he and the sisters walked, shimmering flowers bloomed from the vines climbing over terraces, up along the sides of houses. Their petals were incandescent, silver and purple hues glowing as the light faded.

Hours had passed, yet Brokk's pulse jumped, anger flaring, as he replayed one moment repeatedly in his mind.

The look in Emory's eyes as she had walked away.

With.

Marquis.

Maher.

"Brokk, I'm telling you, we have to leave," Riona repeated. She was at his heels, eyes nervously taking in every face, trying to spot where the threat could be.

A gut-wrenching growl was his only response as he wove through the street.

It wasn't logical; it didn't make any sense. Had it only been last night, their promises lingering on their lips? That heat had flared through them both, devouring and savoring. His world had stopped last night, he and Emory the commanders of their time, only to return to the new day as strangers. As *liars*. They had made love, and Emory had thrown it away as if it meant nothing. His stomach clenched, and the ghost-like memory of their bodies entangling barreled through him.

"Riona's right, Brokk. It's time to make our move. Now." It was Kiana's soft plea that undid him completely.

"No. Both of you, *no*. I have not come halfway around the world to let this—this *lie*—drive me away! I have not endured torture at the Oilean's hands, lost my best friend and possibly my rebellion, to lose Emory now too. I have not fought so hard for her to push me away. I'm telling you, there is more to this."

Kiana shared a look with her sister, and that was answer enough for him as he maneuvered his way through the crowd, heart in his throat. He searched for her inky hair. For a flash of green eyes. She had promised to choose him. Brokk would not accept that Emory would use his emotions against him. He understood these were unprecedented times, and that she thought helping Marquis was the right choice. He had felt that there was a lot she wasn't telling him, and as the weeks passed, he knew they had drifted apart. Until last night.

Panic built in his chest, layering heavy until it felt like he was having trouble breathing.

No matter what, he would not leave the woman he loved behind.

He rushed into the middle of the square, and a flurry of movement exploded around him. Women and men in their intricate clothing jumped in front of him and behind him. Riona and Kiana were instantly swallowed in the mass of bodies, lost to Brokk. The music stopped, and it was like the entire world held its breath as he stood there shaking, feeling the strangers' gazes burning into his back. The moment cracked as the music jumped back to life—the harmonies blending into slow, melancholy notes.

Sweat dripped down his temple as he felt a cool hand intertwine with his own, the pressure sure.

Don't look up. Don't do it. Emory was his weakness, and if she truly was engaged to Marquis, she had wondrously played him. His emotions were a wounded animal going out into the open where Emory waited to land her killing blow.

Wrenching his gaze forward, Brokk instinctively pulled Emory closer, his left hand resting on her lower back. His right hand held hers as they swayed to the dance. His pulse spiked, and it was if he were lost among the stars or discovering uncharted land. There was this intoxicating, sickening silence that pulled between them, and he couldn't find a single word to say.

Her black eyes softened as she took him in, his name a featherlight whisper on her lips. "Brokk."

She looked sick. When did her irises turn black? Her skin was too ashen, deep bruising under her eyes. His gaze swept underneath her jaw, where blackened veins webbed through her pale skin.

"Em, you don't look . . . well. But please tell me I'm wrong. That you're not . . . you're not . . . That last night wasn't a lie?" The broken sentence came out like a caress as they stared at each other, chest to chest. Heat flared from Emory's body. Brokk noted blood on her clothes, red marring her painted silver makeup and jacket.

Pressing her lips together, with the tiniest shake of her head, she whispered, "You have to leave. Brokk, go to the Rebellion."

"That's it? I've just been your pawn all along? Another maneuver? Bring us here to . . . what? You and I, was that just another ploy? To make me trust you. To fall in love with you." He paused, his voice breaking. "Just for once, let me in. Please. What happened to you?"

They rotated, the dance holding them together—a king and a queen who had never been free. Not from politics or from this war. The fact slammed into him that no matter what paths they went down, history was bound to repeat itself. The one thing Emory Fae had been eternally bound to was her duty. The Rebellion had damned his happiness and his heart from the beginning by pushing her to be what she was born to be.

Lowering his lips closer to her, almost grazing her cheek, he breathed, "Em . . ."

This couldn't be true. The memory of her lips on his, their promised whispers in the heart of the night ravaged him, making this reality irreparable.

Her name had been the first word that had damned him when he had stepped toward Emory in her apartment on Earth. Now, her silence spread through him again like a poison, ripping him apart. Pulling back, Brokk searched her face for any emotion leaking through that would tell him he was wrong. He *had* to be wrong. As she leaned in, her breath was hot on his lips, and slowly the music climbed, their lips brushing, rough and fleeting.

Emory pulled away and stopped dancing. The woman who stood in Hriste's square said nothing, but her answer lay in her silence. In her hard, steely gaze, there was no warmth.

CHAPTER THIRTEEN

EMORY

Closing her eyes for the briefest of seconds, Emory tried to memorize his warm scent—reminding her of a mix of honey and amber. Woodsy. Home. Emory allowed Adair's ability to flow within her, the claws sinking into Brokk's mind, possessing him. He refused to accept she was truly staying on the Isles—the bleak truth stared her in the face.

So, she would make him.

Relishing in the rush, she ordered, emotionless, "Turn around. Go to Riona and Kiana. Go to the docks where a ship is ready for you. Sail to Kiero now." Emory watched the effect of her ability possessing him, wiping the Brokk she knew away. Internally, she felt his mind bowing and agreeing to her instructions, but as she watched the spark fade within his gaze, his mouth slackened. His arms rested by his sides, his breath even. All the emotion she saw bubbling to the surface minutes ago—gone.

Tears threatened to spill over as Emory took a steadying breath. "Take as many people as you can with you. Follow Diedre; she will take you to the waiting ship. Find Nyx, ignite the Rebellion.

Save them; prepare for war. But know that the Isles await your call. After this, I will come."

I love you. Wait for me, please. After all this is done. Maybe you will understand, one day, why I must do this.

The music that had once filled the square had stopped.

Brokk—emotionless—turned, weaving through the crowd.

Swallowing past the lump that had built in her throat, Emory pushed the connection of her possessing him to the back of her mind, where her instructions stayed clear and unwavering. Brokk wouldn't come to until he was far away from the Isles.

She looked up to the night sky where a few stars peeked out behind the thick clouds collecting above. Most of them were hidden. The night reflected her mood—an endless darkness that swallowed them all whole.

How many times would she have to hurt him? How many times would she have to lie? Exhaling hard, Emory spotted Diedre across the square, giving her a curt nod. She would make sure he was safe. Brokk would get out *alive.* Or else it was all for nothing.

Sending a silent plea to gods unknown and unseen, Emory set off at a jog, her muscles tugging at the sudden movement.

They are coming. They are coming. The thought filled every crevice of her soul, her breath coming in panicked pants. Picking up speed, she relished in the power flowing in her body, answering her call that it was time to fight.

The square was decorated to its finest, the natural beauty of Hriste the backdrop to the celebration: the rolling valleys and rock-faced cliffs; the ocean with the hidden caves; the flowers blooming in deep, cool hues, so unlike the burning expanse of trees on Kiero or even Earth. Fall was a time the entire world was lit in golden fire. But here . . . everything was crystalized.

She ran past the opening for the festival, the empty streets beckoning to her; she pushed faster. Harder. This was her mother's land. *Her* land. It was time she acted like it. Like one magnet flying toward another, her ability climbed and climbed, humming toward the darkness harnessing the land. The rise of panicked voices was her signal, the screams curdling with fear.

More time, Marquis, I need more time.

Emory dove into her ability, her veins burning with raw power; her vision became doubled. In her mind's eye, she saw Brokk as he went to Diedre, Riona and Kiana flanking him. They were ushered through the panicked crowds, down to the opposite side of Hriste. She watched Brokk clamber down the hidden staircase that would bring them to a private port, spiraling down to the ship that awaited them. Sweat dripped down the back of her neck, and Emory lessened her connection but kept a firm hold over Brokk's mind and body.

As she slammed back into the present, goosebumps rippled over her skin. She sensed the energy change within Hriste; it was eerily quiet like a storm was about to erupt over the land.

And now, she waited.

The world turned to nothing but a mass of color as she focused on the shadows in front of her. The air seemed to shimmer, and one inky claw hooked inward, slashing through the magical barrier that protected Hriste. Like a curtain tumbling in the wind, the barrier between them and the outside world was torn. The bottomless eyes of the Oilean bored into her as they appeared fully in front of her. Their skin was stretched too far, too tight, and their lips were in a permanent grin over sharpened teeth. Long arms held blackened blades . . .

The Oilean had found her.

They had found her.

More claws appeared, ripping and shredding the magical barrier that kept Hriste hidden. Behind the Oilean, the diams appeared, licking their bloodless lips, glaring down at her. Their snarling wolf masks were unmarred, their violet eyes burning in bloodlust.

For Brokk.

For the Rebellion.

She held her chin high as her ability sparked beneath her skin, rolling through her blood like a sea of flames. There was no time for fear.

Roaring, she charged, feeling the small amount of energy pull as Anithe ignited, the once blood-red blade now ebony. *Breathe, Emory.* The ground shuddered beneath her. Emory watched the diams jump from the cliff's ledge, cutting through the air with ease, landing a few feet from her.

"Emmmory Fae, come with us willingly or watch all your friends die."

Keep running. Keep running. Hair flying, she drove Anithe down, slashing at the nearest diam's shins. Staggering back, the cannibal moved so fast, she was a blur before she snapped down to where Emory should have been.

Chuckling darkly, Emory appeared behind the diam in a plume of black-and-purple smoke. "A neat trick, right? You should have never come here with the Oilean."

Not waiting for a reply, Emory cut Anithe through the diam's neck effortlessly, watching her head roll. Her three companions started howling. Emory was already moving, adrenaline making her vision tunnel.

The Oilean still stood far above them, watching the fight unfold. Screaming, Emory kicked the chest of the next cannibal charging at her, fingers covered with bone-tipped claws. As Emory twisted her body, Anithe cut into the diam's arm, making her body sag as she screamed. The cannibal's heart was an easy target, Emory's sword biting into her chest. Emory felt fingers curl around her neck, pressure building as she wrenched Anithe back.

Wheezing, she slammed her right knee into the third diam's gut. The cannibal hissed, doubling over, and Emory used the split second to fling her to the ground. The diam's nails ripped through Emory's neck, releasing her hold. Hot blood trickled down Emory's collarbone onto her clothes from her wound. Emory panted, watching the headless corpse rip her fellow diam apart with her hands, driven by bloodlust. Killing her companion.

Screams filled her world. One remained.

Emory turned to the last diam, sparks floating from her fingertips. "Leave. Now. Or you will share their fates."

Violet eyes flitted side to side as the remaining diam faltered before her. Emory saw the opportunity, seizing it. Charging, she felt gravity leave her, billowing as she flew in smoke and ash. Landing behind the diam, gripping Anithe in both hands, Emory tried to decapitate her. The diam rolled, coming to stand. In a blur, the diam was charging her.

Anithe collided with the diam's dagger. Parrying, the creature said, spittle flying from her lips, "Your mistake, *Queen*, to bloody your hands. You thought you killed us once, and you were wrong. Why protect this kingdom of broken iron? Why protect Marquis Maher? We told you that you would be found. Accept your end."

Each word brought a vicious blow shuddering through Emory. Tremors ran along her spine, down her arms, into her very core. She spat, "One of my last promises to the Dark King was that I would never bow. I intend to stay true to my word."

"You will never bow, and yet you would die for another country," the diam mused.

They were empty statements, this verbal sparring.

Emory sauntered up to her, eyes flicking up to the Oilean for the briefest of seconds. Her pounding heart reverberated in her ears as she counted mentally to herself. *One.* Her ability surged as Emory flew, gravity indefinite, slamming into the diam. Nails bit into Emory's flesh right before she was tossed, dots lining her vision when her head cracked against a rock, blood filling her mouth. Black smoke leaked from her palms, and all she saw was sharpened teeth. *Two.* Staggering, Emory threw a right hook, her fist cracking against the diam's jaw. Anithe dropped, the sword now lying to her left. *Three.*

Come on, Marquis. Come. On.

Lunging, she grabbed Anithe, swinging the blade too clumsily, and the diam's taunting chuckles floated around her. She spat blood, and the ground trembled beneath her boots, but Emory smiled. It was the ghost of Adair's voice that cut across her mind: *Assess your enemy. Find your footing—and then end them.*

The diam slashed her dagger, aiming toward Emory's throat, but Emory ducked, the blade slicing into empty air. Digging deep, she found her strength and rolled as her palms connected to the earth, dirt shifting—the field split. The diam dropped into the pit, her screams silencing the farther she fell into the core of the Isles. The bodies of the other three fell inside as well.

Exhaling, Emory stood on shaking legs, the crack slamming back together. Sweat, blood, and smoke covered her, but she looked only for the Oilean.

End. Them.

Her thoughts pushed her to meet her true enemy. She had been waiting for this moment since the Oilean's dark magic had taken over Adair all those years ago.

"Too afraid to come down?" She didn't recognize her voice as she called to the Oilean. Fury laced every word, a promise of darkness that reflected their own. She wouldn't give them an inch of fear.

The Oilean hissed, hands lengthening into pointed blades. The picture of the four sisters was one born from nightmares. Then the sisters giggled, tilting their heads. "Where is your little prince of Nehmai, Emoorrry Fae?"

Bracing herself, Emory held Anithe in front of her. "He is gone. It's me you want anyway."

Anithe burst into flames.

The Oilean jumped off the cliff, an army of demons behind them materializing from thin air. Hundreds of smoky bodies howled behind the Oilean, mimicking the dabarnes. *Impossible.*

Emory watched the black smoke churn, yellow and orange eyes blinking down at her. Hundreds of salivating, saggy-skinned gray monsters snapped their maws. Her hands shook as she gripped Anithe tighter, a sharp ringing filling her hearing. She tripped over her right foot, and the ground trembled more as the massive army spilled into Hriste like a wave, winking out any light source as they charged toward her.

Steeling herself, Emory ran, loosening a battle cry. Black flames jumped from her, twisting and building like a shield, not burning her but building strength. The wind picked up, sending her sparks flying, and as she ran, Emory knew she wasn't alone anymore. Jumping, she collided with the first sister, flames swallowed by their shadow.

"We know where he is," the Oilean mocked.

Heart dropping into her stomach, Emory shoved her back. "Well then, you have to get through me first."

Their deadly dance became a blur. Lunge. Parry. Duck. Roll. Attack. Block. The Oilean hissed, as if anticipating her defeat in their odds of four against one.

Sweat dripped into Emory's eyes, the strength of their attacks making her arms tremble. The Oilean circled her, hissing and snarling. Muscles burning, she slammed the pommel of Anithe into her closest opponent's arm, bone splintering from the impact.

"Emory!" a shout echoed behind her.

In the distance, Marquis ran in the field, armored bodies of the people of the Shattered Isles following his lead. Her heart swelled at the sight. Then, they slammed into the Oilean's army, disappearing in a second beneath a mass of smoke and claws.

Everything tasted of ash when flesh connected with Emory's jaw, causing her head to snap back. Emory hit the ground, pressure building on her chest. The punch was fast, and the Oilean hissed down at her in pleasure. Emory howled as she felt steel cut deeply through her pants into both of her upper thighs. *Heal.* The thought reverberated through her core; her ability answered, mending her wounds.

Cracking her forehead against one of the Oilean's, she rolled to the right, staggering up. Blood trickled from her lip, and more gushed down her legs.

The outskirts of the city erupted with sickening battle cries. Darkness overtook everything, and fear crawled up her spine in waves. She couldn't see, an unnatural night having fallen over them all. Finding Anithe's hilt, Emory swung wildly, moving in a continuous circle, trying to anticipate the Oilean's next attacks.

Giggles answered her in the darkness; their whispers circled her. "Well, this will be fun."

"Show yourself!" Emory roared.

More giggles.

She was panting; the air smelled like blood. The screams of Marquis's army rattled all around her.

Adair's voice sliced through her core once more. *With my ability, I could raise an army of the dead. With my ability, I am unstoppable.*

Remembering what she did in the Noctis Woods, the animals' remains answering to her call, Emory hurriedly slammed Anithe into the ground. As she pressed her palms to the damp dirt, electric shocks began running down her arms. *Please, help me. Please.*

Her intention was about to burst through her heart. Anithe's flames grew despite being lodged in the earth, allowing a semi-circle of light.

The Oilean stepped into her sight, circling her slowly, their necks cracking, their joints elongating. Their hands morphed into claws, and their teeth glinted as they whispered, "Now, Emory Fae, you will *die.* We have longed to taste your blood."

"You can put that notion right up all your—"

Her speech was cut off when a howl cut through the night. The Oilean's heads snapped up in unison, fear filling Emory as her thoughts immediately went to Brokk.

Had he somehow overpowered her ability when no one else had?

Grabbing Anithe, Emory staggered back as she watched hundreds—no *thousands*—of skeletal animals charge toward the Oilean and their army of dabarnes. Huge stags flew over the Isles' soldiers, their antlers sparkling in the night, their skulls bowing forward as they rammed into the demons, animalistic chaos erupting. To her left, what looked to be a skeletal wolf flanked her. And another to her right.

Tears pricked her eyes as Emory spat at the Oilean, "No. It's your time to die, you fucks."

Ripping Anithe from the ground, she charged, the undead army following her lead.

PART TWO

BLOODIED SPIRITS AND CRYSTALIZED HEARTS

CHAPTER FOURTEEN

NYX

Nyx Astire stopped to look in the full-length mirror, her lightweight pants cinched at her hips. Her top was intricate, the silver and black beads scooping low, accentuating her cleavage, her skin exposed at the open back. Her vibrant purple hair was braided, and despite what had happened, she felt . . . powerful. Beautiful. Which only made the bitter taste in her mouth that much more evident.

Sighing, she began to pace, her sandals padding against the boards. The room smelled of oiled wood and musk.

A couple weeks had passed since Memphis died.

Memphis . . .

Hands shaking, she counted her breaths, the panic settling into her chest, sucking all the air out of the room.

The weeks had passed in a numbing blur, her grief dissolving all her ambition. Everywhere she looked, all she could see was his broken body, his empty eyes. The crack that fissured through her felt roughly mended knowing she had killed Zander. Yet, guilt still pricked at the back of her mind. She had let Memphis down; she should have done *more* to try and save him. Now, when she wanted to do nothing more than mourn, she was handed control of the Dust Clans.

Every day that she woke up, she swore to herself she would get out of bed and try. She owed Memphis that.

Those fleeting moments at the end, when she had heard his thoughts, had felt his peace at succeeding in one final mission . . . Memphis had given her a chance at winning over the raiders.

Memphis . . .

Throat tightening, Nyx blinked hard against the tears that threatened to come. Every night, every moment she was alone, they fell down her cheeks until the numbness filled that vicious hole in her heart. Grief and anger soon pressed into a coldness that hardened her. That sharpened her. Today, of all days, she needed that strength.

Shooting one final look at herself, she straightened her back and left.

She passed through the hallway to the stairs, and the lush house seemed overbearing now, the remnants of Zander making her want to burn every inch of it to the ground. But one thing Nyx had learned quickly here was that the raiders prized one thing above all else: tradition. As the new leader of the Dust Clans, Nyx's delicate alliance balanced on her obedience to uphold such traditions.

Taking a deep breath, she threw open the door, greeting the bustle of the day like an old friend. The sun was nestled high in the sky, the heat of the Risco Desert already ribboning through the air. The market was set up and in full swing, the sellers' voices hitching as high as the sky—their bartering skills impressive.

Arching her eyebrow, she slammed the door shut behind her, purring, "Hello, Kyrie."

Kyrie appeared from the shadows, dressed in his usual sleeveless black armored vest and loose tan pants; his smug smirk made her want to drive her palm into his perfectly straight nose. Kyrie Oijen was—annoyingly—the epitome of devilishly handsome. His golden skin was unflawed, and he had toned muscles and twinkling silver eyes. And surprisingly to her, they had become quick friends. How else could she navigate her newly claimed title? That was, if she didn't want to be woken in the night by a knife to her throat. Nyx knew she had needed to find allies, and fast.

At his silence, she asked, "Where's Suri?"

"Already waiting for you. I was instructed to pick your grumpy—"

Chuckling, Nyx threw a punch, which he dodged with ease. "Don't even finish that sentence, Kyrie. Let's go. It's a big day."

Jumping into the throng of raiders with ease, she allowed her stomach to lead her, feeling Kyrie's stare burning into her back as she walked. The Oijen twins had been the first of the raiders to help Nyx get out of that arena, and they tended to her. That kindness Nyx would never forget, and they had become fast friends. Bonding over their hate for Zander had helped—and three bottles of mulled wine that had followed that initial night. Grief resides deep within one's heart, and Nyx had welcomed the numbness alcohol had provided, if only temporary.

The crowd was white noise as she approached Olly's cart. The fruit was ripe, the deep greens and purples entrancing. Nyx picked up two, and the elderly man grinned a toothless smile as she dug in her pockets for coin.

"Not today, young mystic. Today, for you, it's free."

Young mystic. The annoying nickname had stuck after she killed Zander in the pit. Stilling, Nyx raised her gaze, meeting his kind brown eyes. Holding their breakfast, she was about to protest when Kyrie stepped in, flashing a heart-stopping smile to Olly. "Thank you for your good fortune."

"May the gods smile down on you both."

Clamping her mouth shut, Nyx turned away, sure her nails were about to rip through the soft skin of the fruit.

"You may want to stop looking like you want to puke. Nyx, today is the day you must decide if you want this or not. There is still time if you are having doubts."

Tossing a melon to him, she grumbled, "Memphis died so I could be here. I told you and Suri a thousand times . . ."

"Yes, yes. *I know.* I'm just saying you have a choice in this."

Setting her jaw, she bit into the fruit, practically wanting to swoon when the juices flowed over her tongue—flowery, light, and to die for. The raiders traded with the Shattered Isles for such delicacies—a land she had thought was long destroyed. And, *of course*, there was another king she thought dead: Marquis Maher. She took another huge bite, juices spurting, dribbling down her chin. She couldn't get through the day on an empty stomach.

Walking in silence, Nyx and Kyrie wove through the sandy streets with ease. Heads turned and whispers chased at their heels. Nyx exhaled hard. A small white stone building waited for them in the distance. Suri stood waiting, dressed in deep purple, her style of clothes matching Nyx's. Squealing upon seeing Nyx, Suri ran across the courtyard, slamming into her. The hug was quick, sandalwood overtaking Nyx's senses.

Chuckling, Nyx pulled back. "Come on, Suri."

Breaking away, Suri tucked a loose strand of her onyx hair behind her ear, her grin growing from ear to ear. "What? I can't be excited for you?"

"You've only known me a couple of weeks." Nyx walked beside her, shaking her head as the woman glowed.

"Time is irrelevant when souls recognize one another. You and I were destined to be friends."

As Nyx's lips tugged down, a pang sliced through her heart. Suri radiated light, which she liked to say was because she was gifted with seeing into the unknown. In the passing weeks Nyx had been here, she had gotten used to Suri's unyielding conviction to her unseen gods and to her sight as the clan's seer. Suri described her sight like seeing behind a curtain—only for a fleeting moment and not necessarily seeing what she wanted.

As she looked to Suri, a pull of jealousy ran through Nyx—she wished she had such conviction and optimism after years of eluding Adair. Chewing on the inside of her cheek, Nyx didn't know what she believed in anymore, and her grief threatened to drown her beneath it, again. Swallowing hard, she nodded as Suri ushered them inside.

The living room was empty, cleared except for the bowl in the middle of the table with a delicate flower resting in it, its inky petals like velvet.

The air seemed to disappear. Kyrie stopped at her side, giving her arm a squeeze, his voice gentle as he said, "Remember, we will be with you every step of the way. But are you certain of this?"

Words died in her mouth, but Nyx nodded tightly, grabbing the bowl.

Suri looked ethereal, her inky hair loosely plaited back, her honey skin glowing flawlessly as she led the way, her silver eyes churning with excitement. "Trust me, Nyx, everything will be okay."

It was all Nyx could do to command her feet to move. Like ghosts, they moved through the house, and then Suri opened the back door.

The world exploded in a sea of blackness. Raiders filed in from the streets, the crowd in front of them startling. They bowed their heads upon seeing Nyx and the twins. The sun clung in the clear skies, beating down, searing Nyx's bruised and weathered skin.

Everything ripped from her as Nyx locked her gaze with the crystal tomb, her heart pounding. Memphis could have been sleeping. His pale hair soft, his features peaceful. The raiders had used a preservation magic, so after his body was clean, it wouldn't deteriorate, keeping him in his crystal tomb for this moment.

Nyx faltered, and a hush fell across the desert.

A strangled moan broke through her lips. Tears she didn't know she had left slipped down her cheeks. Nyx couldn't move; she couldn't breathe. *He died on the promise of an alliance. The promise of working toward a life of peace.*

Trembling, she was thrown back through time, to a room where a commander had given her a choice to join the *famous*

Academy. Nyx had been half dead, but Memphis had saved her, the Academy giving her purpose when she was lost. And she had loved him, would have done anything for him. Now, for him, she would dig deep, finding the sheer will to keep going, to fuel her.

Jutting her chin out, Nyx walked down the aisle, Kyrie and Suri flanking her sides. The crowd parted as she reached Memphis's tomb. Gently placing the bowl at her feet, she drank in the clear skies and rushing heat—small comforts before the ripples of war finally found them.

She reached out, her palms connecting with the smooth surface as light flared underneath them. "Rest now, Memph. I'm so sorry it came to this."

Nyx could hear Suri murmuring incantations under her breath; heat surged, racing up Nyx's forearms. Kyrie stood beside her, whispering too. White flames ran along the casket, the last looks of Memphis shimmering before her.

"Whatever you do, don't break the connection. Or else his spirit won't be able to find *rishe*. He won't be able to be at peace," Suri instructed.

Nyx nodded tightly, the flames grew, and the crystal started to hum, the energy pulsing up her arm. Trembling, Nyx held the connection as everything turned to a blinding light.

The tomb turned to dust as the fire roared, sweeping up toward the sky. Nyx staggered back, and Kyrie grabbed her hand, squeezing it hard when tears started down her face. It was chaotic and beautiful, the crystal shards flaring under the sun, a thousand colors searing down to the ground below.

The entirety of the Dust Clan bowed their heads as Suri's smooth voice rose, the sound achingly haunting.

Kyrie's voice filled Nyx's memory, one of his many lessons about the Dust Clans: *One's soul needs help finding the doorway to* rishe. *In our culture, the god of fire, Danu, receives them if they are reborn from the white flame, leading the soul to the afterlife.*

Blinking up into the sun, she wasn't sure if she believed in this Danu, but she hoped that wherever Memphis was now, he would find his rest.

Letting go of her hand, Kyrie held her gaze, a fierceness steeling within them both.

It was time.

Her nervousness started like a heartbeat, low and powerful.

Stepping forward, Suri finished her lament on a clear, high note before bowing her head to meet Nyx. "Nyx Astire of Black Dawn, you came to the Dust Clans for aid in the war against King Adair. You came to us, freeing us from the binds Zander had created through his maliciousness and hate. Freeing us from a life of hatred, repeating a bloody history. You come to us now, bearing your own wounds for all. Now, do you accept the terms of our tradition, to survive the trials presented by Danu? That only after you have succeeded can you become leader of the raiders?"

"I do."

Suri pushed forward, coming eye to eye with Nyx. "State now who you wish to protect your body in case you shall fail."

"Both of you, Suri and Kyrie Oijen."

With a shallow nod, Suri picked up the bowl, white flames licking the edges. She held it out, saying, "Breathe in the sacred flower of maire. This plant is grown within the generations of our leaders, passed down for centuries. It is the portal, a channel, to raw power. Some even say to other worlds. It is there you will answer your test, Nyx, to see if you are worthy to be our leader."

Nyx's heart stopped at Suri's words, at the tales of their tradition. The tendrils of smoke rose toward the breaching afternoon light as Nyx whispered, "Suri, where does this flower grow?"

"The Arken Mountains."

Adrenaline flooded her body. Lowering herself, Nyx breathed in deeply, the smoke filling her nostrils, her throat, her body.

And then she fell.

Lurching, she felt her *spirit* rip from her body, tumbling through time, through space, becoming another entity. The maire swirled on her tongue, drying her mouth.

Wind howled around her before Nyx slammed onto the hard earth. Dust swirled as she coughed and heaved. Confused, she stood, reaching for her blade, which was not there. Slowly, her surroundings came into view: the arena that haunted her every moment. There were no torches or leering crowd. No Zander. No Memphis.

Alone, she shivered, every sense pricked up against the quiet. Her pulse thundered—she was unsure of who or what she waited for.

The crack split across the pit, spinning, sending her heart in her throat as Nyx stared at the body slowly coming into view.

CHAPTER FIFTEEN

BROKK

With the Black Sea crashing around them, Brokk looked to the smoke curling up toward the stars, blotting them out like ink spilling from a well. He was barely able to breathe as the veil and orders that clutched his mind lessened, inch by inch.

Their ship raced, the wind behind their backs.

The sounds of war haunted them, haunted *him*, from the Shattered Isles.

"Brokk." Kiana's voice was hard. Expectant.

Riona slowly twirled her hammer beside him, murmuring, "What the sweet hell happened?"

Swallowing, he bowed to the emptiness as his mind connected the dots, his heart sinking with every realization. "We got played. From the beginning. Emory . . ." Swallowing past his horror, Brokk spat, "The necklace. When she killed Adair, his ability got trapped in the necklace. Somehow, she has his ability now. She knew I wouldn't leave her." He looked toward the Isles. "So, she made us. Now, we can go to the Rebellion because of the tolls they have already paid."

"Marquis told you about Memphis?" Riona asked.

Kiana blinked, ignoring Riona, and whispered, "And in the meantime, Emory used herself to bond the Isles and gained their trust in time to rally against the Oilean."

Brokk nodded. "Creating a diversion, using her . . . ability to get us out." He paused. "And yes, Riona, I know about Memphis."

Kiana and Riona sidled up to either side of him, gingerly placing their hands over his, not saying anything more. Tears pricked his eyes.

The waves crashed, bleeding into their silence, adrenaline slamming his heart against his ribcage. Another explosion thundered out to them, and Brokk flinched. How many more lies? How many times would everyone have to be completely broken before their world could mend? As he clenched the rail, the wood splintered beneath his grip, beneath the ripples of rage flowing through him and masking his grief. Becoming cold and addicting.

"Brokk?" Kiana asked.

How many years had he spent his entire life wondering what his future would hold? And then, when his future was only the darkness, how many times had he promised himself he was above it all? That life was worth fighting for? That the lives he had taken wouldn't mean anything?

He was different, after all. Being tortured, he had clung desperately to his reasons. The Rebellion, their hope. Emory, their fearless weapon. His friends, his family he had chosen, blood not tying them but love. He never had forgotten . . .

. . . until now.

As he looked to the night sky, it bled red, a distant reflection of the war Emory was now fighting. *Without him.* The betrayal cut deep. Those reasons Brokk had held so fiercely to his heart began to slowly slip, leaving him in the darkness Emory had created.

"Brokk, what *now*?" Kiana's frustration pooled in her words.

"We sail to Nehmai. We bring the refugees there, where they will be safest. Where we can begin to rebuild." He stiffened. "As for us, a change of plans."

Riona perked up, eyeing him.

"We won't sail to the Risco Desert on the whispers of Marquis Maher. For all we know, it's a dead end. I say we bring this war to the Dark King, while he has his attentions elsewhere. Nyx can lead the raiders to us if we make ourselves apparent in Kiero."

"Now that's what I'm talking about," Riona exclaimed.

Kiana scowled at her sister. "We don't have an army."

"To our knowledge, neither does he. Why hasn't he come yet? Why aren't militias of thousands marching through Kiero? Why haven't we heard a word since a couple weeks ago? He is either waiting for something, or he *can't* leave."

Chewing her lip, Kiana paced. "It's an unnecessary risk."

"I'm tired of waiting for the day someone else figures out a way to end this all. Emory made her choice. She made it a thousand times over. It's time I start doing the same. The Rebellion is still a priority; we will find them. But to start, let's end the Dark King. I'm tired of running."

Exhaling, Kiana pinched the bridge of her nose. "Fine. *Fine.* But we do this *together.*"

His heart felt encased in ice. Brokk breathed, "I wouldn't have it any other way."

Riona and Kiana dove into plans, and as he listened, Brokk couldn't rip his eyes away from the blood-red night sky. Their voices faded, white noise falling away with the lulling of the waves, memories overcoming him.

You and I, always.

Emory's voice, her promise. Just a lie layered on another lie. She had manipulated his heart. Brokk had risked his life, time after time, thrown away his soul, bound himself to her, and for *what?*

Tearing himself away from the railing, Brokk stormed through the crowds of shivering people, through the crew jumping to action while Diedre shouted orders. The temperature had dropped, and his ragged breath was no more than misty puffs. One thought chased his heels. One thought fueled the energy licking through his body.

That maybe, just maybe, becoming a monster would not be so hard after all.

CHAPTER SIXTEEN

NYX

Azarius Walsh looked just as confused as she felt. His flaming-red hair deepened in the sunlight, making the spattering of freckles on his face more evident. His skin paled. Her heart sank as she took in his bloodied clothes while he slowly walked toward her.

"Nyx?" he breathed, a slight tremor running through his hand, his body.

Breath hitching, she swiveled, looking around. Kyrie and Suri would be watching over her body, she knew. She trusted them. But where was *she*?

"How are you *here*?"

He shrugged. "I should be asking you the same thing! You do know this is . . . some sort of dreamscape, right? In between reality . . . and whatever this is?"

Huffing, she threw her hands out. "You're interrupting my initiation to becoming the raiders' leader, you know."

Running his hand over his mouth, Azarius stopped, shaking his head. "I didn't peg you for the sacred type. You and Memphis are still with the raiders?"

A beat and then another passed as if the entire world were frozen.

"Nyx? You and Memphis are okay, right?"

Nyx bit her quivering lip hard, drawing blood. "Memphis knew coming to the raiders would mean a slim chance of survival for him. He didn't tell me. The old leader here . . . had it out for him since the second we arrived."

Azarius stilled.

"The clans are different. They're dictated by tradition, no matter the cost. Memphis *knew* that. He demanded a trial, one that would ensure an alliance if we won."

"You didn't win."

Nyx stumbled over the words. "Memphis was k-killed. I ensured his murderer answered the same fate."

"And in the same swoop, getting the Rebellion allied with the raiders by becoming their leader."

Her heart sank at the cost. When would it stop, this vicious circle of mistakes, of having to live with the consequences, always alone?

She nodded, watching Azarius pale further.

"Nyx, I'm sorry—"

"Save it. Now, tell me something good before time runs out."

His silence hit her like wave, pushing the air out of her lungs.

Azarius's head suddenly snapped up, his eyes growing wide. Closing the space between them, he grabbed her shoulders, each word like a blow. "Listen to me, Nyx. Our time is over. Wait for us. Wait for me. We're coming."

A dust storm slammed into them, wiping the scene clean, ripping Azarius from her. Choking, Nyx stumbled, grappling for anything to hold on to. Her entire world was a giant churning mass. She screamed as sand filled her nose, clotted her throat, blinded her.

Any light flickered out, and she dropped to her knees. Nyx screamed again against her clothes being ripped, her hair being pulled loose from its plait.

There was a hard tug. She slammed onto the ground, and her ribs cracked. Coughing, she spat out the brittle sand mixed with saliva, dry heaving. The heaviness of the desert was wiped clean, and the first thing Nyx noticed was the air. Clean, light, airy—nothing that clung like the warm aroma of the woods or the dry heat of the desert.

Blinking hard against the sudden light, Nyx stood on shaky legs. Heart dropping into her stomach, she took in the Arken Mountain Range, instantly transported to another lifetime. The mountains were looming, stretching up so high that even when she craned her neck, they pierced through the clouds, disappearing.

There was the mouth of a lone cave ahead of her. The crumbling gray rock was weathered, the mouth waning into pitch black the farther it went. Warily, she bounced on her toes, trying to keep her blood roaring instead of letting the pain in. Pushing Azarius's words from her mind, she stated to the cold air, "I can do this. I *will* do this."

All around her, forest stretched, snow clinging to the branches, encasing the world like glass. She was *freezing*, still in the satin clothing geared toward the unrelenting heat of the desert. She rubbed her arms, trying to stay warm, and timeless silver leaves trilled around her, chiming like bells, calling to her. This reminded her of that night in the Forgotten Bogs and the stranger who sought her out. The beenighe. Was this out-of-body experience another moment before a dream became a tangible reality? Or another warning?

Desperately wishing for her regular assortment of blades, she sent a silent plea to anyone listening before walking into the mouth of the cave. Flickers of silver streaked in her vision, then she was met with the inky blackness—and she plummeted.

Screaming, Nyx spun, limbs flailing, trying to feel anything, to grip anything. And for a second time, in a matter of minutes, she slammed against a smooth surface. Coughing, the copper tang of blood filling her mouth, Nyx stood on shaky legs.

"What in the blasted hells . . ."

A white flame sparked to life before her, and all words died on her tongue as she focused on the scene breathing into life in front of her.

The mural was massive. The expanse of the cave was transformed with paints, her heart stopping at the scene.

"Welcome, Nyx," a familiar voice said behind her.

Jumping, she twisted, all thoughts and retorts dying on her lips.

Memphis stood behind her, solemn, but his cerulean eyes were warm and welcoming.

"Memphis?" She threw her arms around him. His familiar musk filled her, sending shivers down her spine. "How is this possible? How are you *here*?" She was breathing in too hard, too fast.

He hugged her fiercely, and his breath tickled her ear. "I don't have much time. But you must listen to me. This is it. Nyx, you have come so *far*. And have been incredibly brave. You know that, right?"

Letting him go, she took him in. He wore a simple white shirt and black pants; his hair was tied back. "Being brave has nothing to do with it. Memphis, I can't forgive myself for what happened to you. I should have stopped Zander. I should have tried harder."

A whip-like crack echoed through the cave, loose rocks falling from the ceiling as the ground beneath Nyx's boots trembled. Stumbling, she looked at the mural; the colors were swirling, becoming sharper with every second.

Memphis stepped closer. "Nyx, listen to me. This ancient magic pulls at your hardest trials. Think about it. What is your weakness? What would the maire prey on? What does it mean for you to rise, to become a leader? What secrets must you face?"

Heart pumping, Nyx turned, squinting through the glow of the fire. The mural raced; her life splayed before her in heart-wrenching detail—the past she had suppressed into nothing more than a whisper. Her eternal nightmare. The weight of facing it now brought Nyx to her knees.

The green flames were so realistic; Nyx was thrown back within the memory. How the ash had fallen like snowflakes when Adair's soldiers came. Her community was erased in the blink of an eye. Living in the Arken Mountains had fed her soul, but now every dream of building a life there with her sister was gone.

Harper's face shone back at her, the painting capturing her honey skin; her tumbling, thick golden hair; her tattoos of constellations tracing from her throat and traveling up to her cheekbones. How many years had Nyx tucked this memory close to her heart, not breathing Harper's name aloud? Nyx had drained Harper's memory, killing it in herself as well. Harper had been her twin flame whom she had told her closest secrets to—the older sister she had looked up to.

Most of the rebels at the Academy had forgotten what it meant to allow themselves to remember *life* before Adair had begun his reign. To hold on to the lives they all had before.

Next to Harper's portrait was an image of Nyx traveling back through the forest, Adair's soldiers trailing behind her, unseen in the shadows. How carefree she had been, entering their home, greeting Harper, her warm laughter welcoming her back.

Harper had been the first to die.

"I don't want this. I never wanted any of this to happen!"

The walls around them cracked, rock falling more vigorously. Memphis stood before her now, pity blooming in his gaze. "Stop living your life bound by your demons, Nyx. It's time to be free of them." Memphis's lips tugged upward before the white flames roared, then he disappeared.

The chuckle that echoed around her was low and dark. Another figure emerged from the side of the cave, coming to meet her.

The trial had finally begun.

Harper swung a blackened blade lazily, her grin razor sharp. Pain laced through Nyx, like her stomach was being gutted, heat flaring and ice running through all her nerve endings at once. Tears slipped from the corners of her eyes as she backed away, whispering, "No. Absolutely not."

More of the cave fell away, crashing around them, the earth shaking beneath her feet. The mural spun, growing on the cavern's wall, surrounding Nyx and Harper. Snippets of the years without her sister glared in the background, glowing in the white flame.

"Why are you here?" Nyx's voice was hoarse, as if she had been screaming for hours.

"Why do you think?"

Taking in Harper, Nyx tried to memorize her face illuminated in the dancing flames. Nyx had failed her, and now, standing in the crumbling cave, Nyx wasn't ready to admit that. After Harper had been murdered, Nyx had broken, never quite healing. She became guarded—cold and rigid—the exact opposite of what she had once been.

The ground shook beneath her more intensely. As she clenched her fists, Nyx's mind raced, her heart pounding beneath her ribcage. Nyx *knew* what she had to do. To escape this nightmare, to allow herself to face her past, she had to save Harper.

In doing so, she would forgive herself and let go of her guilt, of the pain that was eating away at her. The fire flared, and Harper charged, more rocks crashing around her.

Nyx spotted a pair of luminous eyes in the corner, flaring.

She sprinted, intention filling her entire core. *Don't make the same mistake again.* Sweat snaked down her spine as she wove, flying over the debris. Harper laughed at the shadows, confident, unafraid. She always had been.

Screaming, Nyx collided with the monster, fists tearing at its rancid flesh, her skin scorching at the touch. In the flickering darkness, she couldn't make out much besides gleaming teeth and razor-sharp claws. A low chuckle rumbled through the cave as her screams climbed, a breath suddenly hot on her neck.

She looked up, and the world tilted, Adair's dark gaze piercing into her.

"Hello there."

Shrieking, Nyx slammed her fist toward his jaw but only met air. Panting, she twisted, the shadows churning, the cavern swallowed by flames, encompassing her. Panicked, Nyx curled into herself, breathing hard through clenched teeth. Harper's voice filled her mind. Every second, Nyx slipped like she had on that day, watching the blade pierce Harper's heart. Watching her body fall. Watching Harper slip through her fingers.

Nyx had done *nothing.*

In the distance, drums pounded, and she didn't know if it was the memories drowning her or something else. What was reality, and what was nightmare? Coughing, she staggered, reaching out while rocks crashed around her—she caught a chunk of Harper's thick hair.

"HARPER!"

Adair smirked at her, appearing behind Harper. He grabbed Harper's face, tearing her back, slamming her against his chest. Nyx screamed as his blade slid into her sister's back, protruding out of her chest . . .

The ground was ripped out from underneath Nyx when she was still running, trying to reach them.

Harper's voice grazed around the edges of her mind. *The answer has always been here, Nyx. Come back and find it. Come home.*

Landing once again, Nyx stood warily, blinking against the sudden sunlight. She now stood in the middle of a barren desert. Tears rolled down her cheeks, her stomach turning. With trembling hands, Nyx curled her fingers into fists. *I ensured Harper's memory would haunt me. How could I bury her so deep?*

Wiping her cheeks, looking up to the shimmering sun far above, Nyx almost thought she was back with Kyrie and Suri.

"Nyx Astire, you have come."

That voice. Slowly, Nyx turned, and she was transported once again back to that night in the Forgotten Bogs, to the ancient magic that had bled through the night. The tang of it collided with her senses.

"So, we meet again."

The cloaked figure lowered her hood, and Nyx stopped. A youthful woman stood before her, not at all the demon Nyx had made up in her mind.

Setting her chin, Nyx stalked toward her. "Has it always been you, then? In the Bogs? Bringing me to this place? What the bleeding hells do you want?"

"The maire is a projection of personal trauma. Of pain. What you saw before me, you have been carrying. I'm only here to get what I want, and we don't have much time. Call this a crossroads, if you must."

The heat rose, climbing, but goosebumps ran along Nyx's skin. "A crossroads of *what* exactly?"

"The world is burning, falling into shadow. What if I said it was possible for me to help you end this war? In return for something, of course."

She could hardly breathe. "What?"

"Come now, Nyx. Think about it. Memphis lied to you for years, using you only to discard you when he got Emory back. The entire Rebellion, a waste, only for Emory to go to the enemy. Where is she now? Where is Brokk? Your friends have left you on a whim that you can pull out an alliance to win this war. What if I could help you more than they could? What if I know where the only weapon is?"

Trying to stop her shaking hands, Nyx said, "Azarius is coming for me. Lana. Alby. I'm not forgotten."

"Who do you think gave Azarius and Alby the ability to find you?" the woman asked.

"Who are *you*?"

"A friend."

"That's so specific. I'm definitely going to trust you now," Nyx shot back sarcastically.

The woman chuckled. "I always did admire your spirit. Especially in someone who carries such agony."

"Everyone has pain. My mistake has been allowing it to make me forget my past, forget what is important. But I highly doubt there is some secret *weapon* that will give us an advantage."

"If you genuinely believe that, then please leave. Kyrie and Suri await you. Your life as leader of the raiders awaits you."

"Tell me what you know," Nyx shot back.

Flames shone in the stranger's hazel eyes. "As I said, you have a choice."

She should walk away. Go back and accept her title. But what was the worth of an alliance if they were destined to lose? Her gut screamed at her to walk away, but she was entranced. "Tell me who you are."

"Ancient magic once divided Kiero before men. Centuries ago, I thought I had died, but my magic preserved me. I had been asleep for a long time, until something stirred. A magic reawakened, and here I find myself toying with the threads of humans for years. You should know that Adair Stratton is dead. A stronger enemy than you could ever fathom has surfaced." She paused. "I find myself asking, what world do I have if this Dark King wins the war? I have done everything for *you*. I want to ensure that the world thrives once more, but the Oilean and their *king* are leeching it. Trying to bleed our world dry."

The news hit like a knife, shredding through the last bit of hope Nyx was clinging to.

The woman was so close to her now, almost nose to nose with her. "How do you think this Dark King is even in Kiero? How do you think it went after you left Pentharrow? The Oilean were waiting for the Rebellion in the Draken Mountains."

The stone in her stomach dropped, sinking further.

"I can tell you everything that I know, Nyx. I can help you gain the tools you need to defeat the spreading darkness. All I ask for in return is something small."

"What do you want?"

Licking her lips, the woman leaned in closer, whispering, "You. I want you, Nyx."

"What do you mean?" Nyx took a step back, a cold sweat breaking out on her forehead.

"I have been trapped, bound to the Forgotten Bogs. Centuries ago, I was somehow cursed, my soul bound here, eluding death. Magic has always worked in peculiar ways." Her smirk was razor sharp as the stranger continued, "I want to rebuild my sisters, and your soul burns with such a *fire*, it's intoxicating. You could help free me—the price is your mortal soul. Become immortal, giving this curse that binds me something to sate its hunger. Your soul, to end it all.

"Before kings and queens took over Kiero, there was a service that was the deepest form of respect. My name is Hesen, and I am a warrior of Nehmai. I awoke in the Forgotten Bogs, able to protect the borders against the darkness that is sweeping over the lands. I have been watching you, Nyx Astire, and in return for my help, I want you to bow, to become an immortal warrior, forever swearing to protect Kiero. It's a sisterhood that was ruined by another war generations ago."

Time stood still.

Hesen stepped closer, hazel eyes flaring. "Haven't you searched your entire life for your purpose? You have the raiders behind you, but after this war, do you really want to swear your life to the Dust Clans? Lead them to victory, and then pass the torch . . . I have seen your soul, Nyx Astire. I have walked your dreams." Hesen's hand reached up, cupping Nyx's cheek as she sobbed. "The wildness in you isn't your weakness but your strength. Your loyalty has not been your downfall but your liberation. Your heart isn't your enemy, but your guide to recognize that you have tried your best given the circumstances. Is it such a bad thing to be a part of something bigger than you could have imagined? Could have dreamed?"

Your soul in exchange to free this land. Your soul.

Stepping away, Nyx hiccupped. "And how do I know you're telling the truth?"

Waving her hand, Hesen looked pointedly at Nyx as a pool erupted in between them, the water smooth as glass. Swallowing, Nyx recognized the pool. "You wish for me to look in the future?"

Hesen shook her head, a sly smile on her lips. "I wish for you to look into *my* past."

"I . . . What more do I have to lose, right?"

Nyx sank to her knees, lowering her face over the water, so close that ripples disrupted the surface from her breath.

CHAPTER SEVENTEEN

EMORY

The Shattered Isles had been sliced down to their marrow and were bleeding out. Crouching behind a boulder for a reprieve, Emory shook from the sheer exertion of her ability, of energy, of every little piece of her soul thrown into this battle. Screams rained down all around her, the fight having raged in the infernal night, and from what Emory could make out, they were losing.

An explosion erupted to her left. Bits of rock and dirt flew, making Emory cringe. In front of the boulder, a man from the Isles staggered into view. Drenched in blood and sweat, the man trembled, walking in circles, his sword in front of him. Emory tensed, preparing to lunge to rally with the soldier when a dabarne sprang from the shadows.

Emory watched in horror as an emerald-green gas seeped from the creature's open jaws. Swirling, the gas surged into the man's open mouth and through his eyes. His body spasmed, and the dabarne released him, turning and disappearing in the night. Emory took a step back, the man blinking at her with pitch-black eyes.

He's gone. Turned into a mindless puppet for the Oilean. His skin warped, like it was being stretched too tight, and blackened veins she was all too familiar with ravaged him. He turned, and Emory's stomach twisted as she saw exposed bone, the flesh torn from his cheekbones.

The Oilean's most desired way of killing was to thrive off their victims, feeding off corpses or turning them into weapons.

Forcing her body to comply, Emory stood, Anithe poised in front of her. Trying not to focus on the pools of blood and gore that now soaked into the earth, she treaded carefully. Bodies of the fallen men and women of the Shattered Isles had started to pile up, mixed in with the skeletons of the stags and wolves. Everywhere Emory looked, she saw the discarded, empty husks of the fallen. How had she been so confident that they would win?

We never had the advantage. The thought was ugly and loud, guilt sinking into her core.

A growl sounded through the night; Emory barely had time to react. A dabarne flew at her, yellow eyes gleaming, claws outstretched toward her throat. Ducking, Emory landed heavily on her right knee, swinging Anithe in a curve, the steel cutting into the underbelly of the monster. Hot blood coated her skin, intestines falling from the wound. The dabarne howled, collapsing behind her.

Shaking, she wiped her eyes, trying not to throw up. Ahead of her, a massive crevice in the middle of the grotto was filled with green flames roaring toward the starless sky. Emory scoured the plain and the never-ending night. *Now. Go, Em. Go.*

She shoved past her pain and the numbness, and her fear kept her alert as she ran. How many times had she *thought* about war, ignited by politics and greed, about the thousands of people who had served their countries on Earth? How it must feel to bleed for the world and for your freedom. To die for it. Emptiness and sadness had welled in her for the sacrifices made on Earth, from the first world war to the second, so that the generations that followed may live a better quality of life.

Now, she was being torn by magic, by power and politics. But as she ran into the thick of the fight, her love for Kiero resonated deeply within her core. That slow-burning fire fueled her fighting for the chance that survivors would live to strive for a better world than what her parents had left behind.

A flash of silver was her only warning, a blade that appeared from nowhere slamming down toward her neck. Grunting, Emory blocked the attack at the last second, the impact shuddering up her arm. Her eyes flickered down to see a black boot slamming against her chest, sending her flying.

"Em? EMORY!"

Wheezing, she tried to focus on catching her breath through the fire spreading too fast in her left lung. Her vision swam as she felt the sticky blood fill under her armor, her ability swelling, trying to heal the wound. The broken rib sent searing pain through her chest, and Emory tried not to throw up.

"Emory, *black skies*, I thought you were gone. I thought everyone else was gone."

Standing before her, Marquis looked guilty that he had kicked her. His armor matched hers, once silver but now spattered with black blood. His words wrapped around her like a wall.

He offered his hand to help her up, and Emory leaned heavily on him, regripping Anithe. Stabbing pain laced up her side like fire searing through her ribcage. Commanding her ability to heal the broken bone quicker, Emory tried to breathe.

"I would hug you if we weren't in the middle of this bleeding war," he said.

She coughed and her chuckle was dark as she shook her head. "I told you. Marquis, the others . . .?"

"Gone. I haven't seen anyone alive, and the Oilean . . ."

"*Emory Fae.*" In a whisper, her world disappeared.

Disoriented, she blinked against the empty world around her. The room was still, but those black marble walls sent her reeling. Declan sat on the broken throne, toe tapping, looking amused. Bodies were strewn on the floor all around him, their empty husks gray and shriveled up. Emory's breath hitched in her throat.

"Well, well, Queen. It looks like we meet again."

Trying to ignore the pit growing in her stomach, Emory assessed him. Adair's eyes stared back at her. His body, the familiar quirk of his mouth. She seethed. "It's over. Stop playing me, and let's talk."

By fire and flame. His lips peeled back over his teeth in a sickening grin. She wanted to cry, memories of Adair assaulting her like a rising tide.

"Your friends dying is good motivation for you. But I knew we would talk soon anyways. You like being coy, don't you? My assault of nightmares usually breaks people down first, but not you. This place, between reality and dreams, is only ours, you know." He sighed. "The darkness that I command and that you are suppressing has its perks, doesn't it? Each time you think you have escaped me, I have always been watching. I will always be there. Because you have a part of *me* running through you veins. We are connected, Emory, in the most intimate of ways."

"What do you *want*?"

The Dark King stretched, and his gaze swept over the room, over the bodies. "You know, I was confused at first, why it was so *hard* to break into this world. My assassins, the Oilean, had been stuck here for years, biding their time and preparing this vessel for me. I was dying in our old world—Daer. You can imagine my thrill of finally being able to come here. But it strikes me—the passion in this world, for survival. To fight against your certain doom."

They were eye to eye now. Nose to nose. Anger fueled her bravery. "You will never have this world. *Never*."

His fingers brushed her chin, then up along her cheek in a caress. He had moved so fast, she flinched. "Trust me, before this war is done, you will come to me. Now go and fight, my queen. Go bleed and be ravished. I won't deny, I am enjoying this."

Slamming out of the reality, Emory puked as she felt the wet ground beneath her once more. The waves of the Black Sea crashed in the distance. It was jarring to be back in the thick of the battle.

The throne room was gone in a whisper, but the Dark King's voice lingered, sinking its claws into her soul.

"My queen, you will come."

"EMORY!" Marquis's scream wrenched her to the present as she rolled, an inky blade sinking into the earth right where she had been. The wind cut through the blanket of darkness, howling like a pack of wolves. The Oilean stood above her, blades pointed at her heart.

"You thought you could hide from us? You have lost, Emory Fae. And your army was *delicious* to devour. Especially the leaders from the clans. Terdes Harbor has fallen. Oakland Wharf has fallen. Harbor of Newsoll has fallen. And Hriste is next."

The taunting words sank into her, acid clawing up her throat. Diving into her ability, she rode on her exhaustion. Her power rippled out through the ground, acting as an electric current right before it slammed into the Oilean. Emory watched as the black smoke drifted up their feet, over their legs and arms, down their weapons. Freezing them, caging them.

She frantically found her feet and grabbed Marquis's hand. She pulled hard, and they fled; Emory didn't know how long she could hold the Oilean.

"Come on, Marquis!"

Between her half-healed wounds and Marquis's weight, they were being slowed down.

There were too many faceless bodies, the war raging around them still; they had no clue who was still fighting for their life. There was a crack like thunder, and the Oilean materialized in front of them.

Skidding to a halt, Emory shoved Marquis away from her. "Run. Survive. But *run.*"

It was the last thing she could think of. The Oilean wanted *her.* War had come because of the power she bore; she could do this one more act. To save Marquis. Her hope diminished, ripping her apart.

There weren't any more options. Her last bit of light sailed off this island hours ago. She had killed Adair and come back into this world, this war. Her parents tried so hard to make their family sit on a pedestal as Kiero's fearless leaders.

It was time for all that to end.

Raising Anithe, her arms shook as the Oilean growled. Emory was starting to understand what it meant when she had left Black Dawn Rebellion—what the true cost of her sacrifice was.

"You have exceeded yourself, young queen."

"This isn't over yet." Her voice was hoarse.

Her heart leaped in her throat as Marquis's voice floated out behind her.

"Really, I thought you would all be taller. You know, since I have heard how dark and menacing you are. It's rare anyone truly lives up to expectation. Emory here is a perfect example of that."

The Oilean's hisses floated around them as Emory spat at Marquis, "I thought I told you to go."

"I'm not abandoning you."

There wasn't enough time for her to react, to digest. The Oilean pounced, bones cracking, their limbs moving jerkily. Their teeth elongated, curving over their lips in black fangs. Their wrists broke and reset, their nails growing into razor-sharp talons. Screaming, Emory jumped, slashing Anithe up, slicing through the belly of the closest demon. Black blood poured out before Emory was thrown back. Claws sliced through her right side, from her ribcage down to her hip bone. Blood poured freely onto the dirt.

Emory screamed, and the Oilean pressed her clawed hand harder against Emory's chest. "I can tasssste it in your blood. Our power. I will drain you slowly, just like the rest of your pathetic army." Lowering her marred face to Emory's wound, she licked the blood.

Panic clawed up Emory's throat, bubbling from her lips, and it was all she could do to punch and kick, trying to buck the Oilean off her. Anithe had been dropped in her fall, and her nails ripped at dirt and rock, trying to find the hilt.

"Stop fighting. Come back to me. Come back."

Always Declan's voice. Adair or the Dark King, it was always the same. Never allowing her to heal, to let go of the friend she once had. Had once loved. Always haunting her waking steps and her nightmares.

Emory threw a punch that connected with wet flesh, and the pressure on her chest was alleviated. Blood ran down her clothes, but her ability charged like an electric current running under her skin. She dipped further into that deep well, healing her body. Frantically, she tried to spot Marquis.

Running, he emerged from the shadows, gripping Anithe in hand. "Em, now!" he yelled.

Anithe flew through the air, and in the same motion, droplets of water materialized from the ground. Marquis's brows furrowed as the water went flying toward the four Oilean.

Anithe clattered to the ground in front of her, and Emory scooped the sword up. Under her hold, black and deep-purple embers pulsed within the steel, flames reigniting along Anithe's blade. Sweat beaded on Emory's skin as she set her next intention, imagining the fire from Anithe growing, surging toward the Oilean.

The churning water slammed into the Oilean first as the fire grew, building a wall between them and Emory. Steam hissed, the gurgled screams of the Oilean soon drowned out. They maybe had seconds, and Emory already felt her grip on the flames waning.

"Marquis, I'm hoping you have a plan?"

His back slammed into hers, and she could feel his body shivering as they both watched the water turn to ash, the Oilean straightening. Their empty eye sockets seemed to grow, their growls cutting into the night, black flames now turning green.

Emory felt her hold being tugged away.

"My plan? Survive this broken kingdom together. Survive this *together*."

His words struck Emory as a plea or a prayer to anyone listening. But as the Oilean sprang toward them, she stood by Marquis, facing hell with him. Her friend.

The line between her ability and her physical self was barely there anymore. Emory urged the flames toward each demon—it did little to delay them. Their own green flames ran along the ground toward them. The heat made her blanch.

Their blades collided, sparks flying from the impact. Three Oilean attacked Marquis, his yells lost under their snarls. Emory slammed Anithe's hilt into the Oilean facing her, and its head snapped back. Then Emory attacked. Steel sliced the Oilean's knees, making the Oilean buckle. Green gas oozed from her mouth, her screams clawing up into the moonless night. Emory swung Anithe with all the strength she had left, and the steel passed cleanly through the Oilean's neck.

The body collapsed, the Oilean's head rolling.

Emory watched the remaining sisters freeze, watching the blackened blood pour onto the earth. The green flames encircled them and swallowed the corpse, the headless Oilean becoming nothing more than ash.

Watching the inferno of her flames incinerate one of her enemies sparked Emory's defiance, her blood thundering in her ears. A sliver of hope that they would walk away from this war unfurled within her.

Only three more to kill.

CHAPTER EIGHTEEN

BROKK

Brokk wasn't sure if time had no relevance anymore or if he had truly gone into shock. Sitting down in the bunker alone, he listened to the crashing of waves, the low murmurs of Kiana and Riona outside his room. Above deck, Diedre barked orders at the refugees from the Isles.

"Wash the deck!"

"Don't tie that knot like that!"

"Are you trying to ensure you go overboard?"

Under different circumstances, he would have found her barking orders amusing. Now it only reminded him of a lifetime ago when he and Memphis had tried to run a rebellion.

He sighed and his frown deepened. He ran his hands over his face. How was it possible to feel so run down, so tired that it was bone deep, leeching everything out of him, and yet he had to go on? How could he find strength when there wasn't anything left to take from?

All of this was a constant reminder to him that they had been there with *her*. That Emory had, once again, sacrificed herself.

As he exhaled hard, the lack of sleep made Brokk's eyes burn and twitch. If he rested for a second, Emory flashed behind his eyes, the last look on her face pleading with him to understand. Her lips on his. How it had felt, those hours long into the night, tracing his fingers down her side, curving over her hip bones. Their bodies moving as one. How she said she loved him.

He had continued to be loyal, to allow himself to fall more deeply in love, to choose to believe in what she had said, but in turn, she had used her promises as weapons. Shattering his hold on everything Brokk thought he believed in. He was left now with a fury that consumed him, addicting and unrelenting. *She trusted her secret with Marquis more than you.*

Anger and jealousy licked in the pit of his stomach; he stood too fast, slamming his head on the bunk bed. "Shit." He rubbed the back of his head, the skin beneath his touch throbbing.

Riona leaned against the doorframe, arms crossed. "Hey there."

"Hey, yourself. I didn't hear you come in," he practically barked. His voice was hoarse from lack of use.

"Do you have a minute?"

Sitting back down, Brokk gestured to the empty opposing bed. "Like I have any other choice with you?"

A ghost of a smirk crossed her lips, and she raised her brows. "You know we are hours away from landing back in Kiero, right?"

Hours. Hours? How could he have let himself slip so violently into his own mind, retreating into a shadow for days? Trying to calm his raging heart, he nodded.

"Brokk, I'm going to be blunt. I didn't like you when I first met you. Generally, unlike my dear sister, I'm pessimistic and don't see the good in people. I'm fighting for a city the entire world has forgotten about. Our traditions. Our heroes. The war our warriors fought long before you were even alive. The kings and queens of

Nehmai have been erased. What do I owe Kiero? What did I even owe you? Nothing at all. I shouldn't have to potentially die in this bleeding war."

The waves crashed against their ship, and Riona paused, chewing her lip.

"Kiana annoyingly reminds me every day that our past can't weigh down our narrative. That even with us being separated for years, there is one thing no one can change for all of us."

"What's that?"

"We can start believing that maybe there is good in this world worth risking everything for."

Brokk huffed. "May I remind you—"

'I'm going to stop you right there. If you want to become our leader, if you want to go down that path, you and I know that you will. Kiana and I swore our lives to you a long time ago, and as naithe warriors, it's our honor to do so. Despite my general feelings toward humans, I can see the hope in you. Storming after Emory to the Isles was never the key. I don't know if storming into this Dark King's kingdom is smart, either."

"Are you going to be another person to tell me what I should do?"

"No. I'm just going to be that annoying voice making sure you *honestly believe* it's the right decision. I want to make sure you're not leading us to our deaths. And don't even begin to harp on me, saying that I don't know what you mean. You have found the truth of your past; allow it to fuel you and help shape your future. But I will be damned if I sit by and let you throw everything away because Emory broke your heart."

At his silence, Riona stood, for the first time looking awkward. "Lifetimes passed before I allowed myself to think Nehmai could have a bright future, Brokk Falkov. I'm begging you not to take that lightly."

Riona left the room and tugged the door closed behind her.

As Brokk cupped his head in his hands, the two halves of who he was crashed into one another. A rebel turned to royalty. He knew his anger was becoming a raw, monstrous thing. Ravenous, it begged to consume him. How many years had he convinced himself that it was *all for Emory*? He had the chance, now, to choose his path. Given the chance, would he let Emory go?

Lurching up, he paced, shivering even through his layers of clothes from the Shattered Isles. From his clothes to his memories, everything was a constant reminder that Emory had made him leave. He had never felt so powerless as he had in that moment. He had been her puppet. After everything, she had lied to him and forced him out.

No more.

Exhaling hard, Brokk dove into his second ability, and the bunker on the ship fell away. Traveling the channels was like flexing a muscle; each time Brokk wanted to access it, it got easier. His answers were in the glittering world in between reality and fantasy. At first, he wasn't sure what he was looking for. But he screamed down his mental connection, nestled between the present and past.

No more lies!

A thousand voices cascaded around him, a gentle hum encircling him, luring him in flares of breathtaking light.

Brokk.

He rushed toward the voice. Brilliant golds and silvers washed over the scene, and he blinked hard against the light flare. Slowly, more detailed shapes and objects flooded into view. The room was familiar and yet was as much of a ghost to him as his past.

Tracing his fingers over the wooden chairs, the smooth table edges, he looked at the woman cooing down at the baby in front of her. The bedroom was elegant, rich covers on the bed, the bay window overlooking the sprawling city below. Memories were strange, and his ability even stranger. Sometimes it was like he was watching a scene, but rarely was *he* in a place.

Recognizing the city, Brokk's heart lurched. Nehmai. Which meant—his *mother*. Meera.

"Brokk, you could have the entire world at your feet," Meera cooed right before a golden-haired man—likely Brokk's father, Kavan—sidled up beside her, breathing in her ear.

The memory slammed down, ripping him away from his parents, his home, his past, bleeding into the unknown again, and he was falling, blood pounding in his ears. Brokk grappled, trying to hold on to anything, but he was pushed down deeper, farther away. Like crashing waves, images spurted in front of him, just flickers at first, but then weaving together a more complex story, propelling him further into its depth.

Meera stood with her arms crossed, looking skeptically at the stranger. "Why should we trust you?"

Kavan paced behind her, his agitation overwhelming. "Meera, they know what we desire. Is what you are saying possible?"

The messenger cocked her head in a sickening movement.

"My king grows impatient. I have traveled great lengths from Daer on the whispers that you want a child. Now, do you agree to my king's terms or not? You can have the baby boy if you never tell him where he came from. You will tell your people here that the boy was born in Nehmai. You will never tell the child that he came from Daer. Never. Those are my king's terms."

Meera looked to Kavan, tears pricking her eyes. "Kavan, we could have a *child*. You know the news my healer brought. I'm not able to have children. Please do this. For me, for us."

Kavan's golden eyes looked to the messenger of Daer. "We agree. Bring us the child."

A deep tug pulled within his gut as Brokk was slammed out of the memory. The realization ripped him into threads as he screamed against the truth, against what he saw. He screamed until his throat was bloodied, until he fell, slamming back into the present moment, tears streaming down his face and over the scars, pattering on the wooden floor.

CHAPTER NINETEEN

MARQUIS

Marquis had been surprised to find that he trusted Emory Fae with his life. This queen brought back from the dead had surpassed his wildest daydreams of what he thought she would be able to handle. Gain his trust? An impossible feat. Survive his trials? No one ever had. Adjust to the politics of the Isles and surrounding clans? *He* hadn't even mastered that art.

But through the weeks, his wall slowly broke down until he saw a woman who was just as alone and lost as he was, and he found himself wobbling on the rope—the same rope he had walked with Adair. He *cared* about what happened to Emory. She had become his friend. Marquis often found that would lead him into situations he didn't want to find himself in.

Blood sprayed up along his arm, his sword splitting the Oilean's forearm open from her elbow to wrist. Howls cut through the air as Marquis fought his way back to Emory. His exhaustion mixed with his ripe fear; he could sense a losing fight. Emory's silver clothes were blackened with blood and gore, the remaining Oilean circling her.

The sister behind Marquis roared; he ran faster.

Baring his longsword, Marquis looked at the sea of demons that stood in his way. He sliced through another howling dabarne, but all his focus was on Emory. The green flames consumed the Oilean, their ring tightening as he heard the whispers on the wind: "The Dark King wants her aliveee. Aliveee, sisters. But it doesn't mean we can't have our fun."

Running, Marquis pushed harder, slamming into his memory of the day Adair had looked at him that same way. Not as a person but as prey.

Marquis shivered as the tendrils of his ability snaked down his legs, into the earth; the wind picked up, threatening to become a gale. Cutting down another dabarne, he collided with Emory, and they rolled. The winds slammed into the world, ice pellets slitting surface cuts along their cheeks and necks. Thunder rolled into the late autumn night, the storm growing.

Scrambling, Marquis found Emory's hand, gripping it tightly. "Em, we have to get out. *Now.*"

Her gaze pinned him. "It can't all be for nothing. It can't."

"You won't be any use dead. Now come *on*," he snapped.

He ran, towing her along. He knew this land better than anyone. The rolling plateaus, the hidden caves, and raging sea. The slick cliffs to the city burning behind him. They sprinted toward the roaring wall of fire, and taking a full breath, he called upon his ability, digging deep.

Thousands of droplets of water rushed up to meet them, following their path. "Hold your breath!"

Glimpsing the briefest moment where Emory nodded, he gripped her hand tighter. The water grew, becoming a giant swirling mass as it swallowed them. It flowed up his nose, trying to choke him, but he couldn't let go of her as they were suspended in the water.

Marquis threw their weight forward, out of the water. Steam hissed around them as everything turned to smoke. *Hold on, hold on, hold on.* They cleared the flames, leaving the Oilean, for the moment, behind them.

Dirt and blood filled his mouth, his jaw cracking against the wet earth and pressure built on his chest. Emory blinked down at him, stunned, blood trickling down her temple. Swallowing hard, he adjusted to the clamor all around them.

"MAR!"

A new voice carried across the carnage—too many people he knew lay dead, sprawled across the field. Guilt tore through his mind as he saw each one. He had killed his father to ensure the Isles were able to grow past their bloody history, not go back to it.

He spotted who had screamed his name in the middle of the battle, and relief coursed through him. He thought all his friends had burned with his city.

Siobhan sliced through the body of the dabarne in front of her, blackened blood spattering her face as she charged them, every part of her face etched with the same sorrow that pulled at his seams.

Emory was already running to her.

Scrambling, Marquis tailed her. Sprinting past the dabarnes, he took in their empty eye sockets, their fangs covered with blood, and their roars shattering through his resolve. *Don't look back.* Sweat plastered his skin; his lungs burned as he ran faster. To his left, a dabarne launched itself, landing on a dead soldier from the Isles and lowering its maw to feast on the man's flesh, its serpentine body curling around its meal.

Rooted in horror, Marquis couldn't move. The massive head turned to him, blood burbling on its lips as the beast realized it had live prey in its midst. Its claws dug into the dirt as it stood on its hind legs, roaring, bloody spittle flying. There were hundreds of these demons ripping apart the city that had been his refuge, his heart, his *life.*

Hriste burned as brightly as a star dying behind the monster.

The darbarne's lips peeled back over its mouth as it galloped, angling its head down, and all Marquis could do was stare at those pitiless yellow eyes, all the time seeing the Oilean. Their darkness had spread like an infection, killing the Shattered Isles.

Emory was in front of him before he could react. Marquis took in the flames leaping from her sword right before the steel cut through the neck of the dabarne, its dying roar swallowed up by the clamor of war.

Emory, wide-eyed, yelled at him, "Marquis, move! Now."

Siobhan came running up behind Emory, alone.

Hriste burned on, illuminating the skeletal silhouettes of the Oilean's army.

Siobhan gripped his arm. "Mar, it's gone. We can't save it. We can't save anyone who might be left."

The air was too thick. Their voices too loud. Panic clawed up his throat, squeezing, cutting off his air supply . . .

Emory was before him again. "Dying won't bring Adair back. Neither will letting them win. Now, is there an armada that can get us out of here?" At his silence, she snapped, "Marquis, is there any way of getting off the Isles?"

He stared into those pitch-black eyes, the flames reflecting in the pools, and he could see it—how much Emory didn't understand. Yet, she had come back to Kiero, had walked straight into the unknown. Emory Fae was a lot of things, but her bravery was the spark now leading them. Standing before him now was a friend he could follow. He believed in her.

Tears slipped down his cheeks as he looked over his shoulder. Green flames engulfed the empty frames of the homes, which were crumbling into embers. The demon army fed off his friends—his family. The remains of Emory's skeletal army charged the dabarnes only to be torn apart. The wind picked up, the moisture hanging in the air solidifying under his ability, turning into thousands of pieces of icy shrapnel.

The Oilean appeared, their green flames following their every step, ravaging the grassy plain.

Marquis sent the sharpened ice through the air as true as an arrow, pouring all his rage into the momentum.

Go.

Siobhan's fingers wrapped around his bicep, pulling him back, and he tried to shrug her off. Emory's yells and Siobhan's tugs—both were trying to pull him back from drowning. But always, he heard him.

"Let me go. Survive. Survive. Survive."

He could never disobey Adair's whispers in the back of his mind. Running, he grabbed Siobhan's and Emory's hands, towing them in his wake. In his peripheral vision, he saw the dabarnes' heads turn, nostrils flaring, their scents scattering in the wind.

Forcing his legs to move faster, he swung Emory and Siobhan in front, yelling, "The waterfall—NOW!"

"You can do this. For me, you can do this, Marquis."

He swallowed his fear, looking at the hundreds of dabarnes crawling out of the debris, over the field of scattered bodies. His once-thriving city had become a catacomb in the blink of his eye. The thundering of the footfalls shook him to his core, his pulse ringing in his ears.

Marquis crouched down, his fingers grazing the earth. The soil was warm, coated with blood underneath his touch. "I give this land up from its protection; I give this land up from its protection."

A woman appeared in front of him. Her purple gaze pinned him; she looked no older than twenty, her bound silver hair plaited back, her black robes catching in the winds. Exhaling hard, he saw that the battle around them was frozen—everything was, all except them.

"Ah, Marquis Maher, you called?" The witch tilted her head, weighing her words. "It would seem you have gotten yourself into an even messier situation than last time with your father. That is surprising."

"I don't have time for this. My bargain—"

"You mean when you traded your father's life for your kingdom's protection? Please continue."

Marquis stalked toward her. "The Shattered Isles are lost. Do what you will with my vow and this kingdom. With my father's bones. But I need your help. Get us out of here. *Please.*"

Her voice was smooth as she circled him. "You never stood a chance in this war, you know that? This enemy from another world is unlike anything Kiero has ever seen. Death always does bring an odd kind of peace and closure, wouldn't you agree?" Curling her luminous hair between her fingers, she eyed him. "You know what it would mean, letting those walls down, Marquis? Your beloved land, for the taking. The mysterious Shattered Isles finally put back on the map, only to be wiped off. No more secrets, and no more hiding."

Her voice carried on the wind; it was everywhere. She pulled in close to him, her hot breath against his ear. "What changed your mind, young king? What has finally pulled you from the shadows?"

He exhaled hard, and the world spun, his hands trembling. "Why, in black skies, do you care? Don't spend your magic shielding the Isles any longer. Keep my father's bones, his blood. But just *help us.*"

Tilting her head, she scraped a long nail down his cheek. "Your friend killed my kin. The diams were witches once, before your father banished them, and they were driven to insanity. Driven to be nothing more than monsters. Locked in their watery tomb. Becoming ravenous filth."

Marquis's heart stopped.

"Yet, your path is an interesting one. I see the light and dark within you, Marquis Maher, and I would like to see what becomes of it. I release you of your vow with me to protect these lands. But I ask that another one be made in return."

"What?" he asked.

"I will help you escape the clutches of these demons. I will even get you to your remaining fleet at Durdover Port . . . Only if you allow the young queen to be captured by the Oilean."

The entire world dropped.

Stumbling from the witch, shaking from head to toe, he rasped, "I can't betray Emory. I *won't.*"

"Then you will die here."

Turning, she took one step before his voice quivered out, barely audible, "Wait. Is it the only way?"

She stopped, turning to face him. "Yes."

Marquis was standing on that cliff now, about to leap off. How many times had he envisioned his future and wished for actual allies? Crossing the space between them, feeling like he was going to puke, Marquis forced out, "Fine. Yes. I accept your terms."

Her lips peeled over her pointed teeth, her violet eyes flashing. She grabbed his wrist, a blade appearing in her other hand. "You know what comes next, young king."

The blade was brought down with force—steel slicing through his flesh. His blood pooled over, dripping off his palm and hitting the ground. He hardly felt the pain as she mimicked the same wound on herself.

They pressed their palms together.

Marquis's whisper was low. "By my blood oath, I promise, in exchange for my freedom, I will sacrifice Emory Fae to the Oilean."

The witch snarled in pleasure as she replied, "By my blood oath, I will save you, letting this world burn along with the young queen to pay the blood spilled of my kin."

In unison, their whispers built, weaving, "With the black skies as my witness, it will be done."

Tilting her head up, the witch pulled her hand back, licking the blood off her skin.

Marquis, with tears staining his cheeks, did the same.

CHAPTER TWENTY

EMORY

It was not in her to run anymore. Siobhan shoved her back hard, yelling, "Marquis knows what he is doing. We have to go!"

The impact from the other woman's hands should have been enough to bruise, but all Emory could feel coursing through her veins was magic, thrumming through all her senses. On the shore, this close to the waterfall, water slicked her armor, making the blackened gore coating her slowly wash away.

A buzzing filled her ears, drowning out the war around them. Emory glanced behind them. Hriste and the field splayed out behind the city were unrecognizable. The blackened mass rushing toward them had infested everything that had once been wild. The pit raged with green flames, the Oilean leading the army right toward them.

Marquis was a mere silhouette against the night and the flickering shadows. Squinting, Emory watched as he moved as if talking to someone else, his hands moving rigidly. Then, trembling, he brought his palm to his lips, breaking away.

"Emory, do you have a death wish?" Siobhan screeched.

Emory brought herself back into the moment and wariness grew in her stomach as Marquis ran back to them.

"No. Of course not."

Siobhan grabbed her hand, throwing their weight forward, jumping into the freezing water.

Every sense of gravity winked out. Water slammed into them like ice, dragging them down into the pool's depths, rushing into Emory's nose and down her throat. Emory pressed her lips tightly shut, wanting to scream as they were dragged down, Siobhan's nails biting into her wrists, piercing through Emory's skin. Twisting, she saw a shadow up above, the body hitting the water with lithe force, as Marquis swam down beside them, eyes wide.

Kicking, Siobhan tugged her hard, whipping her out of her trance. As they swam through the darkness, a small light appeared at the bottom of the pool, pulsing. It lit up Siobhan's flaming hair as she was the first to reach it—all the while holding Emory's hand. She wrenched a massive stone out of the way, revealing a tunnel just large enough for a body to fit through.

Nodding, Siobhan looked at her as if to say, *Trust me.*

Pulling away, Emory dropped her hand, clawing through the water, pushing down the thought of her lungs burning, her heart slamming against her chest. Every movement was labored, painful. Siobhan cut through the lake with grace, clambering into the tunnel. Disappearing.

Emory kicked her back legs, trying to propel herself forward, when glorious oxygen crashed into her. Dropping, she hit the sandy lake floor, heaving, clothes sodden, shivering.

"Em."

Marquis was there, helping her up. He had created a temporary air pocket for them, and she tried to catch her breath. "What are you doing? We have to go."

He just stood there, holding her trembling hand, his emerald eyes wide, blood trickling down his face.

"Marquis?" she asked.

Suddenly, Emory was crushed against his chest, his arms wrapped around her body in a tight hug. As they stood there, his ability protected them from the freezing water and his breath tickled against her ear as he whispered, "I'm sorry."

His hands connected with her shoulders, shoving her backward. Water crashing over her, Emory couldn't do anything as she was sucked backward, screaming against the pull, watching Marquis grow smaller and smaller until the inky blackness took over once more.

***

Emory blinked, and the first thing she registered was chunks of ash tickling her lip. Wheezing, lying on her back at the edge of the pool, Emory tried to focus more. The waterfall crashed by her, the night never ending as she tried to move, to get away—to do anything.

A bone cracked above her. Tears slipped from her eyes, a low moan escaping from her.

"Sissssterss, look."

Marquis betrayed me. Left me.

Rolling, Emory dragged her body across the bloodied soil, eyes adjusting to the stilled army behind her. To the three women in front of them. Their white dresses were stained with blood.

They tilted their heads, walking in unison toward her. "You could never win. Look at what your friends did to you. So willing to leave you behind for us."

Feebly, her ability raised its head. She scrambled to stand. Her skin tingled against Marquis's phantom hands, his whisper echoing in her heart. *I'm sorry.*

The steel from the knife was freezing against her throat. A pale finger brushed her cheek, pressing the blade in harder, warm blood trickling down her skin. "I can smell your fear, Emory Fae."

Another sister whispered to her left, "Should we carve her like we did her prince? Would she break then?"

And behind her, the third crooned, "Declan never said what state she should arrive to him in."

Giggles floated around her, but Emory steeled herself. *One.* She had to rise. *Two.* Fight. *Three.* Survive. Throwing her weight, she felt the steel slicing her throat and her ability rushing up, trying to heal the wound, trying to keep her alive.

Was that thunder in the distance? Were people still screaming?

The world swam, falling deeper into shadows.

Hands clamped onto her ankles and her wrists, ripping her hair. There were too many. How could there be *so* many hands? Fingers clamped over her mouth, and she bit down hard, blood filling her mouth. She couldn't focus. The world was a churning mass of smells, of sound.

The Oilean's whispers circled her, the roars of their army climbing, but Emory heard only one thing: "You are ours now, Queen. And you will wish you were already dead."

Her head was wrenched back, exposing the thin line—that was scabbed now—on her throat. "She would slit her own throat to escape us, sissterrrs."

Emory couldn't stop the tears from pouring down her face as she felt a tongue licking the wound. "So long, we have hunted you. So long, we have waited."

Emory was slammed down on her back, then she was nose to nose with an Oilean, those empty eye sockets full of dancing shadows against the green flames consuming the world around them.

"It is time, Emory Fae, to learn the consequences of your decisions."

CHAPTER TWENTY-ONE

MARQUIS

Monster. A term he thought a lot of people fit throughout the years, but never once did he think he would become one. But as the king of the Shattered Isles dove into the secret tunnel after Siobhan, the taste of blood lingering on his tongue, he knew there was no turning back. Marquis cut through the water with ease and shimmied past the rocks, then broke through the surface with a gasp.

"Mar—black skies—what are you thinking?"

Siobhan, severe as ever, stood above him, dripping but alive. Relief flooded through him. Lifting himself up, he collided with her. Her head was pressed against his chest as he rested his chin on top of it, trying to still his tremors. Trying to forget what he just did.

"Siobhan, you have to trust me, okay? No questions right now, but I promise you I will tell you everything. Can you do that for me? We have known each other all our lives."

As they broke apart, she opened her mouth, but not before movement behind her had them both drawing their bloodied swords.

"Her screams are ripping this world apart, you know." The witch raised her eyebrows, picking at her teeth. "Truly, those demons will be distracted for a while."

Turning white as a sheet, Siobhan stood, opening and closing her mouth, but those violet eyes pinned Marquis as the witch breathed, "To Durdover Port, I presume, Marquis?"

Looking to the crumbling staircase behind them, Marquis snapped, "I'm assuming you're getting us there *now* as promised?"

Sighing, she offered her hands to both.

Move. Don't think, just do this. Grasping her palm, he stared daggers at Siobhan to do the same. Like a ghost, she followed, all the time looking at him like he was a stranger.

Grabbing Siobhan's hand, the witch mused, "My bargain was with you, Marquis Maher. Always remember your wording."

"NO!" he screamed.

Where Siobhan was standing, flames roared to life, devouring her flesh.

Marquis hardly registered what had just happened when a deep pull wrenched in his gut as he was squeezed through time and space, the wind howling all the while, brine and seawater filling his senses. Then the entire world disappeared, brilliant sparks of silver and gold streaking through the air. Sweat rolled down his spine, and in the distance, shrill screams of terror echoed.

Just as fast as it happened, he slammed back into reality, the ancient witch holding his chin. "You're wording wasn't very specific. Remember, I will be watching you." Her lips were on his, her tongue parting them, breath hot and sultry. Pulling away, she dissolved in smoke, and Marquis dropped to his knees, shaking and alone.

Durdover Port was as he remembered it from when he used to visit with his father. A thousand miles away from the capital, the quaint town was quiet, its residents asleep and totally oblivious to the fact their entire country was now lost. The Black Sea rolled, and in the slivers of dawn, Marquis spotted the silhouettes of part of his fleet, untouched, docked at port.

Nails digging into the moist earth, he emptied his stomach, acid searing through his throat, tears pricking his eyes. He imagined what Diedre would say if she were here: "This is already a freedom bathed in blood. And that will be forever on you. Like father like son."

The words burned him alive as traces of dawn broke through the night.

Like father like son.

***

The hours slipped past him. Like a ghost, Marquis navigated the town, heading for the barracks. The Port's military captain, after a startling realization of who he was and after hearing Marquis's story, had raised the alarm. In hushed cries and hurried packing, the town vacated.

"My King?" The captain, Ryker, was too young in Marquis's mind to be skilled in war. But he stood before him, stoic, calmer than Marquis himself. Hundreds of civilians had piled their lives on these ships, the entire fleet consisting of fifty ships. And half his army.

Grief wormed into Marquis's bones, weighing him down.

Clearing his throat, Ryker tried in a gentler tone. "My King, in such times, the people are awaiting your words. To remain calm, and to find strength."

King. Blinking against the term, Marquis couldn't tear his gaze from where Hriste lay and the funnels of smoke filling the sky.

His land, burning. Siobhan burning.

Emory, burning.

His voice was hoarse, his whisper barely audible. "I'm not worthy to be your king."

The blood dripping on the ground. The taste on his tongue. The look on Emory's face as his hands had connected with her, pushing her away. He might as well have driven his sword through her heart—it would have been a kinder fate.

Ryker's hand gripped his forearm. "I'm not trying to overstep, but there is no one else now. The news of the entire capital falling has struck fear into the bravest of us. Of the deaths, the political figures that were there and have fallen. We need you to push what you have been through aside for a few more minutes. *Please.*"

He had kind eyes. Green, but soft, like buttery sunlight on moss. Short, cropped hair, knives on his belt attached to his hip, everything about him meticulously groomed. *Emory would have liked him,* Marquis thought.

Nodding, Marquis swallowed, ripping his gaze away from the shoreline of the Isles to where the ships were packed. Pale faces of men, women, and children of Durdover Port looked hopefully up at him. Mouth running dry, he was too aware of his blood-spattered clothes, his wounds. Too aware of the hundreds of clans he was leaving to burn as he addressed the crowd.

"I'm sorry about all of our losses. The families and friends who lived in Hriste. The surrounding clans that made up the Isles."

My betrayal will not be in vain. He believed that what he was doing was for the best. There was a certain innocence in that. Untouched by nightmares, unmarred by demons.

"You should all know the truth. We sail to Kiero to rally with a rebellion. The Mad King's death didn't put out the country's flame, and we will not turn our backs on them. The time for hiding is done, and I must apologize to all of you. I have made many mistakes in ruling, but I realize now that I can't hide from this path any longer."

Selfish.

"War has come. But together, we rally. Together, we will rise."

He shot a glance at Ryker, and the captain nodded in approval before barking commands to his men.

Taking his cue, Marquis cut through the crowds of people, their questions clambering over him. All he heard was white noise and Emory's screams replaying in his mind.

Sails were hoisted, and Marquis shot one last glance at the jagged cliffs, the sandy beaches, and the shorelines that held his heart.

The Isles are lost.

Turning his back, he called on the winds, strong and true, to carry them across the ocean. The winds whispered his message that the merpeople and sea dragons—the caines—would hear.

The Isles are lost.

Shivering, Marquis lurched below decks, trying to hold on to his empty stomach. The ships creaked against the water as their anchors were lifted. Jogging, Marquis made it to the first empty room and shut the door, sliding down to the floor. He felt the ship cut through the water.

Biting on his knuckles, he screamed.

And screamed.

And screamed.

He felt his skin break. Blood flooded his mouth. Squeezing his eyes shut, he was greeted by the image of Emory being sucked back, the water overpowering her. *Him* overpowering her.

"Marquis."

That. Voice.

He glanced up, and blood trickled on his lips as the witch tilted her head. "Don't punish yourself for having your best interests at heart."

Hysteria bled into his voice when he said, "I betrayed my friends and lost my country in one night."

"Emory's path always led her to the Oilean. But your road ahead isn't an easy one."

"Why are you even here? Haven't you already done enough?"

Cocking an eyebrow, she squatted in front of him, her fingers brushing his cheeks, the touch cool. "As I said before, I'm curious about you. And remember, I wouldn't have bargained with you if it wasn't an interesting outcome." She paused, sighing. "Hold on, Marquis Maher."

With that, she turned to smoke and ash, her words lingering in the dimly lit bunker.

Marquis allowed grief, anger, and guilt to flood in. He let it take over, consuming him until he was just a thought. Just a murmur against his emotions.

Not a man.

Not a king.

PART THREE

MAP OF SOULS

CHAPTER TWENTY-TWO

NYX

Nyx tumbled into Hesen's memories, overwhelmed and addicted to the power. At first, the scene around her was unfocused, and Nyx could just *feel* the emotions rushing into her chest, spreading through her entire body.

Hesen's voice whispered in the back of her mind, *Watch, Nyx. Believe me when I say I can help you.*

Her vision churned as the sprawling city before her came into focus. Stunning, the unmarked white cobblestone roadways twisted past towering buildings. Fountains burbled merrily in the square, and incandescent flowers bloomed, mimicking moonlight from hanging pots attached to lanky lampposts. In the square, Nyx spotted Hesen among ten other armored women. Their streamlined chest plates were dark onyx, their cloaks snapping in the gentle breeze. A petite woman stalked back and forth in front of them.

"New recruits, today is the day your life changes. You have been chosen by either myself or my sister to be groomed to become a part of Nehmai's prestigious naithe warrior army. You have all completed our training in the months that have passed, and for that, I applaud you. Now comes the final step. Follow me."

Nyx watched in fascination as they were led through the weaving streets, the woman looking prideful. *How long ago is this, Hesen?*

Hundreds of years before your time, easily. Now, no more questions.

Nyx watched the memory curiously as the woman led the recruits farther away from the elegant city until the air shimmered and a doorway of knurled tree roots appeared in front of them. One by one, they passed underneath it, and they were suddenly in a forest Nyx recognized. The ancient trees were doused in lush green leaves, the sun streaking through them suggesting it was summer.

Lining up, the women looked to their leader, who stood in front of one of the largest trees, its bark covered in thick moss.

Nyx watched Hesen smirk. "Kiana, you're telling me that—"

"The gealltan, as you all might know from your history lessons, is known as the *map of souls*. Every single fey that has become a naithe warrior has finished this ritual. To exchange your mortality for a life as a naithe warrior. To protect Nehmai and our magic, it must be completed. As your turn comes, I advise you to look closely. You will learn more by watching than you ever will listening to me."

Kiana motioned for Hesen to step up first. Kiana pulled a long, curved dagger out from her belt, and the steel glinted. Without flinching, she dragged it across her palm, blood welling from the cut. Dipping the tip of her finger in it, Nyx watched as she drew a crescent moon on Hesen's forehead, speaking smoothly in an eloquent language Nyx didn't recognize.

Hesen's eyes rolled into the back of her head right before the tree in front of her came to life, long branches sweeping down under Hesen's armpits, lifting her up, away from Kiana; a splintering white light flashed through the woods.

Nyx saw it through Hesen's eyes; the forest bled away and all around her, particles floated through the air. Hundreds of swirling incandescent star lights hovered around her and filled her mind with hundreds of whispers.

Blinking, Hesen stepped forward, and the scene blurred.

"Hesen Raygner, you have come like the hundreds of sisters before you, ready to exchange your soul for immortal life. Giving your soul into this most ancient ritual, you are ensuring that Nehmai's power thrives. Your soul provides an exchange of energy, of *life,* that within the channels mapping through Kiero, births magic. Are you ready to protect that at all costs?"

"Yes," Hesen whispered to the unseen voice.

Another scene came into view, churning faster, and Nyx's stomach dropped.

"The gealltan wishes to provide you with a warning. There will come a time when our ways are threatened, our magic depleted instead of replenished. You will find yourself in a bind, but you must wait for this woman."

The image of Nyx—purple hair vibrant, alone in a desert, dressed in her attire from the ceremony—appeared.

Hesen's back arched, her mouth opening in a silent scream. Nyx watched a pale gold light seep from her mouth, disappearing in the void before it all went black.

The memory jumped. Nyx watched Hesen run, her clothes bloodied and worn, the beautiful city behind her burning. Explosions of green gas poured from every angle, the dark magic making her skin crawl. A bloodied sword hung loosely in her grip. She ran down the abandoned street, screams raining down in the night.

"Hesen!" A woman appeared in front of her, a massive hammer clenched in her hand.

"Riona—"

"There isn't time. Nehmai is falling—"

Nyx recognized when panic flitted over Hesen's features as she gasped, "The Falkovs—"

Nyx felt the deep tug that Hesen had felt that night as gravity fell. Riona and Nehmai disappeared. Blinding white light flared, connecting with Hesen's chest. Instead of the cobbled streets of Nehmai, freezing cold water swallowed Hesen and Nyx whole, flipping their body. Nyx screamed, landing in hot, blinding light.

They were both on all fours; Nyx felt mossy ground underneath her palms, the sudden humid air suffocating compared to the clear air of Nehmai.

Disoriented, Nyx saw Hesen stumble, clearly confused how she had gotten there. Nyx could see nothing but the Bogs for miles, fear slithering up her spine, Hesen's emotions colliding into her through each moment of this memory.

Hesen threw up, and Nyx felt the phantom pain burn her sinuses. Beside her, Hesen looked around the dense swamp and low brambles.

They both stilled. There was one figure standing in the distance.

The memory swam, becoming fuzzy. All Nyx felt was fear immobilizing her body, fear Hesen must have felt. Nyx was wrenched back to reality, Hesen standing in front of her, a small frown pulling her lips.

"I will spare you my heartbreak and pain from what happened the rest of that night. To this day, I still don't know who transported me out of Nehmai. There are things about Kiero that would make your stomach curl, and people with vast powers. That *demon* cursed my body and soul to the Bogs, as I have remained for centuries, unable to go back to my home, to know what happened to my sworn sisters. Trapped, just watching Kiero rot."

Wetting her dry lips, Nyx didn't know what to say, trying to sift through the possibility of Hesen's story. Of her role in it.

"I will start in saying that the ritual of gealltan was a timeless tradition of Nehmai, and I know there were other power sources that the naithe warriors used. There are channels of raw power webbing through Kiero. That only naithe warriors can access."

The Arken Mountains. My home.

"Since Nehmai has fallen and our magic has bled into all of Kiero and its inhabitants, I'm sure these power sources have changed. Despite that, I know that these sacred places hold an untouchable magic, the same that runs in my veins, above anything else in this land. A certain energy that could be channeled if one so wished."

"And in return for my soul . . ."

Hesen stepped closer. "Nyx, don't you see what's happening? Over centuries, cords of fate have brought us both to this exact moment. I swear to help you. I know you are aware of what we could accomplish if we could open a channel, or harness that energy."

Blasted hells.

"How do you know about the channels?"

"Fey were here long before your time, or the time of the Academy. You don't think that we caught whispers and glances of the secrets Kiero has, giving our soul to it? I *know* that there are worlds connected in a web, and Kiero lies at its center."

Nyx's mind raced. She had no idea if Brokk was still alive, or if Emory was. With Azarius coming to the clans, here was the chance to grasp at hope for the remainder of their broken rebellion. If Hesen knew the truth about the channels, then helping her could provide access to one, all for the price of immortality.

Do it for Harper and Memphis; they deserved better.

Do it for you. Stop hiding your heart. Stop running from your fears.

That nagging voice whispered against her doubt, and Nyx finally stopped pacing, raising her gaze to meet Hesen's.

"Okay. I agree."

Closing the space between them, Hesen gently held Nyx's hands, guiding her to sit on her knees. "Thank you." Then dropping Nyx's hands, Hesen lowered her lips to her forearm, Nyx flinching as she watched the woman bite into her own flesh.

"What the—?"

Blood welled, dripping into the sand. Hesen acted quickly, dipping her finger into her blood. "Trust me, and hold on, little mystic."

Hesen's finger shook slightly, tracing her own blood onto Nyx's forehead. Placing her bloodied hands onto the sand, she began whispering.

Suddenly, fire erupted within Nyx's veins, her vision swimming from the pain. Nyx felt her back arch violently.

***

"Nyx? Nyx, can you hear me?" Nyx lurched up with a gasp, her chest heaving.

"Steady now. I've got you." *I've got you.* Those three words seared Nyx's soul as Suri's kind eyes stared down at her. She smirked against the blaring light.

Mouth running dry, Nyx blinked against her friend's comfort, not knowing what to say. *Where is Hesen? Did it work?*

Kyrie frowned down at her behind Suri.

Suri leaned down, smiling. "Nyx, come now. You have come back to us. Touched by Danu, surviving the sacred maire trials."

"Is Hesen here? Is she okay?" Nyx rasped.

"I'm not sure who Hesen is. Nyx, come with us. Everything is okay," Suri murmured.

Nyx grasped Suri's hand, warmth spreading up her arm. She wanted to scream, to curl up and disappear. The lie was so blatant, coming from her friend. *Touched from the gods.* There wasn't anything further from the truth. *Perhaps making deals with a devil.*

Had Hesen been real or just a figment of the maire trails?

Nyx swallowed down her fear as Suri raised their interlocked palms to the flaring skies, screaming, "Bow to your new clan leader: Nyx Astire of the Dust Clans!"

The answering bellows of the waiting raiders were thunderous, and despite everything, a heaviness lifted from Nyx's shoulders. *I did it.*

Nyx was practically lifted off the ground as Suri gripped her in a tight hug, whispering in her ear, "Now the fun part begins."

Kyrie nodded when Nyx glanced at him, shadows still dancing in his eyes.

They ushered her through the crowd, praises being sung every direction.

"I knew you could do it, little mystic."

"May your reign be the start to our golden years."

"May you be a just ruler."

"May you bring peace."

"A light finally through our dark years."

Nyx hoped the right words left her mouth in response to those who spoke. She also hoped the raiders couldn't see the emptiness behind her words or the tense jolting of the muscle in her jaw.

"What now, Suri?" she asked.

"*Now,* we are getting prepared for the best party in your life."

"Seriously?"

"You deserve it. The maire trials have their own bloody history. You're one of the handful that hasn't died during it."

"And you didn't think to tell me any of this *before*?"

Shooting his sister a death glare, Kyrie spat, "I told you she wouldn't take this well."

Swatting her brother, Suri shot her a brilliant smile. "Nonsense. Nyx was the obvious candidate. The clan needs a fresh start. Besides, I saw it in Danu's flames. The raiders who are left . . . Let's just say, if any of them were in charge, it would be worse than Zander."

"Even your brother?" Nyx waggled her eyebrows, and Suri beamed.

"Especially *him*."

Chuckling, Nyx shook her head. "In all seriousness, I need to rest."

"Sorry, but it's mandatory."

"And what if that was the first tradition I would change?"

Shaking her head, Suri took her hand. "Tonight is mandatory, but next year? Who is to say?"

Heat flared through Nyx, pooling in her stomach, and she couldn't resist. Those soft eyes and the curve of her lips—Nyx pushed down the onslaught of emotion.

She couldn't let anyone else down.

At her nod, Suri squealed, pulling her faster into the depths of the raiders. For the moment, Nyx allowed herself to be happy, even with Kyrie scowling behind them.

***

The next day, looking around the empty house, Nyx sipped on her water, murmuring, "Any of you guys want Zander's old place?"

"It's—"

"Tradition, I know." Nyx eyed her friends. "But I can't stay here. Every inch of it reminds me of him and Memphis."

"We will find you another accommodation," Kyrie's voice was gentle, and Nyx nodded her gratitude.

"Which brings me to my next topic."

The twins ate, the bread soft and warm, the date jam melting on it. Chewing thoughtfully, they granted Nyx space to talk honestly. In the weeks they had known each other, they always had.

Swallowing, Nyx played with her glass. "Something happened when I was under the maire's influence. And I need you to both trust me on this." Nyx leaned forward. "I need to go to the Arken Mountains."

Kyrie's eyes narrowed. "During your trials, the gods offered advice?"

"Not advice, but an option of aid. To end this war."

"It's unheard of." Leaning back, his arms crossed, Kyrie inspected Nyx. "And *why* would they choose you?"

"Kyrie, are you grumpy I didn't die?" Nyx snapped.

Rolling his eyes, he answered between mouthfuls, "I just think an expedition up north is pointless on a whim of what you *think* . . ."

Suri sighed. "The winter is for rejuvenation. To be happy. War can wait, Nyx. This can wait. You need time to mourn, time to process, and, more importantly, to heal."

Narrowing her eyes, Nyx met her gaze. "Don't sit there and tell me what I should or shouldn't feel. I'm going with or without you." Shoving her chair back, she added, "This war is already at our doorstep." With that, she stalked out of her house, leaving the twins without a second glance.

The blazing heat pummeled her like a wave. She slammed the door behind her, and the raiders bustled past, baskets of food and fine wines balanced in their arms. Nyx prowled in their midst, not hearing the high praise, not caring if she looked as foul as she felt.

Little mystic. Hesen had spoken those words, and she didn't even know if the immortal had been *real.* She wanted to set those words on fire, to erase them. She had fought so hard in the last weeks, but now that she was here—what? Parties? Late nights? Being lost in pleasure? She could see it play out, the temptation sitting behind her in that house. Her body yearned for the simple pleasures of human touch. Her old habits begging to find oblivion and an endless night.

It would be easy to let all notions of the Rebellion go. It was never her responsibility. The fate of the Academy, of their world, was sent spinning by politics Nyx had never cared about. Yet, she was caught in the throes of wanting freedom so bad she had lost everything for it. If Suri and Kyrie wouldn't back her, who would? The raiders were happy to sit behind a leader that relished in bloodshed for sport but not one who wanted to band together against a bigger enemy.

Clenching her fists, she looked to the endless blue skies, still not used to this infernal heat. Voices overlapped, and she caught snippets of the conversation before her.

"Apparently that arrogant man—what's his name?"

"Marquis Maher."

"Yes. The Shattered Isles have gone up in flames. Overnight, the capital has fallen. Wiped off the map like that." The man snapped his fingers in his companion's face. "Rumor is that this Fae queen didn't make it, that she was visiting Maher when it happened."

The entire world ground to a halt. The words were hushed, excited.

Nyx stalked toward the two men leaning against a stall piled with greens. "What did you just say?" she demanded.

They were young, maybe eighteen or so. Their honey-brown eyes went wide, long lashes fluttering as they realized who spoke to them.

Her ability crashed through her, and she grabbed the closest one by his shirt. "I asked what you just said!"

"Our spies reported news from the south. That the Shattered Isles have fallen, along with Emory Fae."

Nyx staggered back; her hands went cold. "How long?"

"A day or two maybe."

Shaking, Nyx spun, running back to Kyrie and Suri, exhaustion and anger nipping at her heels. Hesen's voice repeated in her mind: *Your soul in exchange to free me. Your soul, Nyx, will be the only price to pay for the key to stop this war. A place of ancient magic in the Arken Mountains can open a channel.*

Everything was a blur.

She forced the door open, making both Suri and Kyrie jump in surprise.

"The Shattered Isles have fallen. Emory . . . Emory Fae is reported to be dead."

How fast the joy from the room was stripped. The reality of the situation crashed down on them all.

"We need to prepare *now*. No more parties. No celebration. If I have earned the right to be your clan leader, I have the right to make sure my people stay alive."

Suri opened and closed her mouth. Features softening, she finally whispered, "I didn't see this happening."

Kyrie stood, his gaze severe. "Some things can't be foretold. I will gather our most skilled swordsmen. What's your plan, Nyx?"

As she paced, her hands shook. "Give me a minute. Please."

At their silence, Nyx allowed her ability to fill her as she thought of one thing. She needed to know if Azarius was alive or if he was just another hallucination of the maire trials.

Her telepathy stretched like a web, searching through the hundreds of voices filling the void of her mind until she heard the two voices she was looking for.

"Alby, I told you a thousand times already."

"Azarius, our entire company got eaten. Ripped apart before our eyes. You're saying that what happened was all in my head? That Lana sacrificing herself and Pentharrow falling was for nothing? Now you were looking into those pools weeks ago, acting like someone else was there when our friends were torn apart behind us!"

"Don't remind me of Lana, Alby. Ever. Now let's focus on getting to Nyx, brother. We need to leave what happened in the Bogs behind us."

Slamming back into the present, Nyx keeled over, nails digging into the table. A cold sweat clung to her body as she rasped, "Suri, stay here and look over the clan, readying them to travel. To vacate to the Arken Mountains. Tonight. Kyrie, how fast do you think we could find my friends just shy of the Forgotten Bogs and the Risco Desert border?"

"Nyx, be reasonable," Suri scoffed.

Why did Suri have so much doubt? So much hope that this war would elude them, that her gods would protect them? There was no one looking out for them now. No one except Nyx.

Nyx slammed Suri against the wall, a soft vanilla scent wafting up to her, and she inhaled deeply, arms shaking. "Suri, you will die if you stay."

Kyrie had surged up, but Nyx was faster. "We both know the battlefield isn't where you belong, Suri. But I can teach you how to protect yourself with what time we have left. There are many other ways you can assist. But I need to find my friends, and then we need to head to the mountains."

Slowly releasing her hand from around Suri's throat, Nyx stepped back. "We don't have much time. I can promise you the wrath of this darkness will find us. We will lose if we aren't ready. But if you allow me a second, I can tell you what happened during the maire trials."

Suri's eyes were wide, but she nodded mutely. Kyrie looked between them tensely. He ran a hand over his face, then he wearily sat down.

Settling down again, Nyx felt like she was speaking out-of-body. "You two will be the first to hear this, to know that before this war and the Academy, I had a sister. Her name was Harper, and she was my best friend. She brought out the best in me."

Diving into her tale, Nyx told the twins about Harper and the cave during the trials. How she couldn't save her yet again, like all those years ago when she didn't realize Adair's men had been tailing her. A primal part of her had been broken when she watched Harper die in front of her.

And then her entire community followed.

Next came Hesen.

Suri's eyebrows kept raising, and Kyrie crossed his arms, frowning deeply as Nyx finished with, "I need to see if Hesen is with Azarius. If so, then it means the gealltan worked, that my soul freed her."

"And you're immortal?" breathed Suri.

Nyx nodded. "If it was all real, then yes. Gods above, I think we need a drink."

Kyrie moved fluidly, his silence enough of a tell-tale of his churning thoughts. Nyx watched him grab a deep amber bottle and three glasses. Distributing them, he poured. "Since we will be missing round two of our celebration tonight."

Meeting his gaze, Nyx smiled meekly. "You believe me?"

"Unfortunately, yes." Kyrie drank deeply, hissing through his teeth as he set his glass down.

"Suri?" Nyx asked.

"It has been hundreds of years since the clans have been involved in the workings of Kiero. I believe it is time that changes, and that is why you have won your title. I think it must have been a powerful intention that this Hesen came to you during the maire trails." Suri tipped her glass back in one swig, matching her brother.

"Okay then," Nyx said, drinking the alcohol, welcoming the burn that radiated from her toes to her fingers. Setting down the glass, she said, "Let's find out if Hesen is real."

***

She navigated upstairs, already prioritizing what she would pack. Alby and Azarius needed her. And Hesen . . .

Nyx's stomach flipped, and hope and uncertainty prickled along her senses. It scared her to think that she had sold her soul to free another, and yet she desperately hoped that the ritual had worked.

They *needed* her. *Do not fail.*

As she walked into her room, the words haunted her, gnawing away at any fear she had. Standing straighter, she began to let go of the woman she once was. Too stubborn, too hurt. Jealous and selfish.

She would be there for her friends. They would live through this—and anyone who stood in her way, she would kill.

A small smile tugged at her lips. Nyx felt, for once in her life, that she was stronger than she ever thought possible.

CHAPTER TWENTY-THREE

NYX

Nyx, Kyrie, and a handful of soldiers from the Dust Clans traveled relentlessly through the night.

She had learned that the laghairts that had once attacked her in the arena under Zander's command were gentle at heart. Zander had abused the creatures and poisoned them over the years, driving the animals to insanity. Once Nyx learned this, she made it her mission the first week after Memphis's death to bond with the laghairts, making sure they would never know the cruelty of man again.

The sands beneath the laghairts' giant hooked claws still emitted warmth from the long day that had passed. Nyx liked to imagine thousands of suns captured beneath their feet, radiating long after the moon bathed the land. It helped this barren, treacherous land seem beautiful to her.

Tipping her head back to the waxing moon, she allowed its glow to wash over her as she tried to clear her mind.

"Do you believe what Hesen said was true?" Kyrie leaned forward, the massive laghairt he rode keeping time with her own. Their saddles were smooth, thick leather, her padded pants she wore making sure her legs weren't rubbed raw. Her heeled boots were secure in the stirrups.

Nyx affectionately ran her hand along Dira's smooth scales. "I want to. Azarius and Alby—they are part of my life now. I refuse to turn my back on them."

"But if you say we are in as much danger as you let Suri believe . . ."

Making sure the men that followed in their company were out of earshot, Nyx said, "Kyrie, we are probably in more danger than you can fathom. Which is why this is so important."

I can't let the Rebellion die.

Flicking her braid over her shoulder, Nyx scoured the sands for Alby and Azarius. They had to be close.

Kyrie's wariness was burning beside her, but he said no more.

As they traveled in silence, Nyx chewed over her nerves, trying to fixate on Hesen.

Your mortal soul, to free me.

Even in the darkness, Hesen's voice whispered to her like a pulse—a presence she couldn't shake. Had her life always been leading her to this point? Destiny was always something she had scoffed at. After Memphis had brought her back to the Academy, she swore to never think about Harper. She had buried her past, deeply, then had happily fallen into her new life with Memphis.

Years had passed with her trying to fill the gaping hole in her heart where her secrets lay. But in doing so, maybe she had ensured the truth of Hesen's vision, every decision and mistake leading her here. Here, where she was backed into a corner with no other options, with nothing more to offer other than herself. But, by flame, didn't she owe Harper's memory as much? If the price for Harper's death was to bow to ancient magic, Nyx would. A thousand times over, she would.

A flicker of shadows had her pulling on Dira's reins; she spotted two collapsed bodies in the distance and another leaning over them. Clucking her tongue, she squeezed her thighs, urging her steed faster.

"Whoa, Dira." Pulling to a full stop, Nyx leaped from the saddle, hitting the sands at a scrambling run.

Kyrie protested at her back, but she didn't care.

Sand shifting beneath her boots, calves burning, she came to Alby and Azarius. Hesen straightened, hazel eyes lighting with amusement before she said, "Nyx. Finally."

Kyrie came up behind her, sword drawn.

"Kyrie, stand down. This is Hesen." *The gealltan worked.*

Heart in her throat, Nyx also digested that Hesen being here meant she was now immortal.

Kyrie's voice was white noise as Nyx noted Alby's and Azarius's chests gently rising and falling, their breathing shallow. The twins' freckled skin was blistered and burned, dried blood and gore staining both their clothes.

Carefully, she undid the water canteen from her hip, whispering, "Hey, there."

Azarius's eyes fluttered open as he rasped, "Hey yourself. I . . . need water."

Lifting his head, she slowly poured a little over his cracked lips into his mouth. "You haven't become less demanding, I see."

He gave her a low chuckle before he closed his eyes once again. Laying him back down, she gently tended to Alby next.

Kyrie appeared beside her, still pointing his blade at a smirking Hesen. "Nyx, look."

Following his gaze, she saw in the distance—hundreds upon hundreds of miles away—a green glow shooting up toward the stars like smoke wafting after destruction. Dread pooling in her stomach, her teeth clenched, she said, "We need to move. Now."

Kyrie went to lift the twins when warm wind suddenly slammed into them, sending the sands scattering. Shielding her eyes, Nyx looked away from the unexpected sandstorm. Warm desert air caressed her exposed arms, particles of sand trying to clot in her nose and down her throat.

Staggering back a step, Nyx looked up, trying to see what was causing such powerful winds. Eyes burning, she saw a massive black shadow in the skies before it landed powerfully in front of her. Nyx blinked, not daring to believe who was coming into focus.

"Nyx!" Kyrie shouted from behind her, sounding worried.

"Kyrie, stand down," Nyx said hoarsely.

Aella's incandescent fur shone like moonlight, and the peryton pawed the sands, dipping her head. Her iron antlers gleamed. Closing the space between them, Nyx hugged her massive nose, tears slipping fast down her cheeks as she reached out to Aella's mind.

I'm so glad you are safe, friend. I was worried.

A deep rumbling started in the peryton's chest, almost like a purr. Images erupted in Nyx's mind, one after the other. First was a towering forest, the dappling green light spattering over Aella's fur as the peryton walked, alone. This image repeated, Nyx catching on that Aella was showing her the passage of time since she left Memphis and Nyx with Zander. Through the memories, Nyx was slowly filled with the fear and sadness that Aella had felt.

Swallowing hard, Nyx stood straight, petting the peryton's nose as the next image filled Nyx's mind: Lana's face bloodied and bruised but smiling.

"You two got close while we have been apart."

Numbness spread over her body, and she felt as if she were seeing a ghost. Nyx stepped back to take in Lana smirking from Aella's saddle. Trembling, Nyx was speechless as Lana dismounted.

"I remember you being a bit more talkative last time we saw each other." Lana tilted her head.

Pulling Lana in hard against her chest, Nyx sobbed, cries that shook her whole body. Her hands felt Lana's body, her *realness.*

"You are alive! Are you okay?" Nyx sniffed.

Kyrie eyed Lana skeptically, blades out as he drawled, "And who the hell are you?"

"Kyrie, easy," Nyx said, pulling herself together. Breaking the hug, Nyx glared at Hesen, asking, "You said Pentharrow fell. Did you know she was alive?"

Hesen shrugged.

Lana asked, "Where's Memphis?"

Nyx's company, though not Kyrie, sheathed their blades, the answer in the words no one spoke, that none of them could find.

"Nyx—"

"He's gone," she rasped. Her iron wall disappeared for the woman in front of her, allowing her bleeding wound to show.

Lana was there, folding Nyx against her chest, lending her support. Nyx's exhaustion—her tears—clawed through her body as she hugged her friend back. Together, they would find the strength to go on.

"I'm so sorry. You're not alone, Nyx."

Not alone.

Breaking away from Lana, Nyx steadied herself, gently guiding Lana to the two unconscious bodies behind them—and Hesen.

"Lana, this is Hesen. She's an . . . ally. I have a lot to tell you on the journey back."

"A pleasure," Hesen murmured coolly.

Nyx wiped her tears, and it cracked her heart as the windwalker froze, her gaze landing on the body in front of her, her golden skin draining of color. No words were uttered, but the energy that crackled through the air, heat flaring, was groundbreaking.

Lana's body was a blur until she stilled by Azarius's side. Nyx couldn't move as she watched Lana's shaking hand, so unsure, gently tracing the curve of his jawline. Her tentative fingers lightly brushing over his cracked lips, tears glinting in her eyes.

Azarius's eyes fluttered open, taking Lana in. In the intimacy of that moment, Nyx grinned under the brandishing night, and for the first time in a long time, everything was perfect.

Azarius's tears slipped down his cheeks, and he grabbed Lana's face between his hands, kissing her fiercely. Even the brutal-edged raiders cast their eyes away, blushes creeping up their necks.

Nyx looked up to find Hesen staring at her. Heat climbed up her neck, and she quickly looked away.

***

The journey back to the Dust Clans was blurred, but Nyx's uplifted spirit soared as she counted Aella's powerful wingbeats far above in the skies. Hesen was behind her on their sentry's laghairt, her gaze burning into Nyx's back.

Kyrie muttered, "Truly, you live the most complicated life."

"Complicated, sure, but I have the best taste in friends, wouldn't you say?" she quipped. There was a quirk of his mouth, and Nyx pressed on, "War is complicated, Kyrie. We are all fighting for a chance to learn what a normal life may look like. For that reason, *please* try to open your mind to my friends and their alliances."

As quick as it came, Nyx's happiness waned at the constant reminder of the price she had already paid for this war: her soul.

Kyrie nodded. "I can guess what you're thinking, and it will be okay, Nyx. The fact that the gealltan worked is conflicting to you. If you need to talk, I'm here for you."

"Thank you, Kyrie. Really."

Smiling, he gruffly continued, "Did you hear any more of the whisperings? Of what happened on the Isles?"

Sucking on her bottom lip, Nyx slowly replied, "Not any more than what I told you and Suri."

His eyebrows shot up. "That's all you have to say?"

Nyx shot him a glare. "Kyrie, what do you want me to say? That Emory Fae is somehow alive? That the rumors are all fake? That this Dark King's army didn't destroy the entire *Isles*? That deep down, I agree with Suri and think we should sit, waiting for an entire armada to come knocking on our doorstep?" She sucked in a sharp breath. "For years, we have all lived in fear. For years, I have watched our Rebellion fail time and time again. The Shattered Isles being destroyed is just another reason for us to take this seriously. To get to the Arken Mountains as fast as we can."

Kyrie nodded. "The winds are changing. Can't you feel it? See it within yourself? For the first time in centuries, the clans have broken tradition. They have accepted you. People are bound to be more desperate to fight when we give them real hope."

Bitterness filled her mouth, insecurities creeping up her throat. "Do you truly think the clans will look at me and see hope?" He playfully waggled his eyebrows from his mount, and she clucked her tongue. "Kyrie, seriously!"

"You know what I see in you, little mystic? Despite your pain?" He paused. "Dreams. I see dreams of love and hope. Dreams that our families weren't slaughtered and the only things we have left of them are dissipated memories. Dreams to fight for our country. To do what no one else dares to. I see *that* burning in you. And that bravery is something I will follow until the end."

With her heart swelling, Nyx was at a loss for words.

Kyrie smiled and urged his laghairt in front of her, joining their comrades.

Thankful for the privacy, Nyx wiped her eyes, her throat tightening.

Was it only months ago she thought of herself as nothing more than a soldier? That Memphis was her entire world? Her desperation for his love, his attention, his *approval.* That envy in her had turned her existence into chaos—the blood of her friends staining her hands, her betrayal feeding into her guilt. Never letting her forget. Yet, despite her mistakes, despite that constant battering she felt, Nyx was here with people she loved. People who were willing to help her and willing to fight.

As they rode back to the clans, tucked within the sands, one fleeting dream pushed her fear and secret aside. She, Nyx Astire, had driven herself—without even realizing it—to find a place to call home. But home wasn't a place; it was within her, and surrounded by her friends, she had made it there.

***

She pulled Dira to a halt, and their company arrived back to the Dust Clans with the new light of dawn streaking the skies. Nyx barely dismounted before a blurred body shot toward her, Suri crushing her in a tight hug.

"You guys are okay." Suri exhaled, lessening her hold, beaming at her brother behind Nyx.

"We are." Nyx stepped back.

"The journey was relatively smooth, considering recent events," Kyrie quipped.

Powerful wingbeats sent the sands scattering behind Nyx, and Suri shielded her eyes. The laghairts skittered nervously as Aella landed, Lana sliding off, and Hesen rushed to help support Azarius and Alby.

Nyx rested a reassuring hand on Dira. "Suri, this is Hesen"—Suri's eyes widened as she took in the immortal—"Lana, Azarius, and Alby. They need healing."

Snapping at the sentries, Suri commanded, "Help bring them to my quarters, and we will need a basin of boiled water. *Now.*"

Questions still burned against Nyx's heart as Lana locked eyes with her. Panic flared within her friend's eyes. "I need to go with Azarius. I can't leave him again."

"Go. We will catch up later." Nyx nodded.

A flurry of movement ensued as the raiders jumped to action, hauling an unconscious Azarius and Alby away, Lana at their heels.

Suri pulled Nyx aside. "Our clan is ready to travel."

Our clan. Turning her back on Hesen, Nyx said, "Thank you, Suri. As much as I would love to say we are ready to leave now, Azarius and Alby need to be conscious and somewhat stable."

"How much time do we have?" Suri asked.

"Not as much as I would like. I saw strange signs along the border of the Bogs."

"I will get Dira watered and your saddles prepared for you while you rest. You look . . ." Suri searched for the word with an apologetic gaze.

Nyx laughed. "Yeah, I get it, Suri."

Suri's eyes wandered to Hesen, and Nyx mouthed *go* to her before finally turning to confront the immortal.

"You've been abnormally quiet," Hesen said.

"You do *not* know me."

"Aren't you happy the gealltan worked?"

Yes. No.

Hesen grabbed her wrist, warmth spreading beneath her grip. Nyx decided to avoid answering and instead asked Hesen her own question. "Did you know Lana was alive when you first came to me?"

"I'm not the only one who omitted truths."

Pulling free from Hesen's grip, she stalked away.

"Nyx! We need to remember why the price you paid to free me is important. Please. I'm on your side here. Lana is lucky to be alive after the ramblings I heard from her partner in the desert. If we can talk for a moment, I know how—"

Nyx turned abruptly and grabbed Hesen's throat, squeezing hard. "Don't ever presume to know how I feel." Shoving Hesen back, she snapped, "In an hour, we will talk with the others at Suri's. I'm sure you're resourceful enough to find it."

***

Her room felt desolate as she paced. More than twenty-four hours of staying awake, and Nyx's eyes burned, dry and strained. Her face was puffy, exhaustion weighing down her limbs. Did immortals even *feel* such human ailments?

She looked around at the king-sized bed, the crimson pillows propped up where she left them, the book she had borrowed from Suri about the raiders' bloody history still dropped against them. Despite this house and the haunted memories that lingered within its walls, Nyx appreciated the beauty of the headboard with the carving of two clashing swords and the healthy number of maps and books downstairs. In the weeks since Memphis's death, these had provided her some comfort as she memorized the dips and curves of the workmanship or lost her reality to the pages of a book.

Sighing, Nyx stopped pacing, rubbing her hands over her face, trying to process the last couple of days. Adair was dead. Now a new foe had risen, one more dangerous. One that was able to leave an entire *country* burning, reduced to ash, Emory Fae with it.

Looking to the side table, Nyx was already across the room, chucking it against the wall, heaving. The wood exploded, the shards scattering across the floor.

It reminded her of when she was ten. Her community held an annual festival celebrating the holiday of Tuturan, translated roughly as "the mountains becoming one with the stars." It was believed that protection was bestowed upon them. The stars, once a year, would rain down their renowned magic, shivering through the hulking mountain like blood vessels and providing prosperity for anyone who had contact with the stone. In return, her town, Yuli, would spend all day preparing a feast and their gifts. When night came, each member would lay their present at the base of the mountain range, dancing and celebrating underneath the stars while thriving in the washes of moonlight.

This Tuturan, when she was ten, Nyx was exceptionally proud of what she had prepared. Normally, she and Harper would bake cookies, but this year, she wanted to do something that meant a lot to her. She had worked relentlessly, and now, the celebration was upon them, twilight tingeing the skies in purple ribbons, unfurling among the clouds.

Her parents and Harper waited in the door frame. Her mother called back to her, "Darling, we are going miss the first round of pucas if we don't hurry."

Carefully, Nyx clutched her offering to her chest, motivated to not miss her favorite dessert delicacy. The promise of that thick dough and powdered sugar had Nyx bouncing out the door. Families crowded outside, the twisting streets lined with hundreds of candles, their flames glowing like the stars themselves. Trailing their parents, Nyx and Harper took it all in, endless joy squeezing Nyx's heart.

The trek to the Arken Mountains from Yuli was a slow incline, Nyx's calves burning within minutes. But she didn't care; the only thought clutching her mind was how much she was looking forward to her family's faces when she revealed what she had made.

Happy chatter filled the air as a line started to form, Nyx watching as her neighbors and friends placed fruits, paintings, and flowers at the base of the mountain. Heart in her throat, Nyx watch the line disappear until finally it was her family's turn. Harper went forward with their parents, placing the baked goods at the base of the mountain. Bounding forward, Nyx rested the painting beside an inky onyx rose. Absolute silence followed.

"Nyx . . . You did that?"

Nyx beamed up at her parents, but her face fell at seeing Harper's furrowed brows.

"Mom, it's what I want to be when I grow up—a warrior! Someone who can defend Kiero."

Her painting depicted her in silver armor, her purple hair unbound, killing her opponent. The vivid dyes of the flowers she had spent days collecting made the blood spilling from the man's neck look deep in the firelight as her blade was imbedded within his flesh.

Behind her, laughter broke out, and her parents' faces flushed. Her dad snapped, "Nyx Astire, we come from a line of bakers, and this . . . this offering is just absurd! This cannot be your dream for yourself. Your hope?"

It had been those words that had started the pool of hot anger, lighting it within her belly. Tears blurred her vision as the laughter grew, building and toppling. Rushing back to her work, Nyx grabbed the side of the stretched canvas when flames burst from it, consuming it. Horrified, Nyx looked to her fingers. Had her mind done that? She stumbled back, and the fire grew, her parents' and Harper's shouts drowned out by the noises of their community.

All of the Tuturan gifts went up in flames.

Blinking out of the memory, Nyx swallowed that same anger down. Later in life, she had learned it was rare that a telekinetic could channel elemental powers, but that day, she had learned the extent of her power and the lack of control she had over her anger.

Nyx still battled with it.

Harper had helped soothe that part of her, but it had destroyed her relationship with her parents. Later, Memphis had enraged it—that consuming anger that made her react before thinking. Nyx used to think that part of her was broken. But now she understood it was fueled by her emotions, mostly by her fear.

Standing there with her broken nightstand, Nyx realized that she couldn't allow that terror to devour her any longer.

She flopped on her bed, the blankets puffing around her. First, she would allow herself time to digest that the gealltan ritual had worked. Then she would talk to Hesen about what *exactly* that meant for her. Her stomach flipped with the idea of being immortal for eternity.

Palms over her eyes, Nyx tried not to think about the next steps—moving the raiders up north and the possibility of opening a channel. First, she needed to talk to Lana and Azarius and learn what happened in Pentharrow and what kind of enemy they were up against.

Pentharrow had consisted of hundreds of people. Only three walked away alive from that attack.

***

The cool edge of the steel pressed against her throat. Waking, Nyx froze. "What in the—?"

"Shh, I wouldn't advise moving. Or talking for that matter, little *mystic*. I won't think twice about slitting your throat."

Blinking, Nyx took in the three raiders hovering over her in her room. Disoriented, Nyx noticed then the dwindling light filtering in through her window, the cooler temperature a tell that evening was upon them.

Slept too long.

The man with the dagger wrenched her up, his grip hard enough to bruise her arm. His eyes were dark and hooded, his caramel hair curling around his ear. He was dressed in a black chest plate and loose high-waisted pants. His bare arms were muscled and scarred, but he looked familiar. Her memory connected the dots, fast, as his face sparked her memory of when Zander and his crew captured her and Memphis. Up close, she realized he was not a man—just a teen.

Taking a leap of faith, Nyx tried to sound braver than she felt. "I'm guessing you lot are a bit unhappy I killed Zander. Why wait weeks to do something about it?"

Seething, he pressed the blade harder. "Shut *up*."

He towed her out of her room, and his comrades unsheathed their knives, stalking through the empty house.

Please let Kyrie be with Suri. Please don't let him get caught up in this.

Relief washed through her as they went down the stairs, passing through the empty living room and outside without seeing the Oijen twins or any of her other companions.

The raiders quickly shoved her behind the house in the dying golden light of the Risco Desert. A cart waited for them, often used to move imported goods from the Isles, and this one was empty besides the tarp. Nyx tried to slam her elbow into the raider's gut, but the knife pressed harder, making a trickle of warm blood run down her throat.

"You were ignorant to think we would bow to an outsider like you," he drawled.

He shoved her hard, and Nyx stumbled, slamming her mouth against the back of the cart. Blood filled her mouth, gagging her. Strong hands gripped her bare hips, her crop top torn and bloodied.

She was thrown into the back, the tarp instantly drawn over her and tied down.

Hesen. Help.

The thought was desperate as she tried not to panic, barely able to breathe because the cover was suffocating her. Sweat dripped off her nose, and the cart jostled forward, moving fast.

Nyx was taken, anyone that could help her none the wiser.

***

Concentrating on her breathing, Nyx thought of all the ways she could hurt these bastards. The tarp wouldn't budge no matter how much she beat against it, and conveniently, it somehow had neutralized her abilities. Her throat was swollen and thick from her yelling, sweat beading on every inch of her skin.

Those bastards.

Cramped in the back of the cart, Nyx was curled on her side, feeling every jostle and bump as the raiders towed her to only-gods-knew-where. All she could do was wait and try to fall into her soldier's training by emptying her mind. Memphis used to prep them in case they were caught by Adair's men. Give up nothing and always be prepared to lay down your life for the Rebellion. Back then, she wouldn't think twice—what *better* way to die than fighting the villain that stripped their world of humanity?

Now, she didn't know if being immortal meant she had already died.

Exhaling hard, she tried to not throw up in the confined space, the air becoming thick and too warm. Nyx's vision spun and her stomach heaved. She gave her last futile attempt at screaming, "Let me OUT!"

The tarp flew back, hands gripping her shoulders hard and throwing her out. Landing in the sands, Nyx blearily took in the three raiders grinning down at her in the night.

This is wasting time.

The surge of her ability rushing back into her body left Nyx stunned. The raiders were upon her, binding her wrists behind her back.

"What is the benefit of this? I can *help*—" Nyx's head snapped back from a punch, blood spraying the sand.

The closest raider grabbed her chin, forcing her to look at him. "Shut up. Now. Or you will wish you were already dead."

"Luka. You said this was just to make her stand down," one of his comrades pleaded.

Snapping her attention back to Luka, Nyx seethed, ignoring the pain blossoming across her jaw. "All this just to run me out of town? I'm flattered, boys. But we *all* have a bigger problem coming. My friends and I might have an alternative to gain the upper hand. You must really have a death wish bringing me out in the middle of fuc—"

"Do you ever stop talking? I'm not asking again," Luka snapped.

Smiling up at him, Nyx settled for the moment, watching the panic flare in the other raiders' eyes.

"Luka, we aren't killing her. She won her title rightfully," the young raider said.

"Nir, I told you that you shouldn't come, little brother. Zander at least had some self-preservation when it came to our clan. Stay out of Kiero's politics. And now, I can't stand the sight of everyone I love falling underneath this *bitch's* spell."

A cold knot formed in her stomach.

Luka unsheathed a knife from his belt, hand shaking as he pointed it at her heart. He was washed in moonlight, and Nyx realized he was no older than eighteen, fueled by revenge.

"Well, Luka. You made your friends tow me out here, but it seems you are at a crossroads. What do you intend to do?"

His hand shook violently as he bit his lip. Nyx watched the internal struggle, her life in his hands.

CHAPTER TWENTY-FOUR

EMORY

"Em." His voice was soft, a tickle against her ear. Eyelids heavy, Emory felt the corners of her mouth twitch. She took a quick peek, and the gray traces of dawn filtered through their room. They brushed along the bookshelves, highlighting their clothes laid everywhere.

"Em, I love you." Hot breath snaked along her neck as Brokk started a trail of kisses, his lips soft and hungry.

Pulling the blankets around her tighter, she murmured, "Brokk, come on. Just five more minutes of peace. I was having a terrible nightmare."

"Peace has always been a bit overrated, don't you think?" he asked.

"*Peace* is what we have given up the majority of our lives for," she breathed. Content. Warmth spread from her fingers down to her toes. Flipping, she poked him hard in the chest only to freeze.

Blood ran down from the corners of his golden eyes, thick and fast. Brokk's skin turned ashen, fresh blood pooling at the corners of his mouth. His healthy body crumpled in on itself, as if being deflated.

"No!" Roaring, Emory lunged forward, trying to grab him, to hold on.

He disappeared to ash beneath her touch.

What is happening? Panic surged through her as she stared at the spot where Brokk had been. She blinked, and her mind felt sluggish. Emory lightly touched the rumpled sheet. *What was I dreaming about?* The thought tugged at the back of her mind, but the answer was out of reach. Staggering out of bed, she heard a small giggle from the corner of the room. Chills snaked up her spine.

The bedroom in the Isles that looked normal now emitted an emerald-green hue, making Emory stop. Underneath the bed, green gas curled lazily toward her. The bookcases and other furniture pulsed as if they were living, breathing organisms. There was a small dresser on the far right, and the curtains moved with the air flow in a gentle sway. It must have rained last night because the dampness clung to the breeze.

The back of her neck prickled as Emory took a step closer. "Who's there?"

Again, the giggle drifted through the room, fear making Emory's heart jackhammer. Crossing the room, with shaking fingers, she threw back the thick ivory curtain—

Nothing.

Exhaling hard, Emory pulled away, only to feel fingers lock around her throat from behind, breath hot and sticky against her neck. "Rise and shine, Queen."

Pressure built on her throat; she thrashed, trying to get away.

Pain exploded along her spine, hot and consuming. The world started to peel away, singeing at the edges as dream and reality crashed together. The bedroom dissipated.

She blinked, and as the light adjusted, a few things came into focus.

You were captured and are being tortured. Marquis betrayed you to the Oilean.

Smooth, dark marble floors stretched out before her like the night sky had been captured and frozen beneath her feet. Gone was the fresh salt air, the crashing of waves of the Black Sea. Tremors ran up her legs, dread pooling in her stomach. Fear, hard and unrelenting, grasped her.

"Hello there." Perched on the throne, the Dark King looked at her, his gaze ravenous. The three Oilean stood around her; one slashed the back of her knees, forcing her to fall on the hard marble. "We captured her on the Shattered Isles, transporting her here with our magic after we had a little fun first."

"And Foster?" Declan asked.

"He escaped."

A beat passed. The king ran his long fingers over his mouth, standing, his footsteps echoing within the room.

Blood pounding, Emory gazed at the floor in front of her. The Oilean had bound her hands behind her back, their magic like a poison coursing within her body, confining her. The poison was constricting, and despite the gains she had made, her body soon gave out from the loss of blood. The open wounds behind her knees bled through her pants. Her ability coursed under her skin, feebly keeping her alive. Like a faint pulse, a dimming light, it was there, her constant lifeline, but it was unable to fully heal her.

The Dark King waved off his assassins. "So be it. Where is Lasair? I would think she is the one I should be thanking for your success."

Claws ripped into Emory's shoulder before she was thrown forward, her moan low as tears seeped from the corners of her eyes. Blood spattered on the floor, and she slipped in it, her jaw cracking off the ground.

"This pathetic human killed her."

Warm hands gripped her, lifting her up. "No, please. No." Her murmurs were low. Declan smirked down at her.

"So, you went to go see Marquis Maher? After all my efforts searching for you, you were with him? An interesting choice. An obvious waste of time. But you see, I ran into a little problem since I saw you last. I can't leave this room, this kingdom, without the darkness you stole from Adair—the ability I can smell running through your veins even now. It is the key that I have been looking for. One that I have been lost without."

Licking his lips, Declan leaned forward. "You and I are going to have some fun now, Emory Fae. Didn't I tell you we would be together? Didn't I promise you?"

Whimpers broke through her lips. Hot, radiant pain laced through her shoulder, sticky with her blood.

Declan smiled. "You will wish you never came to this world, Emory. I can promise you that much."

Addressing the Oilean, he said, "Make her pay for your sister's death. Then bring her to me. She will not want to miss what I have planned next."

The Oilean dragged Emory by her hair from the throne. She screamed and thrashed, not believing she was back in the Draken Mountains. Back with *him*. She almost didn't catch the Dark King's next words as her body left a bloody trail.

"You should know that Brokk Foster will come here, Emory. And when he does, I plan to use you as leverage."

There was a flash of his teeth, and the door slammed, leaving her with the Oilean. She stumbled between them as they navigated the once-lively hallways. Carcasses were everywhere, empty husks—forgotten. Down in the bowels of his kingdom, screams clambered up to meet them.

"The army is getting hungryyy. Your world won't stand a chance, and now that our king finally has you, we will all be free."

Their whispers doused the flickering hope she had left. The Oilean giggled. "Let's begin."

CHAPTER TWENTY-FIVE

BROKK

The ship creaked like a weathered branch in the wind. Brokk listened to the Black Sea methodically lapping onto shore as above deck, shouts and thundering footsteps rained down. Kiana's, Riona's, and Diedre's shouts cut through the chaos as cold sweat dripped down his spine.

Brokk went over his plan for the hundredth time. He looked over to the cracked mirror; dark circles puffed beneath his eyes, his face pale and gaunt, scars he still wasn't used to raised and roping down his neck. Donning a simple black shirt and pants, which Riona had taken from a man from the Isles, he sat, tying his leather boots too tight. His arrangement of swords looked too small as he strapped two curved, half-moon blades to his thighs. Two knives went into his boots next. The longsword was heavy in his grip; he strapped it across his back.

He was ready. His feet carried him down the hallway, the winter air pricking at his exposed skin. To his left was a group of men from the Shattered Isles.

"Do you have an extra cloak to spare?"

"Of course."

Too trusting. Too easy. Nodding his thanks, Brokk latched the button around his throat, pulling the hood up. The man was still talking, asking about readying for their new life, but Brokk was already gone, the man's questions and doubts swept up with the wind.

Riona and Kiana were above deck, trying to corral the anxious survivors from the Shattered Isles. Ripping his gaze from them, he knew he only had one window.

One chance.

Pulling his hood over his head, he kept his features doused in shadow. Following the group in front of him, Brokk took in Kiero for the first time in weeks: the lush forests of the Noctis Woods, the Draken Mountains piercing through the gray clouds, snowflakes starting to fly through the air around them.

His breath came out in frosty puffs. Keeping his head down, Brokk walked off the ship slowly. The port they had docked at hadn't been used in years but was enough out of range from the Dark King—for the moment, at least, anyways. Heart thundering, he noted the foundations and frames of buildings that had riddled the coastline, now nothing more than skeletons. Had Memphis grown up close to here, looking out to the endless sea, dreaming about the man he would become?

Passing by the group, breaking ahead, Brokk was maybe ten steps from the forest line. *Don't look back.*

Five steps.

Four.

Three.

Two.

Passing underneath the canopy of trees, he was free. Bones cracking, his body shifting, he dug his nails into the frosted earth, heaving. Scents assaulted him, and a low growl ripped from his chest.

Death. Decay. The scent was everywhere, like the earth was infected; he turned to the east. As he bolted, his muscles relished in the run, his paws pushing him harder and faster than he had ever ran before. Weaving through the trees, he left his friends behind. His court behind.

Wouldn't a prince do what was necessary to ensure their country survived? He felt his heart cracking in two, and he sent a feeble hope that Kiana and Riona wouldn't follow him, wouldn't try to stop him. That they would build a stronghold in Nehmai and get everyone to safety. That they would always continue to fight.

His whole life, he had been afraid to use his second ability after leaving Emory on Earth. To be able to go back in time and see memories lost to anyone else, to be able to find the truths that were hidden there—no person should have that power, let alone the ability to travel *channels* connected to other worlds like secret doorways only he could access.

Brokk had convinced himself to bury that part of him so deep, he was not only afraid but ashamed. It felt like it was a poison running through him, tempting him to use it more and more. He had been content for years just being Brokk, second in command in the Rebellion. A shapeshifter, sure, but equal among his peers. He could see the irony of the situation—after *all* these years, losing the fear of his ability had set him free. *Brokk Falkov.* In his mind, he repeatedly played what he had seen.

Now he knew who had the full story.

***

Night fell swiftly. Padding along the forest floor, Brokk tried to keep his hackles down. Far above, the waxing moon flitted ribbons of silver over the trees, the purple leaves glowing. This forest was bathed in old blood and destruction.

Narrowing his eyes, Brokk spotted the base of the Draken Mountains. He had watched, waited, for hours, padding along the same line, smelling the same scents. He severed all thoughts of Kiana and Riona, of all he had promised to be, all that they *thought* he was. He huffed, and a flicker of movement caught his eye to the left. As he moved toward it, the heavy scent of iron and blood filled the air.

"The king said to bring her body in. That it may still be useful, even half decayed now. It's been weeks."

Slinking low, Brokk used the forest and foliage to his advantage. He was one with the shadows, and the man and woman didn't suspect that they weren't alone.

The clearing was charred. Trees stripped of their bark, branches bare, skeletal limbs stretching white as bone. The decayed body of the woman was being held up by bloodied rope. A circle of ash on the ground was where the man bent down. He was young, his inky hair sweeping almost in his eyes. He wore Adair's old sash, his outfit bathed in blood.

Holding a knife, the woman started sawing through the rope, her face indifferent.

"Do you think he will know if we took a little bite? I'm *starving*." The man stood, circling her, watching something else. Or someone.

Creeping closer, Brokk skittered underneath a thicket of brush, finally getting a clear view of what they were working on.

The corpse's lush hair was now matted, chunks of her scalp broken off, and dried blood covered most of her body. Where her eyes had once been, empty sockets remained, maggots wriggling over her flesh. Brokk flinched as the body dropped.

The Dark King's soldiers heaved her up, making their way back. Brokk had made sure to stay downwind, knowing what the soldiers were capable of, given who had created them. The Oilean bred nightmares; this new army was no exception.

Quietly, Brokk stalked behind them, avoiding rustling any bramble.

"This will likely be one of his last meals, and then we will be able to feast," the woman whispered, eyes scouring the forest.

Inhaling deeply, Brokk took one last look at the moon. Shifting back in one motion, he was upon them. His boot connected with the back of the woman's calf, slamming it down so hard her bones splintered through her flesh. Unsheathing his sword, Brokk swung it with accuracy. His blade protruded from her chest, and he wrenched it back with a sickly squelch of blood.

She turned, smirking. "It will take more than that to kill—"

Her head rolled, decapitated from her neck. Brokk palmed his hilt, his shoulder muscles burning with his fluid movements.

Her body dropped as Brokk pinned her partner against the tree, his voice pure venom. "You will want to listen to me unless you want to end up like you friend here."

Those eyes. Staring, unyielding, blackened. Poisoned, like Emory's. Bowing to another master, empty of humanity.

Brokk pressed harder, and the man's trachea crunched under his hold. "Leave the girl. You're going to show me the entrance and then forget you ever saw me tonight. Understand?"

Wheezing, the man spat in his face. "And why exactly would I do that?" he rasped.

Brokk faltered. It was a risk, but one he was willing to take. It was all he could offer. "It would seem the Dark King has no problem wasting away his soldiers. Show me, and I will give you an entire new world to feast on."

Tilting his head, the man leaned in closer, nostrils flaring. "It's—you? The shifter."

Lessening the pressure just a hairsbreadth, Brokk whispered, "How do you survive without any bodies to ravage?"

"How do you know I won't just deplete you?"

Brokk sheathed his sword, stepping back, smoothing down the front of the soldier's shirt. "Why would you want one when you could have an infinite number?"

Licking his lips, the man whispered, "Just me, right?"

"Only you," Brokk promised.

The soldier looked to his partner, her blackened blood soaking the ground. He nodded. "Come with me."

***

They walked through the forest; snow drifted lazily down around them. The November air nipped at his face, and Brokk inhaled deeply. The winter often reminded him of Bresslin Stratton and the first war he had seen as a teenager, where snow and ice had been used to bind him, to hurt him. Shivering against the thought, Brokk looked to the intricate flakes against the silhouettes of the forest, and for the first time, he found it peaceful. Alluring even.

"This way," his guide murmured. He pointed to the rubble, and Brokk could taste the magic oozing from it like it was an exposed fissure. "Now, what you promised."

Drawing up his ability got easier every time. Stepping into that still place of power, Brokk sent the ripples out, his intention binding. Taking a step toward the husk of the soldier the demon bore, Brokk seethed, "I hope you rot in hell."

The soldier's eyes widened, mouth gaping.

Time and space fell, the opening revealing itself as Brokk shoved the man through the channel, his screams swallowed up. As fast as it happened, it was over, and Brokk dropped the ability, calming the rage inside of him.

Traveling the channels had always been risky, and he had known that without him as a guide, the soldier would freefall. Dying and lost in infinite space.

Crouching down, Brokk touched the weathered stone, closing his eyes, feeling the magic shuddering through his skin, his very core. The word felt condemned on his lips as he whispered, "Ceol."

It was like all the years ago when he had used the word to break their binds, when he and Memphis approached the war raging in the Academy. The rocks turned to dust, revealing the hidden entrance into Declan's kingdom. Soft light pulsed through the staircase as Brokk whispered to the winking stars, "Memph, watch over me."

CHAPTER TWENTY-SIX

EMORY

Tears rolled down her cheeks, her gaze flickering around the room. The space where the four-poster bed had once been was empty. On that wall, reflected in the mirror, she had donned Adair's sash and held the dream of freedom close to her heart. The room had seen her tears, heard her wishes, her fears. Of what being Queen of Kiero might mean. It was where she nursed her bruises, her wounds, as she slowly learned. Where she grew stronger each day with Adair Stratton.

The Oilean had brought Emory back to this room to break her.

The iron chains cut deeply into her wrists and ankles. Her blackened blood dripping onto the floor. The gore-spattered clothes from the Shattered Isles had been stripped off her, a thin plain white dress in their place. Bone and sinew were exposed where the Oilean had torn through her shoulder with their claws. Goosebumps prickling against the cold air, Emory sucked in quick breaths.

The room had been stripped bare, except for a steel basin in the far corner, four unlit candles by it. Digging inward, she tried to feel the familiar hum of the ability running beneath her skin. Silence echoed in its wake until the door slowly creaked open.

"Ah. Sissteers, she's awake."

Emory took in the Oilean as the door shut behind them. Their feet slapped against the cold floor. Jutting her chin out, cringing at their stretched grins, she forced herself to look them in the empty eye sockets.

Brokk is safe. He is safe. Safe. The thought granted her strength as she raised her chin and croaked, "Just get on with it."

Tilting their heads in unison, they said, "It's funny you should mock us when we can smell your fear. Pungent and rancid."

As they circled her, Emory nodded to the candles. "What do you plan then?"

They giggled, their bodies too close. Emory inhaled, and the sweet scent of rain and moss washed over the room right before she was plunged into darkness. Green flame ignited, lighting the candles as they were placed in four corners around her. Shadows climbed and danced along the stone wall.

"You know, at first he didn't scream. Brokk Falkov was strong, but we eventually broke him. Our knives cut into his flesh repeatedly, and his blood flowed. Until his only wish was for it to stop."

Their whispers bounced around her; Emory seethed. "Yet, he bested you. And found out the truth when you lied to him."

Hissing filled the space, and Emory craned her neck, trying to spot them. Adrenaline made everything seem too sharp, a dull roaring filling her ears.

"Our first mistake. You two did beautifully with that information you found, didn't you? Running to one another. Loving one another. Two royals, following their destiny while the world burned."

Snarls erupted in the room, the Oilean becoming silent beside the animalistic sounds coming from the shadows. Emory fought against the shackles, warm blood trickling down her bare legs. The candles flickered around her. Were they about to perform a ritual?

Cold steel brushed her chin, up along her cheekbone. Pausing. Calculating. "No one will hear you when you scream, young queen."

Pressure built; the knife slowly cut into her flesh. From her temple along her jaw, agonizing. Emory cracked her skull against the Oilean, forcing her to stagger back. Blood was falling so heavily, and Emory blinked rapidly, trying to ignore the flap of flesh from her cheekbone. Bones cracked as the sisters crawled toward her.

"Oh, this *will* be fun."

Cutting through the space, the knife lodged itself into Emory's other shoulder. She screamed against the pain, and the sisters were in front of her, chanting an old stirring language that made shivers climb up her spine. The thick smell of iron filled the air, and again, Emory screamed at the top of her lungs.

Candles flared brightly like dying stars; Emory felt herself slip. Wind howled, and she tasted bitter ash on her tongue, fire consuming the marrow of her bones.

Another hallucination. It's just another hallucination.

The room was gone. The Draken Mountains disappeared.

Standing in her shift, blackened with her blood, Emory realized Kiero had been swept away. The new landscape sprawling in front of her was gray and ashen, leeched of all life. She could imagine the once-rolling hills, lush and vibrant. The forests that once grew here were now skeletal trunks. In front of her, thousands of bones stuck up from the ground like grave markings.

"This will be your world's fate, young queen."

She spun, and the three women who stood behind her were breathtakingly beautiful. Olive skin, deep-brown eyes, chestnut hair braided back from their soft faces. Each held a bone dagger. They tilted their heads and their lips peeled back, revealing their sharpened canines. The *Oilean.*

"What happened to you?"

Walking in unison, they chanted, "Like you, we understand what it means to be in love with someone, that you would do *anything* for that person. We all loved Declan, and in return, he promised us a life where we would be invincible, the best assassins in Daer. No longer fey women, but something more sinister. We made sure an eternal night devoured our old world, and we will make sure Kiero serves that same fate."

Shivers crawled over her skin.

"We fed our world to the Dark King. We won't be stopped by a *girl*. Now, run, little queen. Run for your life."

Smirking, they disappeared in plumes of emerald smoke. Heart pounding out of frustration and agony, Emory tried to think about what to do. The wind swirled coolly around her, her bare, bloodied feet going numb. How many times had she run in the last month? Running to Adair. Running to Marquis. Running from her past or toward it, she wasn't so sure now. Pushing Marquis for his fleet, falling into his political games, helping him win over the Shattered Isles.

Now, there was nothing to be won over.

In this echo of a world long past, Emory couldn't help but think she had made all the same mistakes her parents had.

"Emory. Emory, darling, come here."

That whisper. That voice. How many times had Emory yearned to hear it again, to have it guide her? Writhing in pain, Emory lifted her head. In the distance, ribbons of smoke stretched toward the sky, deep blues and purples rippling through it. But before that, in a small alcove in the rolling plains, was a pulsing golden light. Radiant. Pure.

Emory stumbled, exhaustion nipping at her heels.

She couldn't feel the pulsing lifeline of her ability beneath her skin. Stripped of it, she was just a woman. Memories and time slipped through her fingers as she walked.

Of never-ending nights when she went to the movies with friends or on dates. Of sitting in her car, alone, looking at the stars, dreaming of the worlds that existed within the galaxies. Or during a thunderstorm, Emory would lounge by the window just to see the lightning streak across the sky. Or after the first snow fell and she would walk through the woods close to her old apartment on Earth, soaking in the crystalized beauty of the world captured in a frozen state. The snow provided peace in blanketed silence, and within all of these moments, Emory felt comforted.

That same deep pleasure, that feeling of safety and wonder, ripped through her core as Emory dropped to her knees in front of Nei Fae.

"Is this real?" Gasping through the tears, Emory grabbed her mother's hand, crying out when her mother's warm hand gripped hers right back; Emory fell into her. She hiccupped through the deep raking sobs, and her mother hugged her fiercely, that golden light bowing around them. *Like a shield.*

"Mom, what can I do? Are we safe?" Pulling back ever so slightly, Emory noticed her mother was young, golden hair spilling around her kind face. She looked no older than Emory was.

She whispered in Emory's ear, "For the moment." Nei tilted her head, and her lips pulled down. "You let them find you."

Emory's tears fell faster. Harder. "I didn't mean to. Please. I thought it was the right choice. To go where you were born. To ask the Isles for help, to call for their aid. And now . . ."

She drifted, the ash and charred earth still ripe in her nose. The hundreds of bodies. Hriste erased in the blink of an eye.

"I should have never come back. I should have died that night when I killed Adair. I was mistaken to think any differently."

"No. You have fallen and gotten lost. But you know what happens after? Even when we are broken, bruised, raw, and exposed the most?"

The wind of the growing storm howled but did not touch them through the golden shield. Swallowing hard, Emory asked, "What?"

"My darling, you must rise. You *must* fight to get back on your feet."

Her words ripped through Emory's chest, which felt like it caved in on itself as she rasped, "I can't. Not anymore. I'm not strong enough to beat the Dark King."

Her mother rested her forehead against Emory's, warmth rippling through Emory's skin. "You have always been stronger than you know. Listen to me now. You must fight. And you must allow what scares you most to guide you. Let it in, Em. Let what you have taken from Adair *truly* become a part of you, and you can defeat them all."

Thunder rolled, wind howling just outside their tiny sanctuary. Shaking, caked with her own blood, Emory locked her gaze with her mother's.

Nei stroked her cheek. "Don't be afraid anymore, my darling, of the darkness inside you." Hand still cupping her face, her mother smiled sadly. "You must do this, Emory. Go, and stop Brokk. He needs you now more than ever. You must rise. *Now.* And remember that I am always with you, in here." Laying a hand over Emory's heart, she bowed her head.

Emory blinked, and her mother was gone, along with the warmth of her touch. Emory dug her nails into her palms. Across the ashen plains, a storm raced toward her, eerie purple-and-green hues illuminating the pitch-black clouds. Another crack of thunder followed the lightning. Emory stood, shoving against her pain, against the will to give up.

Rise. Help Brokk. Rise. Help Brokk.

Her mind clung to those two commands as blood dripped down her collarbone, her vision spinning. She always thought that the darkness was ripping her apart, Adair's magic untamed. That there were no other options.

Let it become a part of you. Don't be afraid.

Sheets of rain fell, the skies opening. Freezing cold water collided into her. She blinked furiously against the three figures illuminated in the lightning, their bone daggers clutched to their breastbones.

"Look, sisters. The young queen walks to her own execution block with the last of her dignity." Giggles floated all around her. She slipped in the mud, and her body slammed to the ground. The rain fell harder, smudging any definition this bleak world may have had. Steel kissed the bottom of her jaw when an Oilean tapped hungrily against her skin, the sisters all in front of her.

"Stand up and die, Emory Fae."

Emory rasped, "Why would you care about my dignity?"

More giggles floated through the storm. "What fun is it if you don't fight, don't want to live? Come now, where is the queen this world has been waiting for? Where is our worthy opponent?"

Let it become a part of you.

In the pouring rain, as Emory was caught between nightmare and reality, the steel kissed harder into her flesh, and the Oilean roared, "Stand UP!"

What other choice did she have? She lifted her gaze, and standing behind the Oilean, radiant as the sun, was her mother, nodding, a hard glint in her eyes.

For Kiero, for Brokk, this would be the cost.

For *herself*, this would be the cost.

Standing slowly, fear coiling in the pit of her stomach, Emory stared at the Oilean, the storm raging around them. *This is your chance.*

Her entire will dove deep into the forgotten crevices of herself where bits of her soul were tucked away. Her intention forced her body to stop fighting the ability she had stolen. To accept the darkness that had been ripping her apart. That had been killing her because she was resisting it, afraid of who she might become.

The last thing she saw was her mother smiling.

Agony exploded through her chest. It tore through her lungs, and blood seeped from the corner of her mouth, her body collapsing back into the mud. Vaguely, like looking down a tunnel, she saw the Oilean howling with laughter.

But Emory held on. Her body was immobilized, but she still felt the ability rise, as if the entire time that part of Adair was waiting for her. Waiting for her permission.

"Em?" Adair—his kind, dark eyes and unkempt hair—appeared, shyly reaching his hand down to her to help her up. The corner of his mouth twitched. It wasn't fear that flooded through her but relief. No trace of the Mad King was left in him; that emptiness that she hated in his eyes was replaced by familiar warmth. The man who had killed her parents, who had ripped Kiero apart, was nothing more than a nightmare—one she would gladly wake from.

She reached for him and his hand grasped hers. He lifted her up.

"Adair? How is this possible? Aren't you . . ."

He nodded then looked behind them at the Oilean, who had been blocked by some sort of shield. He was buying her time.

"To answer your question, yes, I'm dead. But where you are is a neutral place between the living and the afterlife. You can shape it whichever way you wish. In your case, when you were here last—"

"My parent's study."

"Exactly. But this time, Foster isn't here to travel it, and the Oilean shaped it to make you believe you are in Daer. But your mother and I have been waiting for you since last time. Well, our souls have."

"There is so much I want to say."

His eyes softened. "I know. But we don't have long."

Heart pounding, Emory whispered, "You have to understand. I never wanted it to happen the way it did. I believed I could *save* you."

Warmth surrounded her as Adair pulled her in close, hugging her fiercely. "And you have to understand that it was never your fault. I should have reached out for help when I was young. I should have opened the walls I forced up. I should have told you about my dad abusing me. The Book of Old's magic sang to me, to my dark desires, and I believed I was alone. After that, it was too late. Adair was buried, and the Mad King took over."

Tears welled, her throat tightening. "But you never were alone. I was there, and I wanted my best friend."

The sob broke from her chest, ragged, when Adair whispered, "It's not your fault."

Stepping away, Emory shivered. "You know what I have to do now, right? Is that why you have come?"

"You have always been strong, but you know you can't beat the Oilean or Declan with just your ability. Or even with *my* ability wearing away your body every time you use it. Allow it in. Make it yours, Em. Truly this time." Adair paused. "I'm here now. They can't see me." Adair intertwined his fingers with hers, squeezing reassuringly.

Crippling pain crept up her calves, slithering along her thighs, passing her hips and stomach. Racing down her arms. It blistered through her fingertips. Up her throat.

"Hang on, Em. I'm lowering our defenses."

She swayed but managed to stay upright, watching her blackened veins bulge and spread all over her body. This pain was like a void; it swallowed her whole until it had her pinned, and she wished it would take her.

"Look, sisters. She has accepted her death."

What kind of queen will you be? Will you rise? Will you rule this broken kingdom with me?

Different memories clashed and burned together in her mind, but as a tear slid down her cheek, she turned to look at Adair, who let her hand go. A sad smile tugged his lips as he mouthed, *Be strong.*

The rain poured harder, and the Oilean holding the dagger stepped forward, snarling, "You never deserved this quick of a death."

Emory's pain peaked, making her want to rip her bones out of her own skin, her vision spinning. She tasted blood in her mouth.

The Oilean walked up to her, so close Emory could smell rotting flesh on the Oilean's breath before the dagger was thrust straight into her heart.

Blinding pain erupted, and Emory felt gravity leaving her. Suddenly, she was splayed in the mud, her pulse beating, hard, fighting to stay alive. She was numb, yet it felt like she was burning alive at the same time. Opening and closing her mouth, she gurgled, choking on her own blood. Darkness overwhelmed her senses, the pain finally starting to ebb.

The last thing she saw was Adair's hand gently brushing away her soaked hair from her face.

***

"What should we do with the body, sisterrrs?" The drawl was slow, calculated.

"The Dark King won't be happy we have killed her," another voice piped in.

Emory slowly stirred as the hissing faded. Now she only heard the thunder's rolls as the mist of freezing cold rain drizzled over her. She was lying in the mud, thoroughly confused, and her heart pounded. *I'm alive.* She reeled from the impossibility of the situation, and her nerves buzzed, Adair's ability throbbed beneath the surface of her skin.

It was growing.

It had become something uniquely her own, something new.

The sheer might of the power had her inhaling sharply. She felt *amazing.* Remaining still, Emory tried to look for Adair. Unable to see him, she assumed he was gone, leaving her alone to seek her revenge. Sorrow tugged at her heart, and Emory mentally said goodbye to Adair, wishing they had more time.

"He won't have a body to mourn over after we are through." Snarls of pleasure suddenly circled her, and Emory felt the cold steel from one of their swords. The tip pressed on the base of her neck.

Twisting, Emory realized that her previous wounds were healed. Gone, like they had never existed.

The pain was truly *gone*. In its place was adrenaline at the sheer might of what lurked within her. No echoes of Adair. No echoes of the Oilean. No echoes of darkness. The dark magic had bowed to her will, creating harmony with the light ability she'd possessed. A sweet equilibrium that made something more powerful.

Emory flexed the completely reborn ability to her command.

Standing, she grabbed the first Oilean's wrist, her ability burning in her veins.

Their shock was evident in their silence. Emory smirked before raw energy exploded from her chest, throwing the Oilean easily a hundred yards back. The force ripped mud from the ground, sending it flying with her enemies.

Before, the act would have made Emory expend the ability more, made her dive deeper into the darkness while fearing a loss of control, of Adair's ability killing her. If anything, now, she was invigorated. The thought that this beautiful power could harm her was gone.

It was her salvation.

She flexed her right hand, and the hilt of Anithe appeared, her beloved sword materializing. Its obsidian steel was a familiar sight in this void.

Emory watched the three remaining Oilean rise, coated in dirt. The storm had stilled, and within this barren wasteland, Emory let it fill her—how much these demons had hurt her family, friends, and Kiero. They had inflicted years of pain and loss; *they* did not deserve a quick death.

And it was not just hers to relish in.

Exhaling, Emory threw all her concentration into the idea, her expanding energy rippling out from her in invisible wavelengths. *Mom? Adair? Are you there?*

They appeared, washed in golden light before her.

She reached to grab their hands and expected her fingers to meet thin air. Her ability built within her, and instead, she was met with flesh and bone. Her bottom lip wobbled as she nodded toward their enemy, saying, "Together."

A lopsided grin spread across Adair's face, dimming the memory of the Mad King. *This* was her best friend, the man whom she had shared every secret with when she had been young, who knew her dreams and worries unlike any other person. Squeezing his hand, Emory caught her mother's gaze.

Nei said, "Together. But first I need to do this."

The golden light intensified around them. The back of Emory's neck prickled, the hairs standing on end. Emory could sense a shift in the balance of energy weaving through the air. Emory spotted her father—Roque—as he appeared behind them.

He hugged her. "Emory, we are all so proud of you."

Stepping back, tears burning her eyes, Emory watched now as hundreds upon hundreds of souls appeared. She assumed it was every person that had been killed by the Oilean.

Anithe ignited, black flames crackling hungrily. Nodding at her parents and Adair, Emory ran, thundering footsteps echoing behind her.

Adair appeared beside her, roguishly grinning before vanishing. He reappeared behind the nearest Oilean, and Emory shoved her. She swung Anithe, and the steel cut through the demon's neck, blood and bone spraying over her face. Gasping, Emory saw the body drop. She lowered Anithe, and the screams of the remaining Oilean cut through the air. The others didn't have time to react before the body burst into inky flames, incinerating under Emory's touch.

Adair came up beside her. "Em, look."

The remaining Oilean stood hand in hand, emerald gas drifting from their interlocked fingers. Leading the charge were Nei and Roque. Unexpectedly, a towering wall of green fog loomed in front of them. Nei passed through it first, and Emory watched as her mother dissolved into golden particles. Her father followed.

"NO!" Emory screamed.

Stepping back, the two Oilean looked pointedly at her, their sinister grins pinned back on their pale flesh as they tilted their heads. Trying to run, Adair grabbed her arm.

"The fog has spread too fast. They're gone, Em."

Her rage overcame her, a sharp ringing sounding in her ears. The ground shook beneath their feet.

Adair whispered, "Use your anger, Em. Those moments when we were in the Noctis Woods training were the closest times in years I felt like myself . . . that I felt human. The Oilean took everything away from us. Give them every reason to fear you."

The earth beneath the Oilean opened, black thorny vines curling around their ankles and wrists, lifting them up off the ground as they screeched. The thorns embedded themselves into their calves and arms, black blood dripping. Willing the vines to stop, Emory walked up to them, Adair beside her.

The green fog grew closer to them, but Emory continued to walk toward it until she was so close, she could reach out to touch it. Her ability thrived under her command; any wish she conjured in her mind became reality. The fog spun, forming into thousands of gas orbs before solidifying into individual green snowflakes. They caught the muted light and gleamed like gems until they melted.

Satisfied, Emory went back to face the Oilean. "Your time is over."

Looking back at Adair, catching his gaze, she said, "This is for my friend you took everything from. He deserved better."

They cackled, spittle flying from their lips. "The *Mad King*? He was always—"

Reaching up, Emory lightly touched her fingers to the Oilean's cheek, interrupting her, "You will kill your sister while we watch, and then you will end yourself."

She didn't break eye contact, and a black substance absorbed into the Oilean's skin, snaking from Emory's fingertips. Emory felt every second as her ability took over the Oilean's mind and will. Emory pinned her gaze on the remaining Oilean, who shook her head, staggering back. For the first time, Emory could *smell* the fear within them.

"You will obey me."

She stepped back, exhausted, and the thorns lowered the sisters to the ground.

"Sister, what are you doing? Get her! GET HER!"

Emory watched as the opposing Oilean launched herself at her sister's jugular. She sank her pointed teeth into her sister, eating her flesh, black blood spraying from the wound. Screams pierced through the silence, but as much as Emory wanted to look away, she watched the remaining Oilean destroy who she held closest in this world. She ripped her sister's heart out, and the body dropped.

Trembling, the last Oilean brought her nail up to her throat. Emory could see the demon fighting against her ability, trying to resist the order.

Emory was stronger.

The Oilean's nail grew into one long, bone-white, steeled edge.

Emory felt Adair's fingers interlace through hers, and she turned, folding into his chest. She heard gurgling as the Oilean choked on her own blood, then the thud as the body dropped. Tears slipped down Emory's face as she hugged Adair, sobbing.

"Emory." His voice was soft.

Sniffing, she looked up, only to see the side of his face start to dissolve into golden particles.

"Adair, thank you," she said.

Gently, the particles drifted through the air. She reached up to run her finger along his jaw, but he vanished in a gentle wind, back to wherever his spirit rested.

Drawing a deep breath, she stood taller, not taking one second to look at the bodies of the Oilean. They were nothing but a bloody and ugly mark on Kiero's history.

Wiping her cheeks, Emory expanded and pushed her ability straight as an arrow behind her. In a whoosh, she heard the fire ignite, could feel the magic destroying their flesh, overriding their power.

The demons that had hunted her were reduced to nothing.

Dropping to her knees in relief, Emory tried to steady her breath. The ground lurched underneath her as the graveyard around her bled away. She felt cement form underneath her knees, smelled the burned scent of melted wax. She snapped her eyes open; she was back in the Draken Mountains.

The Oilean are dead.

Emory rose to stand, her ability flowing within her, stronger.

The Dark King was next.

CHAPTER TWENTY-SEVEN

BROKK

The passage was narrow. Slipping into the shadows, Brokk adjusted to his surroundings. A mustiness clung in the air. Pausing, he pressed himself against the wall. Footsteps echoed toward him, hurried and sure. He unsheathed a blade from his thigh.

The man was before him, nostrils flaring as he turned empty eyes to where Brokk was hidden. Moving quickly, Brokk slit the man's throat. With a gurgle, the man dropped. Brokk was already gone, diving deeper into the kingdom. Wiping the black blood on his pants, he sheathed his knife, controlling his breathing as he looked around the drab tunnels. No one stirred, but nausea collided with him as he saw the husks of bodies strewn around.

They had been sucked dry.

He was unnerved and sweat dripped down the back of his neck. Clenching his fists, he stepped forward right when the curved knife appeared from behind him.

It was cool against his throat, and the voice was a frigid whisper in his ear. "Not so fast."

Closing his eyes, he said, "You've got to be kidding me."

He twisted, and Kiana's silver eyes flared as he gripped her wrist, shoving the knife out of his face. "What are you doing here?"

Her magic curled around his limbs faster than he could react, immobilizing him. Kiana seethed, "We are leaving now. Are you insane? Did you actually think you could slip away?"

"I didn't ask you to be here. I don't *want* you to be here, Kiana."

"After everything we have been through, you decided to abandon us without a word?"

"Kiana, as your prince, I'm telling you to leave. This isn't your concern."

"And as your friend, I'm asking what you have found out that has made you come back to this graveyard." She lessened her hold, grabbing his hands with her shaking ones. "Please tell me."

Behind them, there was a slow clap before a smooth voice broke out. "Yes, do tell."

They spun around.

The Dark King stood in the tunnel, black eyes glinting with a feverish hunger, a smirk on his face. His skin was shallow, and there were dark bruises underneath his eyes.

Kiana shoved Brokk behind her seconds before her magic exploded from her in a silver wave, making the earth quake beneath them. Brokk watched as it collided into Declan. Staggering back, the Dark King snapped his fingers, black flames erupting from him, racing forward. Fire rippled in front of them in a blinding display—Declan walked through it, too fast and unnatural.

Grabbing Kiana by the throat, slamming her back, he drawled out, "You are nothing more than immortal filth."

Shifting, Brokk snapped his massive canines, growling low. Another wave of rippling silver magic expanded from Kiana.

"Now, I would stop that if I were you," Declan said. He reined his fire back, still holding on to Kiana, choking her. "I was wondering when you would come, young Falkov. But what extraordinary circumstances that you should come on this day. Do you have any idea who is in my assassins' grasp as we speak?" Kiana wriggled underneath his hold; Declan pressed harder, looking at Brokk as he said, "Emory Fae."

The world stilled, and Brokk couldn't move. His mind scrambled. It could be a ruse. It could be a lie—a trap. Flicking his eyes to Kiana, he shifted back to his human form in one motion, feral. "Let her go."

"Why would I do such a thing? A naithe warrior who is sworn to you? What a delight. What *leverage*. Does she know the truth about you, Brokk?"

"I said let her go."

The Dark King smirked. "No, I don't think I will."

There was a whisper on the wind, and their world bled away.

Brokk blinked, and they reappeared in what looked like a throne room, the ceiling open to the snowy skies above. Declan threw Kiana to the ground, and Brokk rushed to her side, checking her over. Her flesh was charred where Declan's grip had been around her neck. Tears slid down her face, but before Brokk could react, he was thrown back. Kiana's screams echoed around them.

Brokk lunged, trying to get to her. Inky chains appeared, binding her hands, her feet. Brokk recoiled as he realized the links were embers, and the smell of burned flesh filled the room.

"Now, where were we?" Declan paced nearby. "Ah yes. You and I. Should I tell your warrior about what kind of prince she is fighting for? That everything her army died for was a lie? Years of her life wasted, searching for a false prince?" Brokk couldn't move. Kiana's screams rained down as the Dark King took in his expression. "You knew the truth, and yet you didn't tell them?"

Those words pinned him, and Brokk locked eyes with Kiana across the room.

"Well, well, *well*. Isn't this interesting? The valiant Brokk who survives the direst conditions. Who has slipped through my Oilean's grasp one too many times. Why would such a noble character like yourself seek me out alone? The Dark King who plans to ravage this world, shredding everything you hold dear."

Licking his cracked lips, Brokk whispered, "I want to bargain with you."

Narrowing his eyes, the Dark King prowled around the room. "First, tell her the *truth*. Of why, alone, you have come to me."

With shaking hands, Brokk looked at Kiana, his stomach twisting with nerves. He was dying from the inside out, the truth a poison.

"My parents lied. To Nehmai. To you. I . . . I have learned I was only their son by adoption." Kiana's tears and blood spattered onto the marble floor. "I am a fey prince from Daer. I used my ability to see the memories, Kiana. It's the reason my ability is different, the truth my parents tried to keep from me, died protecting me from and—"

Declan cut him off. "The Falkovs thought it was a gift—bearing peace between two worlds. They couldn't have a child, and our father, well . . . he made it seem like a loving peace treaty between Daer and Kiero. Our father found it fair, seeing as he had two boys. Though compassion surely wasn't his strong suit. Not that you would know that, though. Such a golden life you have had. Such love you have known."

"And you . . ." Brokk couldn't say it. Wouldn't say it.

Declan laughed in pleasure. "A long-lost family reunion it would seem, *Brother*."

Kiana's gaze flickered between the two men, her face pale in disbelief. Snapping his fingers, Declan gagged her when she went to speak.

A ring of inky, ravenous fire appeared, enclosing them.

"I knew when you found out the truth, you wouldn't be able to stay away. You must have so many questions. Not only will I have Emory's stolen magic back but you as well. We will devour this world, together, Brother. Finally unstoppable."

Brokk growled. "Family isn't defined by blood. And you are a ghost of a human. A ghost of a man. A *murderer.* I came because there is something you don't know."

The Dark King paused. "Oh?"

"The last thing our . . . biological father did." *The only figment of truth the Oilean knew. That they had thrown in with the lies. My life altered. I was bargained for. I was a light in my parents' life. How would they know I was cursed?*

"A curse," Brokk whispered. For Emory, he could do this. He had always been condemned; he just didn't know it. The sand had finally run out of the vial.

Declan chuckled darkly, but a light flickered in his eyes, curious. "And how do you know this?"

"We both know how he was. Or at least, I saw how he was through my ability, through traveling through the memories. He was a maniac, bloodthirsty. He never cared about us, but about how much leverage he had. There was something he always hated more—*Kiero.* He gave my parents—who couldn't bear children—a cursed child they would grow to love, never knowing that my life was tied to something much more unstable. He thought that was the ultimate punishment."

Brokk didn't have to explain further. Declan knew how his ability worked. How twisted their father had been. Using them as political property. Pitting them against each other. But this was the last unspeakable thing he had done before he had given Brokk up.

"A curse binding us together. If you die, I die."

Finally, the Dark King stopped. Doubt flickered within his dark gaze. "You're lying."

"Why else would I walk straight into the heart of your kingdom? Without backup?"

The knife was in Brokk's hand before Declan could react. Poised right over his heart.

"Now it's your turn to listen, *King.*"

CHAPTER TWENTY-EIGHT

EMORY

"If you die, I die."

Frozen in the shadows of the hallway, Emory tried to still the ringing in her ears. Tried to quell the fear lacing through her veins. The impossibility of it all.

If you die, I die.

Still in the bloodied shift, Emory palmed the rusty knife she had ripped off a discarded body. Slowly, she peeked into the throne room. Declan was frozen, watching Brokk poise the knife right above his own heart. Kiana was trapped in the iron chains squeezing her body, staring straight toward Emory with wide eyes.

Emory pressed her body flush to the wall once more, and then she exhaled.

She had to get Brokk out. *Now.*

Her ability curled, poising strength in her muscles, energy surging through her nerves. She ran, and the entire room was plunged into sudden darkness. Declan's outrage roar tore from him; Emory was already clambering over Brokk, shoving him away from the Dark King, her hands moving before her mind could catch up.

She felt the curve of his shoulder and up his neck, until she was holding his face in her hands.

Heart in her throat, she whispered, "Brokk. It's me. We have to go now."

"Em?"

In the darkness of the throne room, death brushing so close to both of them, her lips slammed into his. Hungry, desperate. Panting, she broke away. "Please, I'm sorry. I was trying to keep you safe. I didn't want to hurt you. But we have to move."

She grabbed his hand, her knife clattering to the floor, and she hauled him behind her, running toward Kiana. Her ability guided her through the absolute darkness, like a thread pulling her closer. She dropped to her knees, and panic clawed up her throat.

"Well, Queen, it would seem you are a formidable opponent after all."

Emory's hands froze above Kiana.

Thousands upon thousands of swirling orbs of fire ignited, floating throughout the throne room, illuminating the snow cascading slowly down from the gray clouds. Hissing filled the room as the snow hit the flames, vaporizing into steam.

Standing, Emory shoved at Brokk. "Get out. RUN!"

Chuckling, Declan shook his head. "The Oilean?"

"I killed them."

"As surprising as that is, I don't think that's the most interesting thing that happened, is it?" His voice was dangerously low, a caress amongst the carnage scattered within the kingdom.

She could feel Brokk's breath down the back of her neck, could hear Kiana's moans.

Brokk wasn't leaving.

He needed to leave.

Stalking toward Declan, she smirked. "Not in the least." *Keep him talking. Keep him distracted.*

"I can smell it on you. The difference. Before, the dark magic was killing you." Lazily, he circled them, dark eyes homing in on

Brokk. The months hadn't been kind to Adair's body; his hair was too long and his face so gaunt he was like a walking skeleton.

Dropping her feeble weapon, Emory said, "Let them go. Your fight is with me anyways."

"Oh, I don't think so. You know, beneath this hollowed-out mountain your previous king called home, an army unseen by this world now lies, ready for my command. I had been waiting for *you*, but things can change in a second, it would seem."

She tensed as guttural screams erupted behind them. Animalistic. Twisting, she saw Brokk's face erupt into fear, his yell echoing around them.

Kiana had erupted into silver flames.

"NO!" Brokk screamed, lunging, but Emory grabbed him, holding him back. It was too late; the naithe warrior's ashes were already scattering on the marble.

Exhaling hard, Emory looked to Declan who was *pulsating*. Silver light slithered over his arms, legs, and chest. His eyes rolled back into his head.

"Brokk, you have to leave. Please go." Her pleas were desperate.

"You really have to recognize when you have already lost." Declan's voice was low; spinning, he materialized behind Brokk, lips peeling over his teeth.

"NO!" Emory screamed.

Like snakes, black smoke whipped from the Dark King, restricting Brokk's throat, his wrists and ankles bound in manacles as he writhed on the ground in front of her.

"You aren't the only one who can make magic bow to their ability, Emory Fae. Remember that." He smiled. "Now, my brother and I have other business to attend to. Luckily, you weren't the only key to liberate me from this kingdom as I was banking on. The naithe warrior's ability has not only freed me but will go to good use, I promise."

With a wicked, arrogant smirk, Declan disappeared. With Brokk.

"NO!" In the empty throne room, Emory ran to where they had been, dropping to her knees, tears sliding down her face. "No, no, no, no, please, *no*."

Grappling at the empty space, she crumpled, clawing at the marble, deep gouges ripping into the floor, her fingernails ripping off.

The room was silent. Another broken kingdom within her grasp, another body lost on her behalf. Brokk was gone. Imprisoned by his *brother*. How could this happen? After every road they had been down, now she carried this knowledge—this ultimatum. If she were to kill the Dark King, she would be murdering the man she loved as well.

Her eyes were hot and swollen when she looked to where Kiana had been, unable to move, unable to do anything but sit in the throne room. Emory was so tired. She had believed she could save Brokk, and she had failed. How could she keep going, knowing she had taken ten steps back?

Debris floated around her, her ability pulsing like an energy wave, cocooning her in numbness. Her mind replayed the look on Brokk's face—wide-eyed and scared, bound by darkness.

Imprisoned.

She felt like she was about to throw up when a deep rumbling ran up the empty passageways toward her, sounding like it was coming from the base of the Draken Mountains.

You must move. Her thoughts coaxed her, her mind only processing that one command.

Like a ghost, Emory rose, padding quietly toward the door. She peeked out into the hallway—it was empty. Yet the noise rose to her like a cresting wave.

So, she walked.

And walked.

Down, she spiraled, past moldy brick walls spattered with blood and gore. Past empty rooms strewn with clothes and bodies, furniture blown apart. She navigated through the corpses, the people who brought life to Adair's kingdom. The hallways she once walked, a rebel disguised as a princess. As she passed each one, her heart dropped further. They had deserved better.

Coming out to where the market had been held, Emory slid flush against the wall once more, crouching low. There, a door was grating open as hundreds of men and women stood. Their murmurs were monotone, overlapping one another, their chant making the hair on her neck rise.

"The true king rises. The true king rises. The true king rises."

Winter winds howled within the cavern, as row by row, they marched, eyes void of humanity, funneling out, repeating the same thing again and again.

The true king rises.

From the bowels of Adair's kingdom, the army left, likely heading toward Declan.

Toward Brokk.

Swiftly, as quietly as she could, Emory ran through the hallways, panic exploding through her. Her ability funneled out of her chest, leading her back to the room where the Oilean had taken her. Her footsteps echoed like thunder, her breath ragged. Slipping into the doorframe, she saw them: the Oilean's broken bone blades.

Grabbing all three and closing her eyes, she dove into the unexplored power that crawled under her skin, curling around her heart. Holding the picture of Anithe in her mind, Emory whispered, "I call on these ancient blades. I call on the blood spilled from their previous masters. Help me. Carve me a blade born from the darkness. Carve me a blade that will bind worlds. That will have no mercy for my enemies. Please. *Help me.*"

Repeatedly, she begged, hands shaking, tears falling fast.

There was a stir of coldness, and Emory peeled her eyes open. Anithe's hilt held the bone that the Oilean had once wielded. That had once carved into her flesh as she begged for mercy.

The longsword was beautiful, sparks flying off the ends, the steel as dark as the midnight sky. She stood and smoke curled down over her arms, down her legs. She gasped when she watched it incinerate her shift. Her bare skin prickled against the air; the smoke encompassed her body, warm and gentle.

Boots formed first. Sleek leather laced up to her knees. Padded pants were next, thick and warm; her insulated, armored shirt was equally as elegant. Emory felt the harness clipping over her shoulder, a sheath for her sword. Smoke cascaded down behind her, a hooded black cape soon falling softly around her. Tears pricked at the corners of her eyes when she looked down at her brooch, the silver metal fine and elegant. In the middle, like a teardrop and as warm as the sun, a gem winked up at her.

Sheathing the blade, Emory wiped her face.

Rise.

CHAPTER TWENTY-NINE

MARQUIS

The old dock creaked as they slid up beside the other ship. Winter had come, turning Kiero into a crystalized world overnight. Snow collected on the barren trees, the frost kissing the ground as far as Marquis could see. Ryker stood beside him as the sun crested on the fifth morning since leaving, Hriste still burning behind them.

"Friends or foe?" Ryker whispered, more to himself than to Marquis. Marquis would recognize the inky planks of the ship anywhere.

Mouth running dry, he nodded to Riona and Diedre standing on the opposite deck, the promise of death flaring in Riona's eyes. He whispered, "Friends."

Ryker started barking orders to his crew, their ship springing into action.

Riona and Diedre watched as Marquis strode to the railing, stepping off, the Black Sea rushing up to meet his feet, forming steps to cross to the other ship.

"Riona. Diedre. You have no idea how happy I am to see you both," he rasped.

"Marquis . . ." Riona looked over his shoulder, clearing her throat. "I take it things didn't go the way you planned?"

"You could say that."

Diedre pulled him into a fast and swift hug before breaking away, looking over the numbers he had brought with him. Always calculating and weighing their odds.

There was a pull of Riona's lips, shadows dancing across her features. She murmured, "That makes two of us."

Standing closer to the immortal, Marquis could see the dark bruising underneath her eyes, how they darted toward the mountain range. Heart stuttering, Marquis followed her gaze. "Riona, where is everyone else?"

Cold fear gripped his heart when her gaze slid back to his. "I have already led most of the refugees from the Shattered Isles to Nehmai, thanks to your clear passage."

"But Kiana? Brokk?"

Again, her gaze slid back to the Draken Mountains. "Brokk went to the Dark King. Kiana was supposed to meet me back here with him. Diedre was too stubborn to leave me alone, despite my protests." He ran a hand through his hair, and the warrior's eyes glazed over as she whispered, "That was four days ago."

As the sunrise flared into brilliance, tendrils of smoke curled in the distance, black, like poison stretching across the clouds.

Marquis grabbed Riona's hands, and her glare was piercing. "We have to get these people to safety. Hriste is gone. The Shattered Isles, gone."

"My condolences." Her voice was gruff.

"Riona, I was wrong. I'm sorry."

"It's all in the past. We are about to learn the price anyways."

She dipped her chin, and Marquis watched the flush drain out of her cheeks as he looked over his shoulder.

The entire world fell out from underneath him.

Emory broke through the forest line, surreal-looking, an inky cloak flowing behind her. Her armor was sleek, like a piece of the night had been tailored just for her.

Stopping, she glared at him.

How is she alive? How? Running, he pumped his arms fast, flying down the dock. Still, she didn't move, didn't give anything away in her features. She seemed to have aged since they had seen each other last. A deep hollowness echoed within her blackened gaze.

Stopping in front of her, he wanted to fold her in his arms, but clasping his hands, he whispered, "Emory?"

She was unmarred, but Marquis could still hear her screams ripping through him. They had haunted his every waking moment and every crevice of the night.

"Em?" He didn't know what else to say. Didn't know what to do. She blinked as if just realizing who was in front of her.

"You brought part of an army." Her voice was low, intense.

"What's left of it," he replied.

Stepping toward him, she whispered, "You left me behind. Left me to *die*."

Black skies. The air around him stirred as he balked. "Emory, listen to me. It wasn't that straightforward."

The knife was poised above his heart before he could utter another word. "No, you listen to me. I thought . . ." her voice broke. "I thought we were friends. I should kill you on the spot. I promised you I would if you crossed me."

Pressure built, pain lacing as he could feel the steel tip through his clothes, but he didn't fight against her. He deserved every ounce of her anger, of her spite. Closing his eyes, he prepared himself.

But instead, he heard a *thunk* and saw the knife lodged into the frozen ground.

"A debt you will pay another way, Marquis. You're lucky I have more pressing matters than you at hand."

Riona walked toward them as pain shone in Emory's eyes. "Emory. How are you here? Where is Kiana? Brokk?"

Emory's silence was enough as she bowed her head. "I'm so sorry, Riona. Kiana didn't make it."

The killing blow. Marquis watched as Riona digested the news. She buckled, but Emory was there, catching her. Helping bear her pain. Her whispers drifted on the wind, cutting through him deeper than any knife.

"She went back in for Brokk. Fighting against Declan until the end. Fighting for Brokk until the end."

Riona's sobs cracked him as Emory hugged her, her gaze slicing into him.

"What about Brokk?" Marquis asked. He flinched at the dark fury that churned within Emory's black gaze.

She stood, lifting Riona. "Declan has him."

"You are going after them." It wasn't a question, and Marquis glanced again to the smoke curling in the clouds. He grabbed the knife from his feet, slashing the steel into his skin; the blade cut deep. Blood dripped onto the frost beneath his feet as he lowered himself onto one knee, looking up to Emory.

"I know I have made mistakes beyond repair. I betrayed you. I left you for dead with the Oilean. I know this is the last thing you probably want." He stopped and took a deep breath. "Emory Fae, when you first came to the Shattered Isles looking for aid, I was skeptical. I was arrogant. Above everything, I was scared. But you have taught me and reminded me what it is like to have friends. What it means to have broken that bond."

Her black eyes narrowed, but she remained silent. He continued, "I've lost your trust, and I understand that. But the seas as my witness and the skies as my master, allow me to earn the chance to stand by your side. To make it right, or death take me. Emory Reia Fae, what I did—"

"Was to save your own neck. You left me for *dead*."

"Yes," he breathed. "But I am here now, swearing my allegiance to you. I am no longer the king of the Shattered Isles. I am Marquis Maher, and I serve only one queen." Sucking in a deep breath, he bowed his head.

And waited.

An eternity stretched between them, but then he felt her hand clasping his bloody one. "We have all made mistakes. But now isn't the time. You and I will deal with that betrayal after we survive this war." She paused. "I accept your offer, Marquis Maher, and may you serve Kiero or may your death release you of this promise."

A warning and a seal.

Her lips twitched as he stood. "Enough blood has been spilled today."

He looked to his palm, and it was healed. Marveling at her blackened eyes, her unearthly ability, Marquis murmured, "You and Adair's ability have become one?"

Not giving him any more of an answer than a scathing glare, Emory turned her attention to the ships behind them. "Riona, you need to get them to safety."

As pale as the snow around her, Riona nodded, breathing, "We will wait for you in Nehmai. I will try my best to prepare for the coming months."

Arching her inky brow, Emory said, "Good. Keep the army from the Isles safe. Train every able-bodied woman and man. We will need them in the weeks to come."

"What of the other rebels?" Riona asked.

Emory paced, brutally severe, as she stated, "I will find them if they are still alive. But first, Brokk needs me. I will not abandon him. Not again."

Sorrow flooded her eyes, and she pinned Marquis with her gaze; he saw a ghost of what had happened back in the bowels of Adair's kingdom. The pain, the guilt, and the rage that ignited her. The woman he had come to know on the Isles had died, only to be reborn as someone else entirely. Someone that he would follow into the darkness. Wherever this path would lead them, he would stay at her side and truly earn that right.

"We need to go."

With tears in her eyes, Riona bid them a quick goodbye before walking back toward Ryker, Diedre, and the exhausted refugees. Meeting Diedre's eyes, Marquis nodded, whispering his last command on the wind, "Trust Riona, and follow her. I will return."

Diedre looked at him skeptically, and he added, "Yes. I know I have acted like an ass. Let me earn all your respect back by doing this. Help train the army, Diedre. Please."

Nodding, his once-second turned on her heel, following Riona.

Trying to push down his pain, Marquis hoped Diedre would understand why he betrayed Emory. *Because you're a spineless coward?* Stiffening, he looked to the frozen landscape in front of them, wondering if the witch from the Isles was tailing him—and how he would tell Emory that.

The barren branches stretched toward them, and Marquis sucked in a frigid breath, trying to rein in his adrenaline. "Like old times, right?"

Vehemence burning in her gaze, Emory ignored him. Brilliant sunlight bathed the world, ribbons of its golden touch washing out the gray of winter. Emory exhaled hard, and inky embers floated from her hands, melting the snow around her.

As if he wasn't there, she gazed into the depths of the woods, whispering, "I'm coming. I'm *coming*."

With her cloak snapping in the wind, Emory took the first step.

Toward war.

Toward Brokk.

And Marquis followed, snow crunching underneath his boots, ice nipping at his heart. Pulling his hood up, Marquis followed his queen.

CHAPTER THIRTY

EMORY

There was a certain meditative state that could be achieved from walking. Emory hadn't spoken in three days. The harsh throes of winter had fallen over Kiero, but she hadn't stopped, her ability nourishing her, the fire pooling in her gut fueling her. She didn't feel hunger or exhaustion.

She looked into the woods, but nothing stirred; the world was eerily quiet, as if it were holding its breath. Briefly flicking her gaze to Marquis, she noticed that he looked like hell, but to his credit, he hadn't voiced his hunger or his tiredness against her relentless pace.

A snap of twigs had her spinning to face the beautiful doe-like creature in front of her. Giant brown eyes blinked at her in surprise, both still.

His eyes widened as the smoke tightened against his throat. Her throat ran dry, hands shaking. *Declan was ravenous behind her, his dark gaze challenging her.* She should've moved, should've done something.

The panic attack immobilized her as the animal broke out of the trance first, galloping away.

Marquis came up beside her. "We should stop."

No questions, no judgments. She hated that tiny part of her that flared in gratitude. This was the man who left her for *dead.* Trying to hide the cold sweat that washed over her skin, she brusquely said, "Well, that was our dinner that just got away."

"We'll manage."

Sighing, she dipped into her power. Inky smoke lazily drifted around her; Marquis's sharp intake of breath was confirmation enough. Turning, she saw two hide shelters and a small fire crackling merrily in the middle.

"If it attracts attention, then so be it. I don't want you dying from hypothermia because you have something to prove to me. Before you thank me, Marquis, the only reason you're still breathing is because I have more important matters. I have to figure out how to save Brokk."

He acted like he wanted to say something, but he only nodded. Emory watched him settle close to the fire, warming his hands. Still standing, she tried to push from her mind where Brokk was now. What he must be going through. What Declan was doing to him.

All because of her.

If she hadn't used her ability against him, forcing him to leave her . . . Her lies had helped enslave him. Sighing, she perched on a frozen stub of a tree, watching the orange-and-red flames twist around one another.

"You know, you can only punish yourself so much."

Snapping to attention, she looked at Marquis, his short emerald hair like a gem in the fading daylight.

"Oh, yeah? Did I ask for your aged wisdom?" Emory snapped.

"You know that I can relate better than most."

Emory frowned. "How is it possible that I went so wrong, so many times? I broke his heart, Marquis. I lied to him. I betrayed him."

Snow started to fall gently again as the former king of the Shattered Isles leaned back, watching the flakes descend. "You know, humans are capable of amazing things. Don't assume that once we break Brokk free, he won't be the happiest man on Kiero that you are safe. That you are well. Our mistakes are in the past, but our characters aren't condemned by them. You acted out of love. It's better than acting out of fear."

"You don't understand." She couldn't say more than that. The information weighed so heavily on her heart, but she couldn't tell Marquis.

If you die, I die.

Changing the subject, Emory said, "Just so we are clear, our fake engagement is off."

Waggling his eyebrows, he said, "You're not my type anyways."

Swallowing her chuckle, she retorted, "Good. It was a terrible plan. Go get some rest, Marquis. I will take the first watch."

He ducked underneath the first leather shelter.

Pulling her cloak tighter around her, she went to the edge of the camp, resting now against the base of a tree. She rubbed her hands together, but her flesh hardly felt the bite of the cold. Watching the fading light, pink, orange and golden hues washing in the sky, Emory counted the days that had passed. When the sun dipped below the horizon, Marquis's light snoring floated into the clearing, and realization slammed into her.

Today was her twenty-second birthday: November seventeenth.

She exhaled, listening to the brush of frozen leaves that clung defiantly on their branches, the whisper of the winter winds that coursed through the ancient woods. Only in her wildest daydreams could she have envisioned last November that she would be here, marching north after an inhuman army. Fighting for the survival of a country. Learning that her life on Earth had been a lie. That she had fallen in love.

Rage curled underneath her skin, resting in her heart. Every time she closed her eyes, she saw Kiana's and Brokk's faces. They had been so afraid, and she could do nothing against Declan. Her rage helped remind her to keep going—for Brokk. She hadn't fought so hard just to let him slip through her fingers. There had to be a way. They hadn't defied death to lose this easily to Declan in the end. Brokk hadn't wasted most of his life fighting for more just to be sacrificed.

Her hope had always rested with him. If he drew breath and kept fighting, hope would always be there. Blinking, she tried to figure out how they would intercept Declan. She didn't know the depths of her power, and how could she win against an army of hundreds?

Her mother and Adair's voices filled her doubts: *Rise. Rise. Rise. Rise.*

"I'm trying!" she snarled at the ghosts within her mind, her voice carrying through the forest.

Movement in her peripheral vision caught her eye. Silver eyes blinked across the way at her. The creature looked like a fox as it slowly revealed itself, beautiful round eyes blinking at her from across the clearing. Its luminous fur went peerless white to tipped silver.

"Hello there," Emory whispered.

One blink. Another.

"Where are you off to?" It responded with a tilt of its head, another blink, and a flick of its bushy tail. Emory's heart froze as an unnatural scent filled the clearing. Like lemongrass and fall leaves, calming and fresh.

"Is it possible you want me to follow you?"

Another blink.

Looking to Marquis's tent, she said more to herself, "I can't leave him. Even if he deserves it."

There was a gentle huff and a whip of its tail as if it was saying, *Then go get him.*

She stood, the hair on the back of her neck on end, and the flames crackled down to embers as the creature sat, waiting. Crossing the space, Emory pulled the flap of the tent back, finding Marquis sprawled on his back, mouth open, his chest rising and falling.

Smirking, she dipped into the well of her power, a round snowball materializing in her palm, cool against her skin. It was a blur as it smashed against his face.

Sputtering, Marquis shot up. "What the—"

"I need you to come with me." Turning her back, she could hear him clambering out of bed behind her. Twilight had fallen, and Emory took in the shadowy darkness. She locked eyes with the animal, and it slipped into the night.

"Emory, what are we doing?"

"Just shut up and trust me. You owe me as much."

Jogging into the woods, she scoured the landscape for the white streak of fur. *There.* She glimpsed the tip of its muzzle, and it took off, weaving through the trees, tail brushing against the snow. She walked a few steps behind it, her breath visible as misty puffs. How could she explain the shiver of excitement running down her spine? The tug pulling in her gut? She followed the exquisite creature, wondering if maybe she wasn't the only one ready to fight back against Declan's poison.

Minutes slipped by as the snow fell harder, downy flakes coating the land, casting their world into this frost-kissed landscape. Glistening in time. There, in the heart of the forest, a gnarled root stood out among the rest. The bark of the twisted stump was lined with silver, but at the top, a half-carved crescent moon and three stars shimmered.

"The markings of naithe warriors," Marquis whispered.

She had seen those markings before. Getting on her hands and knees, Emory peered into the darkness. Under the trunk there was a hole in which she could fit. Just barely, but she could do it. Taking a deep breath, she laid on her back, going in feet first. Ice and snow scraped along her back. Heart pounding as she shimmied, she took one last look at the forest before she dropped. Wind howled, and the frigid air stung her eyes, her cloak snapping around her. Clamping her lips together, she counted the seconds.

One.

Two.

Three.

Four.

Five.

Marquis's screams filled the passage.

She opened her eyes to see a fine blue dust filling the shadows. Shimmering like a thousand stars, it swirled around her boots, her legs, her torso. Slowly, the dust particles packed together, easing her fall until she gently landed on her feet.

Marquis's face paled as he landed beside her. "Where are we?" he croaked.

Words failed as luminous eyes found hers. The fox-like creature padded farther into the earth, and she followed. Roots hung from the ceiling, damp air clotting her senses. Along the edge of the floor, silver fire danced in cracked glass jars, igniting their way, not wavering. Emory's fingers tingled against the age of this place. The fox sped up. They followed at a breakneck pace as the ground sloped down, loose dirt skittering underneath Emory's boots. The mouth of the tunnel widened, and Emory gasped at the scene in front of them.

Four massive crystals lay before her like pyres: ruby, opal, sapphire, and amethyst. Their guide curled up to the side. There was a small stream filled with ice, and a pile of rodent bones was strewn around it.

"Emory." Behind her, Marquis paused. His eyes widened as he whispered, "I can't pass through."

A wildness shuddered through her. "It's okay. Just wait there."

"Emory . . ."

She stepped forward, and Marquis's voice disappeared as the gurgling of the stream filled the cave. Dropping to her knees, she unsheathed Anithe in front of the peerless stones, looking to the fox. "Why do you want me here?"

A blink.

Leaning closer, she looked at the jagged edges of the crystals, each color reflecting off the dirt walls. Yawning, the fox rested its head down, eyes never leaving her as Emory scoffed. "Comfy, are you? Did you just want some company down here?"

At the creature's silence, she shook her head and turned her attention back to the massive gems in front of her. Her scream bounced off the walls as she saw that in each of the smooth gems, a woman's face pressed against the surface. The bodies looked serene. Their eyes were closed, and they were suspended as if floating in water.

"What the *hell?*"

Each of the woman's eyes snapped open at the same time, their hands flying up to scratch against their smooth crystal cages.

The ground began to shudder; Emory got up, pressing against the back wall, wide-eyed, with the new version Anithe gripped in front of her.

The fox paid no attention as each gem grew brighter, cracks running up and down the sides. Heat flared as Emory squeezed her eyes shut, throwing up a shield around her with her ability just as all four crystals exploded. The blast sent ripples of energy and chunks of gem ricocheting off all four walls.

The dust settled, and the four figures rose, dressed in fighting leathers, their silver hair cascading down past their shoulders. Smoke curled at their feet as they flexed their hands, staring in wonder.

Stretching, the fox trotted over to the woman with three blue feathers peeking out from under the curtain of her hair.

"Tav!" the woman exclaimed, tears pooling in her eyes as the silver fox rubbed against her legs, a content purring filled the cave along with their whispers.

"Yedda, Shreya, Far, are you okay?"

"Blythe, where are we?"

"Why in sky's name are we in a dirt cave?"

"It reeks like my grandmother's—"

"Were we confined in those *rocks*?"

Clearing her throat, Emory stepped toward them, not lowering an inch of her ability that was a buffer between her and the strangers. "Who are you?" she asked.

Silence fell heavily around them.

The fox-like creature—Tav—blinked up at Emory as if stating the obvious.

Sparks flared underneath Emory's palms, and she narrowed her eyes. "I asked you a question."

The woman with Tav strode forward, nostrils flaring, her unearthly features sharp in the dim lighting. "I should be asking you the same thing, human. Are you our captor? The last thing I remember is being a part of a war, so maybe you can enlighten me on exactly where we are."

A war. Shock rippled through Emory when she recognized their silver eyes. She locked eyes with Tav, and the snow fox blinked, waiting for Emory to connect the dots.

Shoving Anithe in the damp ground, Emory breathed, "Are you by any chance some of Kiana's naithe warriors from Nehmai?"

Suspicion flooded the woman's eyes. "How would you know Kiana?"

Shaking, Emory tried to grasp where to start. "My name is Emory Fae. Your fox, Tav, led me and my companion here. To you. You've been here, I think, for centuries."

Growls filled the cave; Emory was slammed into the wall, a hand wrapping around her throat. Kicking the woman in the gut, Emory threw her ability forward. Black flames divided them as Emory panted. "Let me explain. Please."

Like feral animals, the group stared at her, untrusting, through the flames. Having their attention, Emory started from the very beginning.

***

Hours had surely passed. Embers still flickered on the ground, and Emory leaned against the wall, staring at her new company. Yedda's round face and kind eyes seemed shocked. Shreya, quiet and unsure, flicked her gaze to Farrah, her twin sister. Blythe sat with Tav, stroking his thick white fur, not blinking as she glared at Emory.

"It's a lot to take in, I know," Emory started.

Blythe spat, "You bring us news of our leader's death then expect us to be gracious? Who put us in these things? Who did this while the rest of our company died?"

"I don't know. But I'm expecting you to understand because Tav brought me to you for a *reason.* You were saved when Kiana thought you all to be dead. It's not by chance that I pass by, the only person who could possibly break your magical binds."

"Blythe, listen to her." Yedda stepped in from the far corner, cracking her fingers. "The great war almost destroyed us. The Falkovs have fallen, except the prince. Kiana apparently lived in solitude for years, but she never found us. What would she have wanted if our places were reversed? Nehmai's survival is in the crossfire, our beliefs and way of life almost driven to extinction."

Blythe shook her head, pain flashing through her features. "Yedda, she is just a child."

"Who will lose if you don't help me. Kiana believed in Brokk. Died for him, in fact." Emory licked her cracked lips. "That has to mean something."

Shaking her head, Blythe leaned back, seething. "He is not our concern."

Exhaling hard, Emory stood up. "Fine."

Sheathing Anithe, she strode out of the cave without another word, leaving the immortals behind her. Tav whined as she went back into the passage.

Marquis sat against a cave wall, doing a double-take as she stalked by him. "Emory, black skies, are you okay?"

"No."

"What happened?"

"Something I should have known. Fucking immortals."

Chasing at her heels, Marquis grabbed her hand. "Emory, stop."

Tears welled in her eyes out of frustration. "Let's just get out of here. I will explain as we go."

That's when the wall behind them exploded. Jumping in front of her, arching his body around hers, Marquis tried to shield her from the rocks and debris. Emory grabbed his hand, willing her ability through him like an electric current. Marquis gasped as all around them the debris stopped, floating gently before it all dropped to the ground.

Raising his gaze to her, he whispered, "New trick. Also new acquaintances of yours?"

Letting go of Marquis's hand, she saw Blythe and Tav first, the immortal glaring daggers at Marquis. "Let's go above ground, shall we? I feel like we are standing in our graves." Blythe looked pointedly at Emory before she snapped her fingers.

The tunnel disappeared, and the group stood in the wintery landscape, their breaths coming out in fast misty puffs. They blinked; the night was deep and alluring. Thousands of stars gleamed down from the skies, and the clouds had cleared, revealing the waxing moon. The snowy forest was painted in its silver glow.

All four immortals circled her and Marquis as Emory whispered, "Marquis, may I introduce Yedda, Shreya, her sister

Farrah, and Blythe. Warriors from Nehmai who were a part of Kiana's armada."

Shock rippled through Marquis's features, which he quickly tucked away. "How is it possible you are here?"

Blythe appeared in front of him, agitated as she palmed a sheathed knife. "Magic. Someone stored us away, hidden and preserved." Snapping her eyes to Emory, Blythe added, "This *human* thinks she found us for some higher purpose."

Tav yipped at her feet as Blythe said, "Unfortunately, I have been out-voted by my sisters. For now, we will travel with you."

Gratitude flared through Emory's chest, warming her, and she raised her eyebrows to Marquis, whose expression mirrored her shock. Tav leaped over to her, rubbing his thick fur along her legs. Emory patted him, whispering, "Thank you."

Yipping, he trotted off and Blythe glared at her. "Watch yourself, child queen." Blythe turned on her heel, her warriors following, but not without each one shooting Emory a wink over their shoulders.

Nodding to each of them, lips turning up, Emory exhaled hard.

Stopping, she held Anithe in front of her after they were ahead of her and rested her forehead against the gleaming black steel. Closing her eyes, the stars as her witnesses, she whispered, "Hold on, Brokk. I am coming. I am coming."

Rise, Em. Rise.

A tear slipped down her cheek.

EPILOGUE

BROKK

Brokk knew he was dreaming. Thick snow layered the forest floor as he walked toward Emory, her forehead pressed against a sword he had never seen before. It was like a curtain of the night sky had been captured and molded to her weapon. She looked weathered, tired. Her cloak fanned out around her as he knelt in front of her, her conviction breaking him.

Hold on, Brokk. I am coming. I am coming.

"Don't." Shaking his head, Brokk pulled away, biting through his lip, screaming, "Don't you dare walk straight into—" His words died on his tongue as the entire scene changed, spinning.

Lunging, Brokk tried to hold on to her, to feel her warmth, to feel her against him. To feel whole.

Gasping, he awoke, blinking against the pain. He couldn't move, a mask clamping his mouth tightly shut. Hot ember chains burned his wrists and ankles, the smell of his own burned flesh wafting up to him.

"Oh, good. You're awake."

Declan lounged against a windowsill, his dark hair combed back as he looked Brokk over, dissecting him with his gaze. "Now, I must send my condolences to you about your friend. Kiana was her name, right?" Brokk thrashed against his binds, and Declan grinned in pleasure. "It was a necessary kill. Since your queen bound Adair's old magic to her, I needed something powerful to break out of that dreaded mountain. Now, I can finally stay in this physical body. As well as a place fit for a ruler."

Brokk watched him pace back and forth.

"Now, Brother, you must understand my predicament. Your loyalty to Emory is powerful. I can't have it. With you and I bound, it's time to realize that I have won. It's time to purge this world." He grinned. "I plan on beginning with you." Declan was in front of him then, stroking his cheek from his temple to his jaw. "Don't be afraid."

The Dark King plunged the knife deep into Brokk's abdomen. Brokk felt his lung being punctured, pain shooting up his spine. Screams clawed out of his throat as his ability rushed to heal him, blood dripping down from the table onto the cement floor.

"The Oilean weren't thorough enough with you. I plan to break you, Brokk Foster. Then we will see where your loyalty lies."

Declan twisted the blade, and Brokk's screams echoed around him, his whimpers cracking through him.

Declan chuckled, his whisper following Brokk into the dark. "We will see who you serve after I am done with you."

Brokk threw up, his pain blinding. Acid seared his throat, but the pain didn't stop. It only built.

And built.

And *built.*

His cries and pleas went unanswered; the only hope he clung to was that Emory was far away. She was *safe.*

Declan's face came into view. He sneered, withdrawing the knife from Brokk's abdomen, wiping the bloodied steel on his pant leg. "Don't make this harder than it has to be, Brokk. I have avenues other than pain to make you bow."

Spitting in his face, Brokk choked out, "I will never serve you."

"We will see, dear brother. We will see . . ."

Placing the knife down on a table, Declan rolled up the sleeves of his shirt. "Let's begin."

Declan placed his hands on Brokk's temple, and reality fell away.

END OF BOOK THREE

ACKNOWLEDGMENTS

Here we are again, at another end of a book, and my gratitude is overflowing. This series has grown into something I could not have ever fathomed, and that is thanks to a lot of people.

Kingdom of Broken Iron holds a special place in my heart. When I started out writing this book I had no idea what my own personal life held for me. It would hold a two-year health battle with Lyme disease and now Fibromyalgia. I was able to channel that pain, fear, and exhaustion that fight entailed, and my characters and writing helped me heal, to hold on. To claw my way back to my life, to have hope. Despite it being a work of fiction, I hope that my readers take away that sliver of fight, and hope, when Emory thought all was lost.

Thank you to Candace, Christine, and Amy for endorsing *Kingdom*. It means more to me more than I can put into words.

To all my readers. You have given the world of Kiero a home. Through your enthusiasm and support, I can continue to do what I am most passionate about; I can continue Emory and the Black Dawn Rebellion's story. I cannot say thank you enough for this—THANK YOU!!!

To Emerald, thanks for being a great editor and helping me realize what some of my favorite words to overuse are (lol). You are challenging me to be a better writer, and I am so grateful for it!

To Rae and Brenna for also being editors extraordinaire. Your insight helped *Kingdom* be the book it is today.

Thank you to Cora Graphics and Dark Wish Designs for making this novel beautiful inside and out!

To Matt, this one is for you. You are my rock, and I couldn't have asked for a better partner. These past years have been so challenging for both of us, and yet you continue to be an amazing human who helps take away the day-to-day stresses so I can accomplish my writing dreams. You have never doubted me for a second. I love you.

To all the people at Chapters Indigo that help hold my signings (prior to covid-19) and now help support and spread the word about local authors, you guys are honestly superheroes, and you have made my years as an author so much fun! Thank you so much.

To my family, Nate, Mom, and Dad, you know how much I love you, right? Thank you for accepting me and my dreams.

To Link, Leonard, and Lola, our wonderful dachshunds. (And now Luna and Luther, our sphynx kittens!) You have stayed by my side through the tears and the frustration of writing this book. Even if you can't read this dedication, I love you to pieces.

From the bottom of my heart, thank you to every single person who picks up this book, talks about it, helps spread the word. You are helping make my dreams a reality.

I can't wait to meet you all again in Kiero! Watch out for the final installment of the Black Dawn Series—*The Cursed Throne.*

ABOUT THE AUTHOR

Mallory McCartney currently lives in Sarnia, Ontario with her husband and their three dachshunds: Link, Lola, Leonard, and their sphynx cats, Luna and Luther. When she isn't working on her next novel or reading, she can be found daydreaming about fantasy worlds and hiking. Other favorite pastimes involve reorganizing perpetually overflowing bookshelves and seeking out new coffee and dessert shops.

www.ingramcontent.com/pod-product-compliance
Lightning Source LLC
Chambersburg PA
CBHW030547310726
48979CB00010B/2069/J

* 9 7 8 1 7 7 7 5 1 3 2 3 8 *